JUST ONE KISS

"I have desired this kiss since the day we first met, Alexandra," Pierce said. "Show me that you, too, have imagined a kiss from my lips."

The heat of his breath seared her skin and set off simultaneous sensations of panic and pleasure. All rational thought ceased as his lips brushed her earlobe and trailed down her neck. A gasp of pleasure had barely reached her lips before he covered them with his. Their mouths touched lightly, expectantly. Alexandra felt his unshaven roughness as he nibbled from the corner to crown of her lips.

With a firmer pressure, Pierce sought more, and she welcomed his tongue as it stroked her teeth and lips, and dueled with her own tongue. In turn, he allowed her the same exploration before he broke away to rain kisses across her face and down her neck.

Her hands had dropped to the open shirt below his chin. Soft curls of dark hair on his chest tickled her fingers as his mouth once again closed onto hers. . . .

The MacInness Legacy

Dear Romance Readers,

In July of 1999, we launched the Ballad line with four new series, and each month we present both new and continuing stories set everywhere from medieval England to the American West—the kind of passionate, romantic stories you love best, written by the most gifted authors. At the back of each book, we tell you when you can find subsequent books in the series that have captured your heart.

First up this month is **Moonlight on Water,** the second book in the fabulous new *Haven* series by beloved author Jo Ann Ferguson. Will a young woman leave her familiar community behind for a steamboat's dashing captain? Next, talented Annette Blair takes us back to Regency England to meet **An Undeniable Rogue,** the first irresistible hero in her new series *The Rogues Club.* Marrying a fallen friend's sister is a simple matter of honor for one dashing rake newly returned from the war, until he meets the wildly tempting—and very pregnant—woman in question!

The MacInness Legacy continues with new author Sandy Moffett's **Call Down the Night,** as the second of three sisters separated at birth discovers her gift of second sight may lead her to a strange heritage—and keep her from the man she loves. Finally, talented Susan Grace begins the new series *Reluctant Heroes* with **The Prodigal Son** as one of the infamous Lady Cat's twin sons masquerades as the other—and finds himself falling for his brother's beloved . . .

These are stories we know you'll love! Why not try them all this month?

Kate Duffy
Editorial Director

CALL DOWN THE NIGHT

Sandy Moffett

ZEBRA BOOKS
Kensington Publishing Corp.
http://www.kensingtonbooks.com

ZEBRA BOOKS are published by

Kensington Publishing Corp.
850 Third Avenue
New York, NY 10022

All Kensington titles, imprints, and distributed lines are available at special quantity discounts for bulk purchases for sales promotion, premiums, fund-raising, educational or institutional use.

Special book excerpts or customized printings can also be created to fit specific needs. For details, write or phone the office of the Kensington Special Sales Manager: Kensington Publishing Corp., 850 Third Avenue, New York, NY 10022. Attn. Special Sales Department. Phone: 1-800-221-2647.

Zebra and the Z logo Reg. U.S. Pat. & TM Off.

First Printing: July 2002
10 9 8 7 6 5 4 3 2 1

Printed in the United States of America

To Julie Moffett
Fellow romance writer and mentor,
Provider of inspiration and encouragement,
And my loving sister

Author's Note

For those not familiar with the late 1700s in America and Salem, Massachusetts, in particular, the following are a few historical footnotes.

Salem, although small by today's standards, was the sixth largest city in America by the end of the 1700s. Its merchant ships traveled so far and wide around the world that many foreigners believed Salem an independent country. These ships brought wealth to the conservative city, along with the science and philosophy of far-reaching nations. It also brought a steady influx of diseases, such as the feared smallpox.

Controversy arose in 1792 among the citizens over opening hospitals in Salem, for the purpose of inoculating citizens with live smallpox virus obtained from mild cases. Eventually, proponents won (spurred by new outbreaks), and several small temporary hospitals administered the inoculations. The patients remained confined over the following weeks as symptoms of the pox appeared in the patients as it ran its course. Dr. William Bentley, minister of East Church, recorded only the death of a pregnant woman from the practice for the year 1792. Deaths of others in Salem contracting smallpox the natural way stood close to fifty percent.

Nathaniel Bowditch went from indentured servant to mathematician and navigator, writing the standard navigation text used by the U.S. Navy.

Many thanks to Nicole Meer and Dewey Owens for their information on harp music from this time period.

Thanks to John Frayler and the National Park Service in Salem for their wonderful tour of Derby Wharf and the surrounding area, and for answering numerous historical questions about merchant ships and the early commerce of Salem. Even though writing is a solo event, it frequently takes several people to bring a book together. Thanks to RWA chapter SpacecoasT Authors of Romance for their constant encouragement, to proofreader Donna Moffett, critique partner Roxanne St. Claire, and my partner in this Ballad series, sister Julie Moffett. Julie wrote Book 1, *Light a Single Candle,* and the next book in the series, *To Touch the Sky.*

I'd love to hear from readers. Send comments and questions, or request my newsletter or bookmark by sending a self-addressed stamped legal-sized envelope to P.O. Box 410252, Melbourne, Florida 32941-0252. You can also visit my web site at: http://www.tlt.com/authors/sandymoffett.htm.

Prologue

Salem, Massachusetts
October 31, 1692

"Hang the witches! Deliver us from their curse!"

Judge Nathaniel Williams listened in dismay as frenzied voices sliced through early morning fog that clung to the long, wet grass on Gallows Hill.

"Nay," he shouted and pushed his way through the mass of citizens thronging and shoving nearer to a view of the gallows.

" 'Tis unlawful to hang them both," he yelled, spreading his hands wide as if to embrace the crowd and force them to listen to his words. "The court accepted *his* confession, but the woman was exonerated. Release her at once!"

Breathy and sweating from morbid anticipation, a husky farmer confronted the man. "Ye have no say, Judge Williams. Ye quit the court."

Nathaniel bellowed back, "This execution is a sham! Spectral evidence is no credible proof. These people are no more witches than we are."

"A jury found them guilty," a woman screeched and waved a cross in his face. "Get on with it, I say."

"A jury found *him* guilty," Nathaniel corrected. "But the woman was found innocent."

A rude dissenter purposefully knocked Nathaniel's wide-brimmed hat askew and slowed his progress. He brushed back a shock of silver-white hair, secured it under the hat, and forged onward. Three cloaked officials approached, trampling the tall grass with the same indifference they had extended to these innocent victims. Leading the group was the Reverend Samuel Clark, the opinionated self-appointed savior of Salem Village. The minister advanced slowly, spewing Bible verses upon the crowd as though personally protecting them from Satan.

Disgust arose like bile within Nathaniel. There was certainly nothing holy surrounding these proceedings. True madness it was. Sheer ignorance fueled by unreasoning hatred. He looked to the heavens for a sign of hope, but found them obscured in dreary gray.

A slim woman draped in a flowing dark mantle, abruptly leaped from the crowd and grasped the reverend's cloaked arm.

"I implore thee, sir, release John Gardener," she pleaded. "His wife is the only witch here. She bewitched him into confessing to save her evil soul."

"I have heard that concern, but legal judgment has been passed. Justice will be served." The Reverend Clark brushed her away as if she were no more than an insect.

The woman grew rigid with anger. "Ye shall be punished for this deed," she hissed at the pastor's back. A harsh breeze blew the dark hair off her shoulders and away from a bleak face.

The hate in her voice chilled Nathaniel's soul. "My good woman," he said, touching her gently on the forearm, "do not let these events harden your heart."

She turned slowly and glared at him from blue eyes so icy and vicious that Nathaniel took a step backward. Inexplicably, cold fingers of fear gripped his heart. He gasped for breath, clutching his chest.

"Ye are all fools. Fools," she seethed at him, turning away and disappearing into the crowd.

Nathaniel stood rooted in shock, waiting until his heartbeat resumed its normal pace. Light rain began to fall and drops thumped against his hat like the drums of a death march. If ever a witch was present on this day, it was surely that woman.

Not daring to dally further, he hastened on toward the presiding judge, Isaac Tucker.

"Isaac, ye must stop this," he urged, when he caught up with his old colleague. " 'Tis a mockery of the law."

Stony eyes full of self-importance bore into Nathaniel. "The Court of Oyer and Terminer has spoken. Ye have no place here, Williams."

"I come today only as the voice of reason amid madness."

"Ye are softhearted and weak," Isaac replied arrogantly. " 'Tis left to those of us who are strong to see the law implemented. I'll have naught more to say about it."

Dismay at Isaac's indifference fueled Nathaniel's determination. He knew the condemned man, John Gardener, and his wife, Priscilla. They were kind, pious folk, certainly not witches, but he realized the futility of saving those with court-pronounced sentences. The gallows awaited John, but a chance still existed to save Priscilla.

Nathaniel pointed at her, now bound and being dragged with her husband toward the gallows. "That woman has no appointment against her. She is innocent according to thine own court. Will ye commit a murder which ye declare so unjust of others?"

Showing displeasure at Nathaniel's interference, but obviously wise enough to see how a crucial mistake or a loss of control at this execution could ruin his reputation, the judge signaled for her release. A constable collected Priscilla from the throng and struggled amid their objections to see her to a safe location. Nathaniel worked his way toward her, aware that the devastation from her husband's impending execution would make life a much greater challenge than death.

"Priscilla," he called, breathing heavily from the exertion of pushing through the crowd. He grasped her elbow to steady her as she swayed on her feet. "Are ye hurt?"

She shook her head wordlessly, staring at the gallows where

two men were tightening a noose around her husband's neck. The Reverend Clark's reading of the scripture became frantic and more excited.

"Stop them." Tears combined with the rain and coursed down her cheeks. "I beg of thee."

Nathaniel sighed sadly. "I have done what I could, my child. 'Tis now a matter out of my hands."

Still, he watched, appalled, as Reverend Clark asked the condemned man if he had any final words.

"I love thee, Priscilla," John called out, his eyes searching the crowd for his wife.

Priscilla sobbed and slumped against Nathaniel. "And I thee, my love," she whispered. "Always thee."

The men on the scaffold yanked a black hood down over John's head and stepped back. The trapdoor released with a sickening snap. John's body dropped, swaying in a morbid dance. An ominous thunder boomed in the distant hills. The crowd cheered wildly and Nathaniel's stomach turned.

"Let me take thee home," he said, putting a protective arm around Priscilla's shoulder. " 'Tis over now."

It disheartened him that ignorance, fear, and hatred had won on Gallows Hill this day. The same victory would likely come again, for more condemned remained jailed awaiting a similar fate. Nathaniel swore with renewed vigor to try to prevent another blow against the innocent. He must not lose hope.

From a distance, cold, blue eyes watched the hanging with undisguised fury. Months of careful planning had come to naught. John had died, and his wife, the one who should have swung from the gallows, lived on. John's confession in the court to save Priscilla had caught her unsuspecting and had ruined everything.

The watcher had dreamed of giving John the world, letting him taste a power most men would kill for, and showing him wonders he could never imagine. Priscilla, that whimpering, pitiful excuse for a woman, had so little in comparison to offer him.

Hatred boiled over as she watched old Nathaniel Williams lead Priscilla away. Priscilla would suffer for coaxing John to his death.

Her eyes narrowed and burned as she focused on retribution. With all her black knowledge, only a small effort was necessary to craft a spell to curse Priscilla. Damp air filled her lungs with odors of disturbed earth and crushed grass. She closed her eyes and envisioned John's body being lowered into an open grave. The perfect curse came to mind. Any man wedded to Priscilla or her direct female descendants would die in his twenty-sixth year, just as John had. It was a fitting justice.

Wicked satisfaction filled every pore of her being. Sometimes it was true that there were fates worse than death. Satisfied with the plan forming in her head, she made her way through the crowd, listening as people jeered at John's body and praised their own holiness.

Fools, all of them. They had failed to convict a real witch even after all the evidence had been set up.

The day grew warm and suffocating as she plodded home, but her spirits rose, contemplating her impending triumph over John's wretched little wife.

One

" 'Tis a bleak morn to be enterin' this witchin' town," a grizzled sailor mumbled as he assisted a young woman into the unsteady longboat.

Cold, sticky air ripe with rolling fog enveloped the seas off Salem, a place haunted by its persecution of witches nearly one hundred years ago. Though infamous in history, the thriving seaport now drew the educated and adventurous. Alexandra Gables, debarking the schooner *Defiant*, was no exception.

"Surely you do not believe in such endowed humans as witches," Alexandra countered, mildly amused that people still maintained such unenlightened beliefs. "Even Salem has professed shame for the hangings. I do recollect they offered legal apologies and restitution to families of the victims."

The sailor's sun-hardened face, days distant from the blade of a good razor, crinkled in doubt. "Me mariner ears hear many a tale, ma'am. But no doubtin' by me, every tale entwines a true fact. There be witches in Salem."

She nodded politely and glanced up at the *Defiant*, searching for signs of her tiny companion. Crimson spears of sunrise cast a reddish glow on the fog-draped schooner. A truly enchanting morning, if she allowed such a persuasion. But enchanted was not the word she chose.

The ocean rolled gently beneath her feet, inducing flutters in an already tentative stomach. She stepped toward the stern of the longboat, thankful that the trip to shore was a brief one. She settled near the coxswain and tucked the fullness of her cotton skirt and petticoat discreetly onto her lap. Above, a covered birdcage attached to a rope descended slowly from the schooner's deck. An oarsman handed over the cage and placed it beside her on the seat plank.

"Wha' creature ye ha' in there, Mistress Gables?" the Scottish-born sailor asked, puzzled by the cage. "It no' moves like a bird."

"You are most clever, sir. 'Tis not a bird, but a creature I call Newton. He resembles the fabled companion Black Sam used to keep."

The man's eyes widened at the pirate's name as he took a seat facing her and set his oar. She easily noted his desire to hear more. "I see you are familiar with Black Sam's exploits."

The deep-voiced coxswain behind her bellowed, "Aye, Mistress. Any sailor worth 'is salt has heard of 'im and 'is stormy demise."

He switched his attention to squeezing in the last of the passengers and casting off from the schooner. Not until the oars dipped cleanly into Salem Harbor and he had steered clear of the ship, did he lean toward Alexandra again. "I ne'er heard sailors speak of any animal on 'is ship."

"Not just any animal, but a small, rugged, resourceful creature," she replied. "Tales say 'tis why Black Sam kept him. He discovered the creature when filling water casks at anchorage in Hispaniola. Some claim the two locked stares, not sure who appeared more fearsome."

The coxswain and oarsman stared with curiosity at the covered cage. As though in response, Newton shifted in his cage, banging his tail against the thin metal. The men jumped, and Alexandra fought to hide her amusement. With dramatic hesitation, she lifted ever so slightly the edge of Newton's cover. Orange-brown eyes set in a rough jumble of green scales glared out at the men. Like a true thespian, Newton inflated his scaled beard to display a row of short spikes. The men gasped and she lowered the cover.

"That be a devil's creature," the oarsman puffed and glanced suspiciously at her fiery hair she had properly tucked beneath a hat.

" 'Tis simply a reptile," she countered. "A French philosopher traveling from Cap-Haitien gave this specimen to my father."

A sudden shift in temperature brought the discussion to a halt. A quiet foreboding made its presence known in the foggy shroud. Every rhythmic slap of the oars into the harbor brought the longboat closer to shore and deepened her building unease. She knew of no possible reason for these dark feelings. Past scientific forays with her father into the western woods of New York and the wilds of Nova Scotia had offered far more danger than this trip to Salem.

Strange, but some internal voice foretold that the danger didn't arise from bears, snakes, or Indians; it emanated from somewhere far less obvious, from the very essence of Salem— or even from her own soul. She did her best to ignore it.

She pictured Uncle Edmond waving farewell in Boston and wondered if she'd been foolish rejecting his offer of accompaniment and thus protection—what little protection a gout-ridden, spectacled printer could provide. He did, however, know the first mate and had been the principal in securing her passage.

Nonetheless, she was perfectly capable of surviving on her own. Years ago she had declined to be accompanied on every trivial outing, and now, well into her twentieth year, she certainly didn't require a guardian. Granted, this summer odyssey was more than a mere excursion, but she didn't need her hand held on a ship with escorts waiting on both ends. Safely tucked away, she held a letter of introduction for her summer host, whose representative supposedly waited at the wharf.

Originally, her father, a lecturer at Harvard, and she had planned to spend the summer in Salem helping Joshua Williams put in order several scientific collections for the Royal Society of London. Her father had journeyed to London in the fall with hopes of returning by the summer. Now unavoidably detained, he had arranged with Mr. Williams to accept her much needed assistance anyway.

She had trained in the arts and sciences under her father since she was old enough to read, and at least one part of every year was spent away from home on some scientific venture. She easily claimed some expertise in geology, botany, and astronomy. Prominent philosophers of science ran back through several generations, and she had no desire to break that family tradition.

Mist, and the damp chill it harbored, ate through the thin cotton skirt and bodice jacket she had foolishly chosen for the day. She tucked an arm around Newton's cage to keep cool drafts from flowing under the cover. The oarsmen pulled the longboat forward. The momentum shifted her weight, forcing her to plant a foot squarely in the brackish water that sloshed along the bottom.

Lord, she hated sailing. Seawater ruined anything it contacted, and at the moment that meant her leather travel shoes. The simple voyage from Boston to Salem, which should have taken less than a day, had stretched on through the night and into morning due to weather.

Location bells rang as small vessels, blinded by the fog, maneuvered toward the wharves. The coxswain shifted the tiller and the craft turned slightly. Alexandra strained to see through the fog to their destination.

The fog shifted a bit, exposing a lone house on a far knoll. A breath caught in her lungs as the earlier foreboding returned and cold encompassed her heart. She pressed a palm to her chest, and the biting cold fled, leaving behind the knowledge of an imminent encounter with the house's occupant.

"Pardon me, but who lives in that house?" she asked the coxswain while pointing toward the shore.

He glanced up as mist again enveloped the lone house. "No idea, ma'am. But 'spect they be of some importance."

Intuition told her his assessment was correct. Yet the view of that house, almost boastful in its seaside grandeur, produced a fear she couldn't justify. She had no doubt the impression would remain etched in her mind.

Newton squirmed erratically in his cage.

"Ah, you felt it, too," she whispered, comforting her companion. "We'll soon be ashore."

The sound of water lapping against the wharf grew louder, and she now understood the means by which the coxswain navigated. Eventually thuds and scrapes telling of an active wharf floated seaward, echoing in the fog like voices off canyon walls. Shadowy warehouses loomed hauntingly through the fog as the longboat glided with raised oars toward a wooden staircase attached to the wharf. A crewman leaped to secure the boat, and the pine stairs creaked under his weight.

The passengers hastily disembarked, either eager to have reached their destination or fearful the longboat might sink before their eyes. Because of her position in the stern and her desire not to repeat the earlier misstep with her dry shoe, she was the last to step ashore.

At the top of the stairs, the first mate, who had come ashore earlier with the passengers' trunks and to secure sustenance for the return voyage, met each passenger and directed them toward their belongings and waiting stages. He smiled. "Ah, Madam Benson, did you have an agreeable sailing?"

Alexandra smiled at his use of her uncle's name. When her uncle had paid for the passage, he gave his name instead of hers. In no mood to quibble the small foible, she let it pass and swung Newton's cage to the side, searching for a polite version of a rather wretched trip. "I had hoped for a swifter sail, but no man can change the wind or sea for his own ends. At the moment, I'm pleased to once again be safely on firm soil." With a nod, she moved away.

She followed the other passengers to the off-loaded luggage.

Stacks of trunks, leather cases, caged hens, a crated pair of young fowls, and a harp-shaped leather container, around which a French girl from the schooner swooned, littered the wharf. Alexandra bandied about several French names, attempting to remember the shipboard introduction to the girls' father. *Monsieur Calonne* sounded correct.

"Etes-vous une harpiste?" she asked, and the girl beamed, pleased that her talent had been recognized.

"Oui. I have played the harp since my eighth year," she answered smoothly in English, with youthful pride not only of her musical but also her linguistic ability.

Such an unusual instrument clearly labeled this family as aristocratic émigrés of France, a rather unsettled place at the moment with political affiliations changing at the drop of a hat. Alexandra found both the music and politics of interest. "If you stay in Salem, I would find great pleasure in attending a recital."

"The pleasure would be mine. Music is to be shared. I do not know, however, when I will be playing, as my family has yet to secure lodging. You see, my papa has obtained a temporary position as a shipping agent for Monsieur Williams."

"Joshua Williams?"

"Oui."

"Then the problem is resolved. I am a summer guest at the home of Mister Williams. Surely he would allow you to play there. By all accounts it is a wonderful place. I will seek permission when I meet him."

A blush rose to the girl's cheeks. "I will await news. *Merci."* She floated away to catch up with two men now loading the harp into a stalwart wagon.

The porter wheeled Alexandra's two large trunks toward a smaller wagon. The driver, who looked no older than thirteen, hustled toward them. "Need your trunks delivered, ma'am?" he said with a tip of his flat cap. "The stage won't take anything large."

She had doubts whether his scrawny arms could even lift a trunk without help. She gave a simple nod, and with one swift move, he hoisted the trunk with her clothing from the porter's cart to the wagon and let it drop to the wagon bed. She cringed as he reached for the second trunk, containing a precious telescope on loan from her father.

"Wait." She set a hand firmly on the dark leather trunk and studied the boy. Lean and tanned from day labor, he appeared eager to please with enthusiasm that belonged only to youth. "Do you know where Mister Joshua Williams resides?"

"Yes, ma'am. His is a fine place. A distant walk from here, though."

"Thankfully, Mister Williams is providing a carriage," she replied. "However, I doubt he is prepared for these cumbersome trunks. Inside this particular one," she patted the leather beneath her hand, "are rather delicate objects. I will pay well if you handle its transportation with care."

The eagerness returned to his features, and he practically swept the trunk from under her hand and placed it with goosedown softness into the wagon.

With her personal belongings on their way, Alexandra surveyed the wharf for someone from the Williams estate with her own transportation. The longboat had set them ashore near the end of a wide stone-and-dirt-filled wharf that extended from adjacent land like the leg of the letter *T*. Warehouses spotted the length of the wharf, and a path for wagons, carts, and stages remained clear. Obscured by wisps of fog, Derby Street ran along Salem's shoreline at the top of the T.

Joshua Williams, in a letter last week, had regretfully explained his own absence for her arrival, but had promised a carriage for the trip to his home. She watched as the last of her fellow passengers were collected by relatives or squeezed onto a stage. With the ship's delay, she had no notion of the current situation and saw no waiting carriage. It was possible her driver did not wish to bring his horse onto the wharf. That was perfectly understandable, for the confusion and noise were excessive. Most likely, the carriage waited along Derby Street at the end of the wharf.

Newton shifted as though to remind her of his presence. He need not have bothered. Her shoulder ached under the cage's weight, and she had tired of shifting his cage from hand to hand. "I am afraid, my friend, a brief stroll is necessary. Behave, or I'll secure you a berth in a ship's hold that is preparing to set sail."

Newton thunked his tail against the cage. Evidently, he didn't care for her sense of humor.

The mist dissipated into a blinding sun as the wharf met Derby Street. The town writhed with activity. In both directions along the harbor, she saw dozens of docks that catered to small fishing vessels, and men pushed carts of cod, herring, sea hog, and perch toward town for market day. A cloud of dust rose as an open top chair drawn by a horse hastily passed the fish carts and approached her location. Transportation, she presumed, tardy but necessary, had arrived. With precision she surveyed her attire, straightened the collar of her buttoned silk blouse and jacket, and tucked stray strands of fiery red hair under her hat.

The driver, a handsome gentleman, reined in the horse and sat sweeping his gaze across the wharf and waterfront. Proud eyes, sharp and assessing, momentarily caught her interest, then looked beyond into the gray fog. His confident profile, set off by black hair and brows, took what might have been a moody, boyish composure and transformed it into one of mature assurance. A few unruly locks swirled under the edge of his hat, as an apparent attempt to comb them in place held no sway with the humidity of the sea air.

The remainder of his hair was tied back, and he sat tall and slender but with more of a workman's physique than a gentleman's job should entail. A closer look disclosed that his jacket had seen no small amount of wear. If Mister Williams had wanted to impress her with a handsome physical specimen, he had chosen his representative well. Surprisingly, she found herself looking forward to the ride, and rather curious as to the mental acuity of the gentleman.

She laughed silently at the scientific philosopher in her,

detailing every new variable and attempting to postulate a reason for its existence. What profession did this gentleman enjoy that left his coat soiled so early in the morn, and why did he feel compelled to attend to his escort duty in such a state?

She remembered an evening when her father had appeared for dinner in complete disarray but absolute ecstasy. His horse had literally thrown him into a bed of as yet undiscovered American wildflowers. Her mother, God rest her soul, had handed him a damp cloth for his hands and face and then fed him dinner. She glanced again at the gentleman in the carriage and felt something more than just professional interest stir inside her.

He hopped from the carriage, appearing serious and rather annoyed, and, if she read his expression right, slightly inconvenienced at the necessity of this excursion. He secured the reins to a post and hustled toward her.

She contemplated how to respond to the obvious abandon with which he saw this duty. Surely Joshua Williams, her father's longtime friend, would abhor that his representative should present such a welcome. She lifted her chin and closely scrutinized his approach. The first move was his.

The gentleman strode by her in long steps without the slightest ounce of acknowledgment. She watched as he intercepted a dockhand, who pointed toward the mist-shadowed form of the *Defiant*'s first mate, supervising members of the crew in loading supplies into the longboat. The gentleman hustled toward the crew and spoke briefly to the officer. Both men turned, and the first mate pointed in her direction. Again the gentleman rushed up the wharf toward her as though she represented a brief stop on a cross-country journey. She waited, rather amused by the entire scene.

"Pardon, me," he began in a smooth, deep, but impatient voice. As he stepped close, she smelled a hint of tar, fresh sawdust, and manly perspiration. "The *Defiant*'s first mate told me you are Madam Benson. You are familiar, I believe, with the Boston passengers who just disembarked?"

She opened her mouth to answer, but he took no notice and continued.

"It seems I have missed their arrival and cannot find my party. The man I seek is Alexander Gables. Do you recall such a gentleman?" With another strike to polite manners, he looked away once again, scanning the wharf.

The long night had eroded most of her patience, and what was left had just expired with this gentleman's lack of civility. She set Newton on the ground and lightly crossed her arms. He had just made his last mistake. Without a doubt, he was Mister Williams's representative, though a slightly misinformed one. Her vision of a pleasant ride to the Williams estate had just met with an ill wind and sunk. No matter. The time would be better spent teaching this gentleman a lesson in manners. She smiled quite pleasantly at him, thinking all the while how difficult she was about to make his task.

She raised her chin with all the femininity, grace—and dash of conniving—she could muster. "I surely could be of some assistance, as I have just disembarked not more than thirty minutes prior."

"Thank you greatly, madam. Do you remember this Alexander Gables?"

With great ado, she crinkled her forehead, tilted her head, and glanced skyward as though envisioning every passenger. "I don't recall the name Alexander. But a few more details concerning the gentleman might bring him to mind."

"I have not met the gentleman myself, but he is youthful, a good ten years my junior."

She openly studied the lines of his face and jaw, disappointed that such a fine male specimen had some obviously preconceived notions. "That leaves me at quite a disadvantage, sir, as I cannot determine the age of a gentleman such as you. Even though a hat shades your face, the sun has darkened your skin, and as I am sure you well know, sun tends to add age to one's features. Yet the strong build of your shoulders and firmness in chin and build speak of youth. Therefore, you could be inquiring of a youth or a man of twenty."

Frustrated that she had not offered a swift answer that would have sent him on his way, a grim line of irritation pressed his lips and almost sent her into giggles.

"I do believe he is a man of twenty years," he added.

"Mmm. There were several gentlemen to fit that description. Do you have anything more specific, such as height, build, or disposition?"

"He is a philosophy intern, a man of science and books. I can only guess him to be small in stature, rather quiet, prim maybe, and possibly a bit, a bit . . ."

He didn't finish, but she gathered the connotation. The world, including this gentleman, had such a dim notion of intellect. "Yes, there most definitely was a man of such description. I am afraid he departed for town on the last stage."

"Many thanks, madam." The gentleman tipped his hat graciously and stepped away.

She let him take a dozen steps before calling after him. "Excuse me, sir. May I impose greatly upon you?"

Torn between the haste to leave and civil duty, he simply froze before turning slowly toward her. He gave a slight bow. "My services are yours, madam."

How this delay must pain him. She took a slow breath. "My uncle left me in Boston with knowledge of my safe arrival into the hands of waiting friends. He could not have foreseen that our ship would be delayed and the arrival obviously unannounced to those who should greet me. I would appreciate your escort into town, where I can get a message to them."

"It would be my pleasure, Madam Benson. I can deliver you to the stage depot, where I will search for Mister Gables."

With satisfaction and not an ounce of guilt in utilizing his chivalry, she scooped up Newton's cage and leisurely strolled to his side. Men like him were a detriment to science and the advancement of women. He had not considered for one moment that she might actually be the philosopher he sought. If he had such preconceived notions about male philosophers, God forbid what he might believe about intelligent women.

"Forgive my forwardness," she said, "but we have not been properly introduced."

He tipped his brown beaver hat. "Jonathan Pierce Williams. Most acquaintances call me Pierce, a name my mother preferred."

She held back her surprise at the name and gave a slight nod. "I know of Joshua Williams of Salem. Are you perchance his son?"

"The only one, I am afraid."

His response was restrained and in a tone that left her wondering as to its meaning. Instead of exhibiting the pride or position one usually associated with a wealthy name, he appeared almost disappointed she had made the connection. Was there some dissension between father and son? Or maybe he simply desired to be known for his own achievements and wanted to avoid the shadow of his father. If so, maybe he had at least one redeeming quality.

They had reached the carriage, a simple chair type, yet the leather and harnesses showed excellent quality and maintenance. She tried hard to recall what her father had said of Joshua Williams's son. Nothing, not even a mention, came to mind. Was that a purposeful bit of knowledge her father had neglected to pass on, or had he simply forgotten?

Did Pierce's family live with his father? She pictured a horde of his offspring creating such ruckus as to render concentration impossible. She required peace and a steady surrounding to accurately draw and detail samples. No matter, she had to accept things as they were. If Jonathan Pierce Williams had a part in her summer plans, she had much left to discover about him.

She gestured toward the horse. "You have a beautiful quarter horse, sir. I'd wager he is a good fourteen hands."

"Thirteen, madam." He caught her eye for a moment, and she considered correcting him on her proper name and title. The decision to wait came quickly. Women so infrequently had the upper hand with men. The moment became lost with a blink of his dark eyes as he offered her assistance into the carriage. As he climbed in beside her, he asked, "What purpose brings you to Salem?"

She hugged Newton's cage on her lap and smiled pleasantly at Pierce. "Adventure, Mister Williams. And thanks to you, I am well on my way to finding it."

Two

The heart of Salem lay along Main Street, several blocks from the bustling wharf. Crowds thronged the streets as market-day vendors hawked their fresh foods, and shoppers carried on social duties as well as domestic ones. A constable cut off the carriage's path as he escorted a fish vendor and his cart toward the wharf. When Pierce gave him a perturbed look, the policeman pointed toward the offending vendor and held his nose. The fish were destined for a watery disposal, as Salem evidently didn't tolerate sales of old fish any more than Boston did.

Alexandra studied Pierce as he once again set the horse in motion. As much as his wealthy family rated him a gentleman, his attire was another matter entirely. Dressed as he was in gentleman's working clothes of sturdy wool blends and cottons, and wearing tall leather boots that displayed blemishes from the elements, a closer inspection revealed a rougher existence. The curled brim of his tall beaver hat lay flat, apparently trampled by a large boot whose partial imprint remained etched in dust. His waistcoat, partially unbuttoned, failed to hide stains of sweat and dirt on his shirt. For so early in the day, life had taken a surprising toll on him.

His original need for dispatch had subsided as he kept the horse at a slow walk. She assumed he had succumbed to the fact that she had destroyed any further reason for great haste. She, on the other hand, wished to waste no time, at least in the form of conversation, on her efforts to gain knowledge of this unexpected member of the Williams family.

She straightened the cover on Newton's cage and brushed sand from her green cotton traveling skirt. With a light smile on her face and a bold look straight ahead, she launched her campaign. "I had the opportunity to make the acquaintance of your father's new shipping agent and his family."

With a quick twist of his head, Pierce stared at her in genuine surprise. "Here? In Salem?"

She had barely nodded in response when he added, "My father does not expect them for a fortnight."

"They were fellow passengers on the packet from Boston. I believe they had been in Boston for a good while but were anxious to get settled in Salem before the fall."

Decidedly unhappy about this apparent surprise, he issued a *chk* and prodded the horse faster. He cast her a wary look and tightened his chiseled jaw. "You are quite a wealth of information. Obviously, fortune smiled upon our meeting on the wharf. Have you, perhaps, any knowledge of where the new shipping agent has gone?"

"His daughter mentioned they were in search of lodging. Beyond those facts, sir, I'm afraid there is little more I know of use to you. Although, if you forgive my saying so, Monsieur Calonne seemed a bit sophisticated for a shipping agent. Is he perhaps an émigré from France, even possibly an aristocrat?"

A smile appeared at the edge of his mouth. "I would not advise a lady such as you to use *aristocrat* in their presence. Monsieur Calonne is a lawyer and a member of the bourgeoisie, with little love for the nobility. Are you acquainted with the details of the French Revolution?"

She disliked the patronizing tone in his voice. "I have read excerpts of Thomas Paine's book *The Rights of Man,* which defends the entire revolutionary fervor. I cannot say I agree with the means behind the revolution, but they appear to have aims similar to ours."

Pierce's eyes widened almost imperceptibly, and she recognized he hadn't expected such a reply from a woman. Heavens be praised that her modesty held her back from explaining that she had first devoured the French version before English excerpts were printed.

"Why has Monsieur Calonne come to America?" she asked.

Pierce shrugged nonchalantly. "I'm afraid his beliefs are out of vogue in France at the moment. He does not wish to be in the position of Louis the Sixteenth, who is not allowed to leave the country."

"I'm aware of the king's position, Mister Williams, but surely the French will handle these differences of opinion in a civilized manner."

Pierce shook his head grimly. "Angry citizens aren't always accepting of small nuances. Letters to my father from Monsieur Calonne indicate that many good citizens who supported the revolution are now held in French jails."

Alexandra found these new revelations unsettling. She inched forward in the cramped seat to better see his face. "Surely the public will eventually release them and grant them citizens' rights. Our own revolution is a good example."

"A perfect one," he quipped. "We tarred and feathered dissenters and banished them to Quebec."

Irritation bubbled forth at his rather derogatory reply. She contemplated several sharp replies, then decided against possibly aggravating her host. Instead, she fiddled with the cage on her lap and contemplated a more agreeable response.

Pierce obviously mistook her reflections for solicitude. "I apologize, ma'am, for burdening you with such distressing details of French politics. It is not an appropriate topic for a lady."

She blinked at him with resolve to educate him on the intellect of women. "Do you mean to say that the ladies of Salem do not express their views, whether national or foreign? Surely they must be as politically minded as the women of Boston."

He arched a brow warily in her direction. "I cannot rightly say I have held a political discussion with a lady as of late."

"Then I am glad to have remedied that situation." She unabashedly smiled at him and added, "Any time you wish to do so again, I will gladly comply."

With a twinkle in his eye, Pierce shifted toward Alexandra, and gently they touched shoulders. "Only if you promise not to accuse me of boring company."

Even though rather unsettled by the closeness of this handsome gentleman, she refused to back away. She parried his move by leaning close enough to smell the musk of his soap. "So promised."

Slightly taken aback, Pierce straightened, not taking his eyes from her. The carriage horse snorted and shook his mane at a passing rider, drawing Pierce's attention back to the road.

Something ahead captured his gaze, and she followed his line of sight. A young woman dressed in red-stripped silk dipped her head and smiled coyly at him from the steps of a millinery shop. Pierce returned a hearty smile, then nodded solemnly at the girl's mother as she stepped out of the shop.

Alexandra was quite taken aback that a married man acted so indelicately, especially with another lady present. She considered a gentle reprimand. Fortunate that life endowed her with a quick mind, she quelled that thought, realizing nothing had actually been said of the marital status of Mister Williams. She had simply supposed he was married. How judgmental of her not to have considered other possibilities.

"Ah, the Blue Shell is but a block hence," he said, as though never noticing the young woman.

"The Blue Shell?"

"Did you not desire an escort to the tavern where the stage discharged its passengers?"

"Most certainly, sir, but . . ."

"You need not have any misgivings about this tavern, madam. It is a commendable establishment where respectable travelers eat and lodge. The bottle-tipping places are by the wharf."

Alexandra smiled sheepishly at the title *madam,* realizing she had yet to apprise Pierce of her own marital status.

A wagon pulled by two chestnut horses blocked the intersection, bringing the Williamses's carriage to a momentary halt. A tall, stately man drove, and beside him sat a woman whose face hid beneath a fine straw hat gaily adorned with green ribbon. A gangly youth seated in the wagon bed fidgeted, then froze and stared at the carriage, and even more so in her direction.

Alexandra's stomach fluttered with an inexplicable feeling of familiarity toward the wagon's occupants. Her eyes locked on to the woman in the hat. She leaned toward Pierce. "Who is that lady?"

The wagon disappeared down a narrow side lane. Pierce glanced after it as their carriage moved forward. "The man is Reverend Goodwell. That may well be one of his daughters. I would have no doubt if I saw her hair. The elder one, Bridget, has the same fiery shine as yours. The last time I spoke with her was years ago, when she was merely a girl."

Alexandra remained silent as they moved. She searched all recent and childhood memories for some prior contact with the minister's family. None surfaced. Then where did this strong feeling of familiarity derive? Had the good Reverend Goodwell and his family ever been to Boston?

Aware they were approaching their destination, she simply had no time to let such distractions remove her from further examination of Pierce. Political discussions had already deferred the questions nagging at her curiosity.

"Excuse my intrusions, Mister Williams, but may I be so bold as to ask what business it is you undertake that leaves your coat so dusted?" She neglected to mention his tousled shirt and the smear of dirt across his brow.

He subtly eyed her attire, noting the damp hem and wet shoes. She felt uncomfortable and a bit foolish under his scrutiny and imagined he probably felt the same.

"I practice as a shipwright and architect for Mister Elias

Reynolds," Pierce finally answered. "He has contracted with a New York merchant group for two ships. As for my appearance, I heartily apologize. It is the result of a minor accident at the work site and is the reason for my delayed arrival at the wharf. In my haste to intercept my visitor, I had not anticipated encountering a lady."

"Likewise, sir, I had not expected to meet the son of Joshua Williams on my first visit to Salem. I am honored and appreciative of your generosity. I am also impressed at your own credentials. Does not your field of endeavor require studies at a university?"

"Most certainly. I spent three years at Oxford. Later I apprenticed at shipyards in the Netherlands and New York. There is nothing impressive in those credentials, however—only what is expected."

"You are much too modest," she replied. "The profession of shipwright must be most satisfying."

Pierce shrugged. "The work is stimulating, but most time-consuming. It takes me away from various family duties."

"I am sure your wife greatly appreciates such a reputable career, even if it does shorten your time together."

She spied a curious glimmer in his eye. "I have no wife to raise such concerns. It is my father. He has passed a good deal of his business matters over to me so he can pursue his scientific endeavors."

A sense of relief washed over her. She felt pleasure at his unmarried status and assumed the town women must view him a desirable match. The pleasure quickly changed to dismay. Why should she even care about his bachelor status? Uneasily she replied, "The scientific world is fortunate he has a son to take over and allow him such freedom."

The thought seemed to perturb Pierce. "His collections offer nothing useful," he mumbled, "simply a way to satisfy the longings of an old philosopher. His time would be better spent attending to shipping."

"Are you saying, sir, that science has no value for knowledge's sake?"

"I am merely expressing the opinion that science should directly benefit mankind."

She fought back irritation at the narrow-mindedness behind those gorgeous eyes. "It is a good thing Galileo or Newton did not wait for some necessity to arise, or we would still wonder about our position in the universe."

"The genius of those men is not in question," he shot back. "But what use is the knowledge of planets in our solar system?"

"Surely, with your studies in Oxford, you read of Newton's universal laws."

He grinned, almost catlike, and it made her wonder what memories were passing through his mind. "I wouldn't overrate the amount of education that occurred at Oxford. I studied what was practical to my profession."

She cringed at his response. How could he take education, one of the things she cherished most in life, so lightly? "Isaac Newton and Johannes Kepler could not foresee all the future implications of understanding why objects the size of the earth and moon are in motion."

He appeared to sense her irritation, but didn't relent. "I assume you allude to navigation and tides."

"You assume correctly," she answered.

"But the men you have chosen were geniuses and could apply their science to direct needs of mankind. My father is a merchant who dabbles in science for fun."

"And Benjamin Franklin was a printer," she snapped. "Did he have a reason to play with the Leyden jar other than supreme curiosity about the electrical phenomenon? There is nary a church steeple in America that doesn't now sport a lightning rod. Man cannot predict from where the next great invention will arise."

Pierce stiffened and slowed the carriage to a stop at the tavern. From his expression, she knew her passion for science had let her manners and common sense slip away. The scrutiny he gave every inch of her face made a flush chase away the chill of the morning. Her father would be appalled at the circumstances. She had accepted a ride, without proper introduction, with the unmarried son of her host, had misled him as to her identity, and then argued over his scientific beliefs.

She adjusted her hat and fought the desire to bite her lower lip in embarrassment. "You must forgive my ranting, Mister Williams. I do not usually get so carried away with discussions."

"You are duly pardoned. I am afraid your enthusiasm for the subject was rather unexpected. You appear quite enlightened with worldly knowledge. Your family did quite well with your education."

"I, too, was educated in Europe. My father considers ignorance an avoidable sin."

"And your husband?"

"I am not married, and see my fortune in it." She bit her lip, wishing that last bit of frankness had remained unspoken.

The look in Pierce's eyes thanked God that all men were equally as fortunate. "That's an unusual belief. I'm afraid few ladies in Salem will find agreement with you."

"I don't seek their approval nor do I believe my choice is the right course for every woman."

"How fortunate a reply. Had you planned to convert the women of Salem to your ways, I would be required to escort you out of town to ensure my future happiness."

He stepped out of the carriage and secured the horse. As he offered a hand to Alexandra, she extended Newton's cage. "My traveling companion, Newton."

"A seemingly appropriate name." He accepted the cage, unable to hide his curiosity at the weight. He opened his mouth to speak, but obviously thought better and extended a hand back in her direction. His hand, strong and warm, engulfed hers.

With skirt and petticoats delicately raised, she alighted from the carriage. "I greatly appreciate your escort and presume we both will find our parties waiting within," she said as he handed her the cage.

"The pleasure of your company—and I must include the rather brisk discussion—was mine." He motioned in the direction of the tavern door but did not offer an arm in escort.

With no time to hesitate, she glided up the three brick steps to the door, thinking all the way how to politely let Mister Williams know the truth and not lose her ride to the Williams estate. He might think her a complete fool or, worse yet, a manipulative woman, although, considering his arrogant assumption that Alexander Gables was a frumpy little man, he should at least be somewhat tolerant.

Long, open windows brightened the tavern despite the large number of people milling about inside. Tables had been pushed aside after the morning meal, and the business of finding lodging or transportation for patrons had taken precedence. Pierce excused himself to search for his passenger, and she, wishing to keep up pretenses, conversed with the owner's wife, who was placing cleaned pewter plates on a sideboard. Alexandra learned that the Williams estate stood on the edge of town, a substantial walk if she chose not to ride with Pierce.

As Pierce dashed among passengers from her ship, she slipped outside, inhaling the spring air redolent with fragrance of the lush purple lilacs adorning the entrance. The sun shone brightly, and temperatures were well on their way to recovering some of their spring mildness. Newton squirmed, hinting his desire for a morning bask. She set the cage on the brick stairs and bent over it.

"Not here," she whispered. "You would make a spectacle of yourself. I have done enough damage to my reputation for one day without your help."

A horse whinnied near the edge of the tavern, and an eerie breeze of cold air surrounded her body. Chilled, she stepped back from the tavern stairs and swung around toward the sound. Without a breath's warning, she collided with a woman

some twenty years her senior. Both of them gasped in breathless surprise, but their forward momentum held each from
crashing to the ground.

"My pardon, madam," Alexandra stuttered as she peered
into eyes so icy blue that they gleamed unreally. Black hair,
rolled high and back from a widow's peak, disappeared under
a purple velvet hat, contrasting with alabaster skin that Alexandra guessed was cold to the touch.

"Bridget Goodwell," the woman scolded Alexandra with
haughty authority, "what are you doing out here? Have you
no sense but to tarry while the others labor? Surely a door
waits to be held, or cloths for the tables collected." In apparent
haste, the woman pushed away and hustled in a blur of purple
down the road.

Astounded, Alexandra watched her go. The woman had mistaken her for someone named Bridget Goodwell. Alexandra
recalled the wagon with the reverend and his daughter. Again
a familiarity rose, along with the memory of the lad's surprised
face as the wagon had passed. Intuition, which she strongly
believed arose from memory or facts stimulated by some event
or sight but not yet congealed, suggested a connection existed.
Her intuition, crafted since her youth, rarely proved wrong.
Torn between keeping her attention on Pierce's carriage and
curiosity to see this Miss Goodwell and solve the familiar
connection, she drew toward the street corner with frequent
glances over her shoulder.

On the side lane stood the reverend's wagon, partially loaded
with a wooden table from the inn. Had the church plans for a
social? At the moment, no one was within sight. She inched
closer to the wagon, casually searching for the former occupants and wondering what resemblance she bore to Bridget
besides red hair.

The road underfoot vanished as a deep rut sent her stumbling off balance toward the horses. With a desperate grasp,
she caught a harness and avoided a tumultuous fate of scrapes
and soiled petticoats. "Easy, boy," she said, steadying herself

with a hand against the horse's flank. The horse snorted and stepped indignantly but held her weight.

Eerily, at the touch she sensed fear, panic, and dizzying vertigo, as though the horses sped out of control. Stunned, she jerked away as if fire had singed her hands.

The horses whinnied as she stared dumbfounded at her untouched palms. The thudding of her heart rang louder than a call to fire. That odd part of intuition that destroyed all scientific method had struck again. She had sensed a horrible fate awaiting these horses and their passengers.

Over the years she had learned that most people have intuition. Friends had often mentioned the feeling of having seen a place before, or of simply knowing the correct life path, but no one had ever discussed feeling events before they happened, as she had just experienced. Uncomfortable with this unexplained phenomenon, she straightened her skirt, checked the damage to her shoe, and considered returning to the tavern. Surely science had an answer, and her unpleasant shipboard travel and the resulting exhaustion were most likely the prime explanation. Yet over the years, she had learned never to ignore intuition. It often proved quite accurate.

The wish to disregard the entire experience and flee came into direct conflict with her internal questioning nature and the drive to explain all things. Her father had always emphasized, "When a problem arises, clear your mind and allow the facts to enter unaltered by personal prejudices."

With a prepared mind, she stroked the animal's warm chestnut hair and voiced reassurance. Impatience, youth, and vigor emanated from the horse, and she knew it was unseasoned. No details to confirm the earlier impressions revealed themselves beneath her touch. The harness, likewise, produced little response, and not until the rough pine of the wagon lay under her fingers did any additional feelings flash and fade.

Uneasy and yet with purpose, she circuited the wagon bed, stopping to inspect the wheels. The greater the distance from the horses, the weaker any impressions. As she completed the circuit, she stopped behind the horses and eyed the wood dou-bletree that attached to the wagon. A light touch of the wood brought an instant and vivid reaction. Excited, yet emotionally drained, she suspected that the wood was damaged or the bolt holding the pieces together was loose or defective. Carefully she leaned forward and examined the wood within reach. No defects were visible.

A woman's scream, foretelling nothing short of imminent death, sang from the steps of the tavern and cut short any further investigation. An image of Newton whirled inside her head. Oh, Lord, his cage was on the tavern steps.

Quickly she fled in his direction. Ahead on the distant steps, the cage lay open and on its side. A gentleman flailed his jacket at Newton, who dashed for the nearest tree while nearby a lady of robust stature crumpled to the ground.

Pierce barreled out the tavern door. With one brief glance, he seemed to size up the scene. "Sir, please, 'tis a harmless creature," he shouted at the gentleman assailing Newton. "Pray, come help me with your wife."

The man turned, unaware that his wife had succumbed to the ravages of hyperventilation. Alexandra gulped a breath and hustled toward them.

Pierce knelt on the ground and patted the woman's limp hand. The husband arrived as her eyelids fluttered to life. "My sincerest apologies, sir," Pierce said as he placed the woman's hand into her husband's and scooped up Newton's cage. He loped toward the tree.

Halfway up the trunk Newton had ceased his climb, aware that the imminent danger had disappeared. His long, spindly green toes with sharp claws held him fast to the tree. An amazed Pierce shook his head. "You are quite a magnificent specimen, Mister Newton. No wonder your mistress kept you well hidden." He reached out, and Newton hissed and swung his tail.

Alexandra reached Pierce's side. Newton's spiked dorsal crest was raised and tense. The scaled and spiked bag under his throat bulged, and a beady eye trained on Pierce. Indeed, with green and brown scales shimmering, the three-foot-long iguana appeared fearsome.

"Wisely, Mister Williams, I would allow Newton peace until the arch is gone from his back."

"I well agree," he answered, "and am quite aware of the festering nature of their bites. However, let us hope that Newton decides in all haste to relax his temper, or we will be entertaining a crowd of near half this town." He motioned down the street where workmen, paving the street with stones, stared in their direction, and to the tavern, where patrons covered the brick stairs.

"Of that I believe you are correct. I must also thank you, Mister Williams, for rescuing Newton. My father, to whom the creature belongs, and I are greatly indebted. That gentleman could easily have crushed him."

As though Newton was well aware of Alexandra's presence and their discussion of his finer attributes, he began to relax. With caution, she reached out and with tender caresses stroked along his body. Slowly his eyes closed. Minutes later she lifted him back into the covered cage, which Pierce held.

"I think it wise, miss," Pierce said, "that you find your party and remove yourself from this situation. 'Tis not an ordinary lady that carries such a creature. Salem is well known for its exotic treasures, and seafaring men have encountered this creature in the Indies, but the rumor of its romp will spread fiercely and with true haste."

After Pierce's rescue, she felt embarrassed at hiding her identity. The truth might serve to simplify events, but gathering curiosity seekers made this not the time or place for confessions.

"I will surely heed your worthy advice, sir." She swallowed guiltily and glanced toward the tavern and back to Pierce. "Have you located the gentleman you seek?"

"It seems the person you remember is not to be found." He paused, eyes serious and lips tightened as if in reprimand.

She wondered if he had uncovered her deception and now awaited a confession.

He continued, "I can but presume he procured other transportation."

"In that case, sir, could I again impose upon your generosity?"

Pierce showed no apparent surprise at her request, and she felt foolishly dependent on his goodwill. Had she simply informed him of his error at the dock, her current tenuous position might have been negated. As she opened her mouth to confess the deception, a young voice called to them from the distance.

"Madam, madam by the tavern. Is this bag yours?" The boy from the reverend's wagon held up a tiny beaded bag and looked in their direction.

Alexandra instinctively clutched her wrist. The navy cord tying her purse to her wrist was gone, along with the bag. The stumble had wrenched it from her arm. "Oh, how fortunate his discovery," she exclaimed to Pierce. "I had been admiring the horses when Newton broke loose."

"Allow me to retrieve it for you." Pierce stepped away. "Wait," she said hastily, then foolishly wondered how to express her belief to Pierce. The feelings she garnered at the wagon may have been no more than an excited imagination. "I implore you to thank him graciously and offer this advice in turn. I noticed an inconsistency where the bolt attaches the doubletree to the wagon. I beg you, do not let the wagon leave unless it is examined."

Pierce showed doubt but made no comment as he strode off to join the youth. From the distance, she saw the boy shake his head several times. Pierce appeared to insist. Eventually, the boy climbed behind the horses.

The reverend appeared and shook Pierce's hand in a warm greeting. The boy motioned to them both and they bent toward him. A conversation of undecipherable gestures ensued, with many shrugs from Pierce, and eventually eyes were cast in her direction. She gave a modest wave, worried that Pierce might expect further explanation.

Pierce took his leave and walked toward her. With each determined step, the curiosity on his face became more evident. In place of questions, though, he offered commendations.

"By all appearances, your acuity prevented possible tragedy. The bolt was nearly sheared through. Reverend Goodwell assured me the team is young and unsteady, and a horse spooked by a loose doubletree might have dragged them all into disaster."

A knot twisted in Alexandra's stomach. Her impressions had proved correct, yet she had no real explanation of from where they truly came. She attempted a modest response, even though she was assured that Goodwell spoke the truth. "Surely, you make it sound dramatic for my benefit."

"The Reverend Goodwell espoused that very scenario as earnestly probable."

With a serious glance back toward the corner, she added quietly and uneasily, "Then I am pleased to have offered my services."

Pierce returned her bag and extended his arm toward the carriage. "Now, if you have no other errands required of me, shall we depart? Although the men at the shipyard are quite accountable, given ample leniency they tend to tarry."

He dispatched her without ceremony into the carriage. Two healthy blocks lay behind them before she found the courage to speak. "Thank you for retrieving my purse, and forgive my intrusions upon your precious time. I have asked much of a complete stranger. You have done the Williams family name great justice."

"A name of importance is not required to serve others in the manner expected by normal civility. I have expressed pleasure at our encounter and must admit it is of the most unusual quality. I hope you take no offense in my asking, but are adventures such as these a normal occurrence with you?"

"With all honesty, Mister Williams, I must swear to living an extraordinary life."

"I beg of you, call me Pierce. That title will save confusion when both my father and I are present. And I, in turn, promise to hold the name of Alexandra in highest esteem." A smiled widened his lips. "I presume that is how your father addresses you, Miss Gables?"

Her ploy discovered by its victim, she answered somewhat sheepishly, "I believe circumstances will render that name quite sufficient." She hesitated before adding, "How long have you known?"

Pierce laughed. "Since the moment I laid eyes on Newton. No ordinary woman has such a creature for a pet. Do not regret your little deception, though. I wholly deserved the ploy. You are simply not what I expected. My father never spoke of his summer intern in genteel terms."

"And my father never mentioned that Mister Williams had a son."

Sudden suspicions struck a cold discord in the pit of her stomach. Had her father known all along of Pierce and purposely hidden the fact? Had he undertaken some fashion of matchmaking? The father, whom she held in high esteem, had possibly made a mockery of the reason for her summer visit. Shame made her desire to shrink from Pierce and head back to the ship. Instead, she drew on the indomitable Gables spirit and turned to face him. She assumed the expression on his face was reflected on her own.

"You do not suppose my father would succumb to such a low deed as an attempt at matchmaking?" she asked.

Pierce, with a decidedly perturbed look darkening his face, grumbled, "I do not know, but I cannot claim it is beyond my father."

Alexandra recalled discussions before her father's trip to London about her lack of male companionship. "As of late, my father *has* seemed preoccupied with the approach of my twenty-first year and no suitors, at least not one I care for."

"As two educated people, we may be assuming too much of our fathers' actions. My father can be as absentminded as cunning." A perturbed line thinned Pierce's lips. "In this case, I cannot guarantee which is the true case."

"My father has no such excuse," Alexandra added. "He harbors no lack of memory. However doubtful it seems, he simply may never have inquired as to the status of your family. Our fathers' prior meetings have generally occurred in Boston."

"Then, my dear Miss Gables, it is impossible to ascertain whether we both have been duped. However, I suggest future diligence in investigating the matter."

The thud of hooves on the trodden road, and the regular jangle of the harness beat home the truth of the situation. She began to have no doubts that the very father who supported her ventures into the sciences had degraded the worth of this internship by meddling with her private life. With every minute that they drew closer to the Williams estate, she mentally added another seething line to a letter bound for her father in London.

Three

Pierce departed for the shipyard well before noonday, leaving Alexandra to wander the Williamses' gardens in relative peace. She reflected upon the morning encounter with him and allowed herself to admit to his wit and knowledge, amazed that such an attractive man actually had intellect and opinions. So many men, like the ones her father so frequently invited from Harvard College, could not carry on a conversation of any depth or pause long enough to listen to her replies. Most were rich, spoiled, and selfish, and spent more time and money on their wardrobes than women did.

She remembered Pierce's dusty attire. Apparently, he lived by a different standard, one she had yet to define. Still, he had shown a remarkable lack of enthusiasm over her extended visit. Well, what did she expect? He viewed his father's pastime as a trivial avocation.

Newton basked on a dark rock, bobbing his head in obvious pleasure. She yawned and let the warm sun relax her very being. What Pierce thought made very little difference. His father had extensive collections of rocks, insects, pressed leaves and flowers. Her summer supposedly entailed assisting this amateur philosopher in sketching and cataloging various specimens and helping to describe the properties of rocks he had collected. Regardless of the twisted scheme Mister Williams and her father may have created to get her wedded, she would complete her assignment. Science was her first and only love.

A butterfly captured her attention as it spiraled upward from a bush. Eventually, it disappeared around the corner of the graceful Williams mansion and into the tangled overgrowth along an open field. Although the majority of ship owners and merchants preferred a home within sight of the noisy wharves, she had discovered Joshua Williams's was not like most. He cherished solitude and space and had fled two years previously from the bustling wharf district to the far edge of town, where ample space provided this idyllic setting.

Alexandra stood in the spice and herb garden behind the house. Fruit trees still in their infancy lined the yard, and several hardwoods had been planted for shade. Sadly, the ancient trees had been harvested in this area for homes and shipbuilding. No doubt, shade from the new plantings remained a good many years distant.

At the opposite end of the gardens from the house were the brightly painted stables where Pierce had exchanged the carriage for a horse this morning. Alexandra pictured his hasty departure on a black stallion. The horse and his rider had seemed as one, prancing and dark. Rich tones of his voice echoed in her memory. Surprisingly, he had shown no anger at her deception, only amazement that she had dared attempt such a scheme.

Movement interrupted her thoughts. The stout middle-aged housekeeper with a broom in one hand stepped out of the kitchen door and marched past Newton with a wary glance.

"You needn't worry, Mrs. Bisbey," Alexandra said soothingly. "Newton will not bother you."

"Gracious be, mum," Mrs. Bisbey said, appraising Newton, "he is an odd one. But for twenty years, I have survived Mister Williams's oddities. The likes of this creature I can easily keep under a watchful eye."

"I will appreciate your assistance. Some of the household staff may be a bit more apprehensive about Newton's presence, though."

Mrs. Bisbey's large, rough hands scratched thoughtfully at

her rounded chin. " 'Tis only young Rebecca, the housemaid, which gives me concern. She sees the devil in everythin'. Come this Sabbath, she'll have half the congregation convinced Lucifer has come to visit. Me knowledge of this creature is likely to be more sought after than the minister's Sunday advice. Best I learn somethin' 'bout it so I can put truth to the rumors that'll be spreadin'."

Alexandra smiled, reassured that Mrs. Bisbey could easily handle the curious. This woman was all business, and from the kempt appearance of the Williams household, she ran a tighter ship than did any seafaring captain. "I have no doubt your sturdy counsel will assure the population they suffer no danger from evil visitations," she replied. "I will gladly divulge Newton's secrets whenever you desire. Now, may I assist you with the purpose that has brought you to the gardens?"

"Mister Williams has returned, Mistress Gables. He has retired to refresh his clothing and will be with you immediately."

"Joshua Williams?"

"Yes, mum. He asked for you to meet him in the conservatory."

"Thank you, Mrs. Bisbey. I shall secure Newton and be there presently." She reached Newton as the housekeeper slipped past, keeping an ample distance. Reluctantly he retreated into the cage, and Alexandra carried him to the conservatory. The glass room was a necessary yet extravagant feature of the mansion, where Mister Williams grew plants for pleasure and study.

Joshua Williams swept in moments later. "My dear Miss Gables." He collected her hand and patted it while studying her with wise and watchful eyes. "What a wonderful pleasure it is to have you brighten my home."

She set Newton's cage down. "The pleasure is all mine, I assure you."

Mister Williams dropped her hand, and she in turn spent a moment studying her patron. He carried much the same height as his son but had rounded out amply in his later years. His dark hair had also thinned to a shiny bald spot on top with gray salting the sides. A pock marred one cheek but did nothing to detract from the jovial expression emanating from his face.

"Your journey appears to have done you little harm," he said. "You seem rested and fit. One of the benefits of youth, I expect."

"More so the benefit of your gracious hospitality," she replied with genuine admiration for his lovely home.

His gaze moved eagerly to Newton's cage. Carefully and without haste, he bent down and removed the cover. "Ah, the creature the Caribs call *iwana.*"

"Literature, what little mention there is, uses the Spanish version, *iguana,*" she added. Newton stoically held his head high and returned Mister Williams's scrutiny.

Barely containing his excitement, Joshua rubbed his hands together. "Newton is a fine specimen. I have prepared the perfect place for him. It offers both warmth and shade, and a perch where he can observe."

He led them toward a corner beneath a glass window, where enormous clay pots, small trees, and large plants jutted tall. A polished piece of driftwood stretched between two wood posts. Beneath lay gravelly sand, several large-sized basking rocks, and a flat bowl of water. "Mrs. Bisbey has orders to warm the rocks in the fireplace on unavoidably dreary days."

Alexandra lifted Newton from the cage onto the perch. Sun streaked through the glass, warming the wood. She could feel Newton's pleasure and knew he found his accommodations quite acceptable.

"What perfection," she said with thanks, "but I must express concern that he may desire to remain forever in such a wonderful abode."

Joshua Williams stared at Newton, unable to draw his eyes from the fully displayed creature. "The credit due is not mine. I simply followed your father's instructions. But I doubt that, even under the best of conditions, Newton would elect to remain. I understand he responds to you in most amazing ways."

"My father exaggerates," she demurred. "I simply understand this creature's desires. On that note, I believe it prudent to remove the water bowl."

"Surely iguanas drink."

"They do, but most attain ample moisture from vegetables. I must admit with great indelicacy that Newton utilizes the water vessel as a chamber pot."

Mister Williams roared with laughter. "I believe Newton and I will get along famously. Nevertheless, I think it wise we retire to my study, where you can indulge my curiosity with further details on his care. I may even find time to introduce you to most of my collections before supper, when Pierce returns from the shipyard."

Pierce's familiar name evoked a sense of anticipation she could not explain. "Your son was most gracious to spend his morning seeing to my safe arrival." Carefully she studied Joshua's face, looking for any signs of the possible conspiracy with her father.

"Ah, yes. I must admit, I held a small concern he might forget. I can name many an occasion when shipbuilding wiped all other duties from his thoughts." He swept Alexandra along toward a front room next to the library. "Toils too hard, he does. No time for the pleasurable attributes of life. An influence of Salem's Puritan heritage, I suppose."

She refrained from asking which pleasurable attributes he had in mind. Instead, she felt a twinge of exasperation and wondered if this internship was nothing more than an opportunity for two fathers to introduce their children.

"Perhaps your son finds gratification in his work, as I do," she offered. "I, for example, require nothing more in life than a scientific question to pursue and a means to sketch or paper on which to write. Not everyone requires leisure or a large family for self-fulfillment."

He studied her closely with a questioning brow and indicated an embroidered chair. "Making apologies for him already, eh? It's not necessary. I know my son well. No one in this world I would trust more with the business than he. But somehow I neglected to teach him what is truly important in life."

She sat, recalling Pierce's response to the girl at the millinery shop. "His manner did not appear lacking in social grace, nor show any desire to avoid life's amenities. Perhaps children, no matter what age, do not share all their intimacies with their fathers."

Joshua Williams's somber, thin lips widened into a wise smile. "My dear Miss Gables, have you already charmed more than one man of the Williams household? I am not surprised. You are a woman of discernment and wit."

Pleased by the compliment but wishing to set the record straight, Alexandra added, "I will say with gentle candor, short of divulging the privacy of another's heart, his attentions were not toward me. As a matter of fact, when I expressed my preference for a solitary life, he volunteered to escort me from town lest I influence other young ladies. I think you have little to worry about with your son. Time will find him a proper match."

Mister Williams nodded. "You are exactly as your father described—honest and forthright. He also said you hope someday to publish your own work." He nestled comfortably into a sturdy armchair of tawny leather. "On a collection of rocks, I believe. That will be quite an accomplishment for a woman."

Pleased her father had actually advertised her scientific aptitude, she answered, "I set my goals high. And granted my future good health and the open minds of the scientific societies, I will see it accomplished. In the meantime, I earnestly look forward to working with your collections. With your good counsel, I believe my talents will live up to the expectations presented by my father." She wondered which talent her father had actually hawked: intelligence or beauty. How she wished to know the contents of her father's sealed letter of introduction, which lay on Mister Williams's desk.

"I have no doubts," Joshua replied. "I saw your father's study on the pileated woodpecker. Your drawings captured the essence of the bird."

Alexandra puzzled at the genuine excitement he displayed in her work. Maybe she was mistaken about the ploy of the two fathers. "I am flattered. I hope to achieve the same success with your collections."

"The specimens await your hand." He pointed toward a broad worktable set with three large plant presses. Then, with a shake of his head, he smiled at her. "Excuse my excitement, though. I have lost my manners. Is all well with your accommodations? Does the desk in your chamber suffice for your needs? Your father did mention your writing and predisposition to lay out drawings and revise them until satisfied."

"The writing desk is more than adequate. I find your home comfortable yet wonderfully elegant, and it contains to my great good fortune a most prodigious library. I admit to a lengthy browse through many of your titles."

He spread his arms wide. "The library is yours to peruse. I wish more citizens would avail themselves of its resources." He rose to his feet. "Now, shall we start with the wildflowers? I have several undocumented specimens."

Curious to see the specimens, she eagerly stood and for the first time noticed the painting on the wall behind her chair. Pierce's raised sculpted chin and dark eyes gazed proudly from the canvas. In response, Alexandra raised her own chin, then moved to his father's side to assist in his pursuit of what the man in the portrait considered a trivial pastime.

Pierce finished brushing down his horse in the meager moonlight that filtered into the stable. He didn't mind the duty, but exhaustion and hunger made it a more arduous task than usual. Rarely did his arrivals and departures fit with the abbreviated schedules of the hired help. Young men were hard to keep, for the sea lured them away at fourteen, and younger boys had schooling and home duties. His father refused to keep indentured servants, and the wharf grabbed up most other able-bodied men.

Rocks crunched under his boots, and the gardens smelled

of moisture and spices—mint in particular this night—as he walked toward the house. With disappointment, he noted a dim glow from the library window. He had hoped to avoid a confrontation with his father this evening concerning the new houseguest. With a conversation all but inevitable, the prudent course was to avoid all mention of Alexandra Gables.

Mrs. Bisbey waited at the kitchen door. She removed his coat and directed him to a hearty meal on the kitchen table. "I didn't think ye'd mind, sir, eatin' back here. Give ye a few moments peace before the master speaks with ye."

"Is the news that bad?" He arched a brow in her direction and sat eagerly at the table. He dove into the bread and meat with little delicacy and followed it with a slug of cider.

"Oh, no sir, there's no bad news." She topped his mug with cider, then dabbed a dribble off the pitcher. "Methinks he has heard 'bout one of your ships, though. Must be good, because he ate hearty at supper. Sir, I warn ye, he may be a tad upset you missed the meal, with our new guest and all."

His irritation rose that Alexandra was already interfering with his schedule. "Miss Gables will be with us all summer and must be understanding of my situation. When there is enough light to see the hand before the face, I must be at the shipyard."

" 'Tis not me that needs convincin', sir."

The single lit candle on the table flickered as his father filled the doorway from the living area. "I thought I heard voices," his father said. "I see Mrs. Bisbey is spoiling you again."

Pierce rose from the table and gently patted Mrs. Bisbey on the shoulder. "Captains a mighty house, she does. Makes sure every man on this crew is properly fed, even long after the cook is gone." He turned and clasped hands with his father. "What news do you bring from the meeting?"

They headed to the front study, set aside as a place of business. "Revelations far outweigh the news, I'm afraid, son. Between Federalist Derby and the Republican Crowninshield, Salem may never choose representatives. Those two families in the same room create nothing but dissension. We were lucky to whittle the considerations to five men." He poured brandy into two glasses and handed one to Pierce. "Crowninshield's losing a ship didn't help matters."

"Aye, we heard the crier's news. Many of my workers had given their savings for expectations with the crew. Losing such an investment, meager as it may seem, is a significant blow." Pierce sought the comfort of an upholstered corner chair.

His father took refuge in his leather armchair. "At least Crowninshield was insured. Though I don't expect he'll be as generous to the families as Derby would be."

"It is a task I never wish to face." Pierce raised his glass. "May your ships make safe sail."

"Our ships." His father emphasized the words and raised his own glass.

Pierce swirled his brandy. "I need to talk with you about that very point. I have too little time to dedicate to the business. You must take on more of the load until this ship is complete."

"Nonsense. You are doing a fine job with the business. Besides, I, too, have extra commitments."

An image of Alexandra sprang into Pierce's mind and he quashed it as quickly as possible. How could any man concentrate on business with such a fine skirt as Alexandra floating around the house?

His father sipped heartily, a twinkle arising in his jovial eyes. "Yes, yes, our summer guest is one. My sources tell me you succeeded in mucking up a proper welcome."

The subject Pierce wished to avoid had arisen. He leaned forward in the chair. "My muck-up was the complete result of improper counsel. You made no mention I sought a woman," he said accusingly.

"I didn't say? You must have been in such a haste this morn, you missed my direction."

"I saw you for but a moment before I slipped out the door," Pierce shot back. "The only direction you gave was not to forget. I remembered, and besides, once the situation was clarified, I delivered our guest without incident."

"Was that before or after the commotion at the Blue Shell?"

A swift anger rose within Pierce. He downed a choking swill of brandy. How like a woman to prattle on with every little shortcoming a man possessed. "No mention was made, I suspect, of my rescue of the foreign creature Miss Gables left unattended on the steps?"

"I recall no such statement," his father said, "but the housemaid did mention the state of your clothing. Quite an exciting rescue, I presume?"

"My appearance was totally unrelated to the incident." Pierce rose to his feet, annoyed by his father's meddling in his life. "And I must point out the timing of this visit is most inopportune. The nature of my schedule renders it nearly impossible to extend the civilities expected of a host. But what I find utterly incomprehensible is why you would dare to concern yourself in my private affairs."

With innocent eyes and a puzzled face, Joshua looked up at Pierce. "My boy, I am at a loss to comprehend your meaning. I see no evidence of invading your affairs. I merely requested your assistance for an errand during a time when I was indisposed. Besides, Miss Gables will be as one of the family this summer while she interns here. No additional requirements will be made upon your time more than normal civility already requires."

Pierce stared at him, unchanged in his belief. He had wanted to save this discussion for a time when his wits and temper were more under control. "Please, Father," he spat out. "You raised no fool and your earnest endeavors to find me a mate are conspicuous. Mrs. Bisbey is woman enough for this household. I need no one else to cook and slave for me."

His father shifted complacently in his chair and smiled. "That is most fortunate, for I hear Miss Gables is lacking in culinary skills. She is here in a professional manner and most assuredly would find your suggestion otherwise an affront. I'd be careful not to approach her in such a manner. Her wit is most sharp and your sensibilities obviously are not prepared for injury."

"A woman poses no threat to my intellect," Pierce huffed.

"Have I raised a man of such narrow mind? Your reading is obviously in arrears. Have you not seen the latest *Boston Magazine*?" His father tossed him a thin folded document.

Pierce frowned as he picked up the magazine. "Work consumes my sunlight hours. Unlike you, I do not care to read by candlelight."

"I think you will find this article worthy of your time, maybe even necessary for your survival against Miss Gables. It concerns the intellect of women."

Pierce held the magazine near the single candle on his father's desk. Beneath the title, the author's name read *Noble Horatio*. "I have read his columns before. Usually he expresses sensible views on politics and life."

"Then read this column."

Pierce glanced at his father and read the first paragraph silently. "Ridiculous," he said, raising his eyes from the text. "He believes the Bible points out the shrewdness of women over men. Claims men allow themselves to easily fall to the soft passions of women." He dropped the magazine back on the desk. "No man is impervious to mistakes. I can allow this author his difference of opinion. Now, forgive me Father, but I must take my leave and rest. My body believes sunrise comes too soon these days." He downed the remainder of the brandy and left his glass on the desk.

He reached the door when his father said, "By the way, *Salem's Pride* reached Canton. She is now loaded with fine Chinese goods. From her last reported location, I'd expect her home in three months' time."

Elation filled Pierce. Chinese silks, tea, and fine porcelain tantalized his imagination. He had risked half his income earned as a shipwright on *Salem's Pride*'s success. The rest he planned to put into the ship he now built for the New York company. He would show Salem he cared naught for the pampered heritage other wealthy sons enjoyed in this town.

He turned back toward his father and caught a glimmer of

pride in his gentle eyes. "Thank you; the news brings a joyful end to my day." With a quick breath Pierce added, "Father, I will do my best to respect Miss Gables's wishes while she resides under our roof. Good night."

Tired as his body was, he mounted the central stairway two steps at a time. A draft from the open upstairs windows breezed down the stairs and suggested cool sleeping temperatures. Tonight he would offer a prayer for *Salem's Pride*'s safe voyage home. He bounded onto the second-story landing and headed down the hall for his bedroom. Beams of light shone from one of the guest rooms.

He softened his footsteps upon approach. The door stood wide open and an Argand lamp burned at a desk toward the back of the room. Alexandra sat with her back to him, her fiery hair tied into a long red stream down her back. Bare feet were crossed under the desk and rested on a low wood crossbar. Still in her green traveling skirt from the morning, she had removed the jacket and opened several of the top buttons of her cream silk blouse. A pen in hand, she scribbled upon paper.

In all honesty, he hadn't meant to stare. She represented nothing but another tedious obligation. Her hand floated across the page, delicate and inviting. With a single flowing motion, she dipped the pen into the well and continued. The room had a fresher smell than he remembered. He slowly inhaled and imagined a whiff of roses. So she did have a feminine side.

The lamplight cast an ethereal glow on her form. He unexpectedly had an odd urge to see how her face softened in the light. How would those fiery tresses fall about and frame her features? He closed a fist, surprised to feel sweat on his palms.

Now who is being ridiculous? he thought. I've let the brandy go to my head. I have no time to trifle with this woman. He turned to step away.

"You stop to stare, Mister Williams, but refrain from offering a pleasant night." Alexandra's voice filled the darkened hall. "That's odd manners, to say the least."

He glanced back. She slowly swung around in the chair to

match his gaze. Words jumbled in his brain and fumbled from his lips. "My apologies. The door was open."

"I find no disrespect in your curiosity toward a new houseguest, sir."

He feared that ill ease shone on his face. "Please, you promised to call me Pierce."

The hint of a smile formed at her mouth's edge. "I earnestly will attempt to remember."

She rose and came toward him, precluding the hasty retreat he desired. "I wish to disturb you no further," he said, backing up a step.

"That is kind, but my writing is finished for the evening and I plan to retire. Before you take leave, I must offer you congratulations. Your father shared the good news of *Salem's Pride*."

"It is too soon to count one's blessings. The most dangerous stretch of ocean lies along our own shores."

She came close enough to continue a subdued conversation. With her head tilted in a most charming manner, she added, "I predict a successful outcome."

"And upon what scientific reasoning is that based?" he asked. He leaned against the door frame, studying her confident green eyes. Was this attention her way of apologizing for this morning?

"Just intuition, I'm afraid." She kept her voice soft, as though in fear of awakening the household. Instead, the soft tones had the sensuous effect of awakening desires he would rather have kept buried. Had she no idea how alluring she appeared in the shadowy light?

"But if it is any consolation," she added as a few loose strands of hair gently touched her cheeks, "I am rarely wrong."

Amazed at her cocksure attitude and unable to help himself, he reached out and touched a fiery curl. "Quite self-assured, aren't you?"

Obviously uneasy at his touch and suddenly aware of her physical state, she casually folded the top of her blouse together back under her chin but did not button it in place. "Was I not right about the reverend's wagon?"

"Ah, but you must have seen the damaged bolt. Only the consequences were unknown." The back of his hand brushed her cheek as he slowly dropped it to his side.

She flushed and set a hand to her face, unintentionally allowing the top buttons of her blouse to fall open once again. Leaning back against the opposite doorjamb, she demurely cast her eyes downward. "What you say is true. I make no claim to perfection. My intuition did lead me astray concerning our fathers' plans for us."

"Ha!" Pierce let slip with emphasis. He set a hand on the jamb above her head. The rose scent enticed him closer, but he did not succumb. "I see no error in that prediction. I do believe my father had every intent in forcing our introduction."

"Oh, I heartily disagree." She stared up at him, the flush gone and a new strength glimmering. "I found no indication of that in my lengthy discussion with him."

Irritation returned as he thought her bold to admit to such flagrant gossip. "The length of your discussion with my father became apparent a few moments ago." He straightened and leaned toward her in accusation. "Although I do believe the details concerning the Reverend Goodwell's wagon were omitted."

Balanced now on both feet, she crossed her arms. The paleness behind her freckles flamed with anger. "In my most affrighted imagination, I would never bow to the art of gossip, if that is to what you allude."

"I allude to my father having a detailed description of our meeting and journey. Could you not have left a few details out? Must you have pointed out every faux pas I made."

"You jump to unjust conclusions, *Mister* Williams. I discussed nothing of the sort with your father. I simply meant we might have been hasty in our judgment of their summer scheme. By all appearances your father has a healthy dose of work for me. One that, in all likelihood, these few months will barely provide the requisite time to finish."

He leaned an arm against the door again and shook his head. "It's all a ploy. Can you not imagine your father partaking in such a scheme? I see it clear as day."

"What I see is a man whose manners need redeeming. I suggest that you use the evening's rest to put them in order." She took hold of the door and partially closed it.

Somewhere in his memory he remembered redheads were quick to temper. This divinely fair one gave indubitable proof of such a tale. "You are the one in search of truth," he whispered. "I fear though you may be too blind to see it."

The red behind the freckles had now turned scarlet, her chest puffed and her face grew rigid, like a cobra ready to strike. Slowly and concisely she spoke, no longer concerned about keeping a quiet voice. "Forgive my rudeness, *sir*, but unless you have any more comments, I plan to retire."

Although the discussion had turned to a rather invigorating little encounter, wisdom hailed this as the time for him to back away. No sense in poisoning the rest of his summer. The next time he passed her room, he planned to sprint. "Good night, Alex-an-dra." He deliberately drew out her name.

She shut the door, leaving him standing in the dark. *How rude,* he mused. *She offered no good night.* He strode toward his room, positive that women with their emotional instabilities could never equal a gentleman's intelligence. He swung the door shut just a little too hard.

At the bottom of the stairs, Joshua Williams had stood in darkened silence listening to the low murmur of voices. The voices rose, then ceased before a door slammed. A frown crossed his face. Some pigheaded youths required a little nudge in the direction of recreation. Definitely a party was in order, but not just any party. Invigorated with a new task, he twirled on one foot and headed back to his desk. How would he guarantee that both his guests of honor would attend? Ah, yes. The answer was simple. Quite devious, he thought, but what fun!

Four

Alexandra twirled loose the wood bolts of a flower press and carefully removed a dried specimen. This morning she had already completed detailing one plant through a sketch and planned another before adding color. However, this familiar routine, which she had used for years to document her scientific work, did not proceed with the usual precision. A fitful sleep had left a tired residue, and she directly blamed Pierce.

In the shadows of the hall last night, his aura of mystery and strength had loomed silently near her door. Feeling his presence, she had summoned all her patience to fight the longing to turn immediately and capture his attention. Such foolishness was not the reason for her presence in Salem. She should be thankful he succeeded in dousing the desire with his remarks. How dare he accuse her of frivolous gossip!

For the third time, Mrs. Bisbey swooshed past the study to the front entry. This time she carried two large baskets. Alexandra puzzled over the woman's preparations, for market day was not until the morrow.

When the robust woman appeared again, Alexandra called out, "Mrs. Bisbey!" The housekeeper paused. "Pardon, my curiosity, but for what event do you prepare?"

"Cranberries have come due, mum. The Willobys are off to Danvers and invited me to collect berries with them. I plan to fill a basket for Mrs. Hunt, too."

"Is Mrs. Hunt a good friend?"

"A fellow parishioner, mum. Terrible shame, her lot is. Her

husband fished on one of Mister Derby's small boats. A fortnight past, a fierce storm smashed it upon the ledges. Men found Mister Hunt's body lashed to the foremast, floatin' in the water."

Alexandra shivered at the image, fully aware of the cruelty possible from the mistress sea. She had crossed the Atlantic to study in England and had witnessed firsthand nature's fury.

"Such a grievous end for any life," she said with genuine sorrow. "Your deed will be much needed."

Mrs. Bisbey looked grim as she tied on a straw hat. " 'Tis no doubt. She has three young'uns. I may sound cold of heart, but she needs to grieve quickly and snatch a new husband."

Alexandra felt horrified at the prospect, but knew the practice was common at this seafaring town. She suspected the widows outnumbered the eligible men, much like after the revolution—only now women lost men to the sea.

"You offer no indelicacy in wishing a quick end to Mrs. Hunt's woes," she replied as Mrs. Bisbey folded her apron into one of the baskets. "Am I to be the lone keeper of the house today?"

Mrs. Bisbey shook her head. "Don't ye worry 'bout dinner, mum. Cook's here and will take care of ye. The elder Mister Williams is gone till supper. He's busy promoting a hospital and making arrangements for the party."

Alexandra knew of the hospital duty, but the party announcement caught her by surprise. "Forgive me, but I was not aware of any planned festivities."

"Mister Williams said 'tis in yer honor on Friday eve. Don't fret 'bout not knowin'; he just told me this morn." A large carriage pulled up on the packed-dirt street and Mrs. Bisbey picked up the baskets.

"What about Pierce?" Alexandra wasn't sure why she asked. Possibly after last evening's disagreement, she simply sought to avoid his presence.

"Oh, he doesn't know of the party either." Mrs. Bisbey stepped through the door.

Alexandra leaned over the threshold. "No, I meant will he be returning for dinner?"

Mrs. Bisbey shrugged. "Never know, mum. He's his own man. Good day to ye." She hustled down the white granite steps and into the awaiting carriage.

At least, Alexandra thought, she would have little interruption of her day's work. She swung shut the front door, relieved to have some solitude at last.

Light shone in and reflected off several mirrors, brightening the study. She took a deep breath, glad for the chance to stretch and actually examine her surroundings. Besides furnishings related to any study, and the large worktable covered with specimens and her drawing utensils, family portraits graced the walls. The paintings were mostly of pretentious-looking gentlemen in a varying selection of collars and jackets that matched the fashion of their time.

She stopped at Pierce's portrait. The artist had chosen a churning sea as background. Appropriate, she thought, for a shipwright; and it fit his rather adventurous, determined countenance. Even the artist, though, couldn't put a stern look into his soft eyes. At the moment, those eyes stared out as though wishing her gone.

She glared back. "You cast such doubts on your father's contributions to science and on my abilities to assist him. He and I will succeed, Pierce Williams."

An eerie tingle breathed along her neck. She felt a presence and dreaded the thought that Pierce stood in the doorway watching. Had he seen her talking aimlessly to his portrait? She waited until the heat dissipated from her cheeks before casually turning around. The room was empty.

Instead, her attention was drawn to an older portrait. The title, painted in black and gold on the portrait frame, read *Judge Nathaniel Williams*. Long white hair under a smooth official cap softened his face. She felt strangely drawn to the painting. Tentatively she reached out and touched the judge's name.

A powerful surge of darkness mixed with eerie, frightening sounds: a woman's mournful weeping, people yelling, "Hang the witches," and the creaking of a rope weighted and swinging slowly back and forth. In shock, she pulled her hand away. Intuition had always been a friend, but since arriving in Salem this intuition had expanded its nature to include first strong feelings, as at the wagon, and now haunting sounds.

She stared at the judge and let the sounds again play through her mind. This time she listened with practiced scrutiny, and the review produced a horrible revelation. For her, the Salem witch trials had momentarily come alive.

Surely this was impossible. Her intuition always encompassed the future. But these sounds came from the past. She had studied the trials, as had many of the educated in New England, but obviously she had allowed Salem's infamous past to influence her imagination.

To prove such folly came merely from prior knowledge and simple exhaustion, she again reached out to touch the portrait. Anguish and a deep pain enclosed her heart. She swore a shadow of sorrow darkened the portrait's face. She backed away, knocking over the chair at the table, her heart thrashing like a scythe against wheat.

Still shaking, she righted the chair and gratefully sat, afraid to look at the portrait. As her pulse slowed and her wits returned, she rotated slowly to face the judge. The portrait appeared simply as the others on the wall.

She set a palm to her forehead but felt no fever. "I have allowed my imagination full run." Feeling foolish, she once again faced the flower specimens and set to work.

The consuming need to continually check the portrait over her shoulder soon interfered with concentration. She felt as though the judge watched, expecting something from her, but what? She shifted her chair to the end of the table so the portrait was no longer hidden from view, hoping an occasional glance at the wall would rid her mind of the ominous feelings. The uncomfortable presence of the judge remained. As another wasted quarter of an hour chimed on the house clock, she gave in and stared up at the judge.

"The history of your life is unknown to me," she whispered.

"But if some providence declares that knowledge necessary, then I promise to investigate."

She swore the judge smiled. She returned her attention to the specimens, and detailed sketches developed quickly under her talented hands. Morning hour after hour ticked by as she examined every aspect of the plants, adjusted fine points on the drawings, and added color.

Pierce swept into the kitchen and followed his hunger toward a bubbling pot. With half a day's work still ahead, he felt little enthusiasm and blamed the new houseguest for his disinterest. Besides rising early to assure a departure before Alexandra awoke, dreams concerning her more feminine virtues had produced a restless night. Blast it all, the last thing he needed was more distraction.

Frustrated, he searched for a tasting spoon. The meeting with the town moderator over a new bridge design had wasted a good portion of the morning and sapped his energy. He contemplated the wisdom of getting involved, even on an advisory level, in such a building project fraught with politics. Shipbuilding seemed an easier task. A wooden spoon now in hand, he turned only to find the tall Swedish cook, Mrs. Flamm, planted firmly in front of the pot.

"Master Pierce," she began in her Swedish lilt. "No dippin' inta da stew. It must cool a vee bit."

Hunger roiled in his stomach. "I'm surprised my father has not already called for dinner. He usually is adamant about a noonday meal."

"Ya, 'tis true, sir. But he not be home till supper."

"I assume my father is off fighting for that blasted hospital," he said dryly.

"Ya. But no fret, I serve dinner quick for you and Miss Alexandra."

Pierce looked up sharply. "She didn't go with Father?" He had assumed his father would escort Alexandra around town, introducing his new protégée to all his fellow philosophers.

"No," Mrs. Flamm answered as she swung the pot from the

hot hearth. "She no move from da study all *morgon*. Not even for a cup of tea."

Pierce found himself inexplicably drawn toward the study. The stubborn Miss Alexandra apparently had her feet firmly planted in his household and planned to stay despite the ploy by their fathers. For such a supposedly intelligent woman, she seemed determined to ignore the obvious. Even though well educated, what could she accomplish that some assistant from Salem could not also easily produce?

He headed toward the study, actually desiring an encounter if only to prove his point. Unbidden, a smile broadened his lips as he brushed a speck of dirt from his jacket and slipped into the doorway.

Alexandra did not sit in a chair. Instead, she crawled beneath the table, reaching for an errant paper, her shapely bottom stuck in the air. A breeze moved the parchment another inch from her fingertips.

"Bloody paper," he heard her swear as she stretched the extra inch.

He cleared his throat.

A thud followed as she slammed her head into the underside of the table. A square wood pencil dropped from the table edge and landed on the floor. Alexandra backed out from under the table, one hand holding the paper and the other tenderly rubbing her head.

She glared at him as she scooped up the pencil. "You might have given me some hint as to your approach."

"A man has a right to move around his own home."

"Regardless, a proper gentleman would have waited until I was less indisposed." A piece of lead dropped from the pencil tip and a fire lit in her eyes. "See what *you* have caused."

He tried to suppress a widening grin. When on the defensive, color flushed her pale, freckled face and puffed up her rather delicate lower lip. How unexpected that her rather flustered, embarrassed state made her quite adorable.

He took on a mock defensive posture and crossed his arms. "Are you accusing me of some misstep?"

"You damaged my pencil. Those made of pure plumbago from England are not a frivolous expense."

Pierce sauntered toward the table. *"I* damaged the pencil?"

"Most certainly. Sneaking into this room was rather childish."

"I required some papers from the desk," he lied.

She stared at him suspiciously. "Well, since you are here, might I ask you to make haste? Interruptions slow my work."

"Oh, truly? Is that what you call languishing under the table—in a rather interesting position, I might add?" He scooped up another pencil on the table. "I see you have others."

Alexandra flushed and snatched the pencil from his fingers. "These are German white-lead sticks and are filled with impurities. Now, I don't wish to be rude, but . . ."

"You? Rude?" he answered, thoroughly enjoying this tête-à-tête.

Her mouth opened to speak but snapped shut in irritation as she turned her back on him. He had a sudden urge to pat the object that only moments earlier had been so prominently displayed in the room. Instead, he shifted his gaze from the lovely curves of her skirt-draped bottom to the broad table.

The drawings immediately caught his attention. Resurrected in vivid color on paper before him were the pressed flowers. Intricate details documented every vein of the leaves and petals. The skillful and exacting artwork left him amazed.

"Quite impressive," he let slip as he stepped closer to the drawings.

Alexandra crossed her arms, rubbed the dark silk of her buttoned blouse with what he hoped was dwindling irritation, and remained quiet.

He compared the sketches to the actual samples. "You have a deft hand and excellent eye. I have no doubt of my father's ecstatic approval. For years, he has tried to develop skill at recording his collections with sketches. Unfortunately, creating delicate beauty frequently lies more with feminine qualities."

Alexandra faced him with a curious look. "Surely you do

not suggest that men cannot do such work?" She moved along the table toward him, as though to protect her drawings.

He refused to step back as she approached. "Most definitely not," he answered agreeably. "I merely suggest that women, who themselves are gentle, lovely creatures, have a definite predetermination to create pretty pictures." He inhaled hints of rose from her perfume and immediately saw in her eyes that his answer was inappropriate.

"These are more than decorative drawings," she announced succinctly. "I distinguish and document similar characteristics with other plants to aid in classification. One small detail left unnoticed may make comparisons difficult if not impossible. The knowledge I have gained with years of study has blessed me with the insight necessary to effectively compare them."

Tired of her disemboweling every opinion he expressed, Pierce spoke with injured pride. "Can you not accept a compliment concerning your talents, or must you constantly bristle?"

"I do not bristle." She held her chin up and body straight. "However, I appreciate you recognizing my skill, but I sense your intent rather limiting." She leaned back against the table. "Women have more capabilities than you imagine."

Ah, Pierce thought in a moment of enlightenment. He had unearthed her Achilles heel. She sought acceptance in the realm of men.

He stepped in front of her and leaned near. "I tend to believe that by summer's end you will have educated me thoroughly in such possibilities. But assist me to sort out my confused masculine intellect: why do you strive so to equal men?"

"I do not wish to equal men."

He nodded once with approval. "I dare say that is a wise proposition."

"I completely agree," she said as her freckles spread in a soft smile. "That would show a lack of ambition."

His eyes narrowed as he searched for an appropriate reply, but found none forthcoming. Why, that little tease. She had not only outwitted him, but also left him speechless, and was fully aware of the fact.

A triumphant smirk remained on her engaging face. She may have soft dimples hiding among the freckles, but behind them he realized she hid a quick-witted mischievous streak. Her demure beauty was but a clever disguise to hide an irritating ability to aggravate all men. How could her father stand such a daily deluge of verbiage? A twinge of sympathy shot through him. The real reason for her father's extended stay in London became far more obvious now.

Wisely, Pierce ceded the battle and knew a change of tack offered the only graceful way out. "Actually, I could use someone with a detailed eye to sketch my ship," he offered. "Have you any time or inclination to undertake such a project?" He fully expected a negative reply lost in some explanation of her current duties.

Thoughtfully, she moved from leaning against the table and crossed to the open window. Alluringly silhouetted in the frame, she stared out at nothing in particular for several moments. She glanced back over her shoulder. "How detailed a sketch do you expect—one for posterity or something of a more architectural nature?"

He blinked at the unexpected reply. What in God's name possessed him to make such an offer? He didn't allow women on a ship before launching. It brought bad luck. Bloody hell, why did he choose that task and not something more mundane?

The answer lay in his attachment to the ship. A proper sketch of his vessel was no small undertaking, and he knew it a great challenge. He had let his pride set the lofty goal to see if she had the daring to reach for it.

Damn it, she had a way of creating uneasy feelings in a man. With every move she made, he feared he would play directly into her hands. No woman before had ever put him at such a disadvantage. The sunlight set her in shadow seductively against the bright window. How lucky he was she did not use the same tactics to push her feminine wiles. With her astonishing skill, he might have found himself married after their first encounter.

Regardless, he refused to be bested. Defiantly, he drew a long breath. If she wanted a challenge, he would oblige.

"I desire a single picture of the ship from keel to mast tops, with the greatest detail possible for that size. As I do not wish to draw you long from your work here, you may do it at your leisure. You must realize, of course, that the ship is not quite finished at this time. The masts also will not be raised until after the formal launching in late June."

Alexandra gracefully faced him and smiled—a little too easily, his wary thoughts decided. He didn't quite know why that worried him.

"I am honored you wish me to do the sketch," she said. "To complete such a charge sufficiently, though, I will require an examination of the ship. Is there such a time when that might be appropriate?"

Even though indecisive about whether to proceed, he hid his hesitation. "My men do not work on the Lord's Day. This Sunday the ship will not be in a good state for a visit, but the Sunday hence will suffice. If you wish, after services, I will escort you to the ship."

"That sounds like a most pleasant prospect indeed." She gently grasped his elbow and inched him toward the door.

Was this a subtle hint she had tired of his company—and so soon after his offer of a personal ship's tour? With most women, he had the opposite effect. He often had to pry their fingers from his arm.

She continued sweetly. "You and your father are most generous in providing for my entertainment."

"Entertainment?" He cringed at the confused resonance in his voice. He had never heard that particular quality in it until Alexandra had arrived. She had been in the house all of one day and already appeared to know more of this household than he had garnered in a lifetime. Irritation started to build again.

"Were you not informed of the social on Friday evening?" she asked.

"Lord, help us, not again."

Curiosity showed on her face as she released his arm. "I

would believe an unattached gentleman such as you would enjoy a fair party."

"A good one, yes, but you have never witnessed an event organized by my father. One evening it is every unmarried young lady in town, and the next he has a gaggle of gentlemen no younger than sixty years, ogling through a telescope in the yard. I have no guess as to my father's motive for this move. And I thought him too caught up with the hospital to meddle in my affairs."

"Ah," she said, "so you know he is with the selectmen. I think it most honorable he is garnering support among the wards for a Salem hospital."

"Honorable?" Pierce shook his head in disbelief. At last he had encountered one topic in which her education was lacking. "He is out of his mind. Did he bother to tell you that this hospital is for the sole purpose of inoculating people with live smallpox and then harboring them until the symptoms recede?"

She withdrew from a press another plant sample for the afternoon's work. "It's called variolation, and the smallpox used comes only from scabs of those who have had mild cases. The scab is powdered and simply scratched in one's arm." She peered questioningly at him. "Have you ever considered who will undertake your care if you contract the more deadly version?"

Pierce leaned back against the table, trying to see her face as she placed the new sample on the table. "My father has survived the pox. Have you not noticed his scarred face?"

"Most assuredly, and this morning I learned he had lost to pox the sister who nursed him." She stood squarely before him. "Could you truly stay away if your wife or child became ill?"

"I would do what is right for my entire family." He detected a defensive tone rising in his voice and inwardly cursed himself for it. "You realize some who get the inoculation will die."

"A small percentage," she insisted. "But when an epidemic hits, hundreds more will perish. One is foolish to risk such a fate."

"Foolish is risking your life simply to be in control," he

shot back. "Besides, I heartily doubt most women in this town would chance variolation and the pox scars that might mar their faces. A beautiful woman like you speaks bravely, but would you be the first in town to have the inoculation?"

In silence, Alexandra smoothed out a fresh piece of paper and placed a weight on the corner to secure it. She brushed her hands lightly together and walked toward the door. "I believe the cook has prepared a proper dinner."

Disappointment overtook him as she avoided the answer. Even though he had not expected her to agree to such a horrid proposition, he did expect her to admit her inability. Oddly, he felt both a triumph and a loss. At last he had won a point, but somehow it diminished the determination and intellect in her he had come to admire.

"You have yet to give me an answer," he said a little too roughly.

With her body profiled to his view, he watched, astonished, as Alexandra slowly undid the top button on her blouse. His brow raised with interest. What ploy did she now plan to lessen her defeat? Another button opened under her fingers, and then a third.

She stepped through the doorway and stopped. She looked back over her shoulder at him. "No, I would not be first in line," she said quietly. With eyes steadily upon his face, she slid her blouse off the shoulder, exposing her upper arm. A raised pinkish scar broke the satin skin and left irrefutable evidence of an inoculation.

She disappeared, leaving him once again speechless, his spirit and appetite all but vanquished.

Five

Friday, the infamous "day of celebration" as joyfully declared by his father, had arrived, yet Pierce only felt burdened. At work a deadline quickly approached; at home his father had insisted on throwing a party; and in his life an irritating redhead constantly cursed his waking moments.

He collected his beaver hat from a Chinese-style side table in the mansion hallway and strode toward the door. He had returned from the shipyard only for the midday meal and to inform his father—with great delicacy, of course—that he had no intentions of attending the evening festivities. Such trivial pursuits had no room in his schedule. Somehow, the moment or desire to confront his father on the latter concern had not developed.

He tried to focus his mind on work. Caulkers at the shipyard had long completed sealing the hull seams with tarred hemp fibers, and joiners had labored to plane the last of the surface smooth and apply a sulphur resin to repel barnacles and teredo worms. To meet his projected deadline, application of the final hull copper sheathing would have to be completed in the next few days.

"Son," his father bellowed from the study.

Pierce stopped, let out a quick breath for patience, and searched out his father.

"Ah, there you are," his father said as Pierce appeared. "I thought you might have slipped away before I could remind you about this evening. I hear Mrs. Flamm is roasting duck especially for you."

"Honestly, Father, we've already discussed this," Pierce began as he fingered his hat, searching for a proper explanation. "My duty requires a late evening at the shipyard. It is truly my misfortune that the timing of this event should coincide with great activity there."

"Nonsense, your craftsman are well skilled. For a few hours, they can be left unattended. Better yet, allow them to leave a few hours early. You will be remembered for your generosity."

"More than likely my sloth. Besides, the schedule permits no tarrying."

"Schedules are not meant to rule one's life, Son. However," his father acquiesced with a shrug and rose from his chair, "if you must be true to your endeavors, I will gladly pass on your tidings to our guests."

"I appreciate the gesture. Ask Mrs. Flamm to save me a taste of duck."

"Ha. I will try, but that young Chadwick fellow—Edward I believe he is called—is well known for his affinity for the fowl."

Pierce faltered. "Surely you did not invite such a cad to our home. His values are so untrustworthy I would not allow him alone in this house for one moment. Whatever possessed you to extend him an invitation?"

"I believe your judgment of him rather harsh. His father is of the finest quality, a fellow Freemason, and lest you forget, the owner of *Salem's Pride*. And with Miss Gables our guest of honor, I felt it my duty to provide the requisite entertainment of a few unattached gentlemen. Do you not agree?"

"Unattached *gentlemen,* I agree. But Chadwick is a wolf with a voracious appetite for young ladies. Why, he is completely unsuitable for the company of Miss Gables."

"Why, that's a pot calling the kettle black. You, a single gentleman who enjoys the company of many lovely ladies in this town, are in a weak position to judge others. In any case, the good pastor of East Church will surely temper the evening."

"Dr. Bentley?" Pierce exclaimed in surprise. "The evening

will simply offer fodder for his curiosity. Surely you must be aware that he prides himself on knowing everything about everyone in Salem. Needless to say, the evening will surely be an extended entry in his prolific diary."

"Hardly. Dr. Bentley, as both a minister and a man of science, is an asset to this town. In fact, I dare say Miss Gables will find him quite enchanting. He speaks twenty-some languages, faithfully records the arrivals and departures of all ships, and is Harvard-educated. He is even bringing with him young Bowditch, a bright young lad with a unique propensity for mathematics."

"Bowditch?" Pierce said, completely perplexed with his father. "Why, the lad is indentured and works at the ship chandlery. Forgive me, but I am truly astounded at the mixture of personalities you have placed together for this evening."

Joshua raised a questioning brow and grinned with a hint of humor around his eyes. "Are you afraid I have forgotten your own needs?"

"I have no needs for your consideration," Pierce shot back.

"So you say. No matter, I have also invited my new shipping agent, Monsieur Calonne, and his family. I've been told his lovely daughter, Simone, is a superb harpist. She has agreed to share her music with us this evening."

"Ah, now we arrive at the real objective behind this affair. You wish to pair me with Simone." Pierce struggled to control his frustration. "Father, I do not require your skills in matchmaking. I will take care of such needs myself. And this time, considering the family's political position, I must point out that you chose poorly."

"You surprise me, Son. Do you still hold a hardened heart after ten years?"

"The state of my heart is not of your concern." Inside, he felt blossom a plethora of memories that he had thought long buried and forgotten. Memories of a first love so intense and so tender, only to be snatched away as her Loyalist family fled to New Brunswick and the safety of English-controlled territory. The

American Revolution had changed the lives of many in Salem, sometimes in rather unexpected ways.

Pierce stroked the hat along his palm, allowing a jumble of thoughts to play in his mind. An uncomfortable conclusion rose foremost in the haze. Chadwick, who had inherited none of his father's honorable traits, had no place in this house. Left alone for a moment, Pierce wagered the cad would seek out business documents just to judge the worth, and thus stability, of fellow merchants. Chadwick required a savvy escort who could guard the Williamses' interests, whatever they may be.

He looked at his father. "Evidently my presence is required this evening to assist, however reluctantly, in maintaining some semblance of sanity amongst the guests you have so awkwardly thrown together. I only ask the favor that henceforth you cease all activity to match my interests with any young lady of whatever stature and bearing. Upon that promise, I will attend to my host duties."

Joshua Williams strode thoughtfully around his son, eyeing him in a most peculiar, appraising manner. With true conciliation in his voice he answered, "All right, I confess my desire to match you with Miss Calonne. I now realize my error. For that I heartily apologize. However, I protest the accusation relating to the sanity of my guests. I find their uniqueness rather invigorating and relish the hours we have ahead. Did you know Miss Gables is presently setting up her father's telescope for use this evening? Dr. Bentley is well known for tracking comets and just recently had the pleasure of—"

"Father, save me the lecture." Pierce felt his exasperation swell. The senior Williams had the unique talent of appearing to ramble off onto another subject simply to avoid further discussion of an undesired topic. "I have already said I will be present, however reluctantly, for the festivities."

He took leave of his father and rode toward the shipyard. Visions of Chadwick riffling through his father's papers, stirring unfounded rumors among the guests and drooling over Alexandra drove him to distraction. It required no one gifted with vision to imagine the vain and shifty Chadwick catching her in an unguarded moment and attempting to place a kiss upon her supple lips. He chuckled, though, as he imagined her response. Maybe Chadwick deserved a hearty round or two with Alexandra.

The strong salt air filled his lungs as gulls swooped low and a pelican splashed nearby in the harbor. The sea was a harsh mistress, oft wild and relentless, but unmistakably the only one he desired—and clearly easier to predict than the unsinkable Miss Gables.

"Mistress Gables!" Mrs. Bisbey bellowed as she entered the kitchen laden with dinner dishes. "You'll make me lose me job. 'Tis no place for a lady, 'specially one decked in such silk finery."

Alexandra temporarily ignored the admonition as she collected china cups and saucers on a serving tray. "I'll soon be out of your way. But I know with Mrs. Flamm departing early nursing a poor stomach, you and Rebecca have an extraordinary job on your hands."

"Me and the housemaid can handle the occasion, mum. But ye are good of heart to consider us. I should tell ye, the others are gathered in the conservatory examinin' your creature."

The sound of breaking china sent Alexandra and Mrs. Bisbey whirling toward young Rebecca. Gravely, Rebecca held the porcelain chocolate pot that matched the service Alexandra had set out.

Rebecca stretched out a broken handle in one hand, and whined, "Awful sorry. I didn't mean to break the china. But when you mentioned the creature, my hand, why it was forced against the table edge. It's the devil speaking."

Mrs. Bisbey rolled her eyes. "It be the devil, all right—in ye." Mrs. Bisbey snatched the porcelain pitcher from the housemaid and shook her head. "Fine job, young Rebecca. No fixin' this piece. Mister Williams will be a mite upset when he finds ye destroyed his Meissen pot."

"Must you tell him, Mrs. Bisbey?"

"Not tonight, young'un, unless you tarry the remainder of

the eve. Now finish up with the chocolate. I'll find another pitcher."

Alexandra wisely took leave of the kitchen and sought out the others in the conservatory. The guests crowded around Newton's perch, and the French girl, Simone, peered carefully from behind Pierce. Her dark hair swirled into a stunning bun, and lively ribbons offset a smooth, perfect, youthful complexion. Alexandra felt an odd inadequacy as she considered her own pale face covered in freckles.

Joshua Williams stood before the guests and kept them raptly attentive as he talked about iguanas and told tales of reptiles in general.

Pierce stepped back to allow Simone a better view and she bravely inched forward. His father told about workers who unearthed a massive reptile jaw in a French quarry twenty years ago. The girl's eyes widened.

" 'Tis said five men toiled the good part of a day to remove the jaw, which equaled a man's height," Joshua espoused.

"Are those creatures still alive, *monsieur?*" Simone asked, obviously imagining the creature connected to such an appendage.

"Most believe not, but much of the world is yet to be explored. Deep oceans, dark lakes, and endless jungles hold innumerable secrets."

The fourteen-year-old Simone clutched Pierce's arm in horror, then slipped once again behind him, putting some distance between herself and the exotic Newton. Alexandra caught a hint of gentle amusement on Pierce's face, the kind of expression one often saw in a parent's features. All evening, he had been patient and entertaining of the young girl, who glowed with the kind attention of a handsome gentleman.

Alexandra knew Pierce took no great enjoyment in attending this guest-laden dinner. However, every ounce a good son, he undertook his duty to entertain and make a pleasant evening for all. In spite of all her annoyances with him, she had to admire this quality.

"Ah, Miss Gables." Slightly slurred words accompanied by

rum-filled breath permeated the air as her arm became entwined with the voice's body. "I feared I had lost you. Off to take care of some necessary functions, I supposed." Chadwick snickered and stroked the skin of her hand.

She politely attempted to extricate herself from his hold but was unsuccessful. Joshua Williams directed the guests back into the front parlor, where he promised to have Miss Calonne play the harp. Mister Chadwick showed no signs of relinquishing his hold or going in the indicated direction.

"A walk in the garden is most intriguing under the moonlight," he suggested and headed Alexandra in that direction.

"Really, Mister Chadwick. I should suppose one such as you would find it quite boring."

"Ah, then you do not know me well."

Rebecca intercepted their pathway. "Chocolate, sir?" she politely inquired of Chadwick and held up a tray with cups of the hot liquid.

"I have no time for such an aperitif, girl," he admonished the maid. "Especially not at the moment when Miss Gables was about to explain why I would find the gardens boring."

Rebecca flushed, disheartened by his rudeness.

"I'd love to have a cup," Alexandra piped up. "Thank you." She used the moment to reach for a cup and saucer and dislodge Chadwick's grip.

Obviously irritated at Alexandra's newfound freedom, he glowered at Rebecca, who fled to safer territory. Alexandra reversed direction and sauntered back toward the other guests. Chadwick followed, keeping only inches between them.

"It is most disheartening to discover I cannot compete with chocolate," he said. "However, when you are sufficiently satisfied, I will gladly escort you on that garden walk."

Alexandra ignored Chadwick at her sleeve and sipped her chocolate. She scanned the gathering for Pierce. "I sincerely doubt you would discover much enjoyment in the garden this evening, sir. You have blatantly admitted no knowledge of astronomy; the familiar moon is not out; and I, who have evidently given you some unintentional encouragement, have no plans to provide you with any 'expected' entertainment."

Chadwick barely missed a breath as he replied, "My dear Miss Gables, it is the unexpected that will make the venture worthwhile."

Alexandra caught Pierce's gaze from across the room. Putting a grim expression on her face and tipping her head toward Chadwick, she did her best to communicate her desire for rescue from the cad. Much to her dismay, Pierce lifted his hands helplessly and nodded toward Simone, who was preparing to play. He obviously was using her as an excuse not to save her from Chadwick.

As though to let his point sink in, he helped Simone take a seat at the harp. Her fingers plucked a few strings as she played a quick scale. Alexandra had a desire to wrap a few strings around Pierce's arrogant neck. He knew exactly what Chadwick was doing.

The girl stilled the strings with her palms before announcing her selection. "Not so many years ago, a composer fell in love with a beautiful harpist. He wrote this sonata for her and she later became his wife, Madame Jean Baptiste Krumpholtz."

Silence reigned as she began, and all else seemed forgotten in the strains of music that followed. Simone finished the first sonata and with encouragement played another. Alexandra devoured each note and completely forgot about Chadwick until the girl once again stilled the strings.

"A bit tedious, didn't you think?" he whispered in Alexandra's ear.

Alexandra shoved her saucer and cup into his hands and applauded the performance. The harpist beamed her pleasure and appreciation for the chance to perform. As the senior Williams stepped forward to offer accolades on the performance, Alexandra searched again for Pierce. He seemed to have disappeared. She tried to withhold her surprise, although he had expressed no desire or propensity for the festivities. She felt disappointment at the abandonment, but scolded herself for allowing even a small attachment for him.

Chadwick reached toward her arm to secure his hold once again, only to be thwarted as Nathaniel Bowditch slipped between them.

"Miss Gables," Nathaniel said, eagerly seeking her attention, "Dr. Bentley informed me you have erected a telescope. I would consider it a great kindness if you would allow me to gaze through it. Dr. Bentley is at this moment gathering a lantern to light our way through the garden."

Chadwick, even though slowed by the alcoholic refreshments of the evening, quickly recovered and looked down his nose at Nathaniel. "Are you too dim-witted, man, to see Miss Gables is already engaged in company with another?"

Undaunted, Nathaniel pressed forward. "Surely you can spare her for a few moments, sir. The heavens are magnificent at this moment, but clouds threaten in the distance to easily obscure the night sky."

Alexandra gave Chadwick a demure smile. "I do believe now *is* the appropriate time to visit the garden." She reached out and took Nathaniel's arm. "Mister Chadwick was just encouraging me to venture in that direction. Surely he won't mind your joining us."

Exactly how much Chadwick minded was evident on his rather livid face. Had sobriety been his closer friend, his wits might have prevented his losing her to Nathaniel. Instead, he stuffed Alexandra's cup and saucer on a nearby sideboard and staggered after them.

Dr. Bentley met them at the door with a tin lantern and led the group to the telescope, set alongside one of the garden paths. A sheet draped the delicate instrument to prevent condensation on the lenses. Nathaniel shut the lantern down to a mere ray while Bentley removed the sheet. The two men whispered in the night air and pointed near the southwestern horizon for several minutes.

"Ah, yes, there it is, cradled in Virgo," said Dr. Bentley before he set about securing the first object for viewing.

"I am delighted to say this is a splendid scope. The moons of Jupiter are clearly visible." Bentley turned to Nathaniel.

"Dear boy, run get the senior Williams. I promised I'd send word once the planet was in the lens."

The remaining gentlemen allowed Alexandra the first view and waited patiently as she bent over the scope. "I can't help but imagine Galileo's thoughts as he observed this planet," she whispered softly into the night.

Dr. Bentley laughed. "I imagine panic may have crossed his mind. The four moons he found circling Jupiter gave absolute proof to the Copernican theory. Man had now discovered a body such as earth could move through space and not lose its moons. Proof, therefore, that earth and its moon could easily circle the sun. Not pleasant news to a powerful church wishing to maintain the earth as the universal center. I do believe Galileo spent his last days confined to his home."

"I unquestionably would not have flaunted such a proof," Chadwick piped in. "Life is too short to waste defending some worthless principle."

"And what principles *do* you see worthy of defending, Mister Chadwick?" Alexandra chided, finding little in comparison to Pierce, who displayed a willingness to uphold his beliefs.

"Economic ones," he shot back. "And ones of social structure. Take Bowditch, for example. I would never consider inviting a simple indentured servant to a social gathering such as this."

Dr. Bentley straightened. *"Simple* is the last term I would use for that boy's genius. He reads an encyclopedia in his spare time. His mathematic skills have proved worthy to enhance sales at the chandlery, and mark my words, he is destined for some great challenge in this world."

"He will never have a Harvard education such as I," Chadwick huffed.

"No, nor as I," Bentley replied, "but I wager he could calculate the Earth's path around the sun. A talent I might assume your education and mine has left us lacking."

"Why should I calculate what Newton has already accomplished?" Chadwick snapped.

Nathaniel reappeared with Joshua Williams at that moment

and answered, "Because his principles are ever important, and proving them to ourselves assists us in their comprehension."

Alexandra enjoyed the repartee against such a pretentious attitude and joined in. "By way of illustration, Mister Chadwick, if I had a cannonball and a child's ball of leather, both of the same size, and dropped them from the roof, which would strike the ground first?"

Chadwick stayed quiet for a moment, probably aware that the obvious answer might well be incorrect. The darkness hid any signs of consternation on his face.

"Come on, man, the answer is simple if you know Newton's law," Bentley pushed.

"Well, then, I believe . . ." Chadwick waffled. "I mean, common sense dictates that the cannonball will land first."

Alexandra stifled a giggle. "I am afraid we have you rather at a disadvantage." She attempted to sound apologetic, but not quite. "We all have avid interests in worldly sciences. It is unfair of us to press an issue in which you obviously are untrained."

"Are you saying I am wrong?"

"Quite so, I am afraid," she said with simple pleasure.

"Then prove your claim," Chadwick challenged.

"There is no need," Nathaniel said with a shrug. "Newton proved the effects of gravity by calculating that the earth's gravity pulls on the moon just enough so it stays in orbit around the earth instead of launching off into the heavens."

Chadwick raised his voice in a snit. "Not one of you sport Newton's qualifications, and yet all of you call yourselves philosophers of science. Prove, in a way this unenlightened mind can understand, that I am wrong, or I shall claim victory over such pompous predictions."

Hair bristled along Alexandra's arms at his attitude. She remembered Pierce's earlier claim that this was her typical response. Granted, on occasion she did bristle. However, in dealing with Chadwick she felt justified.

"So be it, Mister Chadwick," she answered, formulating possible demonstrations in her mind.

Joshua Williams rubbed thoughtfully at his balding head. "I

dare say, I don't stock cannon ammunition or children's balls in my house. But surely we can find something equivalent."

Alexandra recollected the accident earlier in the kitchen. "A porcelain pitcher and a stoneware bottle have similar dimensions. If you would be so gracious as to donate a bottle and a damaged chocolate pot, I believe the experiment might be successful."

"Broken porcelain?" Joshua's forehead crinkled in concern. "When did this accident occur?"

Alexandra lightly touched Joshua's arm. "After the meal, I am afraid, sir. I sought to set up the china tea service and startled young Rebecca, carrying the chocolate pot. The handle broke off and appears beyond any repair. My apologies for any indelicacies and agitation this may cause you."

Joshua patted Alexandra gently on the back. "My girl, your error is forgiven if we can prove to this gentleman such a sound and simple principle as gravity. Go collect the pitcher and see if Mrs. Bisbey will show you to an upper window of the house. I do believe the one nearest the south end has a clear area below."

Alexandra started toward the house when Chadwick added, "I should like to test the weight of the objects before they are released. Who is to say you won't fill the porcelain to equal the weight of the stoneware?"

"For you, Mister Chadwick," she answered over her shoulder, "I will even fill the stoneware with water and leave the porcelain empty. All doubts must be erased from your mind as to the clarity of the results."

With a bubbling enthusiasm, she sought out Mrs. Bisbey.

Pierce stood in an empty house, puzzling over the location of his father and the guests. Minutes earlier he had taken a moment of relief in his chambers, then retreated to the conservatory to cut an orchid for Miss Calonne at his father's request. While in the conservatory, he heard nothing short of an elephant herd pounding up the stairs before the house fell into complete silence.

He didn't know why, but he garnered immediate suspicions

that one of Miss Gables's machinations was afoot. With that woman in the house, not one moment had any semblance of normality.

He chuckled for a moment, wondering how Chadwick was holding up. From the earlier look on Alexandra's face, she had reached her limit of tolerance, which was rather easy for her. Truly she needed to be more accepting of male inadequacies, just as gentlemen were accepting of female weaknesses. A little time with Chadwick just might serve a useful purpose. Pierce considered he might seem a knight in shining armor compared to that cad and his lack of chivalry.

The young housemaid, Rebecca, clamored down the narrow staircase, muttering something about a possessed woman, and flew into the kitchen and out the back door. Assuming Rebecca knew something about the whereabouts of the guests, Pierce followed. He stepped out onto the brick pathway of the rear garden and heard a cheering din near the end of the house.

Alexandra hung out a window of the third story, holding two containers. The remainder of the guests stood below, yelling directions about how to hold them properly, where and when to let them fall, and who would prompt the moment of release. Mrs. Bisbey held tightly to Alexandra's waist, clearly concerned that the woman might fall to her death.

Pierce shook his head in astonishment. Did Alexandra not realize how foolish she appeared? What kind of man could ever put up with these daily embarrassments?

All grew quiet until his father thundered, "Release!" A great thud and tinkling of broken ware sounded an instant later. A roar went up among the guests, involving much laughter and shouting to the upper window. Alexandra disappeared from the window, presumably to rejoin the group. Pierce crossed his arms and stewed on the brick path. No wonder half the population of Salem believed his father a tad daft.

The dark-shrouded guests in the garden approached, headed for the kitchen door. His father and Dr. Bentley appeared first, laughing and cajoling in a jovial mood.

Bentley thumped his father on the back. "What a treat, your

parties. Your new protégée is quite a sharp and daring woman. I say, if she had lived in Salem a hundred years ago, the town would have hanged her as a witch." The men laughed and passed into the house.

Pierce fumed at Alexandra's childish behavior. Did she have to prove everything in the world? Could she not simply be accepting of the common person's foibles and beliefs?

Chadwick strolled by with a grimace on his face and slunk into the house. Pierce recognized the look as one he had personally expressed with increasing frequency as of late. If he had to guess, Chadwick had taken Alexandra on—and lost. For a brief moment, Pierce experienced extreme joy at the thought. Chadwick was certainly deserving of her—ahem—attention.

Nathaniel strode up with a lantern in one hand and a cloth containing shards of pottery in the other. "A splendid demonstration," Nathaniel said. "The pots hit at exactly the same instant. Did you see them fall?"

"From a distance, yes." In all honesty, Pierce wished he had not witnessed any such ludicrous event in his own home. "I would, however, like to speak with Miss Gables. Would it put you out too much, Nathaniel, to ask her to join me out here in the garden?"

"No, sir. I'll ask her straightaway." Nathaniel disappeared through the kitchen door and left Pierce pacing, trying to decide exactly what to say to the newly declared witch of Salem. He paced out to the telescope and back again, listening to the gravel crunching under his boots.

"Everyone seems interested in coaxing me into the garden this night." Alexandra's voice floated through the night air. "Should I ask straight forth what your motives are?"

Damnation, he hadn't heard her approach. Light from the house barely highlighted her form, and at this distance her face was left in complete shadow. He moved close enough until her eyes shone in the starlight. "I have an apology to deliver."

"Of that I have no doubt," she said with a smug demeanor. "You well knew of Chadwick's poor behavior and left me with him anyway."

He could not help but smile. "Ah, you have jumped to a grand conclusion. By the look on Chadwick's face as he passed only moments before, the apology I owe is to him. I should never have allowed him within your reach without a proper warning."

Both hands flew to her hips and her voice became sharp. "Have you asked me here simply to insult my sensibilities or have you some greater purpose?"

Pierce gently grasped her arm. "I only wish to offer you some advice on survival here in Salem. You have resided here not even a week and have already made a spectacle of yourself in town and in my home. Dr. Bentley, albeit jokingly, declares you a witch. Please, I beg of you, end this behavior unbecoming of a lady."

"Unbecoming? Why, you are simply jealous that I dabble in things you consider of the male domain. Broaden your mind and accept my abilities."

"Your abilities are not foremost in my mind. The reputation of my family, however, is of utmost importance. Hold off on your crusade to prove your intellect to the last soul in Salem, and save yourself and my family from appearing foolish."

Before Alexandra could reply, his father appeared. "Excuse my interruption, but the guests are departing. I thought Miss Gables might wish to join me in seeing them off to a pleasant evening."

He offered his arm, which she obligingly accepted, accompanying him into the house. Pierce took a few moments before entering and stood well across the room from the two.

As the men made their exits, each held Alexandra's hand and lavished a kiss upon it. Chadwick, his bruised ego still aching, made a brisk job of it. Nathaniel, on the other hand, came in second only to Dr. Bentley with a lengthy repertoire on her charming presence during the party. Even young Bowditch had fallen for Alexandra's charms. Naive child. Pierce drummed his fingers against his crossed arms. No one here save he truly understood the woman's motivations. And from what he had discovered of those motivations to date, they were more than any one man should be forced to handle.

Alexandra spent the next hour moving the telescope back into the house and carefully disassembling and storing each part. Mrs. Bisbey and Rebecca had cleaned up the remainder of the evening's accumulations and had retired. Joshua had sent Pierce to escort Rebecca home, for she lived near the wharf, past several boozing dens. Joshua, too, had retired after assisting with the telescope and expounding again on the roaring success of their experiment.

Tired, but still spinning from the excitement, Alexandra carried a single candle into the study. The room with all its portraits and paraphernalia grew more familiar with each passing day. She raised the candle near the judge's portrait, then moved on to Pierce's. The sea in the background seemed to rise in a storm, and his eyes drew her hypnotically toward them.

A breath of air blew out the candle.

She whirled into someone and quickly stepped back.

"I apologize for the fright," sounded Pierce's strong voice. "Does my portrait do me justice?"

"If you are here to chastise me for embarrassing your family, then I shall leave," she said softly but firmly.

The darkness and his nearness disturbed her and made his intentions unclear. She feared not that he might wish to take advantage of the conditions, but that she might find it difficult to resist them. She reached this conclusion with dismay. In Boston, she had believed her life fulfilled without the need for a man's touch. Now such self-assurance fled and left her vulnerable.

"I have no wish to further discuss that topic," he answered. "Instead, the evening has unveiled a new discovery concerning you."

"And just what is that you have discovered?"

"That you are every ounce a woman, a beautiful one at that, and you know quite well how to wield those charms. I have never witnessed so many men taken with a woman in a single evening."

"And are you one of those gentlemen?" The words came out quickly and left her shocked that she had let the thought slip. Her heart beat loudly in the silence that ensued.

He took her elbow and spoke close to her face. "Do you not feel some guilt for what you do to men? You demand treatment on an equal basis and long for our respect, yet in the same breath you utilize the charms that beauty hath bequeathed you. Do you not see hypocrisy in your actions? What is it you want from a man?"

"Hypocrisy? You accuse me of such a belief? And what do you as a man expect: a woman to raise your children, run your estate while you are gone to sea; and yet you leave her with no vote or say in her own welfare? You want a woman capable, bright, and submissive. Do you wish me to accept my God-given beauty and reject the intelligence he has equally bestowed upon me?"

"I only accuse you of adoring the attention your beauty brings. You are no different from other women in that regard."

She reached over to remove his hand from her elbow and recoiled at a picture that flashed forth. An unknown girl with raven hair and arms wrapped around Pierce's neck planted a kiss upon his cheek. A red rose clung to her twisted locks. Alexandra recoiled at the odd flash of vision. How dare Pierce accuse her of desiring attention when that was exactly what he wanted and sought from women?

Irritated with his harsh admonition and the odd picture she envisioned, she was surprised to find herself feeling jealous. She had no need for Pierce, and therefore jealousy had no place. If the image depicted the truth, and the woman with the red rose indeed had a claim to Pierce, then wisdom pronounced it wise to save herself the pain of any attachment to him. As odd as these intuitive feelings, sounds, and now even a picture were, they did have a rather prophetic use.

She brushed his hand off and stepped away. "I am no different from you. You espouse no need for a wife, yet I know you to be charmed by a young woman with a red rose in her hair. You appear convinced women are good for only one purpose."

"Preposterous. And from where have you drawn that conclusion? I know of no woman with a rose in her hair."

"That comes as no surprise. You were too busy with her physical charms to notice."

Pierce turned red with anger. "Woman, you are no better than a common gossip to spout such untruths about me."

"I am no gossip and that is the truth," she shot back.

"And I am a gentleman who does not lie. You are a stubborn woman, Alexandra, but not one I ever imagined would stoop to such petty accusations."

She recoiled at the idea that he thought her petty. He might very well be telling the truth about the girl. Their encounter may yet be in his future. If only she had considered such a possibility before she touted the accusation.

There was only one way to clear his impression of her. She hesitated, knowing what she was about to share would sound ridiculous. "It may be yet to happen," she said softly. "On occasion, I frequently am able to guess as to the future."

"You now claim to be prophetic? Lord help us, that is certainly scientific!"

"I cannot explain exactly how I know," she answered, with a frustration she honestly felt concerning her odd intuition. "But my knowledge is based on sound reasoning. Roses are in bloom and you seem attracted to women with dark hair."

"And you have combined those facts and drawn this crazy conclusion. Why, I might even declare a tad of jealousy is evident."

Alexandra crossed her arms, feeling foolish for sharing such a personal secret. "Forgive me for divulging a truth with you. I can see you are not able to comprehend its true meaning. I am rarely wrong with my intuition."

"Then I should gladly wager that this one will never materialize."

"Then you shall lose."

"On the contrary," Pierce sounded almost incredulous that

he was hearing such ridiculous statements from her. "I think you have honed this supposed sight for dramatic effect, maybe even to garner my attentions."

"Then a simple scamp I am. At least you can claim to be my first victim in Salem." She tried to step past him, but this time he more roughly grabbed her arm and pulled her back to him.

"I meant no disrespect to you, Alexandra. I only offer a warning that you can't have the intellectual respect of men if you flaunt your femininity, too."

The room swirled with impressions and images she knew to be a result of her divided emotions. An ever-present conscience demanded control and a smooth but quick departure from the room. Her senses, however, felt the heat of his body and the fragrance of extinguished tallow and dried specimens in the room. She wallowed in the disorientation of the darkness and the strange desire it produced to cling to Pierce for support.

Once again, she reached for the fingers around her arm. As her fingertips touched the rough firmness of his hand, every nerve tingled. Too late she realized any touch presented a danger to her self-control. A simple grasp around his fingers to lift them away melted every part of her being into confusion. Her mind spun and her eyes closed. She felt the tenderness of his lips on her face and neck, and finally against her mouth. She in turn devoured the softness of his mouth and desired more.

His fingers moved under hers and she gasped, forcing her eyes open. His kisses had been but a vision.

With a complete loss of control, fear sent her fleeing without explanation from the room and the touch of Pierce Williams.

Six

The heat of the pleasant Monday morning was just beginning to make the day uncomfortable as Alexandra approached
the mansion from her excursion to the waterfront. She had put
off chances to explore Salem until a sufficient amount of work
had been completed and Joshua Williams had assurances of
her fortitude. That Salem supported its seafaring trade was in
no doubt. Along Derby Street she had seen sail lofts, spar
makers, ship's chandlers, anchor-and-chain forges, a navigation school, warehouses, and even the seamen's church.

She had barely stepped off the granite doorstep and into the
house when Mrs. Bisbey appeared.

"Picked a lovely day for a walk, mum," Mrs. Bisbey bellowed in her usual cheerful manner. "A hearty breeze cools
down the body and keeps the flyin' critters at bay."

Alexandra smiled in agreement, removed her hat, and delicately dabbed at the perspiration on her brow. "I didn't realize
Salem was such a large town." She set her hat and tiny coin
purse on a side table by the door.

Mrs. Bisbey gleamed proudly. "It can't compare to your
grand Boston, but 'tis the sixth-largest town in America and
has a charm all its own."

"Of that, I quite agree. The weather and nature were so
agreeable, I walked all the way to Ye Neck. I stood upon the
great rocks at the beach, let the salt wind refresh my senses,

and watched the ships sail in and out of the harbor. It was magnificent."

"I'm glad you enjoyed it, mum."

A loud thud emanated from the kitchen, and Mrs. Bisbey winced. When no cry for help followed, she relaxed.

"Rebecca, I'm afraid. She's a clumsy girl, among other things. I best see to her doin's." Mrs. Bisbey had started to walk away when she abruptly turned back. "Gracious be, I almost forgot again."

Mrs. Bisbey hustled into Joshua's study and returned with a letter. "This came for you Friday, but in readyin' for the party, me mind completely forgot about it." She handed over the folded and sealed packet. "Mister Williams keeps paper and wax in his top right drawer if a response is necessary." She disappeared in the direction of the kitchen.

Alexandra glanced at the return address and immediately ripped it open. The letter was brief, to the point, and produced such anger she desired to scream.

Madam,

Your columns on duty to family submitted to this paper are most suitable to our readership. We question, however, whether your father's hand has played a part in the authorship. We must also wonder whether his name should not accompany the byline. We are fully aware of his reputation at Harvard College and assume his direction is also behind the success of your essays used for our "Noble Horatio" column. Therefore, we seek your permission henceforth to add his name to yours for this new column, and as he is the male coauthor, allow it to appear first.

Regards,
Thomas Painter, Editor

Unable to suppress her disbelief at such a presumptuous attitude, she dashed into the study and snatched a paper from her worktable. With a forceful hand and sharpened wit, she sat at Joshua's desk and set pen to paper.

Sir,

I make no presumptions that my work will ever reach the standards of the best of writers. However, the foolish assertion that whenever a lady sets words to paper a gentleman guides her efforts is both preposterous and full of audacity. I allow no one, not even the family I cherish, to see the words I create. Those who know of my father from Harvard should also have had wisdom enough to inform you that he has been in England nearly half a year. I already defer the use of my own name for that of "Noble Horatio" on my present column, and if you cannot see fit to place my name—and only my name—on this new column, then I heretofore ask that it be withdrawn from use.

Alexandra Gables

Livid at the impertinence of the editor, she hastily searched for sealing wax. She addressed and sealed her letter, then rose quickly to her feet. A great drum pounded inside her head, nearly driving her to distraction.

Mrs. Bisbey strolled into the room. "Did you find everythin' you needed, mum?"

"Yes, thank you, Mrs. Bisbey," Alexandra replied, gingerly massaging her temples. "But pray tell, where do you post your letters? Mister Williams took those I wrote earlier this week."

"I'm sorry to say, you just missed Mister Williams on his way to the post office. If only you had returned a quarter hour earlier. The place is not far, though. It sits 'tween the apothecary and Chandler's tailor shop, not far after you get to the paved part of Main Street. Can't miss it, mum. On this morn, 'tis a busy place."

Alexandra was determined to get her reply off in the timeliest manner. "Then I shall set out right away. Do you have anything that requires posting?"

"Me, mum? Heavens, no. There's no time in the day for me to partake of such foolishness."

From her attitude, Alexandra predicted that Mrs. Bisbey did not read or write. Sadly, not an unusual condition, but one Alexandra could start to change this summer if Mrs. Bisbey was so inclined.

With determination to see her reply on its way, she snatched up the sealed letter, took her hat and coin purse from the front entry table, and headed out the door.

The iron yard gate in front of the mansion had barely swung shut when the midday heat began to take its toll. She fanned her face and longed for cooler clothing. A passing horse kicked up dust on the road, and she held back a sneeze. As she rounded the next corner, fortune smiled with a gentle breeze. She breathed deeply and strode onward, not truly minding the exertion. Exercise was good for both the body and mind.

Finally she turned onto the wide Main Street, unpaved along this section. Even though horse and carriage traffic had increased, this direction out of town was still relatively quiet. She passed two captains' homes Pierce had pointed out on her first day. They were set well back from the street and edged with broad, green yards planted with trees and ample gardens. Up ahead she could see small houses more closely spaced, some with shops attached. People strolled in all directions, many carrying baskets. A single horse trotted by, hauling a wagon with two hogshead barrels.

In front of her, a middle-aged woman carried a bulging basket over one arm. A cloth covered the contents, but the leg of a pair of breeches hung loose out the back. With each step, the breeches dropped a little farther until they almost dragged the ground. Alexandra increased her pace, quickly catching up to the struggling woman.

"Excuse me, ma'am, but you are dropping your load." Alexandra caught the breeches as the woman looked up in surprise. Reddish-gray hair framed a pale complexion not so unlike her own, but tiny wrinkles softening her eyes set her age well into the forties.

The woman sighed gratefully and reached for the breeches. Her load in the basket shifted, and more clothing started to slide out from under the cloth.

Alexandra caught the tilting basket and quickly secured the contents.

"Goodness, I had no idea how poorly I packed the basket. Thank you, Miss . . . ?"

"Gables. Alexandra Gables." She had a strong sense of familiarity, as if she knew the woman. "I am headed to the post office. If you are going in that direction, I would be glad to assist."

"Your offer is quite gracious. I am headed to the tailor shop just before your destination. And under these circumstances, I would be foolish to reject such an offer. Oh, gracious, forgive me; my name is Hannah and I do simple stitch work for Mr. Chandler, the tailor."

Easily they each took one handle on either side of the basket and carried the unwieldy load between them. Together they strode along the road in relative silence, Hannah giving Alexandra an occasional searching glance.

"You are new to Salem, are you not?" Hannah finally asked.

"Yes. I have been here not even a week." Alexandra was surprised that in this large a town anyone would notice a new face.

"For what purpose have you come to Salem?"

"I am here for the summer to assist my father's friend. He is a scientific philosopher and needs help cataloging his collections."

"Then you must be staying with the Williamses," Hannah said, much to Alexandra's surprise. "Dr. Bentley had high praise for a young woman he met at a gathering there recently. I hear tell you may even educate a few of Salem's young ladies in the sciences this summer."

Alexandra was amazed how gossip from the party had

spread like wildfire. Dr. Bentley had simply made that suggestion to Joshua Williams. Her brows knitted in curiosity. "But how did you guess *I* was the Williamses' houseguest?"

"Intuition," the woman pronounced soberly, before adding with teasing eyes, "and we are but two blocks from their home."

That this woman was more than a simple seamstress required no grand deduction on Alexandra's part. Hannah had a quick wit and easy manner.

"I hope you don't consider this rude," Alexandra said, "but my own intuition tells me your knowledge comes from more than our proximity to the Williams estate."

Hannah grinned coyly. "That, and Dr. Bentley professed you had hair as crimson as the evening sunset. I remember because there are not many in town so colorfully endowed as you and I."

Alexandra nodded with understanding, noting that in younger years the woman most certainly would have borne shiny red locks. "How foolish of me not to consider such a possibility myself. I apologize for my curiosity, but I have found some things about Salem a little unsettling."

The woman leaned close and whispered, "I harbor no surprise on that account. After all, we are the infamous 'witching town.' "

Alexandra gave a short laugh. "As everyone in town seems to point out. I had assumed a place where such an aberrance occurred would desire the very fact forgotten."

"Truly, most do, but the fear of looming evil is still quite present. The people here are afraid of anything out of the ordinary, whether good or evil. That is truly unfortunate for, say, a woman with special talent to foresee events before they happen. It is a unique and God-given talent."

Alexandra slowed her step and did her best not to show the total disbelief that surged through her at Hannah's revelation. "What do you mean?" Alexandra squeaked out almost defensively. Was this woman referring to her gift of intuition and, of late, a growing array of sounds and sights? And if so, how could Hannah possibly know about them?

Hannah caught Alexandra's uneasy gaze, but divulged no further details. "I do believe a bright woman like you understands completely."

Alexandra contemplated what Hannah truly knew and what the woman sought from her. "Why do you think *I* should understand about these talents?"

"I should think when a person of science experiences the unexplained, they expend great energy attempting to determine the cause. Have you not discovered some talent which science cannot explain? And has it not seemed enhanced since your arrival in Salem?"

Alexandra felt the same cold chill of premonition that had come upon her in the longboat. Was there truly some condition in Salem that augmented her intuition? She suddenly wished she had not so quickly chosen to walk with this woman. Even though that same intuition said she offered no threat, the conversation had twisted onto a most uncomfortable topic.

"You speak as though these unnatural talents lurk unbounded in Salem," she stated with guarded reserve.

"I cringe to say they do." Hannah gazed up at her as though she had the ability to see deep within Alexandra's heart. "Many have these honest talents and use them for good as God meant. But just as men carry good in their hearts, there are some who thrive on evil. Those people revel in the power of these gifts and use them for their own ends. Be wary of those people, Alexandra, for they can disguise themselves as friend or foe. They will not allow the good to prevail, for it can expose their corrupt plots."

Alexandra had now completely stopped and simply stared at Hannah. What were these wild ravings about good and evil? Had Dr. Bentley set the devil's fear in her?

"I see the post office ahead," Alexandra said too quickly, unintentionally letting her discomfort show.

The woman placed a hand upon Alexandra's arm. "Forgive

me, child; I hope I haven't unsettled you. But time is drawing near and you must be wary. I wish you well during your stay in Salem. And remember, Alexandra, believe in yourself."

The woman slipped into the tailor shop as Alexandra stood frozen. Hannah's words and something in the way she said "Alexandra" stirred a deep and youthful memory. An unsettling yet familiar emotion arose, but she could not come close to understanding it or its origin.

Dazed, Alexandra continued toward the post office, slowly allowing the odd conversation to sift through her mind. She had the unearthly sense that a warning had just been delivered.

But why would a complete stranger feel compelled to present such counsel to her? After all, their meeting had happened by complete chance. Or had it? Alexandra exhaled an unsteady breath. How could Hannah possibly know about the intuition that recently haunted her life? Pierce was the first person she had ever really trusted with any explanation.

She reflected back to Friday evening as he held onto her arm and the rush of feelings, so intense and confused, evolved. She knew intuition about her personal life was ofttimes dubious and confused. But was his kiss some vision or simply a heated desire?

Alexandra craved the truth, yet feared the answer. With such determination to succeed in a man's world, how could she yearn for losing herself in his embrace?

Certainly part of the answer lay in Pierce's uncanny way of breaking through the defenses guarding her personal feelings. Lord have mercy, would he have violated her trust and told Dr. Bentley of her strange intuition? Could he possibly flaunt such a private admission? If true, offering personal revelations to Pierce, or anyone in Salem, would have to be undertaken with great care.

She had discovered with certitude why Salem hung on to its odd reputation for witchcraft. She had barely resided in town a week, and the supernatural already haunted her every step. At this rate, the pious Dr. Bentley might very well begin to believe that she truly was a witch.

With Miss Gables gone from the house, Mrs. Bisbey took the opportunity to dust the floors and furniture of the study. She deftly lifted the drawings on the large table and with extreme care moved the plant presses. After the wood table gleamed, she shifted her attention to the desk.

Mister Joshua Williams had left some of his correspondence strewn on the blotter board. The outer addressed paper for Miss Gables's letter lay off to the side of the desk, but whether the letter lay among Mister Williams's papers, she had no way to know. Gracious be, on occasions such as this she longed to interpret the fancy forms people put to paper.

She shrugged and shook her head at the papers. Neatly she collected them and tucked them into the empty wooden letter box on the desk. She knew the pile would grow until the following Monday, when Mister Williams would again spend the morning on his correspondence. Surely he would sort the papers out properly then.

The walk to the post office had become almost a daily ritual for Alexandra, with letters to her mother's sister in Charleston, her uncle in Boston, her father in London, and, of course, a search to secure a new publisher for her articles. Today on her postal journey, she gladly marveled that several days had passed without any incident that remotely resembled anything supernatural. No more sounds or emotions emanated from family portraits. No further warnings were received from strangers on the street, and no further visions occurred of Pierce endowing his affections upon her person.

As a matter of fact, she had seen very little of Pierce this week, for the shipyard had consumed the majority of his days. One of their few times together had come at supper last night, when he paused long enough to eat and remind her of the ship tour he promised to give her on Sunday. She actually looked forward to the event, convinced the new experience would enhance her knowledge of the world, since, in truth, she knew very little of the art of shipbuilding.

Up ahead, a ship's mate lugged a sizable duffel into the post office. She had learned that with each ship's arrival, the post office thrived with activity as the citizens of Salem sought news of their loved ones.

Inside, the sailor handed over the mail-filled bag, named his ship, and declared they had last left port at Portsmouth, England. Alexandra felt her expectations rise that a letter from her father in London might well be inside. She waited patiently while a gentleman posted mail to New York and a woman complained about a returned packet of letters.

After an extensive wait, the postal window was finally free. Efficiently she paid for her correspondence and inquired when the new shipment of letters would become available. The man in the thin window simply shrugged. Unwilling to wait for the normal and often delayed mail delivery, Alexandra offered to pay for a personal delivery if a letter from her father was within. She gave her name and the address of the Williams estate. She left the window only partially convinced the man would follow her instructions.

Alexandra pulled taut the string on her coin purse and slid it back over her wrist. She had barely taken two steps when a familiar woman blocked her path.

"Excuse me, I do believe we met the other day," the woman said.

Alexandra had yet to remember where, when the woman added, "I foolishly bumped into you outside the Blue Shell Tavern."

The memory, one she had tried to tuck into the category of best forgotten, crept quickly and embarrassingly back to the surface. Newton had made his great escape that day, and half the town had noticed.

The woman straightened her shoulders and adjusted the blue

silk fichu tucked mindfully into her décolletage. "I overheard you tell the man at the mail window your name is Alexandra. I'm afraid I mistakenly mistook you for Bridget the other day. I do so hope you will accept my apology. My name is Margaret Trask." She held out her hand to be shaken. "My husband is the town moderator."

Social position obviously held sway with this woman, who introduced her husband's status along with her name. Alexandra held out her hand, attempting to sort out the memory.

As their hands touched, she remembered the raven hair, ice blue eyes, and purple dress from their first meeting. Tentatively she shook the woman's hand. "Alexandra Gables, from Boston. You are completely forgiven, and I had quite forgotten the incident."

Margaret opened the door into the bright day and they stepped out onto the cobblestone sidewalk. The woman began a conversation as they strolled. "Are you visiting Salem, or have you come to stay? I couldn't help but overhear you are currently living with the Williams family."

"Only visiting, I assure you," Alexandra answered. "My father is in London and will return by summer's end. I will then rejoin him in Boston."

"And I assume you are partaking of the company of handsome Pierce Williams. Many a lady in this town would love to be in your position. He is quite an eligible bachelor."

Alexandra was taken aback by this stranger's candor and quickly guessed she spread much of the town's gossip.

"I can assure you the women of Salem have nothing to fear from me," she said hastily. "I am but an imposition to the very busy shipwright. My work prevents any desire or time to develop romantic aspirations."

"I am pleased to hear as much." Margaret gave a smile of odd proportions, and her eyes gleamed with some darker ambition. "For you see, I have a daughter and nieces that have maintained an interest in ending his bachelor status."

Something inside beckoned Alexandra to seek greater

knowledge of this woman. She wondered if a simple touch might stimulate her intuition and clarify many of her questions. In a casual manner, she reached out for Margaret's arm. Non-chalantly, but perfectly timed, Margaret shifted just ever so slightly out of reach. Alexandra missed her target and let her hand fall gently to her side. Puzzled, she felt uneasy. It seemed as though Margaret knew her intent.

"I must say that staying with the Williamses is likely a unique experience," Margaret continued. "They have lived in Salem at least a good century. If I am not mistaken, one of their ancestors had a powerful position on the Court of Oyer and Terminer during the witch trials. They keep it quiet, of course. Intolerance for witches is not something one wishes to flaunt in this more progressive time."

Alexandra was taken aback. Were the Williamses part of the witch trials? She didn't know why it should matter to her, one way or the other, but it did. She recalled the impressions received upon touching the judge's portrait and knew Margaret was correct about their involvement. Yet the feelings of sorrow she had also garnered from the judge didn't make sense with someone who so willingly condemned the victims to death.

They had reached the corner and Margaret said good day. As she stepped back, Alexandra immediately felt a sense of relief at the distance between them. Before Margaret turned away she added most seriously, "Truly, you should research the Williams family history. Knowledge can be a useful tool."

Alexandra stood with mouth agape. Had Margaret Trask just given her advice or a subtle warning? Why did Margaret care whether she knew the details? Did the woman believe she would stay away from Pierce because of a dark family history, or did she, too, know about her strange intuition? A great sense of foreboding overwhelmed her senses. Surely Dr. Bentley couldn't have talked with so many people in such a short time.

She snapped her mouth shut and plodded toward home. Lord, what if the Williamses truly had a history of intolerance toward witches. What must Pierce have thought of her confession to having a talent that she could not properly explain?

The day was yet young, and the courthouse with the town clerk's records lay only a block distant. She attempted to push all suspicious thoughts from her head as she started back toward the Williamses' house. Not far down the street, she stopped. Unanswered questions burned in her mind. She simply had to know.

With a quick turn and unbridled determination, she headed toward the courthouse. Margaret Trask was right about one thing: knowledge was empowerment, and there seemed to be strange secrets that Pierce Williams had hiding in his family history.

Alexandra had seen shipyards from a distance, but never had she had the privilege of experiencing one firsthand as on this bright Sunday afternoon. Chaos best described the piled lumber, sawdust, wood chips, and tools that completely surrounded her, sometimes reaching heights far above her head. Yet in its own way, the chaos had order. If one added the constant sound of the caulkers' mallets, sawing, and the buzz of workmen on a workday, the place seemed daunting.

Alexandra gauged Pierce's ship from different angles as they strolled, assessing the best location to choose for the sketch Pierce had requested. The ship sat cradled in a series of widespread vertical boards and rested on long planks built to assist its eventual slide into the water. For the first time, Alexandra learned that only vessels with square-rigged sails earned the true title of ship. With proud satisfaction, Pierce described every detail of the hull, shape, and build of the ship.

"After launching, the three masts will be stepped through the deck and attached to the keelson," he commented. "I assume it will not be too difficult to add them later to the drawing. I'd also like to make sure the owners' banner is prominently fluttering from the mast."

"I doubt affixing those details later will be a problem," she answered, then added quite pointedly, "if the ship is completed before the summer's end."

"Oh, she'll be ready. I'll stake my reputation on that."

Alexandra thought Pierce sounded a bit too confident, but considering her insufficient knowledge of the subject she said nothing. As she appraised the large vessel, she considered how to size the ship to fully fit the desired dimensions Pierce had chosen for the finished drawing. She easily envisioned a dark mahogany-colored hull, fluttering sails, the American flag off the stern, and brightly colored banners flying high at the mast tops.

She glanced inquiringly at Pierce. "What color will she be painted?"

He moved behind her to point easily over her shoulder. "Above the copper sheathing on the hull and up till the deck level, she will be black with a four-foot-wide swath of white a few feet below deck level."

His breath, tinged with a hint of mint from dinner's tea, brushed lightly against her neck with each word. The sensation produced a flutter in her stomach and completely broke all concentration. He stood too near. She feared that with any touch, the desire she experienced the night of the party might reignite.

Pierce, on the other hand, appeared at complete ease. His tall shadow shielded her from the warm sun, and she relished it for a moment.

"The paint scheme sounds most impressive." She discovered an unsteady quality in her voice and knew it came from Pierce's proximity. "Did you choose the colors?"

"No, the owners have a signature design for all their vessels." He set a hand on her waist and gently nudged her along. "The painters are starting this week. She must look perfect for the launching."

He spoke as they walked, his hand remaining in the small of her back. He proudly pointed up at the fine white pine bowsprit and explained how earlier this week it had arrived from a nearby saltwater pond, where the straight and sturdy tree was pickled for resilience. His touch continued, and it left her wondering if he usually escorted ladies in this manner or if she might be an exception. She considered it rather presumptuous of him, but found she enjoyed the contact. Fondly she recalled it's similarity to how her father escorted her mother on visits to Harvard College.

Pierce continued to speak, and she once again paid full attention.

"If you have never attended a launching," he said, "it is a rare treat. The entire town comes out. Schools close, businesses lock their doors, and the wharves are lined with spectators."

"I promise not to miss such an important event." She smiled from under the hat shading her face. A large brown pelican drifted overhead, casting a momentary shadow. "Now, when do I get to see inside this magnificent vessel?"

Pierce bore a curious expression as he answered, "It might not be exactly what you expect."

"If the outside is any indication, I have no doubt I will be duly impressed with both the ship and her designer." She stepped forward, ready to continue.

He gently took hold of her shoulder and pulled her back to him. Tall and imposing, he lifted her chin to expose the face she hid beneath the hat.

"Alexandra, you misunderstand my intentions. I did not bring you here just to impress upon you my supposed talents." His voice, so confident yet honest, easily captured her attention. "For you to adequately depict this ship on paper, you must understand her very essence."

And yours, Alexandra thought, *because you have designed and created her.*

He still cupped her chin and seemed in no hurry to release it. She anguished at the sensations produced by such a firm but gentle touch. The skin tingled under his hand and fingers and burned the sensation into every cell of her being. Her mouth watered as she feared her reaction to any further contact.

For a brief moment, his gaze searched her face. In that time, she was surprised to read within his dark eyes a longing, deep and needful. Alexandra drank in his intoxicating nearness and wondered with a flash of unfamiliar excitement whether she might hold the key to fulfilling this need.

His hand abruptly disappeared from her chin. The loss of his touch left her weak, as though the strings were suddenly cut from a marionette. Pierce snared every physical sense within her. Only her strength of mind remained to control the unmistakable urge to lose herself in his arms.

The words of the seamstress Hannah returned: " . . . the evil can disguise themselves as friend or foe." Amazingly, even through his pride Pierce maintained an air of integrity. He truly did not act in any way that made her doubt his genteel nature. Regardless of what the town records had revealed, Alexandra sensed no hatred in Pierce, no prejudice against those who might be different, such as herself. Yet, he had laughed at her attempts to explain the visions, and he had apparently discussed them with Dr. Bentley.

On the other hand, the Williams family had shown nothing but compassion in all their undertakings with her. Certainly her intuition was not in error. Evil did not exist within Pierce.

Pierce cleared his throat. "To reach the boarding plank, I'm afraid we must round the bow back to the larboard side."

Adjusting her hat and attempting to forget the feelings arising from his touch, she glanced back over one shoulder. "I assume you are referring to that teetering extension of boards I noticed earlier."

Pierce chuckled lightly, as if completely forgetting the past few serious moments. He prodded her into motion and they started around the ship.

"Come, now," he said in a teasing tone, "the plank may appear a shabbily built affair, but it is quite adequate for the daily deluge of workmen. I am offended you believe I would risk your health on something dangerous."

"Can you honestly tell me no misfortune has ever befallen anyone on that plank?" She firmly planted a hand upon her hat as a gusty sea breeze threatened to dislodge it, and looked to him for an answer.

Before he offered a reply, she rounded the bow and collided with a solid brute of a man. She hastily backed up, and the man looked past her to Pierce.

"Good day to ye, Mister Williams, and me pardons to you, ma'am," he said with a dip of his head. "Methought the voices I heard might be belongin' to ye. I'd seen ye comin', but was aboard checkin' on things."

"So far the only supplies gone missing are from the yard around the ship, Mister Bates." Pierce showed no pleasure at the man's explanation, and his tone affirmed it. "In the future, I suggest you concentrate your security efforts there."

"Aye, aye, sir." The big man tipped his grubby cap and disappeared to another corner of the shipyard.

The stern tone Alexandra heard from Pierce surprised her. She noted that he watched Mr. Bates move away with a concerned eye.

Pierce leaned close and spoke in a lowered voice. "In answer to your question about misfortunes, in fact, a man has fallen from that planking. On the day of your arrival some disagreement ensued between Mr. Bates and a carpenter while climbing aboard. No man will admit to the cause or fault, but I looked up in time to see the carpenter lose his balance and tumble from the plank. Mr. Bates, who stood inches from the man, made no attempt to help."

Pierce quieted, as though reliving the incident and attempting to assess blame. "Fortune had it," he continued, "that I was close enough to break the carpenter's fall. He suffered only a broken arm. Perhaps now you will understand my state of disarray upon arriving to collect you at the docks. I suggest for your own health that you keep a safe distance from Mister Bates, although he typically works the night hours and should not be a problem for you while sketching."

She flushed with shame at having questioned Pierce's dusty attire on that first day. He had risked his own safety to rescue the falling workman, and she had made a shallow fuss over a little dirt. The healthy dose of humility made her feel small.

Pierce ushered her toward the infamous plank system. "Attend to your footing," he said as he enveloped her hand in his and ascended the walkway.

He hardly had to give any warning. She gratefully clung to his protective hand on the precarious perch. Only a fool would take a chance with no rail on what she considered flimsy boards. They easily gave under her weight, yet supported the hauling of materials on board. It took little imagination to envision a burdened craftsman bouncing jauntily along with each step as he climbed aboard.

"I must say, I'm impressed by your bravery," she said with a facetious note in her voice.

"Oh, really?" Pierce jumped onto the deck and turned to lift her slowly and carefully down. "And for what deed have I earned such respect?"

"Walking this plank each day." Her lips came precariously close to his mouth before her feet safely touched the decking. She blushed and her heart thumped at an embarrassing volume. How she hated her body's response to each slight encounter with him.

He smiled at the quip, appearing self-assured and at home on the ship. Contentment and security radiated from him, so much so that she, too, could not help but feel sanguine.

She turned to scan the deck, then stopped dead at the view. The ship lay in total disarray, and even to her untrained eye, obvious parts were missing. Everything on deck appeared in varying stages of construction. The massive bowsprit, which pointed grandly off the ship's bow toward Salem and the western sky, and the large wood wheel were the only easily recognizable objects. Newness hung in the air as she inhaled odors of fresh-cut pine and oak.

She glanced up at Pierce, who caught the confused look on her face before he burst out laughing.

"Oh, I'm sorry," he stuttered in between bursts of sound. "If you could only see your expression."

His reaction foretold she had offered an unenlightened reaction to his ship. Had he not the decency to control himself?

"I don't see what is so amusing about a ship in total disarray," she snapped in embarrassment. "It must be near impossible to tell what is yet to be accomplished. And you bragged so grandly at how close this ship is to launching. From what I see, you have much left to complete."

Pierce ceased his laughing and displayed the serious demeanor necessary for a proper apology. "Forgive me if my reaction disturbed you. But rarely does anyone not accustomed to shipbuilding come aboard until further along in the completion process. But I assure you, to paraphrase Shakespeare's *Hamlet,* 'There is method to this madness.' She will be ready."

Alexandra witnessed his fight to keep straight the quirking edges of his mouth. Irritation rose at his behavior, and any desire for his closeness vanished.

"You might have warned me," she said indignantly.

"I tried. But you ignored my words. You are accustomed to seeing a ship replete with masts, rigging, and carpentry. The carpenters and craftsmen finish up while the fittings and equipment are loaded and rigged after launching."

Alexandra knew he was right, but refused to let him see her discomfiture. With an apathetic shrug, she moved away and wandered around the deck. She noticed sawhorses at various locations, piles of trim boarding, mitered scraps, and small barrels containing stain, varnish, and wooden tree nails. From an earlier conversation, she recalled that the local poorhouse had their occupants making such nails.

Pierce now stood so far away that she practically shouted across the deck. "If you wish me to accurately sketch the ship, I'm afraid I'll need to see it in more finished detail. There are no covers for the companionways; the woodworking and rails are incomplete; and, of course, there are three gaping holes where the masts will go." She carefully balanced and picked her way across a pile of slim boards.

Pierce hastily caught up to her location and outstretched a hand for assistance. She ignored his offer for help and smiled triumphantly as she arrived safely on the other side of the pile.

With strong, long legs, Pierce easily straddled the boards and followed. "This part of construction proceeds rapidly." He pointed to a partially built boxlike structure in front of the wheel. "The binnacle, which houses the compass, goes here. The pinrails and belaying pins will sit there, there, and there." He pointed to various places along the main rail.

She found it hard to resist the fondness he showed toward his ship. He stood on the deck like a proud, handsome captain, firm of hand and strong in character to lead his crew to the far corners of the world. Soon she forgot his mocking laughter and let her imagination envision when the great ship would raise sail with the wind.

She stepped onto the wheel platform and took hold of the handpegs on the giant wheel. She imagined the helmsman battered by the blustery wind, salt spray spattering his face with each rhythmic splash of the bow. She easily took on the role, turning the wheel and guiding the ship and crew onward.

An eerie green blackness quickly enveloped the ship, and she recognized the beginnings of a vision. She tried to shake it away with the toss of her head, but to no avail. Wind whistled through the masts, and waves erratically tossed water across the deck. Ominous black clouds roiled overhead and the captain barked orders to the men. Pierce scrambled to assist as the ship began to rise and roll uncontrollably with the waves. Men screamed as the ship swung broadside to a massive wave. The ship rolled violently, and cascading water swept men overboard.

"Alexandra, Alexandra," she heard Pierce anxiously calling. With a horrified gasp and pained disorientation, she opened her eyes. Pierce cradled her in his arms, once again shielding her from the sun. He waved his hat before her face. Relief showed in his face as she looked up at him.

"You are pale and shaken," he said gently. "Forgive me, I was foolish to bring you out in the heat of the day. You started swaying so strangely as you held the wheel, then simply collapsed."

She opened her mouth to relate the scene she had just envisioned, then halted. What could she possibly say? He had shown no prior propensity to believe in her intuition, let alone the strange vision she had just experienced. The horrific scene still ran through her mind with great confusion. She had yet to sort out its meaning.

The decision to keep quiet also came from one other important and disturbing fact: the haunting knowledge she had garnered from the town records. Judge Nathaniel Williams, the very man in the study portrait, had indeed sat upon the court credited with convicting the innocent victims of the witch hunts. If his beliefs had been passed down through the generations to Pierce, then she truly wished to keep any more knowledge of her strange talent private, at least until she discovered the explanation behind it. Surely science would assist her in that task.

She struggled to sit and leaned partially against Pierce. He reached for her hat, which had fallen on the deck, and offered it to her.

"Thank you," she said, taking the hat and smiling weakly. She leaned away from his supporting hold and unbuttoned her jacket bodice for relief from the heat. She looked gratefully up at him. "You are most gracious and understanding. The day *has* been unseasonably warm."

Pierce offered no admonition about the frail quality of women. He simply looked at her with a serious frankness. "I heartily agree, and I think we have had enough excitement for one day.

When she was ready, he stood beside her and steadied her to her feet. She smoothed her hair back from her face and refastened her hat. He wrapped an arm around her waist for support. "Can you make the climb down?" he asked as they walked toward the plank.

The concern she saw in his face said he truly cared for her well-being. She nodded but didn't speak. Her trembling voice would only divulge the guilt she suffered.

While Pierce assisted and cared for her, she hid a potentially dangerous secret from him, for with almost complete confidence, she had now interpreted the vision. She had seen the demise of Pierce's ship at sea and witnessed his death in the murky ocean depths.

Seven

The frothy waves churned up by the stiff breeze scattered a salt spray against the jagged shore of Ye Neck. Even though well back from shore, Pierce inhaled the pungent smells of dried seaweed and sun-baked fish. Alexandra had walked ahead and disturbed a flock of herring gulls, which took flight, swooping wildly until each aligned with the breeze and swooshed away.

Pierce laid his waistcoat in the carriage, then tied the horse to a scraggly juniper, twisted and bent toward the land by steady and often tortuous northeast winds. He took a long breath, one meant to steady his nerves and prepare him for yet another encounter with Alexandra. Why he had not taken her directly home from the shipyard was a mystery. Obstinate as ever, even after fainting, she had requested a moment to invigorate her soul with the refreshing breeze off the point, and he had acquiesced with annoying ease.

"Ye Neck is but a short ride from the shipyard," she had pleaded in a melodious voice—a voice he apparently had no power to deny. Yet he was not ignorant of her true motive for this brief respite. In those lovely emerald eyes, he read an unabated determination to achieve some secret goal. She had something on that ingenious little mind of hers, and he feared that whatever it was would make his life infinitely more difficult.

He sighed and snapped up a piece of long grass in his path.

The word *fool* leaped to mind, but he had discovered without astonishment that he had little power over Alexandra or himself whenever she was near. He stripped the piece of grass, tossed the strands to the wind, and prayed for her internship to pass briskly.

He trailed at a leisurely pace after Alexandra. She stood far ahead atop the grass-and-rock-covered embankment that sloped steeply to the jagged and rocky shore. Her hat in hand, the breeze whipped strands of hair wildly about her face. She wore the same hunter green skirt and jacket that she had on her arrival in Salem. Unbuttoned, the short fitted jacket blew loosely with the wind, revealing the cream silk blouse and the alluring curves of her petite figure underneath.

As he drew closer, the introspective look on her face worried him. He had yet to determine what her reflective moments meant, but as of late, with china dropping out of windows and claims of strange intuition, he knew enough to be wary. Alexandra had not the predictability of most ordinary women of Salem, and that, he considered with a surprising burst of clarity, was to her advantage.

"Perhaps I have done an injustice bringing you here," he said as he reached her side. "I should have escorted you directly home. Are you still feeling ill?"

She produced a halfhearted smile. "My health is unquestionably fine. I simply have several matters which engage my mind and require fresh air to sort out."

"If I may be of assistance, I am at your disposal." He immediately wondered with what dubious problem he had just chivalrously offered to help.

She played with the yellow ribbon on her hat and gazed out across the harbor. A fishing sloop sailed close and men waved toward the shore. Pierce returned the greeting, waiting for her to speak.

"Today I displayed great ignorance in the knowledge of shipbuilding," she began rather modestly. "That is now changing due to your mentoring. You have been most gracious to extend every courtesy in the manner of information about your craft. I do find, however, a few things are still unclear to me."

"Such as?" Questions about shipbuilding seemed too simple a solution to what he had read in her eyes.

"The helmsman's wheel where I last stood. I don't completely understand its function."

"Simple." He shrugged. "To control the rudder."

She rolled her eyes in agitation. "Even I am aware of that. Please, explain the workings in greater detail."

"How detailed?"

"What your father would expect for a description."

"If you wish." He studied the serious lines made by her pursed lips and wondered why this information mattered. "In a simple boat, the tiller is a pole attached to the rudder. Move the pole back and forth and the rudder follows. However, that can be quite a feat for the helmsman on a large ship.

"Instead, the center of the wheel is attached to a wood cylinder, around which rope is wrapped. The two ends of the rope hang down and go through the deck. Below deck, the ropes are rigged into a setup that attaches to the hull and then the tiller. That translates the circular movement of the wheel into back-and-forth rudder action." He spread his hands wide. "Is that detailed enough?"

"Has all that been completed on your ship?"

He studied her curiously, a bit of suspicion nagging at the back of his mind. "The rudder, tiller, and wheel are in place, but the rigging has yet to be accomplished. Now, may I ask why this is of such great concern to you?"

"Curiosity," she said, gazing out over the ocean, "just curiosity." He followed her line of sight and let himself be caught up in the roll of a wave, watching it approach and crash upon the shore.

"Is the rudder a difficult piece to build?" she asked.

"The rudder is indubitably important, and built of the strongest white oak. Several pieces are connected together by iron straps which serve as hinges."

"Do you double-check the fittings to make sure they are properly attached?"

Pierce saw no possible reason for this question except one, and it raised his defensive posture. She questioned his ability to thoroughly secure the safety of the vessel. "I have personally inspected the rudder and taken every possible precaution with this ship and its construction. The quality bespeaks my reputation. The ship is on, maybe even slightly ahead of schedule, but not at the cost of safety. If it is any consolation to you, I plan to invest a good deal of money in this vessel's future voyages."

Alexandra turned to him, holding back strands of red hair that now blew into her eyes. "I did not wish to question your integrity for safety. You have my apologies if I made you think such a thing. After my unpleasant experience with the wheel, it simply piqued my curiosity."

Without another word, she resumed her walk along the crest of the embankment until finding a place where rain had eroded a shallow gully. She chose her footing and worked down the embankment to a heap of dark rocks, slick and algae-coated from the tidal fluctuations. He dutifully followed, as was becoming usual on this day, and, as with the last set of questions, wondered where she was leading him now.

Alexandra knelt and picked through objects on the beach. Dark and light sands mingled with rocks and shell fragments, giving a bluish hue to the shoreline. She stood with eyes lighted by discovery and stretched a hand toward him with several blue mussel shells. "I understand now from where the Blue Shell Tavern received its name."

She let the shells fall through her fingers to the beach and swung back toward the sea with arms outstretched. "Salem is so different from what I had imagined. The sea is in her blood, and no citizen is exempt from that influence." She swung back toward him. "Has it always been such?"

"The Indians once called this harbor Naumkeag. That means the 'fishing place.' " Pierce pointed to a fishing sloop heading into the harbor. "In all likelihood, that sloop there is returning from the fishing banks off Cape Cod. Since Salem lacks the rich soils of the South, men have fished the seas since they first arrived. Today, we ship dried codfish around the world. The only change since Salem's beginning is the number of ships sailing now and the distant lands to which they travel."

Alexandra steadied herself on his shoulder as she stepped up onto a flat boulder. "Your family has resided in Salem for a considerable time, has it not?"

"More than a century."

"Were your ancestors fishermen?"

"Some may have been, but not all. Most came from England and were well educated."

She stepped down from the rock and began a slow stroll over the uneven beach back toward higher ground. He offered his arm as support and she willing accepted his assistance.

"I have studied with considerable interest the paintings in the study," she said. "One is titled 'Judge Nathaniel Williams.' I am impressed by such an elevated title. Did he reside here in Salem?"

"He first lived in Boston, then in his later years moved to Salem to be close to his sister. He sat on regional courts and traveled throughout the area serving the judicial needs."

"Was he involved with the witch trials?"

Astonished at the question she asked, a chill swept through him. This was the last topic he expected Alexandra to broach; he had not defended the family honor on the issue for years.

He put a fist to his mouth and lightly cleared his throat for emphasis. "Before I answer, allow me to give you counsel for the future on this matter. Many of Salem's finest families had some involvement with that period in history. Etiquette now deems it a prudent subject to avoid."

As he tried to assess her reaction to his caution, he noticed anxiety had replaced the curiosity on her face. "Is there something that distresses you?" he asked.

"My apologies if I appear preoccupied. I was only reflecting on the hardships such trials must have brought." She made no eye contact, but instead scooped a rock from the beach and examined it halfheartedly. "I simply desire to understand more of this awkward subject. Was Nathaniel involved?"

Pierce had learned from youthful experience that any discussion on the subject led to drawn-out explanations and defensive posturing that achieved nothing. People found fault in whatever avenue of argument he pursued. Nathaniel had sat on the Court of Oyer and Terminer, then resigned long before the convictions as the foolishness of the trials ran away with all reason. Still, many believed that if he had remained, the outcome might have been different. Pierce, so long parted in history from the event, had no way to assess either viewpoint.

"Nathaniel Williams, to his credit, did his best to honor the law and those so accused." Pierce chose his words carefully to best ease Alexandra's curiosity and close the topic. "I will say, with the little I can comprehend this hundred years hence, that time has proven his beliefs worthy."

They had reached the place where earlier they had descended. "May I assist you up the embankment?" he offered.

Alexandra silently nodded, and he firmly grasped her hand, dug his feet into the loose, sandy earth beneath, and tugged her to the top. She scurried so quickly behind him that she nearly toppled him with her forward momentum.

He caught and held her close. She made no move to back away. Instead, her gaze lingered on his face, catching his questioning stare.

Softly she said, "You may not understand why, but I wish most earnestly to learn about your ancestor. When I stare at Nathaniel's portrait in the study, I find his aged and wise face of great fascination. Please, tell me more about him."

Alexandra's persistence never ceased to amaze him. The last thing Pierce cared to consider at the moment was his ancestor. He looked down upon a fair face with fiery hair strewn softly in all directions and her chest moving quickly with each breath. A soft pink from the day's sun shone delicately from under the freckles on her cheeks. Her full lips were softly parted as she waited for his response. He gathered every ounce of energy in order to give her an appropriate one. He started by stepping back.

"I have shared with you all that I reliably can. Anything else is only conjecture and hearsay passed down from generation to generation. Surely we can converse on a more suitable topic."

He started toward the carriage but discovered that Alexandra did not follow. Impatiently he turned back. "If we tarry much longer, Mrs. Flamm will have cleared Sunday supper away." He read only determination on Alexandra's face.

"Why do you believe time has proven Nathaniel's actions correct?" she asked.

Irritation fought its way into his system as he glared at Alexandra. Why did she feel it necessary to probe a topic he had just pointed out as unsociable? Did this woman ever listen to anything he espoused?

"You have heard all that I am at liberty to share. I'm sorry, but there is little else I can add."

She swept toward him and touched his arm. "I beg of you not to think me insensitive. I offer no judgment on Nathaniel's life. I simply feel a notable urge to understand this man who gazes over my shoulder each day while I work. Whatever you can share with me, even that which may be undetermined by history, I will value greatly."

No matter how alluring her appeal, Pierce had no wish to indulge further in sharing the family history, and he considered Alexandra quite presumptuous to continue asking. Past history was just that: past. Nothing in the knowledge could possibly assist Alexandra in any of her scientific duties, and it was best she learn that not every curiosity would be revealed to her. This was one time she would lose the battle.

"Forgive me for saying so," he said none too delicately, "but since our stop at the point, you have questioned the safety of my work ethic and unearthed the bleakest part of my family history. Time does not permit any further chances for you to damage my self-esteem." He gestured toward the carriage. "Are you ready to depart, or do you wish to walk home?"

Alexandra stared at him, first in surprise and then in profound disappointment. She plopped her hat back on her head and brushed past him toward the carriage. She clambered in without waiting for his assistance.

"Pleasant evenin' to ye," Mrs. Bisbey said as she shut the kitchen door behind the departing cook. With swelling ankles and sore feet, she longingly eyed a soft cushion on a kitchen chair. Thankfully, the Sunday supper dishes were cleaned and put away, and the chores done until the morrow. With Joshua Williams and Mistress Gables gone to a poetry reading in town, the house lay in relative quiet. The younger Williams had settled into the study and worked with a model of his ship. She had a decent break before he'd be wanting tea.

She poured a small mug of cider and pulled another chair close. Slowly and with great ceremony, she settled onto the soft chair cushion. With a grunt of satisfaction, she plopped her feet onto the second chair. She swatted a fly trying to claim the sweet cider, cuddled the mug in her lap and gazed out a small window.

Sunset still lay a good hour hence, and the birds took advantage of that fact. The crisp *o-ka-lee* of the red-winged blackbird sounded in the distance, and a mockingbird swooshed by, chasing a larger crow. A cool breeze blew through the window and out another across the room, making the kitchen bearable. The sudden clop-clop of horse hooves and the sound of carriage wheels passing down the side yard toward the stable echoed in the room.

She frowned at the latter sound. "Mercy be, is that Mister Williams back already?" Reluctantly she slid to her feet, opened the kitchen door, and peered out. In the side yard, one of the young stable hands held a carriage horse while Alexandra helped Mr. Williams to step down. They immediately came toward the house, and Mr. Williams crossed the threshold without a word. By the look of his pale face, his health was in question.

"Some tea, Mrs. Bisbey. Mister Williams is feeling a bit indisposed," Alexandra called back as the two hurried past and swept up the stairs.

By the pale and uncomfortable look of Mr. Williams, he had overindulged on strawberries and rich cream again. The man's constitution was contrary to sweet fruits, and that made summer a precarious time as cherries, melons, and peaches ripened. Mrs. Bisbey attended to the tea, knowing Alexandra would see to Mr. Williams.

Mrs. Bisbey set out a teapot and started to collect the tea leaves used for poor stomachs, when another sound reached her ears: the distinct clank of the front iron gate. Before she had even left the kitchen for the entry, a soft pounding began on the front door.

"Mercy, what happened to a peaceful Sunday eve?" she muttered on the way to receive the caller.

She opened the door to a young lady dressed in yellow brocade silk, her hair done with dark tresses curled long and tight beneath a plumed hat. In the distance, a driver stood waiting by the carriage. In her hand, she held a small square paper.

"Good evenin', mum. Can I help ye?" Mrs. Bisbey asked.

The lady, probably a mere seventeen but definitely of courting age, smiled sweetly. "I have an invitation to present to Mister Joshua Williams from my parents. Is he perhaps at home?"

"Mister Williams is indisposed, but I'll gladly pass it along to him. Please, step in." Mrs. Bisbey opened the door wider.

She held out a hand for the invitation, but the young lady gave no indication of releasing it into her custody. Perturbed, Mrs. Bisbey said, "May I say who called?"

"Lydia Trask, youngest daughter of the Trasks. I promised my mother to personally deliver the invitation. Is there no other family member available?" She raised her voice so the last question carried well into the house.

Mrs. Bisbey cringed at the name Trask. Those people were

no good. For five long years after her arrival in America, she had suffered indentured servitude in that household. The twenty years since had done nothing to dim the memory. She had witnessed enough greed, manipulation, and political conniving associated with the Trasks to haunt her soul forever.

"I'm afraid, mum, they are all indisposed."

"Mrs. Bisbey," Pierce called from study, "do we have a guest?"

Seconds later he appeared at her side, and the young lady coyly batted her dark lashes. "Why, Mister Williams, I am so pleased to find you home. My parents wished me to convey their deepest regards and invite you and your family to our home." She fanned the invitation under her chin, obviously with no plans to easily relinquish it.

Mrs. Bisbey bit her tongue as Pierce, the inveterate gentleman, easily saw that the young lady planned to take her time with the delivery.

"Please, come into the parlor," he said, offering his arm. "Mrs. Bisbey, would you please prepare us some tea."

The two disappeared into the front parlor while Mrs. Bisbey headed for the kitchen, her ankles swelling and her temper on edge with a Trask under the same roof.

"Tea," she grumbled unhappily. "Everybody expects bloody tea."

Alexandra swept down the stairs and into the kitchen to find Mrs. Bisbey bent over the table, laying out a tea service. As she shifted around the table, Alexandra noticed there were two different settings.

"I do believe one pot of tea will be sufficient for Mister Williams," she said, confused by the redundant dishware.

"Right you are, mum, and I've already made up his special brew." She pointed to the white pot painted delicately with small blue flowers. "He oft gets a poor stomach disposition after a bit too much fruit. A few cups of this will quiet the inner demons."

Alexandra stared at the two cups and saucers set out with a white-and-gold teapot. "And for whom is this setting?"

Mrs. Bisbey appeared terribly uneasy and unsure about how to answer. Finally she came to some decision and sidled up close to Alexandra. "This is a rather delicate subject, mum, but I just must confide in someone."

Alexandra wondered why Mrs. Bisbey practically whispered, but quickly realized she did not want to be overheard. "Does Pierce have a visitor?"

"Yes, mum, and that's the problem. She's Lydia, one of the Trask daughters."

The name Trask quickly piqued Alexandra's memory. Margaret Trask had intercepted her at the post office just days ago and had been the one to suggest she research Pierce's family history. She had also quite blatantly pronounced that her daughter had an interest in Pierce. As much as Alexandra thought she wouldn't mind, she disliked these women encroaching so soon on her territory. Curiosity prodded her to ask, "Where are they?"

"In the parlor. Mister Pierce asked for tea. Pardon me sayin', but I once worked for the Trasks, and they're not the most honorable of folk." She hesitated before adding, "Mark me words, mum, she's up to somethin'."

Over the past week, Alexandra had found Mrs. Bisbey of amiable character and good heart. Alexandra trusted what the woman said. With Mrs. Bisbey's pronouncement as to the character of this woman's family, and Alexandra's own rather uneasy feeling around Mrs. Trask, she had the sudden urge to defend Pierce.

"Is it normal in Salem for the young ladies to deliver personal invitations?"

"I can't say it hasn't been done before, but if ye ask me, she believed Mister Joshua and maybe even ye, mum, were gone from the house."

When Alexandra considered that Dr. Bentley had sponsored the evening reading, she thought it most likely that Margaret

Trask knew the circumstances. "I'd like to take a peek at this woman."

"The entry makes for a decent inconspicuous view." Mrs. Bisbey stepped from the kitchen and pointed down the hall.

Alexandra slipped into the entry, and as promised, a good portion of the parlor was observable. Oddly, Pierce drew her attention first. Dressed in brown breeches and a white cotton shirt hanging open at the neck, he appeared relaxed and incredibly handsome. His dark curls were gathered into a short ponytail, leaving his strong chin and easy smile framed by dark brows. Her heart quickened with a sensation that kindled every ounce of her femininity. She suddenly longed to be the one joining him for tea.

Pierce sat opposite Lydia, politely allowing her to chat. The lady had removed her hat, and it was very evident she was still rather young. Alexandra overheard the word "fashion" and caught Pierce glancing toward the great clock. Without a doubt, he was bored. She discovered a great deal of satisfaction in that observation. A plan to deal with Lydia formed in her head almost instantly, and she retreated to the kitchen.

"I have an idea," she said to Mrs. Bisbey. "Tell Mister Pierce that you have served tea in the conservatory. There is a small table with chairs in there. Explain that a new orchid has just bloomed and he might want to share its beauty with the guest."

"The conservatory?"

"It's private and quaint, and if Lydia is after Pierce's affections, she will believe it perfect. I'll explain when I get back. For now, just keep your eye on that girl."

Alexandra swept up her skirt in one arm before collecting Joshua Williams's tea tray. Efficient Mrs. Bisbey was in charge of the guest, and her sufficient diligence would do until Mr. Williams had been given his tea and tucked into bed.

Alexandra left Mrs. Bisbey behind, looking bewildered and concerned. The tea set chattered as Alexandra ascended the stairs, and she wondered how quickly Joshua Williams could drink his tea so she might return to the more interesting tea party below.

Alexandra sat on the edge of Joshua Williams's bed, dipping a cloth in a bowl of cool water. Gently she placed the cloth across his forehead and patted his hand.

"Mrs. Bisbey claims this tea will have you back to health in a whisper of time." She helped him sit and fluffed a pillow behind his back, then handed Joshua the cup of warm tea.

A soft knock sounded on the door and Mrs. Bisbey hustled in.

"Speak of the devil," Joshua chuckled weakly.

Mrs. Bisbey let the comment slip by without retort. Something else was definitely on her mind. "Mistress Alexandra, I need to speak with ye. 'Tis rather urgent."

"Mister Williams," Alexandra said softly, "if you have no further need of me . . ." She removed the cloth from his head and placed it in the bowl.

"Scat," he said. "I can take care of myself. I don't need a bunch of women fussing over me."

Alexandra rose but didn't leave until she reminded him to finish the tea. Once she was outside the door, Mrs. Bisbey began pacing nervously up and down the upstairs hall, wringing her hands.

"Oh, Mistress Alexandra," she said in a frantic but hushed voice. " 'Tis terrible, just terrible."

"Be calm, Mrs. Bisbey, and explain what has happened."

She clutched at Alexandra's arm. "Why, that girl put somethin' in his tea. She's a smooth one, she is. She thought I'd gone, but I did what ye asked and kept an eye on them."

"Did you stop Pierce from drinking it?"

"No, mum, I didn't have a chance."

"What do you mean, you didn't have a chance?" Alexandra repressed an urge to run into the room and physically throw Lydia out onto the street.

"That girl offered a toast and he sipped the cup down on the spot. I think he was hopin' to hurry her visit."

"Good Lord, do you think she poisoned him?" Frantically she wondered if Mrs. Bisbey had any concoctions to make Pierce retch.

"I don't think so, mum. That Mrs. Trask is an expert with roots and herbs. I've seen her slip things into tea that will make a person do most anythin'. Come to think of it, after a couple of minutes he did begin actin' a bit daffy about the girl."

"What do you mean, *daffy?* What was he doing?" Alexandra questioned sharply.

Mrs. Bisbey grimaced and appeared quite dour as she recalled the memory. "Scootin' his chair closer and placin' little kisses all over her hand."

"If I didn't know any better, I'd declare him smitten by an aphrodisiac," Alexandra mumbled, thinking how impossible it must seem. From all she had read and heard, most had no potency unless taken over days and weeks of time.

"What's an aphro-de-sac?"

"A love potion."

"Oh, my," Mrs. Bisbey moaned. " 'Tis said that the first kiss after such a potion seals the heart for each other. Mistress Alexandra, we can't let Mister Pierce get near that horrid girl."

Alexandra calmed herself, trying to think clearly. Aphrodisiacs came in all forms. Some were boiled from barks and plants; others were eaten, such as pine nuts, truffles, hemp seeds, and various herbs and spices. Only in Greek and Roman legend had she heard of any acting particularly fast. She recalled one name, *Satyrion,* a dry and pulverized root usually added to wine. But no one believed it still existed. The entire situation was rather odd, but nonetheless required swift action.

"Did you serve tea in the conservatory?" she asked Mrs. Bisbey.

"Yes, mum, just as ye asked."

Mrs. Bisbey looked hopefully for an explanation, but it

would have to wait. "Don't you worry, Mrs. Bisbey, I'll take care of it. You just stay by the front door and be ready."

"Ready?"

Alexandra didn't stop to answer and quickly headed down the stairs. She sneaked over to where she could see into the conservatory and observe from a distance. Lydia strolled deliberately around the glass room stopping to smell and poke at different flowers. Alexandra watched Pierce follow only steps away. Lydia pointed out a flower for him to smell. As he bent down, she plucked a feather from her hat and stroked it across his exposed neck.

Pierce playfully reached out to catch her, but she giggled and quickly scooted out of his reach, enticing him to follow. He trailed her footsteps, virtually panting like a lost puppy. Boiling anger riled Alexandra. That woman was going to get what she so thoroughly deserved.

Alexandra shifted her position until she could no longer see Pierce. Newton, however, became visible on his perch. The wily creature's beady eyes opened almost as though he knew she watched. His head bobbed in her direction. Alexandra let her eyes and head slowly move back and forth between Lydia, with her yards of yellow flowing silk and Newton. She let a pronounced frown cover her face when she gazed at Lydia. Several times she did this, until Newton no longer watched her but instead focused on Lydia. Alexandra quickly shifted her position to check once again on Pierce's status.

Lydia stood near several orchid pots and craftily slipped out the silk scarf tucked into her décolletage. She gently flounced her shoulders and dipped her chin demurely. This time as Pierce neared, she paused and seductively draped the scarf around his neck. He laughed and said something Alexandra could not hear. Lydia took his hands in hers and brushed them across her lips before placing them on her hips. Pierce's hands slid around to her back as he pulled her close. Lydia took the ends of the scarf and gently coaxed Pierce toward her waiting lips. With closed eyes and parted lips, she awaited his kiss.

The flash of green on yellow was not visible to Alexandra until it reached Lydia's shoulder. Obviously surprised at the odd weight, Lydia opened her eyes as Pierce's lips were but an inch away from hers. She reflexively whipped her head toward the shoulder where Newton, yellow-orange eyes brightly gleaming, stared back.

The scream that followed was most likely heard well out onto the street. Frightened, Newton leaped into Pierce's arms. Lydia jumped back, terrified, and pawed frantically at her shoulder where Newton had sat, as though trying to remove the creature's touch. Pierce, left off balance and now burdened with Newton's extra weight, stumbled forward into an orchid stand, sending the pot flying to the floor with soil and potsherds scattering everywhere. Newton scrambled onto the floor and stability.

Lydia, whirling in a frenzy searching for where Newton had landed, discovered him lashing his tail and arching his crest spikes about a foot from her feet.

Another scream deafened Alexandra's ears as a blur of yellow silk flew past. A door clicked shut and she knew Mrs. Bisbey had aptly done her job. Alexandra looked back into the conservatory at Pierce and the litter of objects now covering the floor. In Lydia's haste, she had left both the yellow scarf and plume behind. Alexandra leaned against the wall, doing her best to stifle the laughter wanting to explode.

Eight

Pierce, his reactions unexplainably dulled and feeling quite light-headed, collected his composure and straightened himself in time to hear the front door close.

His heart ached strangely as he realized his alluring visitor had fled the house. "Lydia," he called with a longing passion and ran to the door.

Sturdy Mrs. Bisbey blocked his way. "Sorry, sir. She's gone. No sense in runnin' after the girl. She's downright frightened out of her mind. Said she won't be comin' back here again."

"Out of my way, woman. She'll listen to me."

"Sir, I tell you, 'tis not a good thing."

"Move aside now or you will soon find yourself a house-keeper without a house to manage."

Mrs. Bisbey nodded solemnly and moved much slower than her years required from in front of the door. By the time Pierce could step out, the carriage was halfway down the block. For some reason, he felt oddly alone, almost abandoned.

"Damnation! I almost had her in my arms." He stepped angrily back into the house. "That scaly green creature has now twice besmirched my family name." He slammed the front door, picturing Newton's romp at the tavern. "I'll deal with you soon enough," he bellowed toward the conservatory.

Passion for Lydia drove him first into the parlor where they had taken tea. He fully expected to find her hat and partake of its sweet lavender perfume. It provided the perfect excuse for him to go calling. He checked the settee and looked behind a chair, but it was gone.

Mrs. Bisbey stood quietly in the room, watching him with a curious expression. He shot her an irritated glance.

"Can I help ye, sir?" she finally said.

"Miss Lydia placed her hat on the settee."

"I, um, handed it to her as she left, sir."

He gave her an inquiring look. "You did, now, did you?"

Mrs. Bisbey swallowed hard and looked unusually nervous. "Well, if that is all, sir, your father is feelin' out of sorts. He must be tended to." She disappeared before he could inquire further.

His father? Out of sorts? When had he arrived home? A part of him desired to see to his father, but a lonely despair drew his thoughts back to the beautiful lady, Lydia, her pearly soft skin, perfect lips, and waiting arms.

Angrily, he marched back to the conservatory to search for Newton. There, discarded on the floor, lay the yellow feather and scarf. His heart pounded in forlorn misery. He missed Lydia so. Strange, she had never attracted him this strongly before. With tenderness, he scooped up the scarf, gently shaking off the soil. He held it to his face and drank in her lavender essence. Never before had he needed a woman so.

The rustle of Newton's crossing the gravel under his perch drew Pierce's attention. Irritated, he eyed the wily creature. "You've sure made a mess of this one, fellow."

"And you, sir, made quite a mess of the floor," came a soft feminine voice behind him.

He whirled to find Alexandra, attired in the softest powder blue dress he had ever seen. She was casually examining one of his father's plants. The bodice clung to the curves of her body, sensually uplifting her delicate breasts. He wondered if she still smelled of roses, and moved closer to find out.

"I'm sorry your visitor left in such haste," she was saying. The seductive way her lips moved beckoned him closer. "Why did she call?" She seemed to speak almost breathlessly as he neared.

Pierce heard the question but had no desire to answer. The pale skin of her face had such elegant smoothness, and those few freckles added just the perfect touch. He longed to stroke a finger along the smooth line from her chin to her cheek, to reach back and untie that luscious bundle of red curls and let them drape onto her shoulders and breasts. A subtle hint of roses in the air reached him as he swept an arm around her waist and let his thumb glide along her chin.

"Pierce," Alexandra said sharply through the haze in his mind. "Pierce Williams, control yourself."

Her hands pushed against his shoulders and he vaguely realized his hand was now entangled in her hair. "Alexandra, why have I waited so long to profess my feelings for you? No one with your beauty has ever captured my heart so. Without you, my life will never be whole. I beg you. Say you love me and I will hold you dear forever."

He frantically placed kisses on her forehead, waiting and hoping to hear her echo his love.

"Pierce, please," she said, turning her head aside, "your profession of love is a bit hasty. You are not yourself."

She raised a hand to his face, he assumed, to caress it. Instead, she set her palm against his chin and gently pushed his head away. What dismay! He had been so close to devouring her full, rounded lips.

Reluctantly he straightened and gazed down into her eyes. Why did this gentle lady not wish his affections? Tenderly she loosened his fingers clutching her waist and moved out of his grasp, slipping away.

Eagerly he followed, wondering what frivolity she had on her mind. Not waiting to find out, he swept up her hand and held it to his lips. "I have never been more truthful with you," he said with heartfelt honesty. "From the moment I saw you on the wharf, I believed you a beauty. Now that I have learned of the quick wit and mind that are so exquisitely packaged inside, I realize how you have enhanced my life. Believe me, Alexandra, my heart is yours for the taking."

She covered his hand in hers, and the warmth sent fire through every part of his being. An understanding glimmer sparked in her eyes and she tenderly kissed his hand in return. Her head tilted back with tender passion and she smiled so kindly, so blessedly compassionate and full of what he knew to be love. She parted her lips to speak, and he slipped his hand from under hers to lightly trace her lips as those words of love he knew to come were ready to slip out.

"And someday I might take your heart," she said and his heart joyously thumped. "But only when I am assured of your senses. You are not acting rationally after this incident with Lydia."

His joy plummeted, confused at her reply. Why did she believe he had no control over his emotions? She had made this claim more than once. Lydia meant nothing to him. She seemed a distant memory. He was glad the woman had left.

"There is little rational about love," he answered quietly and with great assurance. He moved close enough that her skirt enfolded his legs. Never before had he felt so completely in control of his true desires.

"I apologize if I so hastily have expressed my devotion for you, but my heart tells me the time is right." He brushed one of those delicate red strands from her forehead, longing to place a gentle kiss on the spot it vacated. "Have you not wondered what it might feel like to be entwined in my arms or to allow me to whisper gentle lines of tender poetry into your ear?" He trailed a finger lightly around the edge of her ear.

Alexandra, who at first appeared to melt under his touch, caught his hand and smiled at first uneasily at him and then as though amused by something. He frowned, not understanding her reaction. "Have I said something you find humorous?" The hurt in his voice sounded clearly.

She sighed and lightly shook her head. "No, dear Pierce. I find nothing wrong with your words."

She reached out a hand and softly touched his face, leaving the very essence of his manhood pleading for those fingers to explore every part of his body. "You are a kind and wonderful man," she continued, "and surprisingly I'm finding, quite a romantic one as well. But tonight, the circumstances are such that you have no idea what you are doing."

Alexandra reached onto her tiptoes and with slow and gentle regard placed a kiss on his cheek. He tenderly caught her face between his hands as she started to pull back. Their eyes held each other, searching for words but not finding any that would come forth. He placed a light kiss over one eye and then the other. Trailing his lips along the exquisite skin, he moved on to the bridge of her nose and worked his way nearer her lips. Somewhere from deep inside, he drew on a strength that made him hold back before tasting the final sweetness of her lips. He searched first for approval in her eyes.

She stared directly at him with lips slightly parted, awaiting his next move. Slowly her eyelids closed anticipating the kiss. As his lips lightly brushed hers, he found them soft and inviting. Without further reluctance, he pressed into her moist and welcoming mouth, and the passion he so carefully held at bay exploded. He devoured the lips she offered, and unabatedly explored her mouth. To his delight, she responded in kind, stoking his passion to partake more of her forbidden attributes.

Joy and triumph swelled his soul. At last, he had won the woman who had taunted and tempted him since the day of her arrival. The battle was a sweet victory. His hand slid along smooth silk toward her bosom and she gave an almost imperceptible gasp. Her kiss deepened, and then without warning, she pulled away and disappeared in the direction of the kitchen.

Reeling from the unbridled passion he had discovered within himself, he froze, with no energy to move. He simply stood there with open, empty arms inhaling the rose scent Alexandra had left behind.

* * *

At a safe distance, Alexandra paused and stared at Pierce's confused and hurt face. Her heart melted with guilt. She had allowed pleasure and the seductive attraction of this charming man to overshadow the impropriety of taking advantage of him in his temporarily incapacitated condition. When the potion wore off, would he forgive her or even himself for such aggressive behavior?

All this because she could not control her own affection, a passion she had heretofore declared she could live without. Her shame and feet sent her flying for the kitchen. While looking over her shoulder at the damage left behind, she collided with Mrs. Bisbey.

"Ohh," Mrs. Bisbey exclaimed in surprise. "Slow down, mum, all is well. The vixen is gone."

"No, all is not well." Alexandra pressed her hands against her temples in dismay. "Dear Lord, what have I done?"

"What are you prattlin' about?"

"I foolishly allowed Pierce to catch and kiss me. He now believes I am his true love."

Mrs. Bisbey tipped her head in consideration. "Seems like that's not so bad, mum. He's quite a catch."

Alexandra sent her a displeased look. "I am not the sort of woman to catch a man in such a manner. Why, he didn't even have a second's thought between considering Lydia and then myself. And if we don't keep an eye on him till this wears off, you might yet find yourself the target of his affections."

Mrs. Bisbey turned a shade pale. "I love me job here, mum, and that wouldn't do at all. Me mind's got an idea, though." She hustled to a sideboard lined with several spice jars and began opening lids and searching for something. Finally she opened a jar, gave a brief whiff, and smiled in success.

"The answer." She triumphantly held up the jar. "Its time Mister Pierce had another cup of tea. This one to make him sleep like a baby."

Alexandra brightened at the ingenious solution. "Perfect." Mrs. Bisbey had arrived at a much better answer than the one

Alexandra had heard of, feeding a man liquorice extract for a week. That would be a little slow for tonight's problem.

"I hate sendin' you back out there," Mrs. Bisbey said as she winked at Alexandra, "but someone must keep an eye on him until I get the brew ready."

"Aye, Captain." Alexandra delicately saluted. "I may be a reluctant volunteer, but we have a duty to this good family." She peeked out of the kitchen door and caught Pierce heading their way. "I have only one heartfelt request, though."

"And what's that, dearie?"

"Hurry!"

Later, in the wee hours past midnight, the moon cast an eerie pall over the shipyard as Alexandra stepped silently toward the boarding plank. She alighted with ease, this time dressed in men's clothing covered by a brown jacket and a flat, boyish cap. These clothes had proved their use on outings with her father through tortuous backcountry, as well as in slipping unobtrusively into Harvard lecture halls.

Alexandra dropped lightly to the deck, knowing she needed to discover why the ship lost its steering in her vision. For that was surely what she saw happen: a complete loss of control before the doomed vessel turned broadside to the wave. The only logical conclusion she could come to was that the ship had a flaw, a fatal one, and one destined to destroy the only man ever to have touched her heart.

Even for one unschooled in sailing arts, she knew the basics of what controlled steerage on a ship, and Pierce had filled in several details while on the ship tour. The wheel moved the tiller, which moved the rudder. Something related to that chain of events must be the problem. She was relying on her intuition to guide her to the answer.

She wasted no time heading for the wheel. Ominous in the moonlight, it stood before her, large and lonely. Shivers skittered up her spine, and her hands shook as she tentatively reached toward the hand pegs.

The night breeze blew around her as she stood quietly but garnered no insight, no new clues as to the ship's demise. Disappointed, she considered that the answer might abide below deck. Pierce had said the rigging was not complete, yet down in the dark hold, the tiller might possibly have the answer. A trip below deck seemed to be inevitable.

Alexandra stood before the rear companionway as the moonlight brightened the ladder steps leading below deck. At the bottom, an oppressive and threatening darkness engulfed the lowest steps. Only a fool or a desperate person proceeded into such an area without proper light. She drew in a long breath of evening air, knowing she fit both categories.

Nervous thoughts of Mr. Bates, patrolling the shipyard, reminded her to practice caution. He had been on board during their daytime visit, but Pierce had mentioned that he typically had the late-night watch. She stared again into the black hold and fought down a desire to run.

With her eyes closed, she visualized Pierce's tender yet drugged rendition of the reasons for his supposed love for her. She almost chuckled remembering the deadly serious look on his face. These simple reflections on the softer side of proud Pierce Williams gave her the strength to proceed. She quietly descended the stairs and stepped into blackness.

A minute or two passed before her eyesight began to adjust. The meager moonlight from the companionway served only as an anchor. She descended deeper into the ship, shuffling slowly forward and feeling blindly in the dark. Many times she encountered debris, wood, or tools, but persistence drove her forward, stumbling along the hull to the stern. At last, the wood of the tiller lay in her grasp.

Eerily, sounds of wood creaking, straining against a storm, and the deafening roar of water crashing onto the decks filled the air around her. Fear urged her to run, but she stayed firm, letting the sounds subside. Unfortunately, no new knowledge revealed itself in the strange cacophony. Frustrated, she clenched her hands and only for the sake of silence refrained from giving a solid whack to the tiller. Her unusual gift of intuition and vision had failed to produce further clarity. Without further success, the cost of failure this night could be Pierce's life.

No matter how unusual and unexplained her gift might be, she still believed in the rules of logic. Until she had exhausted every possibility on this ship, she would remain. Somewhere the secret waited for her discovery, even though the location chose to elude her.

An eternity passed as she once again worked her way back to the deck. The fresh night air carried with it a taste of the sea and a mournful memory of the man Mrs. Bisbey had said the town discovered lashed to a piece of mast. Would Pierce and the men of his ship soon be added to a list of townsmen lost to nature's vagaries?

Obsessing over a loss, whether in the past or future, only slowed her progress, so Alexandra moved back toward the planks, stopping at the bow rail to take in the magnificent view of moon-painted Salem. She leaned against the rail, resting her hand on the polelike bowsprit pointed in the direction of town. Suddenly, a blinding flash and deafening boom shook the air and tossed her hand from the wood. Had lightning struck the bowsprit? Dazed, she glanced up at the clear sky, seeing only a few shadowy puffs, faint stars and the brilliant moon.

Uncomfortable from the eerie revelations seemingly destined to follow her every move, she hastened her retreat to solid ground. She glided with perfect balance down the plank and toward her next stop. Gravel and shell occasionally crunched under her feet no matter the great effort she took to tread silently. Eventually, the daunting rudder stood tall before her, running nearly the height of the hull. More fearful now of running into Mr. Bates, she made quick work of her search. As the solution fell under her touch, relief and elation washed over her. She finally held the answer.

A rough hand grabbed her shoulder and yanked her back. Even through the thick jacket, fingers dug into her tender skin.

"Ow!" slipped painfully out.

"What ye up to, bloody thief? Think ye get by Bates, do ye?" He shook her hard. "Speak up, Boy."

His breath reeked of rotted teeth and rum. Alexandra gagged and kept her head low. She dared not say anything lest Bates discover her femininity. Better to take a beating than what this brute might impose upon discovering his captive a woman. The man emitted a bodily stench worse than she remembered. She doubted soap had ever graced his body or clothing.

When she failed to answer, he grabbed the collar of her jacket and yanked her toward a tiny, ramshackle hut on the shipyard premises. "Bates knows what to do with ye. Why, I'm goin' to give ye somethin' to remember. Pain be a good teacher."

The thought of Bates hauling her into such a small space sent panic into her limbs. She thrashed and twisted under his hold. As they approached, Bates gave a vicious jerk, destroying what was left of her footing and pulling the jacket taut under her armpits. The thuggish oaf now had every advantage.

Desperately she searched for any possibility of escape, but with the hut only steps away, hope appeared dim. A scream appeared her last hope, even though it would reveal her female status. Bates literally dragged her around the corner and she gasped in a breath of air, ready to deliver an earth-shattering sound.

Bates stopped abruptly, unceremoniously dropping her to the ground in front of him. Her cap slid over her eyes, blinding her to his intentions. Recognizing an opportunity and not waiting for his next move, she instantly sprang away from him and to her feet. Hope of freedom diminished as Bates grabbed the jacket collar. Struggling against him, she slid the cap back and rather surprisingly stared directly into the face of Pierce.

Pierce caught her barely audible gasp and gave an almost imperceptible shake of his head in warning to remain quiet. No surprise shone in his eyes. My God, he knew it was her, even in the disguise. But how, and did he plan on exposing her to Bates?

"Lookie at what I've caught, Mister Williams. Bates is on the job, yes siree. 'Tis but boys robbin' us blind." Bates yanked upon the jacket, and Alexandra felt her boots leave the ground. She let out a breathless grunt of pain.

"Put him down, Bates," Pierce commanded and moved next to Alexandra. Pierce obviously had picked up on Bates's belief she was but a boy.

"Me pleasure. Would ye want me to whup the tar out of him 'fore sendin' him on his way?" Bates raised a hand and she cringed.

Pierce grabbed Bates's thick forearm and held firm. "You'll do nothing of the sort. Release him now."

The massive Bates glared at Pierce, but did not relinquish his hold. By sheer mass, Bates outweighed Pierce twofold.

Pierce reached out his other hand and grabbed Alexandra securely by the shoulder. Relief sprang through her at his touch, but the obstinate Bates still hung on.

"Don't be foolish, man," Pierce spat out. "Your job is tentative at best. If you had failed to catch this boy, you'd be dismissed on the spot."

Pierce played the game of deception expertly. His strong, commanding word foretold of a plan, and she guessed at what he was about to say. Buoyed by his actions, she warily gauged her status and that of the posturing between the men. Her hopes rose in the moonlight as Bates's hold softened and she was able to peer carefully from beneath the cap. The antagonistic face of Bates, locked squarely onto Pierce's level gaze, melded into confusion.

"Whatcha mean, if I failed to catch him, sir?"

"Unbeknownst to you, I've been on the premises for a good half an hour. This lad here"—Pierce successfully tugged her from Bates's grip and safely swung her behind him—"was challenged by me to test your performance. Have you any interest in knowing how well he succeeded?"

"I doubt he got far. Just 'round behind the ship, sir. I caught him climbin' on the rudder."

"Don't sing your praises too loudly, Bates. This wee lad sneaked aboard, toured both above and below deck, sat on the bowsprit, and completely circuited the ship. If he hadn't crunched gravel near the saw pit where you napped, he would have won the challenge."

Bates sheepishly shrugged and struggled to defend his actions. "I didn't mean to nap, sir. Only I worked an awful long day. 'Twas the extra shift that did me in. Smith usually works the Lord's day and I take over at dusk. But Smith was awful sick. Somebody had to cover."

"I'm aware of the situation," Pierce said, "and this time I will allow you the excuse. I strongly suggest, however, you keep this episode in mind and be aware of my personal interest in security. Good evening, Mr. Bates."

Pierce turned quickly to leave and pushed Alexandra before him as if she truly were but a youth. He seemed to carry the charade a bit far, but then he probably wondered what had taken place on the ship. For how long had he watched her, and how had he known she sneaked about his ship?

They walked in this "master-boy" manner a solid block, and Pierce had yet to slow his pace or even acknowledge her presence. She contemplated what he must think of her actions and how she could possibly explain. For rather obvious reasons, this moment did not appear appropriate to claim that his precious ship was about to sink.

He prodded her up a lane away from the wharves, where a few sailors hung outside a boozing den. At last where no windows opened onto the lane, he caught her hand and swung her around against him. He pulled the hat from her head and whispered in exasperation, "So help me, woman, if this stunt was your idea of an adventure, I'll deposit you back into Bates's hands." He stuffed her hat into her jacket pocket.

She attempted to wiggle free, but found his arms locked tightly around her.

"Your freedom is contingent upon a worthy explanation," he firmly announced.

"And if I choose not to explain?"

"Then I will hold you here till the sun rises and you can explain to Salem your true insanity."

Moonlight gleamed off his eyes and hid their expression. Was he truly angered or outraged, or simply curious? She relaxed and offered the first idea to enter her mind.

"An artist must study her subject in all lights. I could not pass up a moon so beautiful."

"I sincerely doubt the ship's hold glistened in the moonlight," he challenged.

"My lack of diligence forced me to stumble, and I lost a pencil down the companionway. I spent quite a time groping for it in the dark."

"Truly. What an ordeal," he said with mock exaggeration. "Can you show me the pencil, or will I find it on the morrow in the hold?"

He had called her bluff. "If you loosen your arms about me, I'll retrieve it from my pocket."

His hold relaxed and she patted her jacket pockets, then shrugged nonchalantly. "Mr. Bates must have shaken it from my pocket."

Pierce's arms tightened once again, but this time leaving her arms free. She spoke again before he could respond. "Why did you follow me?"

He chuckled into her ear. "Did you think a man could sleep comfortably on that rock-hard settee?"

She laughed softly in answer as his breath tickled her ear and sent little shivers of awareness though her body.

"A creaking stair brought me awake to find myself in the parlor," he continued. "The oddity of such a location for a nighttime rest set my mind fully aware. I thought the figure I saw slipping into the kitchen and then out the door might well be a thief. Such was my belief until I glimpsed your face in full moonlight. Needless to say, I was rather curious as to your motivations." He paused. "I still am."

Alexandra considered that Lydia's potion might still be in

effect. Unsure how that might help or hinder the situation, she wisely decided to experiment. She placed her hands lightly upon his shoulders and said with simple enthusiasm, "You were truly a beacon for a foundering ship. Your rescue was both timely and well executed. Mr. Bates never recognized his error."

"My, your disposition has certainly turned accommodating."

She didn't need to see his face clearly to read the smugness his voice revealed. He hadn't fallen for her change in direction.

He removed her hands from his shoulders and firmly held them between his. "My dear Alexandra, if you falsely believe that sweet voice of yours will erase all questions as to why you dressed up as a boy and ventured onto my ship in the dead of night, or even why I awoke on the parlor settee, you are gravely mistaken."

"I had no such intentions. I can only give you my sincerest appreciation for your intervention. I heartily apologize if I compromised your integrity."

He dropped her hands and firmly grabbed on to the jacket, starting her at a slow pace along the lane. "Bates deserved the reprimand. You, however, acted in an incredibly foolish manner. Had he discovered your gender, he might well have taken you for a local trollop."

That very thought had crossed her mind and still made her exceedingly uncomfortable. "By the way, I didn't sit on the bowsprit," she said to change the subject.

"Really," he quipped. "That must be the only thing I exaggerated."

The baggy jacket made a secure hold difficult, and she half slid out of the jacket and his controlling grip. Before she took another step, however, his hand slid inside the jacket and around her waist. She quickly froze, concerned he might discover she wore nothing beneath the loose-fitting cotton shirt.

"Where in heaven's name did you get these clothes?" he asked. "They are far too small to belong to myself or my father."

"I use them on journeys into the woods. My father claimed such wilds were no place for a dress."

"A trip to my ship is hardly the deep forest."

"Then you should try climbing that plank in a skirt and petticoats."

"Why *were* you climbing that plank at all?" He stopped their progress along the street and took hold of her shoulders. Inches from her face, she saw shadows of frustration flicker across his features. "Damnation, Alexandra, I understand so little about your motivations. Every move you make perplexes me. Did something I say drive you to this ridiculous adventure?"

"You are a gentleman to take the blame, but you are not responsible." She decided to be forthright with him. "I came back because my intuition drove me. Just as I recognized a problem with the wagon, I also see one with the ship. I had thought the tea would keep you asleep until morning."

"Tea? What are you saying?" He pulled her near him once again, his firm hands against her back, pressing her close.

She stifled a gasp as his hands slid along the thin cotton on her back. Memories of the kiss and every feeling it had awakened rose foremost in her mind. The brush with danger and the closeness of this intrepid male drove her to near distraction, and her body responded by moistening in a most troublesome place. How could a mere single kiss make her lust so for a man?

Words stuck in her throat. How much should she tell him of what had happened with Lydia? With a resigned sigh, she decided to reveal all, since Mrs. Bisbey would quite likely someday inadvertently let the truth slip.

"Mrs. Bisbey and I gave you a sleeping tea," she admitted uncomfortably. "We did it for your own protection."

Moonlight illuminated Pierce's incredulous face as he stood in the middle of the deserted lane, staring down at her. "A sleeping tea? Good Lord, woman. From what in all the heavens would I need protection?" His hands left her back and now held her shoulders square to him, forcing her to look directly into his dark eyes.

"I'm not sure if you will believe me." Her voice sounded unsteady, but the honesty rang through. "The tale is quite fantastic and I am unsure as to how much of it you will remember."

"Bestow upon me the high points and let me judge the believable."

She hesitated. "Do you remember Lydia Trask calling at the house?"

"Why, yes, now that you mention it I do believe she came in for tea." He tilted his head with a puzzled look. "I daresay the remaining details of her visit escape me."

"I do not wish to alarm you, but Mrs. Bisbey witnessed Lydia adding something to your tea, and it wasn't cream. Soon afterwards . . ." she faltered and then continued, "we discovered your behavior was, um, slightly altered."

"What do you mean, *altered?*"

She had little choice but to blurt out her reply. "You became quite flirtatious with Lydia."

His lips parted in surprise and he let out a quick laugh. "Surely you jest. The Trasks are the last family I would ever consider going near. Their politics are dubious at best, and their means oft a bit ruthless. I was only acting in the polite manner any gentlemen would to a lady who called."

Indignant, Alexandra crossed her arms. "So you don't remember her tickling your neck with a plume from her hat?"

With consternation, he grimaced and silently shook his head.

"Or when she slipped the yellow scarf from her décolletage and wrapped it around your neck?"

She noticed his breathing had increased and he crossed his own arms in discomfort. "I remember nothing of the sort."

"All right, then, what do you remember?"

He opened his mouth to speak but said nothing. Finally he gave up attempting to recall events. "My memory evades me, but I suppose next you are going to tell me I swept her into my arms and kissed her."

"It was a near event. Newton rescued you from such an indiscretion."

He leaned away from her and slapped his forehead in a mock gesture of disbelief. "Rescued by a reptile. Oh, what a great storyteller you make. Please continue, your imagination is invigorating."

He half laughed while she seethed with irritation. Not so many hours ago he had declared her tales marvelous as her voice lulled him to sleep on the settee. Abruptly, Alexandra huffed and started down the street. He had ceased to believe her explanation, and with his attitude, any serious discussion was utterly impossible.

"Wait! I dearly wish to know what happened to me. Please, do continue."

His voice had risen, and she feared he might actually wake those with windows open wide to the cool evening air.

"Shh," she pointed to an open window.

She increased her pace, but his long legs easily kept up. He allowed her the distance until they neared the commons area. Several tall trees made shadowy figures against the moonlight that watched over cows tethered there for the night.

Pierce caught her arm and backed her up against a tree. "Enough, Alexandra, I want the truth. Why did you put me to sleep on the settee? Did you conspire with Mrs. Bisbey to help you with your excursion tonight? And what in God's name were you doing on my ship?"

"Mrs. Bisbey knows nothing of this excursion and I will not allow you to think such. The truth has been put before you and you fail to believe it. There is little more that I can add."

"How can you confess to the reason for this charade by using the poor Trask girl as a scapegoat? I hardly believed you to be one to blame others for your own actions. And why should you have cared if I did demonstrate any affections toward Lydia?"

Alexandra bristled at his attitude. "Lydia had you by the nose and led you around the room like a lovesick puppy. You are lucky we cared enough about you to take the necessary action. If you want indubitable proof, look at your shirt. It is stained with dirt from the pot you fell into when Newton leaped into your arms. Lydia fled the house at that point and Mrs. Bisbey had to stop you from following."

"Ha." Pierce stepped out into the moonlight, looked down, and pawed at the spot on his shirt. He became oddly still. Slowly he faced her, his face cloaked in thought. "I have the queerest sensation of having kissed someone."

Alexandra preferred to bolt home rather than admit she had kissed him under such dubious circumstances. "That is why we gave you the sleeping tea," she reluctantly confessed.

He grasped her arms and stared into her face. "Make sense, Alexandra."

She turned her face shamefully away. "Mrs. Bisbey and I believe you drank an aphrodisiac and were not safe from the effects until it wore off. You see, once Lydia left, you bestowed your affections upon me."

"Are you saying I kissed you against your will?" He sounded worried and almost panicked.

"No," she quietly answered, "quite the opposite. I allowed it to happen."

"Allowed it?" He suddenly dropped his arms to his side. "Well, I hope I provided the appropriate distraction for your evening." With a shake of a weary head, he started to move away.

"Wait!" She grabbed his sleeve, refusing to let go. "Only in my greatest nightmare would I ever dream of taking from you the honor of a freely given kiss. That is why I forced you to sleep. Your desire was for much more than a kiss."

"Do you push the blame to me?"

"No, I admit to weakening under the words you so freely spoke." She dropped her hold and slowly moved around him. "I never imagined you with such a romantic nature."

"Oh, Lord, I can only imagine what crossed my lips. Do you care to enlighten me as to my words so that, should the need arise again for me to penetrate your defenses, I will have them at the ready?"

"There is no need for sarcasm." Without a thought, she trailed a finger along his body as she circled his position. "I will only say they were genteel words of a kind and tender temperament. You seem to understand more of my nature than I had previously believed. The honesty I read from your heart touched mine, and I shamefully admit it weakened my composure. I heartily ask your forgiveness."

He caught the hand touching his shirt and slipped his other hand under her jacket. "I believe there is a great injustice between us," he whispered and leaned back against the tree, pulling her along with him.

With her weight fully against him, she was not only close, but also provocatively positioned. As her mind spun, trying to decide the appropriateness, he continued. "You shared an intimacy and retain the memory. I believe it only fair for me to have my own recollection of such an event." Both his hands once again stroked the thin cotton along her back. "I see only one way to rectify such a problem."

She knew exactly what he meant. "I am suspicious of the potion still having an effect, and do not wish to further compromise your nature."

He reached behind her head and untied the hair she had bound up under the hat. She had the profound feeling things were fast moving out of her control.

"My nature," he whispered, "will suffer no ill, and I can assure you I act fully under my own desires."

"Even if that is the case," she countered, "I am an unwilling partner if a simple thrill is the truth behind your desire."

Without warning, he slid the jacket off her shoulders, dropping it to the ground. She easily felt the heat of his body through the cotton shirt he wore.

He turned her in his embrace until her head rested against the tree. His arms swept her up and his lips rested against her ear. "I have desired this kiss since the day we first met, Alexandra. Show me that you, too, have imagined a kiss from my lips."

The heat of his breath seared her skin and set off simultaneous sensations of panic and pleasure. All rational thought ceased as his lips brushed her earlobe and trailed down her neck. A gasp of pleasure had barely reached her lips before he covered them with his. Their lips touched lightly, expectantly. She felt his unshaven roughness as he nibbled from the corner to the crown of her lips.

With a firmer pressure he sought more, and she welcomed his tongue as it stroked her teeth and lips and dueled with her tongue. In turn, he allowed her the same exploration before he broke away to rain kisses across her face and down her neck.

Her hands had started behind his neck and dropped to the open shirt below his chin. Soft curls of dark hair on his chest tickled her fingers as his mouth once again closed over hers. She felt an unfamiliar hardness of him against her body and hungered to slip her hands under his shirt.

Pierce slid his hands along her shirt, moving up from her waist. His thumbs brushed past the nipples that had hardened the moment his breath had touched her ear. A moan of pleasure escaped her lips, and Pierce suddenly halted.

Breathlessly he pushed away, his chest quickly rising and falling. Without a word, he scooped her jacket from the ground. He wrapped it across her shoulders and aimed her in the direction of home.

"The night watch usually swings through here in a few minutes," he claimed, his voice husky and quick. "I have no wish to provide his evening's entertainment."

They walked close together in a dazed silence. Alexandra wondered if he had truly experienced the same intense, heady passion that had engulfed her body. He kept his face away from her and she feared his displeasure. As she relived the entire moment, though, she remembered nothing but eager anticipation in his actions.

Not until they reached the house gardens and stood before

the kitchen door did Pierce allow her to see his face. Only pensive and thoughtful expressions were revealed in his eyes. No hints of brazen overconfidence or signs of the conquering male.

He started to reach for her arm, then hesitated and kept his distance. "You still have not explained to my satisfaction your presence on the ship, you realize. Tomorrow, after supper has been cleared away, I'll expect an answer. So as not to awake the entire household, I offer a good evening—or morning, as the case may be."

He smiled gently and held open the door for her to pass, taking a moment to close it silently. She quietly took the stairs, not sure of exactly what had passed under that moon-shaded tree. At the second-story landing, she turned to take a last look at Pierce in hopes of finding at least some hint as to his feelings. Nobody stood behind her or had followed her up the stairs. She was alone and slowly becoming fearful she had overstepped the bounds of a proper woman.

A tear dropped onto her cheek as she relived the touch of Pierce's hands on her breasts. Ashamed and confused, she fled to her only refuge and closed the door.

Nine

Monday proved a long day for Pierce. His head pounded from a lack of sleep and the mix of strange teas from the day before. Thankfully, a town meeting that evening provided a perfect excuse to avoid another heady encounter with Alexandra. The townsfolk had sought his presence to discuss the design and field questions concerning a proposed bridge. Afterward he dallied and spoke with several acquaintances while praying for a silent household upon his return. As he stood before the darkened house, he saw his prayers had been answered.

He suffered no surprise that exhaustion had overtaken Alexandra after the previous night's adventure. Damnation, his body grew firm just thinking of her nipples hardening from his touch, and the way her warm moist lips had invited him in. The soft moan that had escaped her lips had driven to the very core of his being. If he had not stopped instantly at that point last night, he would have taken her on the spot.

So much for his father's claim that she required no more than normal civil attention. Lord in heaven, there was nothing civil in the slightest about his desire for Alexandra. She drove him to distraction both physically and mentally. She was a woman of iron and he mere clay in her hands.

Quietly he entered the house, his mind still occupied with Alexandra. Why did she torment him so with forbidden questions about his family and that reckless visit to the ship? He shook his head to clear the mounting frustration. And what about her daft claim of intuition revealing something wrong with his ship? Did she believe it necessary to belittle his accomplishments? He looked up at the heavens. *Why, Lord,* he mused irritably, *did you not shower our household with a simple woman?*

He knew the answer. Because simple, ordinary, and even beautiful women were all around him, but none had caused him to give them even a second look. It seemed he measured everyone against his first love, a bright, honest, lovely young girl. The distance as well as time since the day she had been wrenched from his arms had dulled the memories but not the feelings.

Alexandra was impossible to compare to his early love. Everything about Alexandra shattered his preconceived notion of the perfect woman. Proud and relentless in nature, Alexandra challenged him on every level and beyond. With some chagrin, he recognized his comfortable notion of youthful, lusty love had changed into something deeper and far more fulfilling.

Unfortunately, this was a damn inconvenient time for such an enlightening revelation. He had a ship to build. Standing at the bottom of the stairs, he contemplated the night's rest. His body was exhausted, but his questioning mind put any sleep a long time off. Turning toward the study, he decided to make use of the time.

The room was dark and he stumbled about until securing and lighting a stubby candle. Stiffly he sat in his father's leather chair. The candle flickered and bent as air stirred from his movement. Shadows danced across the walls. With a resigned sigh, he pawed through the pile of business correspondence his father kept in the oak box on the desk. The first letter came from someone in Gloucester interested in investing in the ship his father planned for sail to the Far East next month. Another requested alms to cover a food shortage at the poorhouse.

The next paper in the box caught both his attention and curiosity. It opened quite simply and starkly with the salutation *Madam.* He lifted the letter out and let it fall to the desk before him. The first few lines left confusion as to the addressee. A quick search of the box produced an addressed cover-sheet. As he read the name Alexandra Gables, he became perplexed as to how it had become mingled in with the family business correspondence. Even though feeling a bit guilty about trespassing into her private life, he read the letter.

Pierce's jaw dropped in disbelief as he read the words "Noble Horatio." He had faithfully read that column for a year and was in awe of the author's breadth of wise, masculine advice. Certainly such a young and female mind could not possibly generate the jewels of wisdom imparted on that printed page.

A moment's reflection made the folly of his astonishment obvious. After all, Alexandra had displayed great knowledge, willingly undertook adventures, and without regret made life-altering decisions, as she had with the smallpox inoculation. Was there anything she couldn't achieve?

Once his amazement had receded, he reread the letter's content. Anger began to burn at the sender's audacity.

"Bastard," he declared and pushed to his feet. He paced the floor, disbelieving that any intelligent man could express such narrow-mindedness. This editor, a wholly unworthy cad, deserved a sound rebuff. First the man strips her of the very right to announce her own authorship of the one column, and then demands the right to put her father's name on another.

"Bastard," he said again and plopped back into the chair.

He searched the desk for fresh paper and set to work. An hour slipped by, but Pierce never paused and ink flourished on the page. When finished, he felt a great relief and, at last, true exhaustion. With a stretch, he rose to retire, knowing that at last a solid sleep awaited his head on the pillow.

Alexandra held no propensity for work this morning, unlike the others of the household. Mrs. Bisbey and Rebecca, the housemaid, hustled madly in the sunny rear yard, cleaning and hanging linens. Joshua Williams had left with his shipping agent for business in town, and Pierce, as usual, had departed for the shipyard long before she rose.

She stood in the study with arms crossed, watching the room lighten and darken at the weather's whim as puffy clouds floated past the brilliant sun. The portrait of Judge Nathaniel Williams seemed completely indifferent to her intense scrutiny as she stared at him from a few feet away.

"I have no doubt you are directly involved with all that has happened as of late," she chided him, frowning and half expecting the portrait to reply. "I expect you even know why these odd visions have begun and accelerated since my arrival."

She began to pace slowly, thinking yet all the while keeping an eye on Nathaniel's portrait. "I wish I knew more of your role in the witch trials. I find it quite strange that Mrs. Trask, who appears uncomfortable with my close proximity to Pierce, spared no words in recommending I discover your involvement. Yet that desire does not logically mesh with the impressions I receive from you. What role does that woman play in all this?"

She momentarily paused in front of Pierce's portrait and felt her heart quicken before moving back to Nathaniel. "I have to admit, knowing you sat on the witch trial court makes me a tad uncomfortable. Also, I am more than a little concerned over what Pierce thinks of my intuitive visions. Not that I'm a witch or any such nonsense, but then neither were the poor souls a century past."

She scratched thoughtfully at her chin and wagged a finger at the portrait. "Do you not agree, however, that I must convince Pierce of the ship's impending demise no matter how I might have learned of it?" Her voice practically demanded Nathaniel offer some wisdom on an appropriate course of action.

When the painting simply hung silently, she began pacing again. "If Pierce is prejudiced toward those with unusual abilities, will he even listen, let alone believe me? Surely he would not think anything so absurd as that I'm a witch."

Her imagination ran rampant as she pictured a pentagram

etched upon her forehead as she ran through Salem's streets uttering spells. Alexandra shook the crazy thought away.

"Pierce might simply believe I am so demented that he will place me on the next boat to Boston. Such would surely be the case if he caught me talking to you. Thank God I can be assured of your silence."

She shuddered at another appalling thought. What if Pierce actually believed that the late-night ship's adventure, the seductive kiss under the tree, and now her tale of his ship succumbing to nature's fury were all part of her attempts to steal his attention and heart? True, she had acted recklessly in allowing his physical attentions. And with sickening clarity of memory, she recalled he even once said her claim of intuition was but an act to seek his notice.

"Oh heavens, Nathaniel. What if my improprieties keep him from believing my sincerity? I've been foolish not to think beyond my own physical pleasures. Even so, I have no ounce of doubt, if he doesn't repair that rudder, he and many others will die."

If she had simply allowed Lydia to seduce Pierce, perhaps she would have maintained her impartial credibility. Then he might more readily accept her explanation and investigate the flawed rudder. She envisioned the tragedy caused from her jealous preoccupation that a Trask might invade her territory and end up with Pierce. Did his affection truly matter so greatly?

She recalled the first day they met when he arrived late due to the carpenter's fall off the plank, yet he was unwilling to credit his heroic excuse. At the Blue Shell Tavern, he had gallantly rescued Newton from a gentleman's wrath and quite amiably accepted being duped at her hands. And she did rather adore his subtle intelligence, witty tales, and willingness to debate his beliefs with a woman. Surely the fact that a simple look from his warm eyes left her weak and longing for a closer encounter had no bearing on any attraction. If only she had not encountered Mrs. Trask. The woman had seemed so set on scaring her away from Pierce, yet the method had produced quite the opposite effect.

She stopped and stared at Nathaniel again. "Mrs. Trask definitely led me to understand that you judged innocent people guilty and caused them to hang. If she found your actions so offensive, then why does she seem so intent on matching her own relations with the Williams family?"

Her foot tapped in a thoughtful rhythm. "I must admit to some confusion. Maybe my first assumptions were in error. I looked no further than to determine whether you were on the court, as Mrs. Trask had said."

Alexandra gently stroked the portrait's frame. "Is there more to your story, Nathaniel?" His brown eyes stared solemnly, yet she swore they held less pain than she originally had perceived.

The clock steadily chimed out ten strokes. The day and the chance for answers were quickly disappearing. She raced upstairs to grab a hat trimmed with blue ribbon to match her light-blue muslin and lace dress, then left the house without informing anyone of her destination.

She was soon at the town clerk's office in the courthouse. The glass-and-wood door of the clerk's office opened before Alexandra's hand even touched the knob. Hastily she stood aside as a lady and gentleman rushed out. As she tried to step inside, the clerk she recognized from her previous visit filled the doorway, donning a hat. The man stepped out, pulled the door tight, and locked it.

"Surely you are not already closing for the dinner hour?" Alexandra said, rather puzzled by everyone's apparent haste.

"The launching begins promptly at noon. I've no desire to miss it."

"A launching? Whose ship?"

"Why, Mister Derby's, of course. Have you not read all the notices?" The man spoke rather indignantly, as though perturbed by the lack of diligence of others. "The office will reopen after dinner," he snapped before hustling down the hall and out onto the street.

As Alexandra retreated from the courthouse and gazed down the street, children, parents, and virtually every citizen in town headed toward the wharves. Notices of the upcoming event graced almost every shopwindow in town. She ruefully realized her focus had been solely on the Williamses' realm. A lanky boy raced by waving a small flag in his hand. Caught up in the excitement of the moment, she dutifully followed.

The streets filled quickly as stores shuttered their windows and people emptied their homes. At Salem Harbor, the wharves and shore were lined with spectators, all gazing toward the yard where Mr. Derby's ship awaited its slip into the water. Only on the Fourth of July had she seen so many people in one place.

Alexandra worked her way past Derby Wharf and along Derby Street, avoiding the few carriages rudely brought onto the crowded lane. Colorful flags waved from ship masts and homes, and in the background she heard faint music playing. She had yet to determine the best place to observe, when a throng of people and a carriage flooded the street, forcing her onto the step of a ship chandlery shop.

A head appeared out the door. "Why, Miss Alexandra. Come in out of the crowd." Nathaniel Bowditch, the indentured servant she had met at the party, invited her into the relative quiet of the shop. "Out to watch the launching?" he asked.

"Truly I had no idea there was one today, but I have since become quite caught up. An amazing affair, isn't it? I even heard music in the distance." Alexandra smiled at the young man and looked past him to a desk behind an equipment display. On the desk, several books were spread out.

"Dr. Bentley mentioned you were an avid reader," she said, nodding toward the desk. "Is that the encyclopedia?"

Nathaniel appeared a tad embarrassed at his noticeable attachment to books. "Newton's *Principia*, I'm afraid, and a Latin text I'm using to translate it. Surely I'll be through the book in a few years." He grinned as though teasing, but she knew that in all likelihood he spoke the truth about the translation.

"Are you going to the launching?" she asked, wondering

how much freedom he had being indentured as a bookkeeper to the shop.

"I never miss one. However, with the owner out of town, I'll probably wait until the last minute to run out onto the nearest wharf. You still have enough time, though, to wander down to White Wharf. That is the best view. Mister Derby will speak a few words, workers will then knock out the restraints, and the vessel should slip down the ways."

Alexandra felt drawn to stay and visit with the interesting young man, but he seemed determined to have her enjoy her first launching. He held open the door and she stood wavering in the entrance for a moment, promising to come again and explore the shop.

A commotion diverted their attention as a large carriage rounded the nearby corner. The driver shouted impatiently for people to clear the way. Alexandra immediately recognized Mrs. Trask and Lydia as two of the four women passengers. She hastily stepped back into the shop and onto Nathaniel's foot.

"Oh, my greatest apologies," she exclaimed, as he slid his boot from under her foot.

"No harm done. Those people frequently produce such re-actions." Nathaniel's expression reflected disgust as he added, "I understand you've met the Trasks. I heard from my sisters that your iguana attacked Miss Lydia. Gossip travels like wildfire in this town. Personally I think they make a perfect match."

Alexandra muffled a snicker.

Nathaniel matched her smile before becoming quite serious. "Watch yourself around that family."

She looked at him curiously. "What do you know about them?"

He leaned out the door to watch as the carriage wound through the people. "The Trasks usually get what they want, often at a cost to others. Their sons and daughters marry only the wealthiest and most powerful in town, save for the Derbys, who will have nothing to do with them. Mister Trask spends most of his days making political alliances all over Massachu-setts."

"I take it Pierce Williams would be a suitable match for one of the girls."

"Perfect. Only I doubt he will ever cave in to their wishes. My sisters say the Trasks have sought Pierce for a match as long as I can remember. My guess is Miss Lydia had that on her mind when she came to call."

"Of that I have no doubt," Alexandra said with emphasis.

Nathaniel stepped away from the door. "The Trasks' carriage has passed. I'd be careful, though. My sister told me of a girl who succumbed to a strange illness after proclaiming her love for one of the wealthy Crowninshield brothers. By simply being a houseguest at the Williams estate, the Trasks may fear you have encroached onto their fertile territory."

She had been thinking exactly the same thing with no little trepidation. Stepping across the threshold, she turned back to Nathaniel. "I will heed your warning and appreciate the hon-esty."

She waved him a warm farewell and followed a horse cart hauling a load of children down the street. Barely two blocks away, she arrived at White Wharf. There were so many people lining the wharf, she considered herself lucky to find a position behind a child, over whom she saw the cradled ship with an unobstructed view.

Men crowded the new ship's deck, proudly waving their hats at friends and family below. Banners and flags flew from poles attached to where the masts would eventually go. The tide rode high onto the beach, as was surely planned by those in charge of the launch, for at low tide much of the shoreline and the areas surrounding the wharves had exposed mud and the stench of wet muck.

A small, finely attired group of people she guessed to be the Derbys and their shipwright milled nearby the new ship along with numerous workers. The launch time obviously approached. Spectators dressed in their Sunday best strolled and chatted along the wharf.

A lone woman walking away from the wharf caught Alexandra's eye. The woman was dressed in white, as were many this warm day, but a telltale swath of red hair was visible under her hat. Without a doubt, Alexandra knew it to be the woman Hannah she had met on her way to the post office.

So many questions flooded her mind that she twice collided with people while scurrying after Hannah. The woman disappeared around the corner of a warehouse, forcing Alexandra to press ahead quickly. She was relieved as she turned the corner to catch sight of Hannah again.

"Madam, please wait," Alexandra called.

Hannah turned, showing no surprise at Alexandra's presence. "Do not rush, my dear, I will wait."

Alexandra breathlessly reached Hannah's side. "Madam, I apologize for chasing you through the street, but I have many questions to ask you."

"Please, I insist you call me Hannah." She inquisitively tilted her head. "And why do you believe I have answers for you?"

Alexandra stood staring at Hannah, not expecting her to have asked the first question. "Why . . . why, you seem so knowledgeable about Salem."

Hannah looked at her with eyes of wisdom, ones that had the ability to see through any facade Alexandra might erect. All logic suggested coming straight to the point.

"On the walk to the post office"—Alexandra rushed on before she lost her nerve—"you mentioned the ability some people have to foresee future events. Why did you share that particular story with me?"

Hannah smiled and nodded with what appeared like relief. "I see you have finally come to accept the truth of your gift."

"I didn't admit to having any such talent."

"But you do, my dear, don't you?"

It wasn't so much a question as a statement of certainty. "Why are you so assured I have any special gift?"

"Because you are here and grasping my arm as though afraid I might run away and leave you without knowledge."

Alexandra looked down at her hand on Hannah's arm. She didn't even remember taking hold. Embarrassed at such a brash gesture, she released Hannah and brushed her hand awkwardly on her dress.

"I do so apologize for my abhorrent behavior. I am simply attempting to understand what is happening to me, and my intuition tells me you have the answers."

"Then your intuition serves you quite well. Tell me, do you trust what the visions tell you?"

Intuitively Alexandra felt right sharing the facts, as unclear or sordid as they may be, with Hannah. "With a truthful heart, I must say I am not sure. Many of the insights I have experienced are vague or have yet to come true. Sometimes I simply get urges of pure intuition. Other times I receive sounds or a single picture." Alexandra swallowed and hesitated. "Recently, though, I experienced a strange, frightful daydream. Nothing like this ever occurred before I came to Salem."

"Have you interpreted the daydream?"

"I have little doubt of the dream's meaning. With great regret, though, I have unintentionally allowed my feelings to become involved. How that influences my interpretation, I cannot say."

Hannah gently took Alexandra's arm and they walked slowly along the street. In a soothing voice seemingly sympathetic to her problem, Hannah asked, "Do you fear what you see?"

"Yes," caught in her throat as she remembered the ship. "Because it pertains to someone I care greatly about."

Hannah's eyes widened in surprise, then searched Alexandra's face. "Do you speak of love?"

"I do not know for sure the true feeling of my heart. However, I have seen his demise and I want to save him."

"Then you must decide how best to convince him of the truth."

"But how? I have no explanation for these visions, and he

shows no propensity to believe me. And what if I am in error? I may have simply daydreamed these demented pictures."

Alexandra paused to calm a rising frustration. "Someone also made me aware of his family history. Research I have done indicates they persecuted those who were different."

"You speak of the witch trials." Hannah grew serious in demeanor and voice. "There is much I have learned about those times, and they were truly cruel. Did the purveyor of this information have your interest at heart?"

"Hardly. She apparently has interest in uniting one of her daughters with Joshua Williams's only son."

"And the woman believed that information detrimental enough to destroy your possible romantic aspirations?"

"I believe that was her plan. Although I have to admit it seems to have had the opposite effect."

Both women strode several steps in quiet, letting the thoughts stew in their minds. Finally Alexandra asked, "Do you perhaps know of Judge Nathaniel Williams? My meager research has determined he sat on the Court of Oyer and Terminer."

Hannah shook her head. "What I know has been passed down through family history. At times, in my youth I discovered it hard to accept what my loved ones imparted. But just as you have done, I searched through church and town records for the truth. I believe you, as a person of science, will more easily accept what your own scrutiny will uncover. Does this judge have some connection to your visions?"

Alexandra drew in a long, steady breath, afraid to reveal such a personal occurrence to a stranger, yet she trusted Hannah and believed it a necessity. "I experienced the misery of the gallows and felt his pain. But that event is so far in the past. Why should it haunt me?"

"Maybe your research will uncover the answer. You might also do well to find the name Priscilla Gardener from those same years. Her husband was hanged as a witch. The history of her family since that time might prove useful."

Alexandra instantly recognized the importance of the first true piece of information gathered from Hannah. But why would this Priscilla's family history be of interest to her? Surely Hannah knew more than she had divulged. "I beg of you, tell me more of Priscilla Gardener."

"I'm afraid, my dear, her story is better told through discovery. Now, you have much to do, and my stitchwork awaits me."

"Please, give me a few more moments. I have so much to ask. How can I be sure a vision will come true and can I change the outcome?"

Hannah gently patted Alexandra's arm and stepped away. "You must trust in yourself for those answers. When you truly believe in your talents, you will know."

"But where can I find you?"

Clearly Hannah intended to relinquish no further details. She quietly retreated up the street until Alexandra lost sight of her.

All these years, Alexandra had considered elderly philosophers of any persuasion to hold the prize for vague and misleading answers. Hannah had just proved them all wrong. For every question Alexandra had asked, Hannah provided not one concrete answer. The only possibly useful tidbit was the name Priscilla Gardener.

Loud and jubilant music filled the air only moments before loud cheering overtook all other sounds. Alexandra hurried back toward the wharf and arrived in time to watch the new ship plunge deep into the harbor, bobbing up to settle comfortably on the calm waters. Unless she convinced Pierce of the sincerity of her knowledge about his ship's rudder, the next launching and subsequent death might be his.

That very thought sent her back to town to await the return of the town clerk. Until she discovered the truth about Nathaniel Williams—and now about this mysterious Priscilla Gardener— she planned on becoming a common fixture around the courthouse.

Ten

Puffy purple-black rain clouds edged the ocean horizon, leaving behind a soaked and humid coast. A stiff sea breeze cooled Pierce as he paced Turner's Wharf, waiting to take his father for an afternoon sail. Thankfully, the rain had passed and the blazing sun indicated a clear Thursday afternoon. Sailing was a most chilling experience if rain soaked one's clothing.

He gazed out across the harbor to his small sloop. A bachelor's toy, one friend called it. Another claimed it a rich man's pastime. Both were wrong. The *Abigail* represented a means for a brief escape from pressures and obligations of shipbuilding, and the chance to do what he had loved since childhood: skim swiftly over the seas commanding his own boat.

The shipyard lay not far from the wharf, and he was begrudging his lost time and the pressing need his father claimed for this trip to Mariner's Island. Actually, *island* seemed way too kind a description for the hunk of rocks where birds roosted at night to escape predators.

The clanging and hustle of wharf business boomed again after the midday dinner break, and fishing boats returned with the high tide. He heard the distinct trot of a horse and glanced up the lane. A carriage with two figures drew near. So his father had brought an extra passenger. Somehow it did not surprise Pierce. Nor did the fact that as the carriage pulled closer, he recognized the passenger as Alexandra. His father seemed to have a ploy up his sleeve for every occasion.

Alexandra dismounted from the carriage and stood talking in an animated manner with his father. Without looking in his direction, Alexandra pointed an arm and finger at him. His father handed over a flat leather valise to her, and as she stepped away from the carriage, he, in a rather unexpected move, drove away.

"What are you up to now, Father?" Pierce mumbled under his breath.

Alexandra walked stiffly toward him, then stopped silently a few feet away, unease obvious in her features. "I had no idea that you were our transportation today."

"Then we are on even footing. I had simply agreed to assist my father on a trip to Mariner's Island. Every morning for the last month, he has put upon me for an excursion to observe the nesting of birds. Yesterday he announced he could wait no longer. He made no mention of anyone else, and you never told me of your plans to accompany him on this excursion."

"Until this morning I was not aware of his plan."

"He oft makes last minute decisions. I can but guess he assumed your assistance invaluable."

"I do believe *assistance* is no longer the correct word." She glanced over her shoulder at the street down which the carriage had left. "Now it appears I will be collecting and documenting all the necessary data, too. Nesting season is coming to a close, and there may be no future chances this year for observations."

"I have no doubt you are perfectly capable of that task. However, I apologize that my father so awkwardly thrust the task upon you."

His father had left them in an uncomfortable position, yet one most certainly intended. These ploys to push the two of them together had to stop.

"Your father claimed the cook's son is gravely ill and requires a doctor's services," Alexandra commented as though trying ease the uncomfortable situation. "He plans to collect one at once and take him to her home."

"How odd he said nothing of it when I left this morning. I assume"—he cleared his throat as if making a point—"the emergency rose quite quickly."

Alexandra gazed past him to the peninsula of Marblehead across the harbor and then to the watery horizon of the ocean. "Evidently so," she said softly, as though not wishing to admit he was right about his father's intentions. "But now a resplendent day lies before us, does it not?"

Pierce stood, hands at his side, searching desperately for something to say. Small talk was not his forte. He gave a pensive gaze at the sky and slowly clasped his hands behind his back. "Quite so, but as with everything related to the sea, the peacefulness might change quickly. To tarry long on the dock is to waste precious time."

"I quite agree." Alexandra moved toward him, ready to depart.

Pierce sized up her clothing before he walked to the wharf's edge. Light wool dress and sturdy shoes were adequate for the short sail and the rocky island. "At least you are dressed sensibly for a day afloat. Can you climb down the ladder to the dinghy?"

Alexandra looked over the edge to the ladder of short pine boards nailed to the wharf's side. Next she carefully studied the wooden dinghy. "I know your father said the island sat just outside the harbor, but are we planning to take this piece of equipment out where there are actual waves?"

He didn't require great brilliance to read her nervousness. My, my, he thought, she didn't like to sail. No wonder she acted a tad ornery the day he collected her at the wharf. A sudden smile played on his lips. No sailor could help but find a certain amusement in accompanying a landlubber on a swift sail.

"This is but transportation to and from shore. I am afraid this piece of 'equipment' is a tad slow for anything else." He spryly clambered down the ladder and into the dinghy. "My sloop is moored in the harbor. Some claim it is the swiftest in Salem."

"There is no necessity to hurry on my account," she said a bit too quickly. His mention of speed obviously did little to calm her rising nerves.

"Oh, my haste has nothing to do with you," he said emphatically, "but with the tides. They are high now. If we dally too long on the island, we must fight the outgoing tide on our way home. Also, at low tide, Salem Harbor is rather infamous for becoming a mudflat."

"I see," she said, preparing to drop the valise into his hands.

"Whoa, is this luggage for an afternoon cruise?"

"Nothing less than a few changes of clothes," she quipped. As he frowned, she added truthfully, "Drawing supplies and paper. Is that acceptable to the captain?"

He held up his hands to catch the valise and she released her hold. Not quite filled with brazen confidence, she hoisted her skirt to carefully descend the ladder.

Attempting to be the polite gentleman, he looked away for a moment. Then, wisely he decided it better to see to her safety, and so what if he caught a little glimpse of something more? The more was actually quite nice, what little of her shapely legs he could see under the petticoat. The dinghy rocked under her feet as she stepped in. Quickly she dropped to the wood bow bench facing him and held tight.

As he gathered in the bow line and shoved off, he brushed against her. She stiffened at the brief touch against her shoulder. He puzzled why she felt such discomfort around him. Surely his aggressiveness Sunday night had been no more than called for by mutual desire. But where was that desire now? He read nothing in her eyes but unease with his presence. Lord, had he seemed too eager, too passionate? All he could remember was pushing back as he experienced his control slipping away. Just the memory created another physical response. He cursed inwardly, glad for today's choice of a longer coat. Damnation, he needed to concentrate solely upon sailing.

With an ease he felt anytime when upon the open water, he set the oars and started rowing. As a rhythmic beat set upon his body, a jaunty tune, accented with each strong stroke, whistled from his lips. Across from him, Alexandra sat tall, cuddling her skirt and petticoat, remaining quiet yet scrutinizing his every move. Oh, he thought, if only there were some way to read behind those gorgeous eyes.

"Last Sunday eve, if I do properly recall," she said as if to impinge on his thoughts, "you quite adamantly demanded a meeting with me the next eve. Why did you change your mind?"

"I decided to allow a few days," he said with huffs of breath in between strokes, "to give you proper time to recognize the importance of being honest with me." Rather stimulating memories of their midnight tryst rose to mind, as well as his uncomfortable encounter with Bates. "Much of the summer remains, and we must learn to work, ah, effectively around one another."

"If you recall, I already divulged the reason for my midnight adventure to your ship." He heard a tinge of defensiveness in her voice. "However, I will again impart the story, but this time I request your indulgence in allowing me a full explanation, no matter how outlandish it may seem to you."

He was rather surprised she intended to stick to her rather vague explanation. By the end of the day, though, he planned to have the true story. Women, with a little creative coaxing, had a weakness for giving away their deepest secrets. Surely the reason for her adventure did not reside at any great depth.

"Promised. But you'll have to hold your confessions until we board the *Abigail*." He tilted his head toward the red-and-white moored sloop they approached.

Alexandra turned to face forward and watched as Pierce brought the dinghy's bow gently against the boat. Alexandra reached up and grabbed hold of a rope ladder hanging over the gunwale.

"Ladies first," Pierce said. She struggled up two steps of the rope ladder before he added, "Don't forget the painter."

She ignored him and continued to climb, inadvertently shoving against the dinghy with her last step up the ladder before finally lying stomach first across the side and none too delicately swinging her feet over.

"What's a painter?" she called as she leaned back over the side and yelled out at him.

Pierce frowned and pointed at the bow line as the dinghy drifted quickly away. He had to row the dinghy completely around in the breeze to again get an appropriate angle to join with the boat. "Landlubbers," he huffed with each extra stroke he was now forced to take. Sailing alone was challenging enough, but with Alexandra aboard it might yet prove near impossible.

He stowed the dinghy oars, boarded the sloop, and secured the dinghy to trail behind the sloop. Upon reaching the island they would require its use once again.

"Why is she named *Abigail*?" Alexandra asked as he uncovered the sails and ran the foot of the mainsail out along the boom.

"My mother's name." He stopped for a moment and turned to her. "I apologize for not preparing a better way for you to climb aboard. I simply was not aware you were joining me today."

"I ask for no special treatment. Whatever you require of me I will do."

"Have you ever sailed before?" He checked to make sure no twists were in the mainsail. He moved on to the jib.

"I can canoe and have been a passenger on various sized boats."

"No, I meant have you ever personally sailed a craft?"

"No, I haven't," she answered a little unsteadily.

"Good, then sit right there and you'll be out of the way." He was amused to see he had struck her pride.

"I have no desire to be simple ballast on this excursion," she answered stiffly. "Just because I have never sailed does not negate the possibility of my learning something about the process. I assume since even the most uneducated do it, I can likely learn something of the craft."

"No doubt you probably will," he said with a slow smile. "And if that be the case, you can assist me in setting sail."

"Fine." She stood quickly and the boat swayed. Her eyes widened slightly, then grew determined.

He figured she might make it out of the harbor without turning green, but as soon as they hit the rolling open sea her head would hang over the side. Oh, hell, he might as well make her feel useful until that moment. He untangled the jib sheet, knowing the day grew longer by the moment.

"Untie the mooring line at the bow," he commanded, "but don't let go. Let it play out a little when I tell you. To start sailing from a dead stop is difficult, so I'd like to use the mooring to give us an extra boost."

Alexandra did what he asked and remained quiet while he finished rigging the sails and then let them luff loosely. Time for the lesson to begin. Since the island lay not far outside the mouth of Salem Harbor, he hoped the trip and lesson would be a brief one.

He set a hand on the boom and smiled at Alexandra. "The entire art of sailing depends on knowing where the wind is coming from at all times. A moored boat such as this one tends to head directly into the wind."

"Then the wind is coming from that direction." Alexandra pointed off the bow.

"Correct. Now, this sloop or any boat can't sail directly into the wind or the sails won't fill properly. Therefore I need to set the boat at an angle and allow the sails to fill. Hold onto the mooring line until we start moving forward, then allow it to drop free."

Alexandra nodded and watched carefully as he swung the jib to larboard and it billowed into a smooth curve. As the sloop swung around to starboard, the mainsail filled and they started to move forward. He signaled Alexandra when to release the mooring rope, and she timed it perfectly. He unpinned the tiller and moved her to act as the helmsman. Giving orders in landlubber terms as to which direction to swing the tiller, they efficiently tacked off across the harbor.

He observed, surprisingly with some pleasure, a transformation in Alexandra. At first she fought the wind against her hat until she eventually swept the hat into the safety of the covered cubby and let the wind ravage her hair. Wildly those strands of fire swept about her face, yet she glowed in enjoyment. The tentative sailor who had first come aboard now changed with each successful tack. The power of sail, even if only in the safety of a sheltered harbor and on relatively calm water, connected with Alexandra's sense of adventure. All talk of Sunday night seemed forgotten.

The protective arms of the harbor approached and soon the sloop breezed out onto the rougher open ocean. The more the waves swelled, the more pensive Alexandra became. He attempted to distract her by talking about the theory of sailing and slowed their progress by tacking further to a beam reach.

He took over the tiller as they neared the rocky, tree-covered knoll not far off the Salem coast. Many a foolish seaman, misjudging his navigational skills in fog, darkness, or storm, had ended marooned on the treacherous pile of rocks. Pierce set anchor and they boarded the dinghy for the short row to the island. Why this place had not been christened Mariner's Rock was beyond him.

He beached the dinghy on a spot of sand not more than a few feet wide between massive, sharp boulders and secured the craft. Alexandra stepped ashore, dragging along the valise. A slight green had appeared on her pale, soft skin. He smiled. At least this was one realm in which she did not have complete control.

"Can I assist you with your supplies?" he offered.

"Thank you, but I hardly believe that is necessary. I can walk across this island in a hundred paces. I could use some help in finding the nests, though."

"I'm at your service, then."

Quite successfully they discovered several nests, some with eggs and others with young hatchlings. Alexandra eagerly sketched and recorded data while from habit he scanned the horizon and also continued the search for fledglings. On several occasions, he caught himself watching her instead of looking for nests. He found it fascinating when she concentrated: her lips pursed and a cute wrinkle appeared over her brow.

She laughed as he climbed a scraggly tree and lifted down a nest so she could document the egg color. Later, when he held her waist and lifted her up several inches to peer at hatchlings, their closeness seemed a natural partnership. These doings certainly weren't the usual activities he associated with women. But he actually found them more stimulating than a dozen cups of tea or even the grandest gala. The hours passed most pleasantly before, with disappointment, he noticed clouds gathering and beginning to move closer.

He leaned over her shoulder as she sat on a rock. "Why exactly did you go to my ship Sunday night?" he asked as she put a final flourish on a pencil sketch.

She looked up at him, quite serious in demeanor. "Do you want the truth or something I believe easier for your digestion?"

"The truth. And I assure you there is little I will find hard to believe." He wondered exactly what she had in mind.

With a nod and worried look in her eye, she continued. "Then the truth you shall have. Once before, I told you about my unusual ability to sometimes know what may happen in the future. You seemed to have doubts as to any person possessing such ability. I fully admit, even I have doubts about this odd intuition. However, some of the things I experienced have indeed come to pass. The Reverend Goodwell's wagon is the most recent example."

He had hoped her explanation lay elsewhere, and felt a little disappointed she chose to remain with this story. He had promised to offer her the benefit of the doubt, however, and on that he would carry through.

She continued. "The day of your gracious ship's tour, I experienced a startling vision at the ship's wheel. I saw you and the ship engulfed in a storm's fury, and unable to maintain a safe heading. The ship and crew were lost. . . ." She paused and then added, "including you. The vision concerned me enough to further determine the cause. Thus I returned to the ship at what I believed a convenient time to investigate."

"A bloody dangerous time," he let slip, feeling most insulted and terribly uncomfortable with the outrageous story he heard issuing from such an intelligent woman's mouth. His new ship about to sink? That was about the most offensive thing he had ever heard. How could she expect him to believe such nonsense, and what did she hope to gain by claiming such a horrid event?

Irritation glazed her eyes at his indignant interruption. He coughed lightly into a fist. "Sorry, please continue."

"I revisited the wheel, sought out the tiller in the dark hold, and examined the rudder. Not until I reached the rudder did I again experience a vivid picture of the ship's demise."

Pierce looked at her, incredulous that she claimed such a problem. "I've personally examined the rudder and overseen its installation. I assure you, there is nothing amiss about it."

"Not the rudder per se, the iron fittings."

"Preposterous!" His voice grew louder and he discovered himself pacing a few steps back and forth on the uneven surface. "How would you, a woman who has admitted no intimate knowledge of shipbuilding, know anything about a rudder or its fittings? Did you see any flaws?"

She matched the increase in his voice. "No, I saw nothing. But I felt a roughness where the bolts penetrated the iron."

Before he let impatience steal his composure, he inhaled and spoke at a slower pace. "Roughness around the bolts on the iron fittings in not unexpected. The process of cutting holes for the bolts and then the installation creates a particular stress at those points."

A frown overtook Alexandra's thoughtful face. With equal patience she answered. "I have spent considerable time contemplating the possibilities for my vision and the iron's roughness. Even though I claim no engineering expertise such as yours, I have read of cases where iron has failed with catastrophic results. Is it not possible that the iron on your ship has a similar problem?"

"Possible? Anything is possible. But the smith who provided the fittings is known for his careful work. There is no time to remove and examine the fittings. The procedure would place us behind schedule for the launch."

Alexandra closed her eyes and set a palm to her forehead. "Dear Lord, this is going to sound even more insane." She opened her eyes and looked at him with assurance. "You will have the time."

"Truly?" He swept a hand out toward the sun. "Have you the ability to create a longer day?"

She crossed her arms. "You need not sound haughty. My predictions may save your life."

"Or forfeit it when I am locked away for insanity." He shook his head at the absolutely serious look on her face. She truly believed what she imparted. "So, just *where* will I find this extra time?"

"I believe it more proper to say *when*. And that will be while you await a new bowsprit."

Nothing she said now seemed to surprise him. Either she strove with great creativity to create a fantastic tale, or he must reluctantly accept that Alexandra had truly crazy beliefs and a vivid imagination. He could not, however, understand why she risked her reputation on such daft statements. "Are you telling me the bowsprit also has defects?"

"Absolutely not. I presume it is in perfect order. But lightning will irreparably damage the wood."

"Lightning?" he repeated. "Unbelievable."

The rumble of thunder in the distance diverted their attention toward the ocean. A dark cloud approached, and his skin picked up a shift in the wind. It was time to leave.

"We have to go now," he said rather abruptly.

"I'm not ready," she announced rather stubbornly after he imparted his decision. "I still have to finish this drawing and examine another nest."

"The subject is not open for discussion," he shot back. "The boat leaves now, whether you are on it or not. Storm clouds are gathering, and I do not care to be stranded on this piece of rock during a squall."

She glanced up at the distant cloud. "I can't believe you are worried about that cloud. It is hardly an ominous storm and is a good distance away."

"Trust me, Alexandra. I know the sea. Those clouds will move fast and be here in no time. In all likelihood, we have already waited too long."

Looking again at the clouds, she acquiesced and quickly packed her materials back into the valise. Pierce sighed with relief at her decision and her willingness to trust him. They boarded the dinghy and he shoved off from shore.

By the time they reached the sloop, the wind had picked up. This time the climb over the side was infinitely more challenging. The waves rocked the sloop, and water had soaked the hemp ladder. By the time Alexandra swung onto the deck she had been partially drenched by a wave. Fortunately for him, she had secured the painter and he did not have to waste time and energy rowing any farther.

He rapidly set them underway. Alexandra volunteered to steer, and believing the trip out represented a decent effort, he decided not to argue, knowing it would take her attention off the impending storm. Besides, he'd have his hands full simply manning the sails if a squall truly hit.

They kept well ahead of the storm, although the waves increased in size. He had sailed in rough weather before and knew how well his sloop handled. How Alexandra would handle the severity of a storm was another question altogether. The dour expression she wore told of the concern hidden inside that stubborn head.

He shortened the sail, preparing for the eventuality that the storm might catch them, and then looked back at Alexandra from several feet away. "Why do you believe the bowsprit will be hit by lightning?" he shouted over the wind.

She raised a hand in protest. "I don't plan to share any further details on how or why I know such a fact. Think me a complete fool, if you wish. But for the sake of the other sailors if not yourself, I beg of you to check out the fittings on the rudder."

He found the genuine pleading in her statement rather compelling, even though her entire story of the sinking and lightning strike sounded preposterous. Surely there was some perfectly logical reason for her strong beliefs. Or maybe he had yet to coax from her the true reason.

She looked at him, rather puzzled. "Why are you shortening the sails? Don't we want to outrun this storm?"

"Storms often move faster than predicted. If it gusts through us and hits the sails, this sloop would be laid over on its side."

Horror appeared on Alexandra's face. The bow splashed hard against a large wave, sending a spray over the sloop and shifting the stern to one side.

"We have to keep on course or we'll end up on the rocks or run aground. Prepare to jibe," he yelled at Alexandra who looked blankly at him.

"Put the tiller over. Now!" he tried again in simpler terms.

She shoved the tiller hard to the windward side and the boat swung off in the wrong direction. Evidently he put it in too simple terms.

"Leeward," he yelled too late as the leading blast of storm wind surged against the partial sails and the sloop's deck rolled dangerously near the water. The squall had arrived in full force and at a most inopportune moment.

Nearby, a sheet of rain pounded the ocean waves and crept toward their position. "Get in the cubby, you'll keep dry."

Alexandra, looking completely disheveled, clamped her hands firmly onto the tiller and fiercely shook her head. "No, I'll stay right here. You need my help."

With any further help like the last, they'd end up swimming to shore. "Please, this is more than any novice expects. Get below while you still can."

Alexandra refused to go and he cursed her for defying his order. He hoped she was ready for a wild ride.

Rain pellets began drumming upon the wooden deck, instantly soaking them both. He lowered the mainsail and left only enough of the jib to keep the sloop headed away from the rocks or shallows. To regain their course, he literally made a series of tacks in a large circle until the sloop was back at the same position where Alexandra had shoved the tiller the wrong way. For each new tack, he now carefully pointed in the direction she was to move the tiller. They continued that routine in a zigzag pattern, slowly gaining headway toward the harbor entrance and calmer waters.

Even with the gusting winds and larger waves, all went well as they approached. The tide had begun to move out, making the currents a little difficult but not impossible to fight. Time had become the biggest foe. The harbor became shallower with every minute, and the storm and rolling waves slowed their progress.

The wind increased as they finally passed the land encircling the harbor waters. The waves noticeably decreased. A bolt of lightning sliced through the sky as it struck atop a hill across the harbor. Alexandra, soaked and now shivering uncontrollably, looked at him with concern. He hurried back toward her. "Please, get out of the wind. We're almost home."

With teeth chattering, she shook her head. Since he had no time to argue with a recalcitrant passenger, he swept off his own drenched jacket and flung it around her shoulders. Chill wind bit through his shirt.

Pierce rushed back to the jib, which had begun to flap as the sloop slipped out of proper position to the wind. "Get ready to jibe," he yelled again just as the corner of the jib worked loose from the line securing it. As it flapped wildly, he reached out for it. Oddly, the boat shifted under his feet, once again in the wrong direction.

"The other way," he shouted. Somehow Alexandra had mistaken his reach for the loose sail as the direction to shift the tiller. In this part of the harbor, with the tide so low, there was no room for errors. For the next two minutes, he tried everything he could until he gave up and simply tossed the anchor overboard. It immediately struck bottom and began to slow the sloop, unfortunately just a little too late. The keel slowly sliced into the muddy bottom of Salem Harbor.

Frustrated but determined to stay calm, he tied down the sails and went back to Alexandra, still huddled by the tiller.

"Have we run aground?" she asked innocently.

He shot her a contemptuous look. Even a novice damn well knew the exact condition of the boat.

"Aground? Here in the harbor where every sailor in town can witness the feat? Surely you must be jesting."

As much as he wanted to, he had no right to blame her. He was the captain of the ship. Sitting there, she looked quite pitiful, wet and shivering, but for some odd reason, no longer pale green.

He slid the hatch fully open to the small cubby below deck and took her hand. He pulled her down and shoved the hatch shut. Hunched over, he settled her onto a bench and searched through a storage cupboard behind him.

"What do we do now?" Her teeth shivered and the words barely came out. A hint of blue showed around the edges of her lips. Pierce could plainly see she required warmth—fast.

"First we must warm ourselves. The cool rain and windy seas rob us of necessary heat. Then we wait for the tide to come back in and the storm to subside. We have no choice but to be patient."

He shook out an ancient wool blanket and sat next to her on the bench. Gently he removed his drenched coat from her shoulders and tossed it aside.

"The only way to warm you up is to get you dry. If you can survive the indiscretion of removing your own jacket and staying close to me, our combined body warmth will help."

Alexandra appeared too cold to argue. He helped slip off her jacket, then removed his own soaking shirt. Her eyes widened with question at his gesture, but she made no comment. He threw the blanket around his shoulders, then settled her against him with her back against his chest. The blanket stretched around them both and covered their upper bodies.

The sheer coldness of her body shocked and concerned him, but soon he felt the cool of her wet blouse warm. He encompassed her icy hands in his and set about thawing them to a normal temperature. She remained surprisingly quiet, and he assumed the coldness of her body and the sounds of the rain on the hatch and thunder overhead induced the mood.

He found little need to talk. At first, the indignation of sitting in Salem Harbor while run aground in the shallows completely occupied his mind. Every man in town would want to know how he let a little squall affect his control, especially once inside the harbor. Surely stories of how he let a woman distract his attention would spread like wildfire. The more he considered the outgrowth of such gossip, the more a grin wanted to creep to his lips. Maybe such tales might help to enhance his reputation among the men. Pierce Williams, human at last, they might whisper.

Accepting his present situation, he found his attention shifting to the woman in his arms. Heat now emanated from her hands, but he continued to hold them between his. Her back and shoulders fit perfectly against his chest, and with a dip of his chin, he rested it against the damp mass of red hair.

The smell of damp wool overtook the rose scent he normally

experienced when this close to Alexandra. At the moment, though, he truly didn't mind.

She stirred, evidently warming, and tilted her head up to smile thanks at him. "I've heard tales of gentlemen planning such circumstances as this simply to deprive a woman of her best virtues."

"I can't imagine," he replied with a knowing smile.

She settled snuggly back against him. "Before, I've always believed the woman remiss for blindly falling into such an obvious ploy, and the gentleman a cad for undertaking such a scheme. At the moment, though"—she paused and looked up again—"I am at a loss for deciding if either of us fills such shoes."

"Speaking for myself, I am no cad. Besides, maybe I should be the one to hold suspicions. I believe you are the one responsible for setting us upon the mud."

He felt her stiffen. "I do believe you are the one who announced the tack and pointed in the inappropriate direction," she shot back.

"I did not point. The jib line had worked loose. I simply reached for the sail."

The hands between his disappeared as she crossed her arms. Obviously her stubborn streak had returned with the warmth.

"Well, I see no reason for us to quibble over a situation when it will not change its outcome," she declared in a trucelike manner. "As you have pointed out, we have a bit of time to pass."

And this might be an appropriate time for him to coax out the real story of her visit to his ship. Perhaps with a little manly persuasion, she might relent to the truth. "With your hair pinned up tight," he said gently, as though concerned with her welfare, "it will never dry. The tide is yet hours from deepening enough to free this boat and allowing us to leave."

She reached up and felt the soaking mass. "I'm afraid the pins are too tangled to easily remove them."

"If you allow, I'll gladly help." He felt through her hair for the pins, and with no argument from her began to untangle the fiery strands. Little by little he played with her hair, taking more time than was actually required to free the tangled tresses. As her hair finally lay damp but long down her back, he held it together in one long bundle and placed it over her shoulder and off her back. The white nape of her neck called invitingly to him. Without thinking, he placed a kiss there.

She stiffened in response, but said nothing. Encouraged, he gently squeezed her shoulders and continued with nibbles around her neck and toward the smooth skin behind her ear.

"Perhaps you can tell me of your time in the Netherlands," she said, her breath coming a little too quickly.

Between kisses down her neck, he answered, "I'd rather hear about how I awakened fully dressed and alone on the settee Sunday night."

Without warning, she leaned away from him, turned around, and studied his face with catlike eyes, green and curious. "Only if you swear to heed my word and examine the ship's rudder."

A heavy sigh of disappointment slipped unbidden from his lips. "Are you still adhering to that version of events?"

"That version happens to be the truth."

Reluctantly he had to accept the fact that this woman, wrapped and presented in a most ingenious package of beauty and intelligence, had demented beliefs. As much as one part of him wanted to encircle her in his arms and never let go, the rest questioned his absurd attraction to a woman with such odd ideas. His heart pained him, knowing that acceptance of wild visions was simply not within him.

If she chose to believe such nonsense, then so be it. Once he had taken the ship on its maiden cruise up and down the coast, the entire scenario would become history.

He smiled gently at Alexandra. "I will examine the rudder as you wish, but only if I receive certain promises from you."

"Whatever you ask, but please, take me seriously."

Pierce pulled her gently back against him once more and

tightened the blanket about them. Maybe friendship wasn't such a bad thing. "I ask that you trust me," he said. "If no defects are apparent on the ironworks, I expect you to forget all nightmares, visions, or fears you have for my health or the ship's. You must promise never to speak of these things again to me or to anyone else. Is that agreed?"

The answer took time in coming. Silence told of a mind weighing facts and deciding the impacts. Finally she spoke. "Your request is acceptable. Never again will I mention those visions—to anyone, you included."

He gave her a light squeeze and received only a slight response. They endured the storm's fury quietly, wrapped in their own thoughts. Finally Pierce's introspection gave rise to a sense of profound loss. Why had simple promises struck between two friends hit such a deep chord? With a building despair, he began to see through the lust and physical attraction he felt for Alexandra. He realized that deep inside there had been a rekindled hope that he had at last rediscovered the nearly forgotten lasting bond of love.

Lonely and tired, he let his head drop back against the bulkhead. He knew well enough there could be no love without belief and trust in one another. As close as they sat together, their hearts were worlds apart. He closed his eyes and tried to imagine the face of his first true love, but the only features that materialized belonged to Alexandra.

Eleven

The carriage horse snorted, as though impatient to get underway. A driver, used only for special occasions and dressed snappily in a black coat, held the creature back, waiting on Joshua, Alexandra, and Pierce to climb aboard.

"Vait," Joshua Williams heard someone call and turned to see who it was. Mrs. Flamm, the cook, ran toward them from the house.

Joshua was surprised as she ran past him to Alexandra.

"Miss Alexandra, vait," she called, approaching her with something in hand. "Please, I gift for daughter of friend. She new bride and must leave town quick. My friend, Mrs. Zorn, cook for Mrs. Trask. She Svedish, too. Please, give to her."

Alexandra held out a hand to accept the small, flat wrapped package secured with a piece of blue ribbon. "I will do my best. Is this the handkerchief I saw you embroidering today?"

"Ya, I no have much time. I write letter on paper for her, too. Thank you, Miss Alexandra." With a pleased look, Mrs. Flamm strolled back to the house.

"I'll carry it for you," Joshua offered, seeing Alexandra had no place to hide it on that elegant gown. She thankfully handed the packet over and he slipped it in his pocket.

He noted how Pierce then politely, yet with too proper a distance, offered a hand to assist Alexandra into the carriage. *Polite* described all too well their behavior lately around each other. After their escapade several days ago huddled together in the privacy of Pierce's sloop, he'd have thought they'd be hiding coy smiles from him. Damnation, he thought, couldn't that boy get anything right?

Earlier this week he would have sworn Pierce had fallen hard for Alexandra. He had spent more time shaving, washing, and cleaning his teeth than in the entire previous year. Yet poor Alexandra seemed to ride a giant wave. Happy as a lark one moment and moody and temperamental the next. He'd tried to get some indication of how things were progressing from Mrs. Bisbey, but the close-lipped woman only snapped at him to mind his own business. He had hoped her curtness meant things were heating up just fine. But from the way the two were currently behaving, it seemed that perhaps some reevaluation was necessary.

This evening, though, if Pierce ignored Alexandra, he must be constructed of stone. She looked absolutely stunning. The hunter green silk-and-brocade gown she wore, accented by touches of gold embroidery, splendidly displayed every feminine virtue she owned. That notably included the fine, rounded rise of her breasts, not covered by any fluffy silk.

He wondered if the exposed décolletage was for Pierce's benefit, whose portrait she frequently stole glimpses of while working in the study, or for the other gentlemen attending this evening. With Pierce's recent lack of attention and her knowledge of psychology, he presumed she just might plan to attract others' attention in an effort to make Pierce notice.

Women, he mused. They always seemed to have some ingenious, manipulative plan in their minds. With his son's attitude, things might go well for her, for pride had definitely befriended Pierce.

Ah, what a wonderful, challenging evening lay ahead. He imagined the Trask women's faces when Alexandra walked through the door. Without a doubt, she would capture everyone's attention with the way several golden feathers accented her fiery hair.

He caught Pierce admiring Alexandra's backside as she settled into a seat in the carriage. "Are you to stand there all night, Son, admiring the view, or are you to give me a boost up?"

"You taught me never to pass up a good opportunity, Father." Pierce cast Joshua a cocky look, then helped him ascend into the carriage before climbing in after him.

Alexandra stared at them both with a rather dour expression. "If you two are through discussing my attributes, I believe we should be on our way. Heavens be, we should behave so rudely as to arrive late to a Trask function." A facetious tone rang clear in her voice.

"Don't worry your head too much, my dear," Joshua replied. "We are simply small fish at tonight's party. The Trasks are after a place in the bigger political sea."

With a raised chin and knowledgeable demeanor, Alexandra trapped Pierce's attention. "I know exactly what they are after."

"Power." Pierce spoke abruptly, as though afraid of what else she might add.

Suspicious of the unspoken conversation that ensued in front of him, Joshua studied them both with a raised brow. "Exactly when did you have the chance, my dear, to meet any of the Trasks?"

"I ran into Mrs. Trask at the post office one day. I also had occasion to meet Lydia, her daughter, when she recently invited herself to tea with Pierce."

Joshua raised a brow. "Tea, with you, Pierce? It appears I missed that occasion." He looked pointedly at his son for an explanation.

Pierce shrugged awkwardly. "You are fortunate to have missed the entire episode. Miss Lydia personally delivered the invitation to tonight's gala and decided to stay for tea. That's all."

Alexandra lightly cleared her throat.

Pierce glared uncomfortably. "I know this sounds rather odd, Father, but our diligent Mrs. Bisbey witnessed Lydia putting a powder in my tea. I drank it before anything was said, and fortunately for me it did nothing harmful."

"A powder?" He frowned and leaned forward on the seat, indifferent to the bumpy jolts the carriage frequently took. "So what in the devil was it?"

"As far as we can tell, an aphrodisiac," Alexandra answered matter-of-factly.

Joshua slapped his knee and sat back. "By George, I'm sorry I missed this."

"Oh, it was all rather dull, I'm afraid," Pierce said, shaking his head ever so slightly at Alexandra as though warning her to go easy on the details. Her expression gave little indication of any intention to heed his advice.

"I assure you, the excitement ended quickly, Father," Pierce said, his eyes still on Alexandra. "Newton chose to dramatically introduce himself to Lydia, and put rather an abrupt end to the meeting. The only lasting effect was a slight headache the next day."

Joshua chuckled. "I do suppose Miss Lydia is not fond of exotic creatures. Her exit must have been quite dramatic."

"Quite," Alexandra said emphatically as a reminiscent smile touched her face. Pierce shot her another glare and she fell silent.

Joshua sat back and locked his hands together in his lap. Miss Lydia's behavior at tea put a whole new view on the evening's events. That cold fish Mrs. Trask had been after Pierce for years as a suitor for one of her girls, but would she truly go that far?

"Do you believe Lydia's designs on you are the reason for our invitation to dinner?" he asked Pierce.

"I can't see why else. Politically we usually oppose every candidate they support. Only the senatorial candidates and a few others, such as we, are coming early. Most of the powerful or well-to-do are not arriving until well after the dinner hour."

"Well, Son, you are fair game at your age and status. Being a proud father, I can't say I blame them."

"Don't be absurd." Pierce leaned forward in the seat and

glared at his father. "I know exactly how you feel about the Trasks—you despise them, the same as I do."

"I must confess, while that is true, you are free to make your own decisions, which might explain why Miss Lydia resorted to such an unusual method."

"Possibly, but tonight I beg of you, Father, be attuned to stymieing any sudden urge I may have to propose to Miss Lydia. There is no telling what I might consume."

To hear his son actually asking for assistance with his personal life warmed Joshua's heart and counted as at least one small victory for the evening. "I will do my best to look after your interests, Son, although I do recall as of late you have asked my to stay out of your affairs."

Pierce glanced uneasily at Alexandra. "That was an entirely different situation."

"Was it?" Joshua brought forth a smug grin.

Pierce frowned at him in irritation and sat back, refusing to say more. Alexandra remained silent, but the slightest curl at the edge of her mouth said she enjoyed witnessing Pierce's squirming.

Joshua patted Alexandra gently on the hand. "I assume if Alexandra isn't too occupied fighting off the attentions of the rest of the gentlemen attending, she, too, will surely assist in watching out for your health. I do think, however, the situation should be mutual. You have put her in a rather delicate position. To the Trasks, she must appear as a competitor—and a stunning one at that."

"Thank you for such flattery, but I can handle myself." Alexandra sat taller, with confidence. "And I have already confided to Mrs. Trask that my position in the household is strictly business. But curiously, Mister Williams, I must ask why you choose to attend the dinner feeling the way you do about the family."

"Simple. For the protection of the candidates. Those willing to serve our new and glorious country should be made aware of whom to watch for behind their backs."

As Alexandra shook her head at him with mock scolding, he knew, as usual, she understood perfectly the logic of his move. Odd it was that although he felt as if he knew both Pierce and Alexandra well, he understood very little of their relationship. Instead, he sensed a strange and almost tangible tension. Whatever had happened between them out on the *Abigail* seemed to have irretrievably damaged what he had seen as an emerging emotional bond. Unintentionally his fingers began to drum on the carriage seat.

He held in his hand the means to change at least one of their minds, but his conscience argued against interfering. *Oh, Abigail,* he prayed to his long departed wife, *if only you were here to assist me.*

After the carriage rolled up to the Trask mansion, Pierce alighted and helped Alexandra out. Joshua stepped out next and found Alexandra staring past the house to the view it held of Salem Harbor.

"The harbor is beautiful at sunset, is it not?" Joshua said as a cool breeze wafted in off the water.

Alexandra remained still, as if frozen in place.

"I . . . I have seen this house before," she whispered in a distant voice.

Next to him Pierce immediately tensed and caught his breath.

"From the longboat, the day I arrived in Salem," she added.

Pierce eased out the breath and rushed to place Alexandra's arm on his and prod her toward the house.

Puzzled, Joshua stared after them and then looked out over the harbor. Dark storm clouds gathered in the distance, mean and billowing, the kind that sweep in heavy and violent. He advised the driver to take the carriage home and return later to collect them.

As the driver departed, Joshua again looked out over the water. What had that exchange just been about? Alexandra wasn't simply admiring the view. Something she recognized about this house sent a chill to her soul. He heard it in her voice.

Damnation, Pierce heard it, too, and by his anxious response knew what was troubling Alexandra. Had the world's virtues such as kindness and caring taken a holiday from these two?

Troubled by his son's lack of compassion, he strode to catch them at the house steps. He longed to offer fatherly advice and reacquaint them both with a little truth and honesty. But he knew that if love were ever to flourish, it had to find its own course.

Joshua scratched at his chin. Since advice was impossible, only one alternative remained: action. With a decisive heart and unflagging desire not to give up, he knew the next step.

One could hardly call the dinner at the Trasks' a small or familiar affair. The group was split between a formal dining room with a long table, and the parlor, where several smaller tables had been placed together. Extra help hustled about making changes in the final seating arrangements as those indisposed sent regrets or new guests were added.

Pierce had practically been swept away by Lydia the moment he entered, and Alexandra had just excused herself from Joshua after divesting him of Mrs. Flamm's package.

She wandered around the table, curious as to the Williamses' placement. Joshua was delegated to the parlor group along with Mr. Trask, his oldest daughter, Phoebe, and her physician fiancé, as well as several delegates. Alexandra and Pierce had places at the main dining table: she next to Mrs. Trask, who sat at the head of the table; and Pierce with Miss Lydia near the opposite end. Alexandra puzzled over why Mrs. Trask even kept her in the same room as Pierce if she suspected her in competition with Lydia.

The kitchen lay just off the dining room and was Alexandra's next destination for delivery of the package. As Phoebe, the oldest daughter, began to entertain with a simple rondo on the pianoforte in the parlor, Alexandra carefully opened the door to the busy kitchen and slipped inside.

An ordered confusion reigned. Helpers for both dining areas

hustled in and out, at least three cooks slaved over food preparation, and a sharply dressed male servant collected a tray with small hors d'oeuvres to circulate among the guests.

"May I help you, ma'am?" a young kitchen helper inquired.

"I'm looking for Mrs. Zorn."

The girl pointed across the kitchen to the large cooking fireplace, then hurried on to her chores. Alexandra hesitated at going farther, not wanting to get in the way and cause an accident. She tried to get the woman's attention but had no success over the din.

Keeping well to the edge of the room, Alexandra slowly worked her way around toward Mrs. Zorn. As a large soup tureen swept by in the fragile hands of an elderly helper, she stepped back against a crude pine table set out of the way from the main preparation area.

She glanced at a cheesecloth rolled into a ball with a loose edge partially covering a few slices of mushroom. A portion of woolly, black-speckled stem caught her eye.

"Why, the fungus *Leccinum atrostipitatum*," she whispered under her breath. That certainly had no place in a kitchen. Anyone expert enough to gather mushrooms knew it caused stomach upsets when eaten.

Instantly concerned, Alexandra flew to Mrs. Zorn's side and watched as she stirred a bubbling pot of gravy. "Pardon my intrusion, but have you already added the mushrooms?"

"Ya, they goot and tender by now." Mrs. Zorn turned and reacted with surprise at Alexandra, dressed in all her finery and standing near a cooking fire.

Alexandra opened her mouth to express her concerns, only to be interrupted by a stern voice across the room. "Not on that table, foolish girl," the elderly helper admonished the girl Alexandra had first encountered in the kitchen. "That is Mrs. Trask's table and no one dare go near it."

The mushrooms and cheesecloth lay on that very table. Alexandra hastily reevaluated the situation. "Are there any remnants of the mushrooms left?"

"Behind me on da table, in da brown bowl. But ma'am, dis is not a place for you."

Alexandra turned and with a pronounced frown headed for the brown bowl. Inside were chopped completely edible mushrooms. Puzzled, she returned to Mrs. Zorn.

"I'm sorry, I should have introduced myself. I am Alexandra Gables, a houseguest at the Williams estate. I have brought a gift for your daughter from Mrs. Flamm." She held out the letter-wrapped package.

The woman's eyes brightened as she swept up her apron to wipe her food-splattered hands. "Das is vunderful." Mrs. Zorn accepted the gift and, with a little kiss to the paper, slid the letter package into her apron pocket and set about once again stirring the pot. "Tell Mrs. Flamm, soon I see her. It so goot of you to bring da gift."

"The pleasure is mine." Alexandra smiled pleasantly.

Endless possibilities for the inedible mushroom played through her mind as she slipped out of the kitchen, just as the first guests approached the dinner table. With a shudder, she speculated that her position next to Mrs. Trask at dinner had ominous implications. No matter, she would simply accept the challenge. The Trasks were not meddling with a naive young girl.

After much ado over the sociable mix produced by the seating, the guests took their seats. Pierce gave a brief nod in her direction as he gallantly pulled a chair out for Miss Lydia. Lydia dipped forward as she sat, exposing to Pierce quite an eyeful of cleavage. He wore no smile, but as usual acted the complete gentleman.

After a parade of brief acknowledgments to God, country, and those of note present, dinner finally commenced. A lively older gentleman and senatorial candidate engaged her in conversation through soup while Mrs. Trask appeared quite occupied with a town selectman whose name Alexandra had already forgotten. As the dinner plates began appearing, one of the servants briefly whispered in Mrs. Trask's ear. She quietly excused herself and left the table before the gentlemen could notice and be required to rise.

Alexandra glanced down the table at Pierce and Lydia. Lydia chatted with both Pierce and a gentleman on the opposite side. At one point, the haughty girl laughed and picked up a water glass for a brief toast. Pierce followed suit, but Alexandra noticed he simply wet his lips and no water slipped down his throat. So he actually believed at least something she had told him.

The memories and hurt from their time on the *Abigail* returned. Pierce showed so little faith in her when he required a promise never to mention her intuitive gift to anyone. Was it some punishment for her forwardness under the tree? As much as she longed for him to believe in and care for her, somehow she had completely alienated him with her actions and the outlandish tale of his ship. He appeared to have lost faith in all her abilities, and she could hardly blame him. Few people like those who are apparently a little touched in the head.

Sounds of thunder rumbling in the distance grew closer. Strong breezes began to blow through the rooms, lifting the curtains in a blustery billow. The servants paused the dinner service to hastily close several windows throughout the house. Fingers of lightning continually lit up the night sky, and the booming grew closer.

As the food service proceeded, a servant placed food-filled plates before both her and the empty place of Mrs. Trask.

"What appetizing fare," a selectman's wife commented from across the table.

Alexandra drew her attention away from the storm to examine the carrots, small potatoes, and roasted hen accented with mushroom gravy. The chunks of mushroom smothered in the gravy held a tint of violet-brown.

With a quick comparison to Mrs. Trask's plate, she observed no similar coloring. Sudden and startling, a crackle and boom sizzled through the air, sending vibrations through the room. Involuntarily, everyone looked toward the window to observe the storm. With the temporary distraction, Alexandra switched plates.

"That bolt hit close enough to singe my brows," the elder gentleman next to her jokingly announced.

Alexandra jumped guiltily at his voice and wondered if he had noticed the switch. Rain began pelting the windows and roof, creating a dull syncopation to entertain the diners. Mrs. Trask slipped back into place, frowning at the weather. The elder gentleman caught Mrs. Trask's entrance and expression and rose in respect as she sat.

"I certainly hope this storm passes quickly," he huffed. "Politics is a difficult enough proposition without having to duel with the hand of God."

"Politics brings out the fierce and hardy," Mrs. Trask chastised him for his doubt. "The storm will pass and the remainder of my party guests will come. The weather simply allows us a long and leisurely dinner beforehand."

The hostess looked steadily at Alexandra. "How is the food, my dear?"

"The smell is heavenly, but I am just now attempting my first taste." She delicately cut a small slice of the hen. With a subtle flourish, she purposefully speared a mushroom piece and added it to the meat morsel. Slowly and daintily, she chewed and swallowed.

"Delicious." She dabbed her mouth with a cloth napkin.

Mrs. Trask smiled broadly and visibly relaxed for a brief moment until she glanced down at her own plate. An angry expression developed.

"Gloria," she hissed at a servant passing by. "Take my plate back to the kitchen. I refuse to have gravy encroaching upon my carrots."

Gloria, with fear of further reprimand upon her face, swept the plate from Mrs. Trask and disappeared into the kitchen.

Alexandra sat horrified. That plate had now gone back to the kitchen, where anyone, Mrs. Zorn included, could eventually devour the contents. By the brief glance Mrs. Trask had taken at the plate, and the irritated, unsurprised look on her face, Alexandra was sure she had not even noticed the switch.

Only one response came to Alexandra's mind. She started to cough, as though choking. Politely she covered her mouth and lightly patted her chest. With a much flustered appearance and head bowed, she continued a light cough, and retreated into the kitchen. As the door shut, she leaned against it and looked frantically around.

"Back again, ma'am?" the young girl asked.

"A plate just came back to the kitchen. Do you perhaps know what Gloria did with it?"

"Yes'um I do. Mrs. Zorn added more gravy and sent it out to Miss Phoebe. She likes it that way."

Alexandra felt her mouth drop open in a thick-witted gape. Mrs. Trask had just succeeded in poisoning her own daughter. Alexandra considered, for only a fleeting moment, waltzing into the parlor and confessing her knowledge to Miss Phoebe, but realized how impossible the task. For a moment, guilt attempted to assail her conscience. But as she recalled that Mrs. Trask had meant the plate for her, it passed quickly. Fortunately for Miss Phoebe, she had a physician at her side and the mushroom would produce only severe stomach upset.

Composed and apologetic and having overcome any consideration of guilt, Alexandra returned to her seat and thoroughly enjoyed the remainder of her meal. The more she ate, the friendlier Mrs. Trask appeared, even going so far as to volunteer a carriage home if Alexandra should become tired before the rest of the Williams family was ready to depart. Smiling, Alexandra thanked her for such a generous offer and said she would see how the evening progressed.

The severity of the storm decreased to a steady rain. Just as the diners had retired from the table and the men had sought brandy in the study, the front door opened to a wet messenger.

One of the servants collected Pierce, who spoke for a few moments with the messenger. Joshua joined them and soon a bleak seriousness played over the two men's features. Her heart thumped, longing to discover the reason. A doting Lydia hovered near the men, precluding any chance for Alexandra to approach them. Mr. Trask joined them himself, as well. Pierce nodded at something that was said, and Mr. Trask left to speak with a servant.

Lydia had a profound look of disappointment as she moved nearer Pierce and produced an appropriate pout for his benefit. She swept up his hand and drew him away from the men at the door and toward a flower-covered side table. Alexandra grimaced at the obvious flirtation, but stood stunned by Lydia's next move.

The girl plucked a red rose from the flower arrangement, inhaled its fragrance, and offered it to Pierce for the same. He politely indulged her with a brief sniff, after which she snapped off a good portion of the stem. With as coy and alluring a smile as she could muster, Lydia slipped the rose into her dark, long curls and gave Pierce a peck on his cheek.

Pierce froze in place as the red rose practically tickled his nose with the kiss. The look in his eyes read complete disbelief. Alexandra knew he recalled her prediction about affection being bestowed upon him by a woman with a red rose in her hair.

His gaze flew across the room and caught her attention momentarily. She saw disbelief, confusion, and fear—a fear that everything she had foretold might possibly be true.

Mr. Trask reappeared with a cloak and spread it over Pierce's shoulders. The two shook hands and Pierce collected his hat and left with the messenger into the wet evening. Lydia stood in the doorway waving discreetly, yet obvious enough to let all in attendance know she was staking a claim.

Alexandra determinedly worked her way toward Joshua, who waited patiently near the door as though knowing she sought him out. Lydia brushed by them both with a triumphant yet irritated look. Evidently pleased with Pierce's attention, she was aggravated that the night had ended so abruptly.

"Why does that woman remind me of a siren?" Joshua said softly as they retreated toward the parlor.

"Because behind that lovely facade lies death on the rocks," Alexandra said, rather surprised at the vindictive sound of her voice.

The servants had hastily cleared, taken down or pushed against the walls the tables in the parlor. Most of the women were gathered there while the men waited in the study until the arrival of the remaining guests.

"What do you know of Pierce's hasty departure?" she asked before Joshua decided to rejoin the other gentlemen.

"A problem at the shipyard. Nothing to worry about, I'm sure, dear. He said not to expect him back."

A commotion sounded behind them in the parlor. Alexandra whirled around to see Miss Phoebe partially collapse upon a settee with a hand to her stomach.

"Please, get me to my room," the young woman said weakly, then quickly put a hand to her mouth. "My stomach is quite indisposed."

Lydia and Joshua helped her to her feet and assisted her from the parlor. Another woman rushed to the study to secure the services of Phoebe's fiancé. He immediately took over from Joshua and helped her up the stairs. Phoebe appeared paler by the moment with each step she took.

Joshua crossed his arms, then set the fingers of one hand against his cheek. "What do you supposed happened to her?"

With only a twinge of guilt, Alexandra answered, "I do believe, sir, she had too much gravy."

Across the room, Mrs. Trask shifted her attention from her daughter to the dining table and back again. In time the woman might figure out what had occurred, but in all likelihood, she would assume Gloria had simply set the plate in the wrong place to begin with. Poor Gloria.

For Mrs. Trask's sake, Alexandra placed a conciliatory and concerned expression on her face. The Trask women were apparently having a tumultuous night.

* * *

The humid night air lay like a blanket over Salem, quieting the clop of hoofs and rendering the stars a hazy blur. As a stable hand retired the horse and carriage, Joshua and Alexandra approached the door. Mrs. Bisbey swung it open, eagerness to hear of the evening events written on her face.

"Why, where's Mister Pierce?" A hint of suspicion rang in her words. "Did he not come home with you?"

"Problems at the shipyard stole him away early." Joshua slipped off his dress coat and hat and handed them to her. "We thought he might already be home."

"No, sir. He's not been home. I'd surely be the one to know. That vicious storm kept me from visitin' me friends. Only someone touched in the head would dare venture out in that gale."

"Thank you, Mrs. Bisbey. My son will appreciate your voice of confidence."

Mrs. Bisbey's eyes widened. "Oh, sir. I didn't mean no disrespect."

Alexandra put an arm around Mrs. Bisbey's shoulders and gave her an affectionate squeeze. "Don't let Mr. Williams's dry humor cause you consternation. Ever since that last glass of Madeira, he has discovered the wry side of many issues."

"Politics," Joshua said with resounding emphasis. "Does it to me every time." He stopped at the stairwell and stood pensively for a moment. "Alexandra, before you retire, please grant me a few moments of your time. I'll be in the study."

The request did not catch Alexandra by surprise. On the ride home, she noted that he had been unduly withdrawn, as though struggling with some decision. Apparently, he had made it.

Mrs. Bisbey looked to her for some explanation.

Alexandra spread her hands in complete ignorance. "Something has set him to worrying. It's best I set his mind at ease. I'll pass along all the gala details in the morning."

Mrs. Bisbey appeared crestfallen at the delay after having waited up to hear the news.

Alexandra leaned close and whispered, "I promise 'tis worth the wait. It's a secret between us, but Mrs. Trask made her own daughter ill on poisonous mushrooms."

Mrs. Bisbey gasped. "Oh gracious, mum, to hear ye tell this story will make me entire day. Don't sleep too late. Me heart might not stand the wait." The housekeeper gathered her skirt and hustled up the stairs.

Joshua stood at his desk, lighting a tall taper when Alexandra entered the room. As the candle flickered to life, he pointed her to a chair. "I realize the hour is late, but I beg of you to grant me a few moments."

"I do not believe after the evening's excitement, sleep will come easily. You may take whatever time you require."

With a slow but decisive ado, he removed a letter from his desk drawer. She immediately recognized the folded paper as the one from *Boston Magazine*.

Her body tensed, wondering if he had read it. Casually, as if it were of no importance, she reached for the letter and said, "I misplaced this a good time ago and had no idea as to the cause of its disappearance."

"I'm afraid Mrs. Bisbey accidentally placed the letter into my effects." He released it to her waiting hand. "Even after I read the salutation, I guiltily confess to perusing its contents."

The pit of her stomach fluttered and tightened into a fist. Anonymity fit better with the advice she espoused in the magazine. Joshua now knew not only of "Noble Horatio," but also of her new column and its failure at publication. She started to respond, but he waved her silent.

"Let me continue. To read someone's personal mail is a grievous offense, and I beg your forgiveness."

"I am as much at fault for leaving it fully unattended at your personal desk. I do ask your indulgence, however, in guarding the integrity of the name 'Noble Horatio.' "

Joshua drew in a long, slow breath, checked the time on his pocket watch, and then sat with solemn demeanor in his chair. "It did not reveal anything I did not already know. Your father bragged to me long ago of your column and swore me to silence. His pride in you is tremendous and well founded. That makes my next confession even more difficult for the injustice I have done to both you and your father. My motives are honest, but possibly misguided. I hope you both will understand and forgive my actions."

Alexandra stared, puzzled at the concern in Joshua's candle-softened eyes.

"My son is a proud man," he continued, "one often unwilling to admit that not everything in life fits exactly into his way of thinking. I was not ready, however, for his apparent disregard of your superb talents. I believed his wavering respect for the intelligence of women required a bit of humility. In the past, he and I have held discussions over your column, where he fiercely defended the ideal you espoused. I thought if he discovered your identity, his opinion might change. Therefore, I left your letter in the box exactly where I found it, knowing he, too, would eventually come across it."

Alexandra inhaled sharply, feeling the color drain from her face.

Joshua smiled weakly at her. "I daresay I have little faith in my son's ability to overcome curiosity. I can but be the one to blame. Unfortunately, the consequences reached a bit further than I had expected."

"I do not understand." Her voice warbled, afraid that all Salem already knew the truth and now even the 'Noble Horatio' column risked the chance of cancellation.

Joshua produced a second letter from his desk. "Apparently, Pierce had some thoughts about the editor's letter and penned a reply. He had yet to seal and mail it when I discovered it on the desk. Having already committed the grievous sin of reading your letter, skimming his came easily. When later he asked about the whereabouts of the letter, I told him it had been posted. I must admit how disconcerting it is the way one small indiscretion blossoms into others."

The folded letter, waving back and forth in Joshua's hand,

held an unknown impact on her life. What response had Pierce written to the editor, and how might it change the ability for her to continue the writing she loved?

"I feel no less like the devil offering a gift in place of your soul," Joshua continued. "But I believe you hold the right to determine whether this letter should ever leave the house. Knowing what it holds, I recommend you make the judgment only after reading its contents. If you desire to refrain from lowering yourself to my depth and perusing the actual words upon paper, I will gladly read it aloud."

"Letters are such a private affair, Mister Williams. Surely Pierce would find great distress if he knew I were to learn his private thoughts."

"Your integrity is well founded, but his letter is a business letter and the product of my fallacy. His words might affect your future with the magazine. Whether or not it is ever delivered will never be known by Pierce. I can honestly tell you, I will never reveal your knowledge of its contents."

Alexandra closed her eyes, the longing to know its contents bending her conscience away from her usual convictions. Did Pierce heartily agree with the editor and condone his accusations? Did he write some personal editorial about allowing women to write columns intended for and supposed by the public to be the thoughts of a man? Whatever he wrote, the letter imparted his intentions toward her life.

"The letter must be sent if those were the wishes of the author. I have no right to interfere with whatever Pierce felt of great necessity." She stood before the desk, solemn but sure. "Please, whatever it contains, helpful or harmful, post it."

Joshua rose to meet her eyes. "You have made your decision and I will follow it through. I do believe, though, a certain fairness in your knowing its contents and preparing for its impact upon your life. Please, allow me to read it to you. In that you have a right."

With the decision made to post the letter, she allowed herself the slight indiscretion of knowing its contents. She nodded at Joshua and sat back upon the chair.

He unfolded the letter and leaned nearer the candle.

Sir,

Miss Alexandra Gables is a philosophy intern in my home, and through an error by the housekeeper your letter has come to my attention. From its contents, I discovered you have little knowledge of the intellectual depth and breadth of this fine woman.

Part of the reason for her presence in our household is the absence of her father to London over the past six months. Surely you can concede the fact that from such a distance his assistance in her writing is rather impossible. I myself have also witnessed the fortitude and remarkable dedication she has to writing. The act she undertakes is not simply putting words to paper, but drawing from the very essence of how she lives life.

In only moments around Miss Gables, the strength of her character and beliefs is easily seen. She accomplishes and undertakes aspects of life the average man would run from in fear. Never before have I met anyone more qualified or capable of penning solid advice, interpreting a man's actions whether political or social, or fighting for the rights of those lacking the knowledge to stand up for themselves.

Miss Gables requires no man's hand to help pen such beliefs. For you to even suggest such indicates how little you know of your author. So strongly do I believe in her, I advise that you place the name Alexandra Gables alongside "Noble Horatio." It is time we give the women of this country the honor they are due.

Yours in knowledge,
Jonathan Pierce Williams

Numbness overtook her entire being. She heard Joshua fold the letter and place it on his desk, but her limbs offered no response. Never in a thousand years would she believe Pierce thought highly enough of her to so ardently defend her to another. Surely he must have penned this letter before she stole onto his ship and so eagerly allowed his advances on Sunday eve.

Slowly she rose and turned to Joshua. "Is there a date on the letter?"

"Yes, Monday."

Stunned, she realized it was after the kiss. She remembered Pierce retiring to the study after their return in the wee morning hours. Had he written the letter then? If so, his words did not reflect the feelings she attributed to him. Had he pushed away from her because he felt too strong an attraction? Had the impassioned kisses he delivered truly come from the heart? If so, then why did he not share his feelings? And why did he not trust her knowledge of his ship?

Confused, she wanted to flee and let the thousand questions work into some semblance of an answer. "I had no idea he thought such of me," she spoke, barely above a whisper.

"I cannot speak for him, but Pierce's rather insolent attitude with the editor may negate future work with the magazine. Do you still wish me to send the letter?"

"Yes," she said slowly, lost in thought. "Yes, I cannot retract such a decision. I will live with whatever the consequences."

Slowly she worked toward the study door and stopped at its threshold. She looked back at Joshua, his face serious, yet studying her reaction with interest.

"Good night, sir. And put your mind at ease. I find no fault with your actions."

"Good night, my dear," she heard while slowly finding her way along the darkened but familiar path to the stairs and the sanctuary of her room.

Twelve

For Pierce, the night held many questions with few answers, and answers that only formulated more questions. Water dripped off his borrowed cloak and squished in his boots as he walked up to the house in the wee hours. A ride had been offered, but he chose the walk to clear his mind and make sense of the uncertainty building inside.

He had been a blind man, a foolish oaf, and all the while thinking himself a sensible man. Believing outlandish claims was simply not in his nature. How then could he explain even a portion of the night's events?

Since Alexandra had touched foot in Salem, his life had changed. No longer could he walk through his house assured of solitude and routine. Now a strange iguana occupied the conservatory and frightened the guests. He knew where lightning would strike days before it happened, and every time he came within ten feet of Alexandra he could never fathom the outcome of each encounter. He bounded up the steps and into the house with a strange, unbridled energy.

With care, he entered as silently as possible, hung the wet cloak and his damp waistcoat on chairs in the warm kitchen, and set his hat upon a worktable. A soft shuffle sounded behind him and he turned to see his father, outlined in shadow with a candle in hand, entering the kitchen.

"You are up late, sir. I hope not waiting for me."

Joshua set the candle on a table. "We arrived home but a

while ago. I had some things to dwell on after that rather tumultuous party."

Pierce raised a brow in surprise. "Save for the storm, I noticed little excitement at dinner."

"You departed too early. The storm kept away a good many of the attendees, which, in my eyes, made for a more pleasant evening. However, two of the more pigheaded candidates nearly came to blows. Then, of course, there was the odd affair with the Trasks' daughter, Phoebe. She became violently ill. Something she had eaten, I do believe. Although no one else appeared to have had any problem."

"Sounds exactly like the social affairs you love."

Oddly, the latter news concerning the bad food struck a chord with Pierce. He suspected one person knew the answer. "By the way, how did Alexandra fare?"

"Quite well, actually, and that brings me to another story."

"I'm almost sorry I asked."

Joshua grinned as though eager to further expound on events of the evening, or at least on those related to his protégée. "Lydia had prepared a song which she dedicated to you."

He rolled his eyes. "My luck be praised I wasn't there to listen."

"Well, when her sister, Phoebe, fell ill," Joshua continued, "Lydia required someone to play the pianoforte. The young physician at the party asked around until he found a replacement accompanist—Alexandra. Only she had no idea for whom she was playing."

Pierce chuckled. "On the contrary, I can well imagine she did. I can easily picture Alexandra missing a few notes and Lydia huffing off in a rage." He imagined the catlike grin as the surely talented Alexandra purposefully thwarted Lydia's plans.

"Quite the opposite. She played perfectly and Lydia never missed a beat. Afterwards the guests pleaded for an encore—of Alexandra's playing. One gracious lady she is, though.

Claimed she could only accompany and not play alone. An awful lot of curious people asked me later what kind of work she was doing for me." His father winked in his direction.

A smile worked onto Pierce's face, and he felt justifiable pride. Alexandra Gables was their intern, their jewel, and in his opinion the most talented woman in all Salem. Hell, in all of Massachusetts. The Trasks had made a grave error including her in their invitation. With complete modesty, she upstaged them all.

His father wandered over to a small table and searched under a cloth for a piece of bread. Finding a sizeable piece, he tore off a chunk. "I assume you had plenty to occupy your time, too, Son. So how extensive was the damage at the shipyard?"

"Some believe a waterspout came ashore. The watchman was rather shaken up but unhurt. After reviewing the entire scene, I'd say lightning did most of the damage."

"Do you have an estimate on the delay?"

Pierce shrugged and wished to sit, but his damp clothing stuck to his skin. "A few weeks at most." He lifted the cloth of his shirt away from his skin, wishing the uncomfortable moisture gone. "I'm sorry to put such an abrupt end to our conversation, Father, but I must get out of these wet clothes and speak with Alexandra. Has she retired?"

"A good time ago. Seemed to have much on her mind. I'm afraid it was my fault, really. We had quite a discussion after arriving home."

Pierce shot his father a stern look. "Not about me, I hope."

"Actually, about me." His father patted him on the shoulder. "Seems that woman has a good deal to teach an old man about sticking to his principles." Joshua sighed. "I'm tired and you're wet. Blow out the candle before you retire." He walked out of the kitchen, leaving Pierce to contemplate his father's words.

Pierce stood quietly, understanding exactly what his father had meant. Alexandra had an honesty about her that precluded any self-interest. Even in the face of his ridicule, she had fought to make him believe her crazy visions. She, the one who sought to understand and define all things, had no explanation for them and knew she appeared foolish in his eyes. By God, how could he have been so closed-minded?

As he snuffed out the candle and let darkness engulf him, he longed for Alexandra's forgiveness. He had so much to tell her, to share with her.

The climb up the stairs took him closer to her chamber and focused his mind on the day he held her in his arms on the *Abigail*. She had fit so comfortably against him. She was so desirable and he so foolish for rejecting the attraction he felt in every bone in his body. Was it too late to rescind the prideful things he had demanded of her?

Pierce stopped and leaned his forehead against the cool wood of her door. Without explanation or even consulting his conscience, he silently entered, closing the door behind him. His sight adjusted to what little light came from the moon, hidden by cloudy remnants of the storm. He made out the still outline of her body on the bed and slowly moved forward until he stood a foot from her head.

He knelt to the floor, lowering himself to her level. A sweet rose scent reached him like tendrils of a vine and drew his hand toward the soft curls about her face.

"Had I known you planned a visit to my bedchamber," she whispered, "I'd have left the door open."

He immediately stood, realizing how improper the situation appeared. What would she think of such an invasion? His mind fumbled for some sort of excuse. "Had I not seen you switch plates with Mrs. Trask, I might not have sought an explanation. My father informed me of the sudden illness at the party. Some odd intuition told me you knew the reason."

"Leccinum atrostipitatum."

"Is that some strange curse, or have excessive glasses of wine slurred your speech?"

"I do not believe in overindulgence." Alexandra rose up onto one elbow, her loose and heavy hair falling across her shoulder. "It is a mushroom, and not an edible one. Mrs. Trask took a special effort to mix it into my gravy. I was fortunate enough to notice and simply had an opportunity to switch plates. Little did I know, she disliked gravy touching her carrots. She sent it back to the kitchen."

"And I suppose that coughing fit of yours was to rescue the plate."

She nodded enough that he could see the shadowy movement. "I'm flattered you noticed. But the kitchen staff had already added more gravy and expeditiously redistributed it to Phoebe. At that point, there was very little I could do. I knew that particular mushroom was not deadly, just discomforting."

"That's quite gracious of you. However, I suppose you made all that you could of the situation. I have to wonder why, though, they wished to make you ill."

"Prolonged wondering is not required. Over dinner, Mrs. Trask offered me a ride home if for some reason I felt disposed to retire early. I do believe they simply hoped to rid themselves of any competition for your heart."

"Lydia is absolutely the last person on earth I would desire. Can you imagine Mrs. Trask as part of my family?"

In the darkness, he swore he heard Alexandra smother a giggle. Silence then reigned in the room for several seconds, which stretched interminably into what seemed like hours. Pierce stood awkwardly in his damp clothes, not sure whether to stay or leave.

"Why are you truly here?" she finally asked.

"Hasn't your intuition told you why?"

"Do not mock me, Pierce Williams."

He knelt again on the floor near her bed. "There is no desire in my heart to do such a thing. The truth be, I simply had to see you before I retired. Not necessarily to wake you, but just to know you were still here in my home and my life. Forgive me, Alexandra. I've been so damn foolish."

She sat up on the edge of the bed and reached out for his hands. Under her fingers, she felt the red garnet family ring he wore on social occasions. "The need for forgiveness is mine as well. Thoughts of how I have treated you precluded any sleep. I gave you no chance to defend your principles."

"You simply shared your beliefs and stood fiercely by them. There is no dishonor in that."

"But I have wronged you in many other ways. I must confess . . ."

Pierce touched her lips to interrupt. "You have no confessions to make. I am the disbeliever, the doubter, and the eternal skeptic. I was so physically drawn to you that I had to find a reason to escape such a hold. I feared what I felt for you, and not believing your predictions made it easier to step away."

Affectionately, she ran a hand through his wavy, wet hair. "Why, you are soaked. Have you just now returned?"

"Barely minutes ago, but I must share the news. You were right, Alexandra. By God, you were so right."

"Whether I am right or not has little bearing if you die of chill at my feet."

She stood and gathered the light summer quilt from the bed. "If you think it not too forward of me, I suggest you remove that damp vest and shirt."

"I will not think it forward at all, only slightly suggestive." As he fumbled unbuttoning his vest and loosening his shirt, he pondered her request, considering he stood in her bedchamber and she was herself barely clothed. Improprieties aside, he considered her fully mature enough to know exactly the situation. Still, he must shoulder responsibility for this woman in his own home.

Vaguely her words reminded him of what he had said to her on the *Abigail*. Had the situation now turned? "How can I be sure of your motivations?" he said with a hint of tease in his voice. "I've heard of similar situations where women have enticed men into their chambers to entrap them into marriage."

"Then my enticement must have been the closed door to my chamber. No, I believe the fly has walked into my web on its own feet."

He grinned and stripped to his waist, finding a certain eagerness in the act. "My pants are also damp," he added, trying not to sound too hopeful.

"And they will dry quickly as your body heats up."

He felt only a moment of disappointment in her reply as she wrapped the quilt around him and he wallowed in the warmth of the gesture.

"Now, sit," she commanded.

"As you wish, but only if you join me. I am sure I will require your extra warmth for my pants to dry properly." He sat against the head of the bed and held open the quilt for her to sit against him, much as they had done on the *Abigail*.

She hesitated and he leaned toward her, reaching for her hand. " 'Tis not as if you haven't sat with me this way before."

"Ah, but before it was upon a hard bench on rolling water, where the state of my stomach dominated my thoughts, not half reclined on the softness of a bed in thin nightclothes." Unaccommodating, she remained on the edge of the bed.

He released her hand, then leisurely yawned and stretched. "If you wish to hear my tale, then join me. Otherwise, your warm bed and my tired eyes might send me to sleep in moments."

"And why should I trust the man who stole a single kiss, then abandoned me to believe I had offered too much with too little resistance?"

He blinked in surprise, confounded that she had thought herself forward for the actions he himself took that night under the tree. "My dear, you have foolishly misread my reaction to that kiss."

With gentle tugs on her body, he persisted and eventually tucked her against him on the bed. "The misdeed was mine," he said reassuringly. "If I had not stepped away from you at that very moment, any respect you had for me would have been completely lost."

He folded the quilt about them and set her back against his chest, wrapping his arms around her waist. Her breath came faster and he knew tonight was very different from the one on the *Abigail*.

"I suggest you tell me at once about the shipyard," she said with a hint of discomfort in her voice. "For at this moment, I have doubts about respecting either one of us."

He lifted his head from her fragrant curls nestled below his chin and inhaled slowly, knowing she spoke the truth. When he had walked into her bedchamber, he was fully aware of the possible consequences. Every moment he spent at the yard tonight, her spirit surrounded him. Without her, he could no longer focus. Lord above, he was amazed that after how poorly he treated her she could feel the same.

"When Lydia broke the stem off that red rose tonight and placed it into her hair," he said softly, "I began to fear everything you told me to be the truth. Then I remembered what you had said about my ship, and I knew with certainty before I ever arrived at the shipyard what had been damaged. Lightning completely blackened the bowsprit and blew the top off the guard hut. Bates, his hair standing on end, told of the massive bolt and the strange gale of winds that followed. I don't know how or why you know such things, but truly I now accept them."

He purposefully let his hands glide across the soft skin of her hands and along the thin cotton of her gowned arms, resting them on her shoulders. "I am a blackguard for not believing in you." She set a hand over his, and the simple gesture told him of her affection.

"I can hardly expect anyone to easily believe what even I cannot comprehend myself," she said thoughtfully, stroking his hand. "Maybe with time I will solve the puzzle of my intuition's source."

"I will gladly support whatever efforts you undertake. Though I must declare," he added, teasing returning to his voice, "your intuition was a bit remiss in the omission of the guard hut roof."

She turned a challenging face to him. "Are you now demeaning the bit of knowledge I shared?"

"Only so as to defy you to delve further into your gift. Did you not foresee what happens tonight?"

She swung around, sitting on her knees. "If you mean, how I throw you heedlessly to the floor and demand your removal from my bedchamber—no."

"I meant nothing of the kind. I envisioned more that you allowed me the courtesy of another kiss and permission to hold you in my arms." He couldn't help reaching into the long, free bundle of hair behind her head.

He leaned forward and brought her face nearer. At first he paused, knowing without a doubt his reaction to sensuous contact, then proceeded, unable to withhold the desire.

She, too, hesitated, and at first he feared rejection. But finally she brushed her cheek against his, then pressed welcoming lips eagerly and tenderly against his. Leaning slightly forward on her knees, she lightly dropped off balance into his lap and arms. He clutched her tightly, afraid this moment might dissipate as easily as fog.

Impassioned kisses he placed on her face and neck as she caressed his hair and untied the leather binding it back. As his hair released about his neck, the freedom served only to enhance his desire. He stroked his lips against hers before devouring her mouth and all its mystery. It wasn't until she gasped for breath that he realized his eagerness.

Guilt began to assail his conscience. "Alexandra, I broke off our encounter the other night because I had no doubt where your touch would lead me. I stand again at that threshold, only this time I have no wish to walk away. I am a man of greater age and experience. I have no right to take your maidenhood before marriage."

"If that is what you are offering tonight, I am not a naive child and understand the consequences."

"And if tomorrow, God forbid, I drop dead, you will have given away your innocence."

"To have touched the only man ever to steal my heart, and shared an intimacy with him as I have with no other, justifies my wish. I will have a memory to cherish every day the rest of my life."

"And what if you found yourself with child?"

Deep in thought, a silent aura enveloped her. She sat up stiffly in his arms. "Could we not stop short of that point?"

The complete innocence in her question gave him no doubt of her virginity. He stroked a finger along her face. "Is it easier to stop a ship under sail, or at anchor in the bay?"

Under his touch he felt a smile blossom. She understood his point.

Absently she played with a tie string on her gown. "For once, with all my studies I fail to know the very necessary details to preclude such a problem. I do know women use barriers to prevent conception, but I simply have never had sufficient reason to learn what they are."

"Alexandra, we can stop now with no regrets." He hesitated and she remained silent. "If not, and you allow me to admit with some indelicacy, I do know of one preventative women practice."

She cupped a hand gently against his cheek. "Please, share it with me. I make no judgment of your past. My only concern is the current state of your heart. My greatest desire is to please you and embrace these new feelings driving my body and soul. If you have some knowledge to allow us such intimacy, I beg of you, please tell me."

Softly he pulled her back to him and whispered, "They soak a sea sponge in vinegar and place it inside their bodies."

Alexandra quieted, and he pictured her mind ticking with thoughts like a well-tuned clock, analyzing available data and attempting to reach some conclusion.

"If I find such a barrier tonight, will you take me again into your arms?"

"Alexandra, there is no rush. I'm not asking you to sacrifice yourself for me."

"I do this as much for me as I do for you. I have lived until now with no need of a man. If life so cruelly wished to take you from me, I would survive alone. But I will never forgive myself if I don't at least discover where my heart can take me. That solution seems quite simple."

She slipped from his arms and off the bed. "Alexandra, wait. 'Tis not that easy."

"Anything worthwhile rarely is," she whispered from across the room. He heard the door to the room open and then quietly shut again.

He sat empty-handed in his still damp pants wrapped in her quilt, contemplating what had just happened. Damnation, if he didn't have more trouble getting close to that woman! Minutes ticked by as he waited, beginning to grow concerned. He didn't have a chance to tell her that the women he knew who used such methods were long married or well practiced. Would she even know what to do with the sponge?

Oddly, he heard a patter of bare feet pass the bedroom and continue down the hall. He crept to the door and carefully peered out. Alexandra slipped into his room and slowly eased the door shut. Curious, he followed.

Alexandra stood against Pierce's bedroom door, feeling every bit the child who had stolen to the kitchen for a nighttime treat. Lord, what crazy thing had she done, and what drove her to blatantly leave all good sense behind?

She had entered into unfamiliar territory in more than one way. Not once this summer had she taken the time to enter Pierce's room, but she required a place now for privacy. Immediately she inhaled the manly smell of leather and musk fragrance. Her eyes closed and her heart began to beat faster as she imagined his touch. Quickly she hastened to the bedside table and placed a small bowl filled with lemon juice and a sponge.

She had gathered the sea sponge from a specimen jar in Joshua's conservatory, and the lemon juice squeezed from Mrs. Flamm's new sack of lemons just received from the West Indies. The odor of vinegar precluded any thought of using such a liquid. The simple stench would drive even the hardiest man to another room. She surmised that lemon juice was an acid similar to vinegar and would most likely suffice.

The next step was less clear. Save for normal hygiene and monthly female bleeding, she had never touched or considered her feminine place. Now, suddenly she had to place something up inside her body. Not one to run from any challenge, she grabbed the fist-sized sponge and squeezed the cold excess juice from its hold. She lifted her gown and pressed away. Much to her chagrin, nothing happened.

Surely such an action could not be so hard. Why, animals mated all the time and they never flinched. She spread her feet farther apart and tried again. Excess juice simply dripped through her fingers, and she shuddered from the cool liquid against such a sensitive place. The harder she pushed, the tighter her body seemed to shut. A tear dropped onto her cheek. Was she unfit for a man?

Warm, comforting arms surrounded her from behind. Her brief surprise at Pierce's presence melted as he gently removed the sponge from her fingers and placed kisses along her neck. "You should have told me you changed venue," he said, his voice low, soft, and sensual.

Quickly she wiped at the tear on her face, afraid he might discover it. "I required some privacy to think about our situation. Maybe I am not the right woman for you. As much as my heart desires nothing more than to be in your arms, my intuition warns me against such action."

He dropped the sponge into the juice and rotated her to face him, holding her so close that his body seemed to scorch the air. "This time I do not believe your intuition has a say. What you need, I believe, is my assistance."

"There is nothing you can do for me." Frustration crept into her voice, but he seemed to ignore her words as he brushed his lips against her ear.

"That is not what you said only minutes ago on your bed," he whispered.

"Minutes ago I did not realize . . ." She stopped abruptly, not sure what to say.

"Realize that putting such an undesirable item inside you, an unseasoned woman, is nearly impossible," he finished. He tenderly placed a kiss on her cheek and wiped away the remaining moisture from her tear.

"How did you know?"

"*My* intuition. Now, I promised you my help. Trust me. Have no fear of your womanly virtues."

He lifted her into his arms with barely an effort and carried her to his bed. He laid her back, pushing aside the bed quilt. Sitting next to her, he lifted her hand and gently kissed one finger at a time. "Close your eyes," he whispered.

He let a single finger trail from her wrist along the skin of her arm and move ever closer to her body. Dots of light flashed in tiny explosions behind her eyelids with each inch of skin traversed. As his finger touched her gown and caressed her side, all thoughts but his touch left her mind. His finger slid past her waist and hip and started down the outside of her leg. When the thin cloth of her gown ended and he again reached skin, an involuntary shudder wracked her body.

He reached her toes and stopped for a brief moment to gently massage her foot. He shifted to use both hands, each on a separate leg, and slowly and lightly slid them back up, taking the edge of the gown with them. Bit by bit, the gown exposed more of her body to him. She offered no protest as he coaxed her hips to lift and the gown slipped past. As her back arched under the heat of his hands, his mouth stopped to tenderly torture her breasts.

"Do you wish to drive me mad so I forget all my troubles?" she protested. "If so, you have succeeded. I want only to hold you near me."

"You shall have your wish in a few moments." He pulled the gown past her head and let it tumble to the floor. "Until then you must suffer under my touch."

He moved away for a brief moment and she heard the tear

of a sponge, and the odor of lemon pleasantly filled the air. So she had foolishly guessed wrong at the size. Content to let Pierce guide this awkward process, she closed her eyes and waited. A cool touch on her chin made her eyes fly open. Slowly Pierce drew the lemon-scented sponge down her chin and neck, leaving drops of juice between her breasts. Down further the cool tingle spread, moving past her breast and navel, toward the place she avowed most private. Hot and cold sensations divided her mind and passions.

No man had ever touched where the cool stream of lemon was headed. The very thought sent every sense crashing together into a gasp as the coolness blended with her moist heat. Pierce's fingers touched places of sheer sensation she had never known existed. Just as the barrage of pleasures almost overtook her very being, she felt a pinch and brief push inside and knew the deed was done.

"Dear Lord," she whispered breathlessly. "If such pleasure be the path to contraception, it is a wonder children ever exist."

"That is only the beginning," he answered as his fingers once again found the places of pure ecstasy.

Between groans of pleasure, she leaned up to him. "If you continue such without allowing me the right to every inch of your body, I shall deem you unfair."

He responded with another caress of his finger. She pulled away from him and reached for his breeches. "Off with these or I shall believe you not capable of keeping your promise."

He moved to work his breeches loose, and Alexandra eagerly helped in the disrobing. No expectations or scientific explanations could have described the sight, within the shadows, of his need for her. He sat up to remove his damp stockings, and she could not help but touch his shoulders and back and wonder what sensations touching him in other places would create.

She nuzzled at the neck under his hair until he twisted around and they both fell into the bed. His very nakedness against her legs and thighs and breasts set off overwhelming sensations, much like the first touch of a velvety-soft flower petal or the cool mist of a rainbow-crowned waterfall.

He leaned over her on one elbow, strong and hot, sweat already beading under her fingers on his shoulders. She let her hand run to his chest and the dark swirls of hair she had felt once before. His hand stroked her side, leaving the skin singed with heat.

Tentatively, unsure of his reaction, she let a hand trickle down his chest to the very part of him unfamiliar to her. Uncertain of whether to touch or hold, her fingers lightly played around the firmness. With a sharp intake of breath, he pressed against her thigh and caught her hand in his.

"God in heaven, Alexandra, do not torture me." He placed her hand firmly against the place she sought. Firm and hot, it radiated his extreme need for her. His fingers sought out her soft place, and once again sensations of pleasure arched her back in sparkles of light. He engulfed her in his arms and rolled her atop him, caressing and stroking the smooth nakedness of her skin. Under her, the length of his body felt strong and warm and able to handle her weight. Her hands slid from the developed muscles of his arms to the smooth skin of his side and then slipped gently under the tender skin of his buttocks. As though triggered by her touch, she felt him move his hip rhythmically against her body. Her body's eager response to the hardness against her abdomen produced a soft gasp.

Quickly he rolled her to his side and leaned up onto an elbow. "Alexandra, stop me if I move too fast. I can withhold my need to devour you."

Short quick, breaths escaped her as he tenderly brushed hair back from her face to kiss her cheek and neck. The sensations served only to enhance her anxiety to continue. "Having never before been with a man," she whispered breathlessly, "I do not know what is deemed as appropriate timing. All I do know is, I have no wish for you to stop."

She reached up, encircling his neck and drawing him down toward her. Slowly his mouth burned a path to her breast and his tongue swirled around her nipple. Her fingers dug into his shoulders with the myriad of wonderful and erotic sensations. In a sudden panic, she lifted his head with her hand. "Am I an improper woman to feel such ecstasy?"

"There is no impropriety in finding pleasure with a man who has your interests at heart."

"And are you such a man?"

"I could never pretend to be something with you I am not. Were I to want anything but the best for you, I could not lie by your side."

She held his face between her hands and covered it with little kisses. "I have lost all control over my body. Everything you touch, every stroke you make, increases my desire. It is as though I am on some journey whose destination must be reached."

Pierce gave a lighthearted laugh. "My dear, for one who knows everything about life, you understand little about the physical love between a man and woman. The journey is one we take together. I will get us to the destination."

His mouth sought hers, ending all discussion, and she let her body and all its senses speak. She ran fingers in long strokes down his chest, and her hands sought every nook and contour of Pierce within reach. Everything and nothing mattered in the next minutes. She tasted the saltiness of his sweat and inhaled scents she knew came from them both. The heat of the night left moisture on their skin as their bodies slid along one another, searching, rolling, and entwining.

They journeyed together until she no longer could proceed without him. So ultimate was the call for him, even as a novice she knew desperately the final need. Strong and steady he held himself above her, touching yet not crushing. Even though his eyes were lost in shadow, she knew he sought the final permission, as if either of them could persuade their bodies to any other path.

She wrapped her legs around his and drew him forward, braced for the unknown but accepting nothing less. Emotionally, sharing a part of her life given to no other opened her soul wide. Physically, the depth to which her body accepted the fullness of him truly surprised and excited her. Her back arched in natural response, and with eager but tender motion they moved together. His lips near her ear whispered unremembered words of love and encouragement, but all senses focused on the sensations coming too fast and powerfully for her mind to discern.

Full and deep they worked together, climbing ever higher to the final apex of the journey. She heard Pierce draw in breath sharply, and his need became faster and more forceful. The ecstasy overloaded her mind, and she closed her eyes. The final rush to the top came with unexpected speed as her body let go in a burst of pleasure and soft moans.

"Oh, God," Pierce groaned as his body stiffened in a firm thrust.

As the quickness of his breathing slowed, his arms wrapped tight about her and he settled them on their sides, her head resting on his arm.

"My dear Alexandra, do you know where we have taken ourselves?" He kissed her forehead and pressed her close. "To the very place our fathers sought—in one another's arms."

"Are the wishes of our parents such that we cannot admit they were right?"

"It's the principle, my dear, the principle."

"What if we are completely wrong about their desires?" She pictured her father and Joshua with their heads together plotting. "No matter, how can I possibly hide this relationship from your father? How can I see you each day and not want to lie again by your side?"

Pierce grew disturbingly quiet at her question. "I will make it easier for you. I must be away for a while."

"Gone?" She rose up off his arm, and her heart sank at the implications.

"I'm not deserting you, Alexandra. The damage at the shipyard has delayed the launch, but not by much. The new bowsprit can be hoisted into place along with the masts after launching. I must travel to New York to speak with the owners and update them on the progress. I'll also spend a day to secure new wood for the bowsprit. To be honest, I do not want to go. I fear greatly leaving you here with all the rather strange occurrences happening. I can but presume, though, that you will be safer with me out of town."

"But you must have time to repair the rudder. It's not safe to sail."

"Trust me, the rudder will be safe."

"Surely you had no time to inspect it tonight. How do you know what is wrong with it? Please, I beg of you, take the time to make it right."

Pierce pulled her head down to his chest and softly stroked her long hair. "After what we just shared, do you doubt that I care about and believe in you? Trust me, the ship will be safe when we sail." He tucked the quilt up over her shoulders against a slight nighttime chill drifting in the window.

The caress of his hands slow and gentle along her back, the warmth of his body, and the drum of his heart worked to ease her concerns. Trust was all she had to give him. In truth, trust was also all she wanted. The lull of sleep and comfort and exhaustion made further thought difficult.

"Will you still be here in the morning?" she said sleepily.

"Until you throw me heedlessly to the floor and demand my removal from the bedchamber."

She opened one eye and looked up at him. "But 'tis your room."

"So it is." He smiled and gently brushed a hand over her face to close her eye and send her into a journey of contented dreams.

Thirteen

The distinctive tread of his father's boots down the hallway brought Pierce fully awake. Light filled the room, and he realized the morning was well underway. Alexandra's arm lay draped across him, and her head, under a mass of red curls, snuggled against his chest. Gently he slid from beneath her and off the bed. She gave a soft, pleasurable murmur but did not awaken.

With due haste before Mrs. Bisbey wandered the hallway, he dug out drawers from a chest and tied them at the waist, leaving the knees loose until he put on his stockings. A board creaked beneath his foot and he silently swore. If anyone heard it, they would now realize he was awake.

He tossed a clean shirt over his head and searched for breeches. Finding a pair, he slipped into them and tucked in his shirt as Alexandra stirred awake. A twinge of guilt played in his conscience. Had he been more of a gentleman would this night have happened? He pushed away such considerations. It was too late for any regrets.

The smile that spread across her face as she remembered their tryst charmed his soul. He held a finger to his lips to warn her to silence and slid next to her on the bed. She held the bed quilt modestly over her breasts but immediately leaned toward him.

"The morning is late and the household is already awake," he said, pulling her and the quilt into his arms. "I suggest you slip back to your room unless we wish to explain our present situation."

Alexandra nodded with understanding as she leaned up to kiss his cheek. Playfully she rubbed a thumb across his roughened face, where his morning beard had started to show, and then tousled his hair. Unable to help himself, he nuzzled at her neck and she quietly laughed, tightening her arms around his neck and pulling him down.

Damnation, he found himself aroused and wanting her all over again. She pulled his shirt loose and skillfully tortured the skin on his chest before running her fingers firmly along his back. He hungered at the smooth skin at her neck and finally enveloped the tip of a breast in his mouth. Almost unnoticed in the background, his ears heard the sound of light footsteps mounting the stairs.

He froze, although his chest still heaved in heady anticipation. With only the sound of quick breathing filling the air, they both silently listened. Immediately he knew Mrs. Bisbey was on the way to his room.

"My hot shaving water," he whispered desperately. "I'm usually the first up and get it myself. But when I'm late, Mrs. Bisbey brings it up."

"What shall we do now?" Alexandra asked. They both glanced around his chamber, realizing no place offered any shelter from curious eyes.

Pierce leaped off the bed, tucking back in his shirt and buttoning his breeches. He scooped up Alexandra's gown, grabbed her hand, and swept her with him toward the door. He put her behind it against the wall, where she quickly threw the gown over her head. Just as Mrs. Bisbey reached the door, Pierce swung it open.

"Good morning, Mrs. Bisbey. I heard your footsteps in the hallway."

"A good mornin' to you, too, Mister Pierce. I have your shavin' water." She moved as though she fully expected him to swing the door open and allow her to place it by his wash basin.

Instead, he held his ground in the doorway and with a grateful smile reached for the bowl. "Thank you for bringing it up. I'll just take it from here."

Mrs. Bisbey abruptly halted and gave him a peculiar look. "It's not necessary, sir. I know me job."

"And I'll save you the extra steps today." He plucked it from her hands before she could react.

She gazed up, puzzled at the guilty smile he knew covered his face. "Ye seem in a chipper mood after gettin' stormed out of last night's party."

"Exactly," he replied. "You know how I detest those social events." He stood with the bowl in hand and put his foot against the door to close it.

Mrs. Bisbey looked down at his naked legs and feet. "Ye want me to get out clean stockin's while ye shave?"

He gave her what he thought was a dazzling grin. "You are so efficient, but they are already laid out. Thank you, though, for offering. I'll be down in just a few minutes."

Mrs. Bisbey glanced past him toward the totally disheveled bed. She stared into his eyes for several seconds before shaking her head and walking away. He pushed the door closed with his foot and discovered that Alexandra had slid down the wall into a ball. She held a fist stuffed against her mouth to keep from laughing.

He juggled the warm water over to the washstand. Alexandra rose and followed, circling her arms about his waist. "I shall remember how well you stretch the truth," she whispered.

"For you, I am afraid I would do almost anything. And that makes you quite a dangerous woman, my dear." He turned and kissed her, well aware they had no time to allow physical responses to take over.

She leaned away in his arms. "And do you again plan to take risks in my presence?"

He gave a hushed laugh. "As an honest man I must admit

I wish this day were past. Then I could once again hold you through the night in my arms."

"And I will gladly risk the indiscretion to be by your side. But how many nights do we have before you leave for New York?"

Suddenly uncomfortable with the truth, he held her head against his chest and answered, "I leave tomorrow."

"The nights will pass slowly," she said softly and then looked up at him. "Will you write?"

"I will send a letter from New York. Do not be surprised, though, if I arrive home before you receive it."

"I'd rather have you than the letter." She kissed him so delicately on the lips that it seemed but a sensuous breeze had awakened the skin under her touch. Again she brushed her lips against his until he held her face and engulfed her mouth in his.

"Alexandra, I have no regrets about last night," he said in between several kisses, "but as a gentleman I had no right to expect so much from you."

Alexandra stopped and placed a hand against his mouth. "Even in the heat of passion last night I held you to no promises."

"And I made none then, but I can't leave without the assurance that you will be here when I return. Now you must hurry to your room before Mrs. Bisbey decides to knock on your door. I will see you for the midday meal and we must try to find a moment of privacy."

"To steal a few kisses to keep me sustained through the day?" she teasingly asked.

"No," he answered and almost laughed as confusion overcame her smile. Seductively, he slid her gown above her waist. "To take out something we put in." To a gasp and her surprise, he touched her most private place.

She jumped back and let the gown fall into place. In a swaying dance toward the door, she whispered, "Do you think anyone will notice if I eat with haste?" She blew him a kiss and peeked out the door. Before he could answer, she was gone.

Morning in her bedchamber gleamed brighter than Alexandra remembered. A few drawings lay on her writing desk, and the colors appeared so vivid, she almost smelled the flowers' scent. She swung open her cupboard to the dresses hanging there and considered which color best fit her mood. Hunter green was too dark, blue too passive, and beige too dull. If she had her way, she'd stay in bed all day and dream about last night with Pierce. It only took another few seconds for her to see the fallacy in such thought. Wiser and certainly more tantalizing was dreaming about the future. A pattern of summer flowers against a white background became the choice for the day.

A light rapping, accompanied by Mrs. Bisbey's voice, caught her dressed only in a chemise and stockings. With a light gait in her step she couldn't explain, she opened up the bedroom door.

Mrs. Bisbey stood with a bucket and pitcher and a wide smile on her face. "Goodness, ye look cheerful this mornin'. Must have been a grand time last night." Mrs. Bisbey hustled over to the washbasin and set the pitcher down.

"One of the more memorable times of my life," Alexandra answered, taking out the flowered dress and laying it on the bed.

"Must have been, what with Mrs. Trask doin' her own daughter in."

"She truly made her only a bit ill, but please, this is just between you and me." Efficiently Mrs. Bisbey dumped the dirty basin water into the bucket, and clean water took its place in the bowl. Alexandra stepped up to the basin and splashed water on her face. In between splashes she conveyed the story about the mushrooms, the switch, and then poor indisposed Miss Phoebe.

Mrs. Bisbey seemed to have no doubts of Mrs. Trask's culpability of such action and offered warnings for Alexandra to stay well away from her.

Alexandra patted her face dry with a linen towel and turned to face Mrs. Bisbey. "Joshua is not aware of what happened with the mushrooms, and I'd rather not worry him. However, Pierce saw me switch the plates, so I had to give him an explanation. At least for a while, the Trasks will have no one to chase. Pierce will be safely away for the next several weeks. I presume I, too, will be left in peace during his absence."

"Where is Mister Pierce goin'?" Mrs. Bisbey asked as Alexandra dug a petticoat out of the wardrobe and tightened it around her waist.

"Last night's storm wreaked havoc at the shipyard. Pierce has to find a new bowsprit and discuss the launching with the owners in New York."

Mrs. Bisbey quieted for a moment as she helped Alexandra with the flowered skirt. "When did ye speak with Mister Pierce? Mister Joshua just said ye had long retired by the time Pierce came home."

Immediately Alexandra recognized her error. "I, ah, heard him wake this morning and stuck my head out the door when he was in the hall."

Mrs. Bisbey tilted her head in thought. "Odd, I just left his room, and he had yet to get stockin's or boots on his feet."

"It was just moments ago," she amended quickly, remembering Joshua's comments about how little lies continue to grow. "I think he knew I was awake and wanted to tell me about the shipyard mishap. He had his boots on, I do believe."

Just as the words slipped from her mouth, she knew it to be impossible. His boots and shirt lay on the floor on the other side of her bed. Weakly she smiled, as Mrs. Bisbey stood with the dress bodice in hand at the end of her bed. Two more steps back and she would be able to see the evidence of her lie.

Alexandra quickly reached for the bodice in Mrs. Bisbey's hands. "Surely you have other duties, and I needn't waste your time."

" 'Tis a pleasure doin' for you, mum. 'Specially when I hear good tales." As Alexandra fastened on the bodice, Mrs. Bisbey walked around her shaking her head. She lifted up tresses of Alexandra's hair trailing down her back. "I can't imagine how a miss slept so wild, though, as to put so many tangles in her hair. I'll be glad to help ye brush it out."

"It's no problem at all. I love brushing my own hair. After all the excitement last night, sleep came with difficulty. Why, I remember tossing and turning most of the night."

"Then you start brushin' while I help make up your beddin'." Mrs. Bisbey turned and tugged on the wadded quilt, pulling it up over the bed.

With a speed and agility heretofore unknown, Alexandra darted around the bed to the far side. As her feet quietly slid the boots and shirt under the bed, she grabbed the quilt edge and straightened it into place.

Mrs. Bisbey ran a hand down the quilt, taking out any wrinkles. "Why, this quilt is damp. Did you get wet last night?"

Sheepishly Alexandra shrugged. "I'd completely forgotten: my gloves were wet and I foolishly laid them on the bed. They're dry now, though. I hung them up last night."

Mrs. Bisbey crossed her arms in consternation. Alexandra sincerely doubted the housekeeper believed even half the things to which she had admitted. Finally the woman shook her head. "Everyone seems so gay this mornin'—and so confused." Mrs. Bisbey strolled to the door, mumbling about having something ready for breakfast, and how parties where spirits were served left everyone in strange moods the next day.

As Mrs. Bisbey's footsteps graced the staircase, Pierce appeared at Alexandra's open door. Quickly and without a word, Alexandra dug his boots and shirt out from under the bed. He slid the boots on at the door and gave her a quick kiss before tossing the shirt back in his room and heading downstairs.

Alexandra sat on the edge of the bed, brushing her hand across the damp quilt, now cold to her touch. Hours ago it had been anything but cold as Pierce cuddled her against him, wrapped in its cotton warmth. Boldly she had demanded he remove his shirt, knowing the impropriety and where her actions might lead. She knew intuitively from the moment he had entered her room and knelt by her bed that he felt the same.

Every night since his kiss under the tree, she had dreamed of his warmth, the scent of his skin, and the strange hardness of his body. Only the disappointment she suffered at his disbelief in her visions had kept any stronger desires at bay. But once the block against her heart had been removed with his letter, the feeling she knew to be lustful love grew without control. She had certainly studied the mating of animals, but nothing had prepared her for the urges, needs, and desires in the mating of man.

She moved to a stool in front of the washstand and began the tedious task of brushing out tangles—the true solid evidence of the restless, driving force that entwined them together, moving, touching, caressing, and losing each other in the act of discovery. With each stroke, she counted the hours, minutes, and seconds until that night when he would hold her once again.

"Wake up, Miss Gables." A man's deep voice, gentle and reassuring, drifted through her hazy dream stupor. Vaguely she felt a gentle shake of her shoulder as someone tried to roust her from a comfortable nap.

"Miss Gables," the voice spoke a little louder.

Her eyes flew open as memories of the day returned. She lifted her head from the papers and books strewn across the hardwood table. Leather-bound volumes of births, deaths, marriages, and baptisms lay scattered and open.

Embarrassed, she peered up at Dr. Bentley, the warm minister of East Church. Even though he had a propensity to garner every little tidbit of gossip that floated around town, she had good feelings about his helpful temperament.

"My apologies," she said. "I simply was resting my eyes against the strain of reading. These old records are not always clearly legible."

Bentley laughed heartily. "I've garnered a reputation for frequently lulling the eyes closed of my parishioners, but never has one fallen asleep in my office. Have you not been receiving sufficient rest with Pierce gone to New York?"

She gulped and gave an innocent smile, wondering if anyone could possibly know what had happened that night two weeks ago in Pierce's bedchamber. "Why should his presence have an impact upon my rest?"

"Come now, my dear. One day every summer week I take a group of young ladies to the seashore to collect and study our natural wonders. I find it a great enjoyment to hear their talk of the eligible gentlemen in this town. As of late they have expressed disappointment at the apparent unavailability of Mr. Williams since your arrival in town. But the real truth lies in your face." He pulled out a heavy chair across from her and sat. "I have seen the look of young ladies in love, and you seem no different. When you speak of him, little smiles form around your eyes and you look away as if remembering some shared secret."

She knew better than to confirm any truth to Dr. Bentley. No matter how amiable and wonderful a minister, he tended to inscribe everything into his diary. "Truly, sir, I doubt any fondness I may have for Mister Williams has any bearing on my exhaustion." She concentrated on keeping her eyes trained on Dr. Bentley and her face calm.

"Perhaps, then, you are taking your research too seriously. I declare, between the churches in Salem and the courthouse you have worn new paths."

Alexandra reached out for Dr. Bentley's hand. "And you have been wonderfully gracious to convince the pastors to give me such marvelous assistance."

"When you came to me two weeks ago searching for information about a woman accused of witchcraft and a judge involved in the trials, you certainly piqued my curiosity. Giving you my assistance is a rare pleasure. All I ask is that you promise to accompany our group to the seaside next week. These young ladies are most curious about our natural world."

"I'll look forward to the outing." She began to close volumes and straighten a wayward collection of notes, inked to the very edges to make the best use of the costly paper.

"By the way, did you find evidence of Judge Williams and that woman . . . ?" Dr. Bentley lightly snapped his fingers as though to prod his memory.

"Priscilla Gardener," Alexandra finished. She frowned, displeased by her lack of progress today. "Judge Nathaniel Williams sat on the court responsible for persecuting the witchcraft victims of sixteen ninety-two. He resigned when the claims became outrageous and spectral evidence was allowed to have influence."

She relaxed back in the wood chair, her mind once again sorting and trying to make sense of the details. "I am not completely clear as to what relationship he had to Priscilla Gardener, though. Records show she was originally on trial for witchcraft before her husband. In all likelihood, John Gardener confessed to witchcraft to save his wife's life. Such a grievous thought that a man of barely twenty-six years should die so horrible a death! Poor John Gardener must have known his wife was several months with child. Church records document the birth. Judge Williams later penned a scathing editorial about the execution of her husband."

Dr. Bentley nodded with understanding. "It is hard to fathom how the people here ever let such fears overtake them. I am aware it is easier for us to look back with wisdom on the past. But it makes me wonder what follies we are hatching today."

Dr. Bentley studied her face, and she knew it reflected disappointment. "I take it you have not discovered all the answers you sought," he said with sympathy and curiosity.

"I must admit my hopes were high. I had followed the line of Priscilla Gardener up to the present, and there it died out. A most unusual history. It seems Priscilla never remarried and raised her daughter by herself. A most understandable occurrence, considering how her husband had perished. Her daughter, though, had several children but oddly was also widowed young. She, too, never found another husband, as seems to have happened with all the females in Priscilla's line. All were widowed early and never remarried. 'Tis almost as though they were cursed," she said nonchalantly.

A light glittered deep in Dr. Bentley's eyes. As thoughts mulled in his mind, his index finger tapped the table. "Considering the great hardship on widows and the shortage of women before the revolution, I do find that most strange. Until only recently, men far outnumbered women and, to put it kindly, sought out any single woman for marriage."

"*Strange* is barely the adjective I would use to describe this family lineage." She hunted out a page of the notes and handed it to him. "Look at the dates on this page. These represent the deaths of each of the men married by daughters of Priscilla's line. Two records stated the age of the husbands. They were both twenty-six years old. In the editorial Judge Williams wrote of John Gardener's death, he mentioned the fact that John died at age twenty-six. I find that coincidence exceedingly curious."

"Having never study genealogy, I cannot say what the mathematical probability of such an occurrence might be. But I do agree with you, it seems highly unusual. What have you uncovered of the relatives alive today? Do they still reside in this region?"

She turned a large volume on the table in his direction. "In your own East Church register, there is documented the marriage of a Mary Hannah Abbott to a Phillip Joseph Bennett. A year later the birth of three girls is recorded. She delivered triplets. So unusual was the occurrence, I found articles in the *Gazette* about the birth. Barely a year hence, records show the death of Mary Bennett and, not long after that, the death of her husband. There is no record anywhere of what happened to the girls. No adoptions, marriages, or deaths."

Bentley frowned. "The daughters were barely a year old then. Surely someone must have recorded adoptions or baptisms. Maybe they went to a family member out of town?"

"Possibly, but Phillip Bennett had no siblings and his parents were deceased. On Mary's side no close relatives were evident, either."

Bentley leaned his ample body forward and rested his arms on the table. "How many years ago are we discussing?"

"A mere twenty, sir."

"Twenty years is sizable enough to make most forget, but triplets are so unique, surely someone must remember. One of my parishioners, Anne Appleton, kept records for a lawyer back then. She seems to have solid wits about her, and might well remember what happened to the girls."

Alexandra practically leaped to her feet, anxious for a new lead in the search. "Will you be so kind as to write a quick note of introduction for me? Whenever it is convenient, of course."

Dr. Bentley glanced at the volumes stacked on the table. "I believe, in the time it will take you to reshelf these volumes, I might be able to scribble down a few appropriate words."

"Thank you, sir. I feel most positive about your suggestion."

Dr. Bentley scrutinized her face so closely, she felt a tad uncomfortable. Some thought obviously concerned him. "May I ask one last question?" he said slowly.

"And what is it you wish to know?"

"Why are you so interested in the line of this Priscilla Gardener? Where did you first learn of her?"

"From one of your parishioners. I only know her by the name Hannah. She has reddish hair, much like mine with a few streaks of gray."

"I know of several women named Hannah, but I do recall the one you describe. A widow, I believe, recently arrived from Connecticut."

"I don't know from whence she came, but you spoke with

her in the days after Joshua Williams's party. You told her of my intent to occasionally instruct the young ladies in town."

Dr. Bentley appeared most perplexed. "Dear Alexandra, I have no recollection of an extended conversation with that woman in the past several months, let alone divulging to her such a fact. I'm afraid you are mistaken."

Stupefied, Alexandra mumbled, "But how did she know?"

"Know what?"

Afraid of sounding completely daft, she smiled weakly at Dr. Bentley. "It appears I completely misunderstood Hannah's comments. However, do you perchance know her full name?"

"Offhand I do not recall. But I record each new face and church member in my journals. Surely I can find it." He selected a volume off a shelf and thumbed through the pages.

Alexandra began hastily replacing church record volumes, all the while trying to make sense of Hannah.

"Here it is," Dr. Bentley gleefully announced. "Hannah Brickford. We have a good many Brickfords in town. She mentioned no connection, but it might be likely she is related to one."

"Hannah Brickford," Alexandra murmured, as something tugged at her memory but no clear picture materialized.

Dr. Bentley set to work writing a note of introduction for the lawyer's record keeper.

"Thank you so much for everything," Alexandra said as the last book and papers were cleared from the table and he handed over the letter.

"Promise you will keep me informed of the results," he said as she swept up her hat from the table, ready to find answers for the new questions now invading her mind.

"Promised," she called back over her shoulder before stepping into the warm sun of the summer day.

Dr. Bentley had sketched a small map on the back of the letter showing the record keeper's house. The Widow Appleton had lived in Salem her entire life. If anyone might remember the occurrences of twenty years prior, she might very well be the one.

With all the information packed tightly into Alexandra's head and the notes from the past two weeks held tightly under her arm, she almost missed the rather ominous warning from her intuition. It easily reminded her of the day in the study when she felt under observation. Discreetly, she stopped and removed a handkerchief while checking the lane ahead and behind. Nothing or no one appeared out of the ordinary.

Calmly she continued, the feeling still present. One lesson living in Salem had taught her was to listen to intuition. Someone apparently had an interest in her movements, but who and why? Hannah came to mind, but her presence had never produced any haunting sensations such as these. Also, quite inexplicably, she knew the strange feeling came from a man.

The Widow Appleton's cozy home sat on the lane just up from the schoolhouse and the whipping post. Two doors down, Captain John ran a respectable tavern. The widow slowly answered Alexandra's knock, but once introductions were complete, she appeared pleased for the company.

Impatient for answers but understanding the necessity for polite intercourse, Alexandra waited for tea preparation and the serving of sweet biscuits. The elder woman served them in the small but very cheery room of the lower floor.

"So you seek information about the Bennett triplets," she said, pouring tea into two white teacups. "I had thought most people in this town had long forgotten those girls. So tiny when they were born, few reckoned they would survive long. But grow they did, into charming, round-faced darlings. I kept one in my home while adoptive parents were sought. Won't ever forget the beautiful hair of that young'un. Much like yours."

The revelation came as a surprise. "You mean red?"

"Oh, yes. Gorgeous curly little red tufts of hair."

Excitement tingled, and Alexandra's curiosity longed for the Widow Appleton to spill every secret immediately. "Please, share with me what you know of the girls' parents, Phillip and Mary Bennett."

The widow sipped on her tea, a hollow look in her soft blue eyes. "So sad how they both died young. Mr. Wynn, the solicitor, found the girls excellent homes, though. I'm sure they were duly loved."

Alexandra sensed that the widow had much more knowledge than she cared to impart. "Why were there no proper records kept of the adopting families? Surely with a lawyer handling the adoptions, somewhere the deed was recorded."

The widow fidgeted, and Alexandra knew she had touched on something that troubled the woman, but she still seemed reluctant to release her knowledge.

With compassion, Alexandra smiled warmly at the widow. "Ofttimes the knowledge of one's family history is not something eagerly shared, but I believe that the girls might be distant relatives and I wish very much to learn about them. As you can see, red hair is prevalent in my family. Please, tell what you know about the girls and their parents. Exactly how did their mother die? The records were quite vague."

The old woman added a warm touch of tea to her cup and raised it to her lips. Her hands shook as she stared out an open window. Moisture sat unheeded upon her lips as she set the cup down. "All these years, I have kept the tale private. Legal reasons, you realize. But now that my employer, Mr. Wynn, is long passed on, I can't see the harm in revealing the truth."

"I promise to keep in confidence anything you reveal to me. I have spent two weeks going through court and church records to search out these girls. Please, allow me the satisfaction of finding loved ones long parted from our family."

A twinge of guilt touched Alexandra for playing to the old woman's good nature and for misrepresenting her family ties. But she simply required answers and would not accept the defeat of leaving empty-handed. She felt strongly that following the lead about Priscilla would help her to comprehend her strange gift of visions and understand how the woman Hannah had learned of her gift.

Unsuccessfully, she attempted to ignore the most persuasive reason for her persistence. The day she touched Hannah's arm at the wharf, feelings of an emotional bond so elusive yet compelling drove straight to her heart. The woman occupied her mind and made concentration on any other tasks impossible. The need to learn about Hannah fired an internal determination not to stop until all was revealed.

Tension played on the wrinkles creasing the widow's forehead. With a sigh, the elder woman started to talk. "Phillip Bennett hired Mr. Wynn as his solicitor a year or so before he met and married Mary Hannah. Phillip and Mary were truly in love and the happiest couple I had ever met. Then one day about a year after the girls were born, the family left town for a good while. On returning, Phillip reported that Mary Hannah had drowned, her body lost to the sea."

The Widow Appleton looked away, tears in her eyes. "I don't think he ever stopped loving her. With the three girls, one would expect he'd remarry, but he never did."

"From the records," Alexandra said gently, "I know Phillip Bennett died a year later. Can you tell me how?"

"He'd been a ship captain since his twentieth year. Made a good living, too. But he died at sea like most men in this town. I was a friend with his mother. She died of the smallpox the year he married." Far-off memories reflected in her eyes.

Not wishing to get away from discussion of Priscilla's lineage, Alexandra softly cleared her throat. "After his death, you said your employer worked to find homes for the girls. Why were no records kept?"

The Widow Appleton hesitated. "I know the truth and will tell you. But if I hear it gossiped around town, I will deny having uttered any such words."

"I promise you, this is for my own edification, not that of Salem. Please, go on," Alexandra prodded.

The widow searched Alexandra's face, then seemed willing

to extend trust. "Well, Mr. Wynn was not just Phillip's lawyer; he was also his friend. After Phillip's death, he helped go through the family's personal papers. He discovered a record of divorce in Connecticut."

"A divorce," Alexandra exclaimed, trying to keep the shock from her voice.

"I am afraid that is so. To avoid disgrace on the girls, Phillip and Mary Hannah evidently went to Connecticut and sought the decree. Few divorces were given in those days, and the church had to approve of the reason."

"Please, if I might delve further into the details, why was the divorce granted?"

"The decree stated infidelity"—the widow paused, lowering her voice to a mere whisper—"of Mary Hannah."

Alexandra bit back her surprise that a respectable mother of three young girls was capable of such a disgrace. Slowly she let the truth of the matter sink in. While perusing the census records, she had come across the fact that Massachusetts granted only four divorces in the year seventeen-ninety. She suspected that years ago even fewer were allowed. Connecticut might have been more lenient, but still it was an uncommon occurrence, made especially more difficult with children involved.

"But you said Phillip still loved her," Alexandra said, a little perplexed. "Was there no way to heal the sin?"

"We will never know, but that is why the records were kept closed and vague. Perhaps Mr. Wynn feared Mary Hannah had not perished but was simply banned from her children and Phillip. Personally I couldn't understand it. She had seemed such a wonderful person."

The Widow Appleton glanced down at Alexandra's teacup. In response Alexandra lifted it to her lips and took several sips.

"To ensure the girls went to a good home," the Widow Appleton continued, "Mr. Wynn hid his knowledge of the divorce from the public. I also know that he later went into town records and destroyed all traces of adoption so that if Mary Hannah ever returned she would have no claim to the children."

Alexandra sat stunned. Could Hannah and Mary Hannah be the same person? The two names were relatively similar. Hannah Brickford. Mary Hannah Bennett. But if so, why would Hannah give her Priscilla's name and want her own sordid background revealed? The more she learned, the less anything seemed to make sense.

She tried to keep uncertainty off her face. "Do you remember who took the girls?"

"I do, but this is a most delicate matter. One child lives in town and may not be aware of her adoption. If you desire to reacquaint yourself with her as a relative, please request her parents' permission first."

"I would never dream of revealing such a thing to anyone without consent," Alexandra firmly reassured the widow. "But I would very much like to know where my relatives reside. Surely you understand the importance of family ties. Please, tell me what you know of the girls."

"I only know of Bridget Goodwell, the Reverend Goodwell's daughter. They live here in Salem. Another went to a physician's family. The third went to a couple with no children. Quite financially set, I do believe, but they moved away soon after. I'm sorry, but I can't remember more."

Alexandra mentally repeated the name Bridget Goodwell: the woman Margaret Trask mistook her for and the woman in the wagon with whom she had felt a familiarity. Suspicions grew that Hannah *was* truly Mary Hannah and had somehow sought her out, knowing she might uncover the truth. Had Hannah played on the sympathy of their sharing a common trait—their red hair?

Only one solution presented itself. If indeed Hannah Brickford was Mary Hannah, then she was the one who held the definitive answers. Therefore, she must be found. Alexandra heartily thanked the Widow Appleton and set off for the tailor shop.

* * *

Hours had passed since the visit to the Widow Appleton, and Alexandra, standing outside the apothecary shop, had little but dust tarnishing her shoes to show for the effort. Hannah remained elusive, as did the answers to more questions than Alexandra had ever compiled.

Hanging from her arm, she had a small basket with herbs from the apothecary for Mrs. Bisbey. Alexandra had promised to pick up the rather extensive collection while in town. Poor Mrs. Flamm's boy truly had a long-term ailment, and Mrs. Bisbey planned to boil and take by a concoction this evening.

Alexandra glanced back at the tailor shop, where earlier today she had spoken with the proprietor. He had not seen Hannah for a week, as she had indicated some family plans. Alexandra had inquired of Hannah with several Brickfords in town, and none seemed to know of the elusive woman. Since then Alexandra had scoured the town and at this point had lost all hope of finding Hannah.

Alexandra set off down the block toward home. At least at the Williams mansion there awaited a light supper and long rest. To obtain that rest, she would have to disappoint Joshua, who had requested her company tonight at a reading, the closest thing to theater allowed in the state.

Up ahead, a young lad not more than eight years old watched her every step. He shifted from foot to foot impatiently, then finally trotted in her direction. "Excuse me, miss. Be you Miss Gables?"

Puzzled at the boy's knowledge, she immediately wondered if this was a prelude to another encounter with Hannah or Mrs. Trask.

"Yes, I am Miss Gables. What can I do for you?"

From behind his back, he brought forth a folded note and handed it to her. As she took it from his fingers, he scooted away. "Thank you," she called after him, wondering about his haste.

With a little trepidation and much curiosity, she unfolded the note.

Have arrived home earlier than expected. Some urgent business requires attention, and then my time is yours. Meet me at Ye Neck before supper.

Pierce

Alexandra's heart leaped for joy. Pierce was back in Salem. After no word for two weeks, she had begun to doubt his intentions. Her heart sailed with joy at the thought of Pierce's arms encircling her body. In the privacy of Ye Neck, they might even steal a few kisses. She remembered his last kiss in the stable before he had left for the wharf. Funny, but even then she had also experienced that familiar feeling of being watched.

Since she was practically standing in the middle of town, she could just make the walk to Ye Neck before supper. Eagerly she turned in the opposite direction from home, suppressing the urge to skip down the street.

A thought suddenly halted her progress. Mrs. Bisbey required the medicines now in order to have the preparation ready for later that evening. Quickly Alexandra considered the time required to return home and then take the carriage back to Ye Neck. It would take longer, but not by much. Again changing direction, she picked up her sore feet and hustled home.

Along the way, thoughts of Pierce occupied her mind. He had sent only one letter to Joshua during his absence to New York, and it solely contained business. Although disappointed that nothing had arrived for her, she had understood that they had made no announcement to Joshua of their relationship. What if New York and all its attractions had cooled Pierce's feelings toward her? At least now, his true intentions would become known.

Alexandra clanged the iron gate shut and rushed in the front door of the Williams mansion.

Mrs. Bisbey rounded a corner and almost collided with Alexandra. "Why, Miss Alexandra, I didn't hear ye come in." Mrs. Bisbey studied her face and gave a small frown of concern. "Best I get ye somethin' cool to drink."

"No time, I'm afraid. I have to meet Pierce."

Mrs. Bisbey's eyes widened in surprise. "Mister Pierce? Lord be praised, he's finally returned. I must get his room freshened. When's his ship come in?"

"He is already here. He sent me word via a young boy in town." Alexandra handed over the note, and Mrs. Bisbey opened it to the writing and stared at it, obviously unsure of the words. Her reading lessons were progressing well using printed words, but Mrs. Bisbey had quite a way to go before being able to easily read another's handwriting.

"The note requests I meet him at Ye Neck before supper." Even though in a hurry, Alexandra patiently pointed out the words *Ye Neck* on the note for Mrs. Bisbey. "I'd have gone straightaway, but I had the medicines from the apothecary."

"Oh, thank ye, mum, for comin' home first. I know ye must be excited to see Mister Pierce. We all are."

Mrs. Bisbey relieved Alexandra of the basket and set the note on the hall side table. "I worry 'bout Mrs. Flamm's wee one. Best he get some of me potion down him real soon."

The sun had dropped lower in the sky, and Alexandra realized she must get underway. "Is Mister Williams at home? I cannot attend the reading with him this eve and must apologize."

"Oh, 'tis no problem. He's run an errand, but I'll let him know."

"Are any stable hands still here?"

"Yes, mum, a boy is out there now finishin' his chores. Ye wish me to have him prepare a carriage?"

A renewal of energy swept Alexandra. Her heart cheered at the thought of Pierce's presence and his desire to see her immediately. Alexandra stepped past Mrs. Bisbey, heading for the kitchen door. "No need. I will tell him myself. Save us some supper."

Her feet moved faster than she thought possible to the stable. The stable hand, moving slowly after a long day, eventually brought out the two-seat carriage. "I can drive ye, miss, if ye like."

"I appreciate your offer, but I can handle it quite sufficiently," she said, wanting to be alone with Pierce. She climbed aboard, took the reins, and trotted off down the side lane before he could offer any advice. The streets and their pedestrians seemed aware of her haste, and the way to Ye Neck became clear.

Fourteen

A cart driver dropped Pierce and his luggage off at the Williams mansion and accepted his fare. New York, with its unkempt streets and animals strolling at will, its people of strong purpose and government, and its thriving shipping, offered nowhere near the serenity of the streets of sweet Salem. With a bag under each arm, Pierce strolled to the front door.

Conflicting emotions made him pause. Each day without Alexandra had seemed like forever. The men with whom he had dealt had bordered on dull, and the lack of a daily heated discussion or two during his journey made time creep by slowly. Most grievous of all, though, were the long nights without a warm body entwined in his and a faint hint of rose pleasing his senses. Damnation, he missed her!

He dropped the bags inside the door and called out, "Father! Alexandra! I've returned."

"Oh, my," echoed from the kitchen, followed quickly by a harried Mrs. Bisbey.

"Why, Mister Pierce, aren't ye waitin' for Miss Alexandra at Ye Neck?"

Pierce stared, rather dumbfounded and slightly confused, at his housekeeper. "I've only just arrived in town. Why would I be meeting her there?"

Now Mrs. Bisbey took a turn at appearing confused. "Because ye sent her a message sayin' so, that's why."

"Message? What message?"

"I'll get it for ye, sir." Mrs. Bisbey disappeared into the kitchen and returned waving a paper in her hand. "A young lad handed this to her in town barely an hour ago. She wouldn't have even come home except she had some medicinal things for me."

The handwriting on the note slightly resembled his, but it took only half scrutiny to see it was a forgery. The words struck fear into his heart. Why would anyone with proper intentions assume his identity and lure Alexandra to an isolated place?

"Did my father read this?"

Mrs. Bisbey's cheeks burned into crimson. "No, sir. Miss Alexandra told me what it said. I simply passed that along to Mr. Williams. See, Miss Alexandra been workin' with me on readin'. I wanted him to think I was doin' good."

A thousand thoughts flew through his mind. His father probably would have recognized the false handwriting. "Is my father at home?"

"No, sir; he went next door to talk with Captain Smith. Plans to be back for supper, though."

"That's too late. Run get him and give him this note. Explain what has happened and tell him to get the constable. Alexandra's in danger."

He thrust Mrs. Bisbey the note and raced through the house and out the kitchen door, heading to the stables at a dead run. His black stallion pranced in its stall and sensed his urgency. He bridled and saddled him and mounted in one leap before tearing out of the stable leaving the door wide open.

Alexandra faced into the onshore breeze, her skirt flapping in an uneven rhythm. Birds sailed past, heading for nighttime sanctuary on the many rocky knolls off the coast. Images of her time with Pierce on Mariner's Island returned with great affection. How many more adventures had they yet to share before she returned to Boston? Summer wouldn't last forever. The thought made her increasingly sad.

Dusk had another hour before claiming the countryside to

complete darkness. She had expected Pierce to be waiting and fought off the impatience to feel his embrace. "Be patient," she scolded herself. "You have endured more than two long weeks; surviving another quarter hour will take little effort."

Vegetation, now mostly in shadow, varied from shades of hunter to pale green. Beach pea, with its purple flowers just weeks from blooming, thrived in the sandy soil. Somewhere in her mental catalog she knew the seeds were edible if gathered young.

The land ended at a steep ten-foot slope to the beach that swept into the water. The beach sand had a bluish hue from crushed mussel shells and was mixed with small pebbles and other broken shells. Occasional piles of dark boulders broke the smoothness of the beach line and gave some hint of the offshore hazards facing mariners. From her high perch, the view out over the ocean and the New England coastline was spectacular. Dr. Bentley claimed he walked here every morning for the dramatic unfolding of the new day, and she easily understood why.

She leaned against an odd granite boulder stretching her height and half again. It stood tall and thin and seemed very out of place when compared with the sandy soil below her feet. Similar strange boulders had been common on her travels throughout New England and Canada. Several philosophers had plotted locations where they had discovered these erratic boulders, and someday she hoped for enough data to build a credible scientific explanation for their origin.

The sun dropped even lower to a point where the trees and brush hid it from view. After another circuit of the area, she settled against the great boulder. The breeze brought with it the sudden apprehension of being watched. The feeling resembled the one earlier on the way to the Widow Applegate's home. She recognized the very isolated nature of the surroundings, and that she was quite alone. Her hand flattened against the rock as she turned to check over her shoulder.

Her fingers tingled, and sketchy pictures of an ominous figure sweeping toward the boulder flashed in her head. Frightened, she made a quick scan of the bushy vegetation. The process brought no revelations and served only to increase the tempo of her heart, now thumping loudly. Was the vision of the past or the future? Not wishing to take any chances, she reached up and liberated a hatpin.

In her mind she reviewed Pierce's note with more scrutiny than emotion. He stated no specific time for their meeting but said only "before supper." That hour might vary from person to person depending on the family lifestyle. And would he have chosen such a remote spot with a chance he might be delayed?

Above in the sky, a circling black crow cawed and alighted on the boulder. He folded his wings closed and watched her carefully out of one eye. The fabled sinister implications of such a bird came to mind and only increased her unease. A chill sent uncomfortable tingles through her body, and the high-pitched scrape of windblown juniper branches raised goosebumps on her arms. A sudden rustle of a small creature scurrying through the underbrush sent her spinning around and scared the crow into flight. Maybe this beautiful but isolated point was not the safest place for her to remain alone. Deciding to leave, she stepped away from the boulder.

"Ahoy, there," a voice from the sea called. The salutatory greetings came from a small ketch sweeping past with two men heartily waving at her. In a natural response, she raised her hand to wave back.

Behind her a small stone clicked, as though dislodged by a shoe. Well aware of the vision's warning, she instinctively flattened herself against the boulder and spun her head toward the sound.

In a jarring blur, a massive figure collided with her shoulder. Having partially missed her, the figure clamped onto her arm and clothing, propelling them both down the steep slope. Sand and dirt were tossed into the air, and small rocks bruised her body as they tumbled together.

The man's body gave a sickening shudder as it struck several basket-sized rocks piled at the bottom. Hope of any freedom was dashed, though, as the arms encircling her barely relaxed.

He almost effortlessly rolled to his feet and began dragging her toward the water. Frightened, she dug in her shoes to no avail. Dread spilled through her as she got her first good look at the man. Long scraggly hair, patched clothing, and weatherbeaten skin surrounded a determined and vicious countenance. A face right out of a nightmare.

Recognizing that this man threatened her life, yet fighting a rising fear, Alexandra let him pull her closer. With all her might, she thrust at his midriff. As the hatpin sank into flesh and struck a rib, the sensation left her nauseated.

Startled, the man swore in pain and released his hold. Grabbing the moment of freedom, pure fear drove her back toward the slope, and she began climbing up it at an angle. Her feet dug into the loose berm, and dirty sand lodged under her nails as she clawed at the scant vegetation for stability. Surely the men in the boat must have seen what happened. Maybe they would come to her aid. But why, then, did the attacker risk being seen by the sailors?

Nearing the top, the answer arrived with a sickening jolt. No help would come from them. They were clearly part of this well-planned attack and had served as the distraction. Instead of simply thrusting her to the beach and rocks below, as the attacker must have intended, he had succeeded in sweeping them both down to the beach.

A hand grabbed for her ankle and she shook it loose, panic again welling inside. Fear drove her forward. Before she could climb another step higher, his fingers locked around her other foot. Despair overwhelmed her as with one firm yank, he pulled her back to him.

He tightened his vicelike grip around her arms and waist and lifted her off the ground. Gasping for breath, she let a scream tear from her fear-constricted throat. The unearthly, shrill sound spoke of the true nightmare she suffered. Hot, angry breath issued from the silent figure bent on her destruction. Jerkily over the uneven ground, they headed toward the water again.

"Please, stop this! Put me down!" Her feet thrashed at the man behind her, but the few impacts produced no weakening of his grasp. Water splashed about them before he tossed her into the waves.

Water covered her head before she could obtain a breath. With starved lungs, she shoved to the surface. Gasping for air, she stared straight at her attacker. Anticipation of her demise glistened in his eyes. He grinned at her apparent fear, his missing teeth making a savage smile. This man apparently enjoyed his work.

The confusion and uncontrollable fear disappeared as somewhere in her mind the need to survive came alive. As her heart beat faster than she thought possible, she assessed her position. At best, things appeared dim. Wet petticoats precluded any chance of scrambling away through the shallows or swimming out deeper. Still, if he planned on killing her, he had some work ahead of him.

Without giving her a chance even to ask why he desired her demise, the man lunged forward. Alexandra flung herself sideways and pushed off, hoping to outdistance him. But the layers of her gown offered a perfect hold for her assailant. He tugged her back toward him and she fired fists at whatever part of him she could reach. Not one impact even seemed to make him flinch. His massive hands took hold of her shoulders, and she heard a bizarre laugh as he forced her under the water.

Not willing or wanting to accept defeat, she pushed with all her strength against the seabed, straining for the surface and air. The effort produced no gain against the boulderlike figure above. Pained at allowing such a horrid, lonely death without Pierce, she struggled for what she knew to be the last time. The murky green water grew darker, and she feared the end.

Breath pounded in Pierce's chest as he crested the slope and slid standing down to the beach. The scream he had heard held a tone of fright from someone surely looking at death. Ahead a rough-looking man stood in the shallow waves, his arms struggling to hold someone under water. Pierce felt his heart tear in two. Was he too late?

Rage, intense and consuming, overwhelmed him. In two running steps, he hit the remnants of a dead wave and launched into the air. His shoulder took the brunt of the impact against the man's back as he locked a grip around him. Both crashed with a resounding splash into the water.

The man shoved off the ocean bottom, twisting out of the hold. As both steadied on their feet in thigh-deep water, Pierce heard behind him gasps for breath, followed by coughing. Incredible relief found its way through his rage, but he could not remove his concentration from the ruffian only feet away.

"Run, Alexandra! Get out of here, now!"

The man lunged at him in midsentence. Quickly Pierce angled to the side toward shallower water and let a punch fly, but the man caught his arm, throwing him off balance. As Pierce stumbled in the sluggish water, the attacker's solid mass tackled him to the foot-deep water. They rolled together and came up with the man behind Pierce, locking one arm in a hammerlock and hooking an arm around Pierce's throat.

Pierce threw his head straight back, impacting the back of his skull with the man's face. A grunt accompanied a crunch, and the arm around his neck loosened. He drove an elbow into the man's ribs, ducked, and spun out of the hammerlock, still holding the man's wrist. This time the ruffian stumbled off balance and fell right into the foot Pierce sent flying his direction.

Blood poured from a gash in the man's head and into one eye. He was slowed but not stopped. Pierce spent a second to look for Alexandra. He glanced up the beach past the man and saw no one. With God's luck, she had escaped. As much as he desired to pound this killer into submission, the way his blows had bounced almost harmlessly off the man's body said it was impossible. The best plan now was to put distance between them.

The setting sun gleamed red off the water and into his eyes. Half blinded, he hastily backed up through the water until beach shells and rocks crunched under his boots. He remembered the gully he and Alexandra had taken on their visit, and dashed in that direction. With surprising agility and much to his dismay, the massive, heavier man followed.

Pierce's longer legs and stride set him well ahead and he bounded up the gully. The incensed pursuer scrambled up a steeper portion of the slope and cut off his escape. Trapped, Pierce began to build a new strategy. A good ten feet apart they poised, hands loose but ready, and stared at one another.

"Why are you doing this?" Pierce hissed with heavy breaths.

The man did not answer.

"Who wants to kill Alexandra?"

The man's chest rose and fell from exertion. He shrugged, but never relaxed his guard as he brought his fists in ready for a sporting, although deadly, round. By the size of the man's hearty arms and signs of past damage on his face, he had seen some action and obviously triumphed. Pierce thought about his fencing lessons in England and suddenly saw their inadequacies. Good strategy, of course, but obviously better if one had a weapon.

All he needed was enough distraction to get past this man and then outrun him. Honor might dictate a confrontation, but then there was no honor in this man's attempts to drown Alexandra or kill him. The man backed him toward the edge of the slope.

His attacker shuffled in with a jab to the head before Pierce had time to further consider the situation. Pierce parried the blow and landed a punch to the ribs. The solid mass barely flinched. A fist came again toward his head, and he raised an arm, slightly deflecting the hit from his jaw but taking it partially in the eye.

With the man in close and not wishing to waste another precious moment, Pierce fired a leg upward into his groin and sent the man buckling over. Pierce doubled his fists together and raised his arms to strike a blow to the man's back. From out of nowhere a board swung upward under the man's chin and sent him flying backward down the slope to the rocky beach. Lying against a jagged pile of rocks, the man didn't move.

Dumbfounded, Pierce stared at Alexandra as she released a driftwood board.

"Cricket—a good game really." She tried to make a joke of her reaction, but her voice bordered on breakdown.

"I didn't think women played," he spat out between heavy breaths. He collected her into his arms, fearful that at any moment she might collapse. Holding tight and pressing her head against his chest, he placed kisses onto the wet, red tangle of her head.

"Do you wish to smother me and finish that man's duty?" she gasped.

He held her back at arm's length and looked into the shadow of her face. "My God, woman, I thought he had killed you."

"We Gableses are a tough lot. But your intervention a little sooner would have been appreciated."

Unable to help himself, he kissed salty drips off her face. "Sooner? You are damn fortunate I arrived at all. I wasn't supposed to be back until the morrow. Did you not get my letter?"

"The only thing I received was a note from a young lad."

An eerie concern left a hollow in the pit of his stomach. Someone had intercepted his letter and felt they had to act quickly. But why? All it had contained was a description of his New York visit and the date of his return.

"We must get going. It isn't safe here."

"What about him?" She tipped her head toward the beach.

They moved to the edge of the slope and peered down into the gray shadows of the early eve. Soft moans said he still lived, but the defeated killer showed no movement. By the way his arm and shoulder angled, there was no doubt he was seriously injured. Alexandra stared in horror. Pierce wrapped an arm around her shoulders, comforting her away from the scene.

"There is nothing we can risk doing for him now," he said gravely. "He may have compatriots. We'll contact the ward constable and have him bring a physician. I have a firm suspicion, though, if he regains consciousness before then, he will be gone by the time anyone returns. He strove to kill, not ravish you. That speaks of some sort of conspiracy."

"Someone wants me dead? But why?" She sounded incredulous and yet concerned at the thought. "Surely the Trasks would not go so far simply for the purpose of matchmaking."

Pierce dabbed a sleeve at the blood on his face. "I agree. There is something more sinister here, a much greater stake."

"But what?"

"You tell me." The feel of taut nerves under his hand on her shoulder revealed her apprehension. "Who would benefit from your death?"

"No one. I can't imagine a possible reason for what has happened here. How can I be a threat to anyone?"

"There is no apparent reason I can see, either, but it might have to do with your father." A funny, puzzled look appeared on his face. "Whoever it was knew enough about our relationship to be assured you would run out here to meet me. And they would have used that knowledge to intercept my letter to you, telling the date of my intended return."

"I have told no one. But I do remember something quite odd: the last kiss we shared in the stable before you left. I thought we were being watched."

"Are you sure it was not my father or Mrs. Bisbey?"

"My distinct feeling was of someone relatively unfamiliar."

"I don't like the implication that someone around my home is part of this. We can ponder these things later, though. Now we must move to a safer location."

As they turned away from the scene, he added, "You didn't have to hit him. I almost had him myself."

"You merely made him mad," she answered, with decent composure considering the circumstances.

"I had him bent over and gasping for air."

"And he had an upper hook coming in your direction." Her teeth started to chatter, probably more from the emotional impact than the chill. "I wished to take no further chance with your life or mine."

It did no good to offer his coat, as it, too, left a trail of drips. Instead, Pierce swung her toward him, where he could feel her breath upon his face and encompass her in his hold. "I gave you a chance to escape. You should have taken it."

"And leave the only man I've ever cared about to face a demented killer? Necessity overwhelmed the risk." She kissed him, preventing any retort.

His heart and breath still pounded fiercely in his head, though now he had trouble distinguishing between exertion and complete joyous relief at their survival. The shadows deepened as the last remnants of day faded in the sky.

With the ruffian's compatriots possibly nearby, they cautiously worked back toward the carriage. Instead of taking the trodden path that led from the road to the beach along Ye Neck, they stayed well into the long grass and skirted bushes and brambles. A large silhouette loomed in the shadow of a wind-twisted tree. The grind of molars on grass and the jangle of a bridle identified it as Pierce's stallion. They collected the horse and continued toward where Alexandra had secured the carriage.

Quietly they watched in the now darkened eve, making sure no one else was about. Crickets chirped and katydids chattered in a swell that abruptly ceased as voices and footsteps approached. Someone carried a torch that flickered boldly in the sea breeze.

"Pierce! Alexandra!" Joshua's frantic voice called out in the darkness.

"Father, over here," Pierce called, before drawing Alexandra and his stallion toward the voices.

Joshua worked toward them in the dark, followed by two men, one of them carrying the torch. "Thank heavens you are all right. From what Mrs. Bisbey said, I feared some terrible end had come to you both." As he got close enough to see their soaked attire and Pierce's bloodied face, he stopped in his tracks. "My God, what happened?"

The man that Pierce now recognized as a ward constable held a torch high to fully take in their state. "You're bleedin', man," the constable said as Joshua withdrew a handkerchief from a pocket and dabbed it aside Pierce's eye.

"I'm fortunate that is all. Our assailant was no small fish. I arrived to find him holding Alexandra under the water. I feared I was too late." His arm encircled her waist and held on as though she might yet disappear.

Pierce related all the relevant facts of what had occurred, from his arrival at Ye Neck to the violent encounter. Tenderly touching his face where Joshua held the handkerchief, Pierce took it from him. He withdrew the cloth, amazed at the amount of blood the cut produced.

"Where's this villain now?" the constable asked.

"Injured on the beach." The words slipped solemnly from his lips as the reality of the fight played back in slow motion. "I'd say this is not the first time he has undertaken such a dastardly chore. The man seemed to relish his job and was quite proficient, too."

The second man lit a torch off the constable's and gave it to Joshua before the two men disappeared toward the beach. The night breeze raised bumps on Pierce's damp flesh. He felt Alexandra shivering next to him.

Joshua noticed and removed his coat for her. "Get her home, boy, and into some dry clothes. But before you go, see if you can explain this note." Joshua unfolded the paper and held it out to Pierce. "I can see plainly it isn't your writing. Who would do such a thing?"

Pierce told his father what he knew, which, when they considered all the possibilities, wasn't much. Joshua seemed much disturbed by the knowledge that someone at home may have had a hand. He made a promise to scrutinize the stable hands and other workers. Overall, though, neither Pierce nor Joshua truly had any idea why anyone would plot to kill Alexandra. If she had not stopped by the house, no one would have known about the note. Later, when her body was found, the town would simply have believed it an accidental drowning. The entire premeditated nature left him shaken. Something quite evil was afoot.

Alexandra snuggled close to Pierce as he drove the carriage, as much for warmth as for the feeling of protection. Joshua and the other men had stayed behind to search for the attacker. Even though she and Pierce had defeated this man, his actions had only opened wider a chasm of fear she had never before experienced.

Shadows threatened at every bend the carriage rounded. Mentally she tried to force the thoughts out of her head, but a simple tree moved by the wind became another lurking attacker. Others were still out there somewhere, waiting, wanting her dead. But who and why? What had she done to deserve such attention?

The thud of hooves slowed as the carriage pulled off onto a practically invisible path into a forbidding stand of trees. "Where are we going?" she asked nervously. "We've hardly left Ye Neck."

"My friend David has a cottage up here. It belonged to his mother, but she passed away earlier this year. I oft stay here if I wish some privacy from home."

"Please, I've no desire to face anyone else new tonight."

"No one is there. David went to sea last month."

The carriage settled to a stop in front of a shadowy structure. No lights or movement were visible. Pierce secured the horse to a post and came around to her side of the carriage.

"Won't your father worry when we fail to return home?"

"I told him of our destination." Pierce sounded self-assured and positive, but she didn't quite understand his reasoning.

"And he offered no objections?"

"I explained I thought it best for your safety. From what

you have told me, we need to scrutinize the employees at home. Until the daylight of the morrow, it is probably the wisest course." He helped her step down from the carriage. "I also told him about my feelings toward you."

She was dumbfounded that in the few minutes he had stepped away to talk with Joshua back at Ye Neck, they had covered such a delicate subject. She longed to ask just how he *did* feel about her, but withheld the question. Instead, they walked arm in arm and entered the cottage into a quaint-sized room. In the darkness, she heard the scraping of flint. Eventually a small flame flickered and a candle glowed to life.

"I will be back soon," he said. "I must take care of the horse."

Candlelight swathed the room in a yellow glow. A carved chest with a bold-colored design stood against one wall of the unpretentious room. A table with a bench and two chairs sat in the center, near enough the fireplace so that an evening's work might be accomplished. A simple sideboard with dishes, few matching but all of desirable and pleasant design, leaned against another wall. The fireplace was used for both warmth and cooking.

Two rooms were off the single main room. One apparently had been the widow's and the other her son's. Alexandra found a chest at the end of the widow's bed, filled with linens and quilts. She removed a light quilt and spread it on the bed before returning to the main room. Setting a fire seemed an easy proposition, for the tinderbox was full and a neat pile of wood was positioned near the fireplace. By the time Pierce returned, she had started a fire warm enough to dry some of their clothes.

He set a bucket with water on the floor by the fire and swept his coat over the back of a chair she had positioned near the heat. Without a word, he caught her in his arms and made up for two weeks of undelivered kisses. He placed a final kiss on the end of her nose before leaning away.

"I brought in some water from the cistern. We can use it to clean up a bit."

"I need to tend to that cut," she said, tenderly examining his head. A thick blood-crusted scab had started to form.

The sideboard had several drawers that contained towels for drying dishware. She found a square linen, soaked it in the water, and made him sit in a chair facing the fire. In the flickering light, she dabbed around the scab, removing the blood staining his face and neck. The blood on his clothing would have to wait for a good cleaning.

As she finished wiping away at the dirt and salt on the rest of his face, he gently caught her wrist. He took the linen from her hand and dropped it onto the table without taking his eyes from her face. He pulled her onto his lap.

His lips lightly touched hers again and again while he pulled out what pins remained in her hair. As he kissed her forehead and ears, her breathing intensified with desire.

"I'm stiff with the ungainly sea," she complained halfheartedly, "and my hair is matted wet. How can you desire me as such?"

He nuzzled at her ear and whispered, "You are a siren of the sea whom I cannot resist. I forget all things knowing I will suffer bliss at your hands."

"Then you are doomed, for I am but a simple human."

"If that be the case, then we will drown together." He fingered at the hooks and eyes fastening her dress.

The thought of lemon passed through her mind. "There is no protection available," she whispered into his ear.

"I must hold you, Alexandra." He let his mouth play around her lips, taunting and teasing. "And besides, it does not matter."

The rather careless words made her heart chill. "But it does to me," she answered indignantly. "Has New York made you suddenly callous?"

"No, it made me aware of how miserable I was without you. When I thought you had drowned, my heart died and I was filled with a rage I have never known. I need you, Alexandra." He undid the dress bodice and loosened the tie on her chemise.

She caught at his hands, trying to slow them and make him

listen. "And every night I now lie alone, I think only of you. But that is not enough to justify the risk we take." So desperately she wished to say that the nights had unfolded the truth of her love for him. But she could not blurt out what might be one-sided. "I have a father who is alone, and a home in Boston."

"You have a home with me." He slid the chemise over one shoulder and caressed the exposed skin.

"Only until the summer's end." She clutched his chin in both hands and made him look into her face. "And I live in your house as Joshua's assistant."

He took hold of her wrists and gently lowered her hands. "Only until your father returns. After that I will make plans to build us our own place."

"Our own home? I don't understand."

This time he placed her face between his hands. "As much as I have always declared no need for anyone, I cannot live without you. Love me, Alexandra, for the rest of your life. Be at my side as I will be at yours."

Joyous relief at his admission, but regret that he had professed need but not love, left her unsure how to answer. "In my heart, I know that I have found the man I thought never existed. I also feel a strange passion I know must be love. I love you, Pierce Williams, but I cannot live with a man who does not feel the same."

Pierce chuckled and dropped his hands to her shoulders. "Why do women always want men to profess the obvious? I may rescue a maiden in distress, but I will only build a house for one I love. Yes, I do love you and want you to be my wife."

"And you will accept my love of science, and maybe even a few exotic creatures into the house?"

"Only with certain stipulations."

"And what would those be?" she asked with a bit of curiosity.

"That they do not"—he lightly kissed her lips—"interfere"—he kissed them again—"with our lovemaking." This time he lingered at her mouth, and his hands pressed against her back, holding her against him. The kiss that followed ignited the sensuous emotions left dormant the past two weeks.

He pushed her to a stand while he slowly removed each layer of her clothing, pausing to admire and caress each part revealed. Eventually, all her attire except the chemise dropped into a wet and ungainly pile at her feet. Before he could finish with the last of her clothing, she lifted off his shirt and reached for the buttons on his breeches.

He stood in front of her now and further loosened the chemise at her neck so it fell past her hips. The fire's warmth spread across her naked back. His hands ran along the same skin as he drew her against his chest and into a deep kiss. The feel of his body, hot and inviting against her breasts, made her fingers fight to untie the drawers at his waist. She pushed his clothing past his hips and he tightened her fully against him as he plundered her mouth. In a gasp of haste and need, he pushed away and sat back on the chair.

Water dribbled out of his tall boots as he yanked them with some difficulty off his feet. He slipped his breeches and drawers off along with the stockings and anxiously pulled her onto his lap. Naked, he held her before the fire, its warmth heating her back.

The look of pleasure in his eyes said he admired her very being. His hands gently brushed the rise of her cheeks and the rim of her chin and trailed down her neck to her breasts. As he stroked her breasts, she caught one hand and kissed the tips of his fingers, much as he had once done to her.

He slid to the edge of the chair and wrapped her legs around his waist. With a solid strength, he rose with her from the chair and carried her to the widow's room. Knowing what lay ahead, the pure anticipation set every sense on fire. Tonight she was no longer a novice.

He laid her on the bed and fell in beside her. "I could do this every night of my life," he said, rolling her on top of him.

"Why, you would need two wives for that." She sat up and shook her head, letting hair fall wildly in all directions. Her hands ran up his chest to his shoulders and back to the soft skin of his sides. "One who can get rest and do the household duties, and the other to keep your insatiable appetite appeased."

"Must you have a plan for everything? I believe it wiser to simply wear me out now and you can have the rest of the evening for dreams."

Alexandra laughed, appreciating the freedom of not being overheard by a household of listening ears. "I have no doubt I can send you into a blissful sleep, but it is you who may have trouble subduing me."

"Is that a challenge?" Pierce reached up to pull her head down, but she scooted back and now straddled a most sensitive spot.

Her finger circled his navel, and she could sense his response. As her hips moved ever so slightly to entice him further, she whispered, "It's one I believe you will let me win."

She bent down to his chest, determined to find every spot on his body sensitive to touch, and torture it gently for as long as possible. Her tongue stroked and caressed his body while her very womanhood teased and eventually welcomed him. He let her play and lead in this new discovery of her body until she begged him to bring her to the end of their journey. Together their unabated breaths and gasps continued until they collapsed into each other's arms.

He could not, however, let her win the challenge. Just as she snuggled against him ready to settle down, he reached for her most sensitive spot and taught her how women had a particular ability left wanting in men. The sensation left her arched under his hand and desperately clutching his neck. All her thoughts closed into a fuzzy darkness as a soft scream left her lips. For passion like this, somehow she didn't mind losing.

Fifteen

Pierce awoke to a chill on his backside and slid back under the quilt. With some difficulty, he succeeded in opening one eye and discovered Alexandra leaning up on one elbow, staring at him with an odd smile.

He reached out toward her and froze in a flurry of pain and stiffness.

"If your body feels in any way like your eye appears," she said with what he thought sounded like a touch of sympathy, "I suspect you will be moving quite slowly this morn."

He rolled onto his back, closed his eye, and set a hand on the swollen skin around the injured socket. "At least I'm in better shape than the other fellow. I think." He gave a little laugh, only to feel a sharp pain with the deeper breath. "Lord, I think he bruised my ribs."

Alexandra cuddled against him, drawing the quilt fully up. "If knowledge can help to console the pain, I stuck a hatpin into his ribs."

Pierce wanted to chuckle at the thought but fought the desire. "You are a dangerous woman, Alexandra. And I must admit, braver than most."

He heard a sigh escape her lips. "I am almost afraid to admit I saw the attack moments before it happened. Not taking any chances, I had the hatpin in hand."

"Good Lord, if news of your talent gets out I will be in poor straits. Much of the town will fear your bizarre claims. The more villainous members will want to whisk you off to some hideout, hoping to glean a prosperous prediction of the future."

"You make it all sound quite exciting. Only what will those villains do when I can't deliver upon demand?"

Pierce frowned in mock thought. "Burn you at the stake, leave you in a desert without water, or maybe just sacrifice you to the gods." He tickled her ribs and then, without even having to open an eye, pulled her onto him.

"You move well with your eyes closed," she whispered and nipped at his chest.

"Practice," he shot back and found her mouth with no hesitation.

She allowed one deep kiss before moving to nuzzle his neck and ear. "Are you confessing that women frequent this place? Have I fallen in love with a true rogue?"

"I make no confessions, but swear I do not deserve the title *rogue*. I am a good, honest cad."

"One who tells wee little lies to his housekeeper."

"I am no worse off than my lady houseguest. When Mrs. Bisbey found the lemon juice in my room, I told her I had used it to freshen the water in my basin. Later I overheard you telling Mrs. Flamm you had used the lemons to rub into your elbows, and the juice in your drinking water. If the two ever combine stories . . ."

"Why, Mister Pierce, are you concerned about your honor?"

He opened his eye and looked up at her. "I think a lady deprived of her wardrobe should be careful of how she speaks."

Alexandra suddenly became serious and sat up by his side. "My clothes. I left them in a soaking heap on the hearth."

He rolled to his side with a grunt of pain. "Do not worry. I spread them on the chairs after you fell asleep. I couldn't very well take you home soaked. My father would question my responsibility."

She pulled the quilt up to her chin. "That's a strange worry considering you shared my bed."

He tugged the quilt down again. "Fathers need not know everything."

She batted away his hand. "Have you told him of my visions? Or even the future I see for your ship?"

Pierce reached out and brought her against him. "I have taken care of the ship."

She quickly raised her head and looked at him. "You found the flaw with the rudder?"

"I found it the day before lightning struck the bowsprit."

"How dare you not tell me!" she said, outraged, poking at his arm.

"At the time, I'm afraid I couldn't accept these strange visions. I simply attributed it to your superb observational talents."

"Well, then, exactly what did you discover?"

"That you were correct. The metal was substandard."

She put a decidedly irritated frown on her face and sat up. "Don't subject me to such a pithy answer. Give me the details or I shall steal the covers."

"I don't believe it wise for a woman to threaten her intended one," he answered quite calmly. "But since I succumb easily to your blackmail, I will acquiesce. The truth is, I had another iron fitting as a replacement in case of damage."

"Why didn't you tell me before? I could have examined the piece."

He raised a questioning brow. "Do you think I'm incapable of recognizing flaws?"

"I'm sorry, please go on." She softly bit her lip.

"Once you mentioned the metal, I took it back to the smithy and we put it through several tests. When hammered, the piece proved rather brittle. The smithy admitted to allowing a new apprentice to make the fittings. It appears he did not have an appreciation for the tempering process. The smithy requested I keep it quiet until he contacted another merchant whose vessel he had also supplied."

"And all the fittings were replaced?"

"My ship will not sink, Alexandra, and I will not die. You have seen to that."

"What if we cannot change what I envision, no matter how we try? I don't have enough experience to know the truth. Isn't it possible for you not to go on this voyage?"

He held her hand, palm against palm, his long fingers overtopping her petite hand. "Shipbuilding is my dream and in what I believe. What faith would I display in my own work if I were afraid to sail on the ship I designed?"

Consternation played on her face as, deep in thought, she traced the stitching on the quilt. "I'm afraid I understand all too well your feelings. Should I be in a like position, I would do the same. For me, I know the greatest hardship will be the waiting."

He leaned up on his elbows. "The person left behind frequently suffers the burden. Surely, though, your work keeps you busy. What did you accomplish while I was in New York?"

The way she raised her head and looked at him told of an uneasy answer to his question. Maybe he shouldn't have asked.

"There is much about me you still do not know. I pray when all is revealed, you won't believe me totally demented. I myself do not understand all that has happened here in Salem."

"I will not change my mind about you no matter how absurd the truth."

She let out a deep sigh. "If only my tales were but imagination. I'd best start at the beginning."

"Beginning?" A spot of doubt crept into his voice and she caught it with a swift glare. "I'm sorry," he replied. "Give me time. This is all a bit difficult."

"And you have yet to hear the tale. Have you ever studied Judge Nathaniel Williams's portrait in your study?"

A bit of curiosity and wariness couched his answer. "I've seen it a thousand times."

"But I doubt you have experienced it as I have." Alexandra recalled the strange feelings and sounds, related to the hangings, that she experienced on her first day in Salem, and told him of her research related to Judge Nathaniel Williams. Then with great trepidation, she followed with the story of meeting the mysterious redheaded woman, Hannah, and later her suggestion to delve deeper into the lineage of Priscilla Gardener.

Alexandra's story fascinated Pierce. "Are you saying that Nathaniel knew Priscilla?"

"Perhaps. He was on the court and very likely participated in some portion of the trials before he resigned. He also wrote a scathing editorial about the execution of John Gardener. It seems most likely that they had known each other."

"Yes, as the town was quite small in those years. I can understand his sorrow and anger at the hanging, but what has that to do with us today?"

"Nathaniel requires something from me," she answered, a bit uncomfortable with the odd implications. "I simply don't know what."

Pierce dropped back to the bed and rested his head on an arm. "Portraits of dead people making requests. Alexandra, forgive me, but this sounds so incredible."

"It's more than that. My intuition tells me what he wants is related to you."

"Me?" he exclaimed, a little puzzled.

"You and your family. I've always thought my visions and your family were connected. At first when Mrs. Trask mentioned Nathaniel's tie to the witch trials, I thought it because she wanted me to distrust your family."

He rose again to his elbows. "I dislike the rather dubious implications every time I hear that family's name."

"But now, I believe it is something more. The first time I met Hannah, she gave me an odd warning, one that has haunted my thoughts."

"My God, woman, why have you not told me all this before?"

"Because even I thought it sounded foolish . . . until now. Hannah said to be wary of people who use their unusual talents for evil. That they will not allow the good to prevail, for it can expose corrupt plots. But the oddest part was when she took my arm and with total sincerity said, 'The time is drawing near and you must be wary.' Rather eerie in light of what has happened. I'm in a bit of a haze about the interpretation, though."

"What else do you know about this woman Hannah?"

Alexandra related the time she spent with the town and church records, and with the Widow Appleton. "But what is rather incomprehensible to me is why Hannah would warn me about strange happenings on the one hand and then tell me to research the Gardeners' trial, which led to my discovery of rather shocking facts about her."

"Assuming Hannah is the Mary Hannah you found out about."

"My intuition tells me they are the same."

"Are you sure you are not one of these triplets? You have red hair."

"I considered it but have dismissed the possibility."

"Why so easily? Is it not plausible?"

Alexandra brushed a lock of hair away from his injured eye. "I assume my parents would have told me if I was adopted. My mother died several years ago and was quite a good, honest woman. We never had secrets from each other. I also presume you have never met my father or heard a description?"

Pierce thought back for a moment and then shook his head.

"What little hair he has left is as fiery red as mine." She swung her hair over a shoulder to emphasize the statement. "No, I think Hannah simply required someone to get answers that she knew would not be available to her. The red hair gave credence during my discussion with Mrs. Appleton about my tie to the family. It is likely Hannah knew the similarity would loosen doubts."

She walked two fingers deliberately up his chest and tilted her rather proud but alluring chin. "I think you should find my nonrelation favorable, for the women in the Gardener line were all widowed young. A number of their husbands, including John, who was hanged, died at age twenty-six."

Pierce let a smug smile cross his lips. "Well, then, I guess I wouldn't have fit well into the family anyway. I am already thirty years." He sat up closer to Alexandra, wishing to wipe away the worry now overcoming her face. "Is that too old a man for a woman with mystical powers?"

"Not for a man who has such magical control over my body—and a man who took unfair advantage of me last night."

He wrapped a hand behind her head and drew her within a breath's distance. "You challenged me, and for once you are in a territory which I know and love well. Of course, if you are a poor loser . . ."

"I never lose." She brushed the tip of her tongue against his lips. "I will gain knowledge through experimentation, and a reversal of fortune will soon be mine."

"And when do you plan these experiments?"

"Whenever the conditions are proper." A hand on his chest forced him back down to the bed. "The sun is not yet fully risen," she said, "and I believe, as do you, in an early start to work." Her fingers trailed up the side of his leg and continued to his chest.

"But I am an injured specimen," he replied with a duly grave amount of self-pity. "Will that not make a difference in your data?"

Her body slid onto his, as if the occurrence were quite common. "Not after a large number of trials."

Ignoring the pains and stabs of sore muscles for the pure bliss of heated love, he spent in her arms the minutes until the sun blazed through the framed window.

Fog swirled around Alexandra as she stood in a dreamlike haze, seeing very little but hearing voices and water lapping against the wharf. Cool moisture clung to her face much as when she first arrived in Salem. She even wore the same green traveling clothes and felt the same trepidation. Through movement of the fog she caught a glimpse of Pierce's ship, docked only yards from her location.

A mere three weeks had passed since the attack at Ye Neck. In that time, Pierce's ship, officially christened *Lucinda* for the owner's daughter, had been launched to the excitement of Salem's citizenry and to her great concern. A band had played, and men, including Pierce, rode the ship as it slid down the ways into the water. After it settled into the harbor waters, it had been towed to a wharf for the mast-raising and final touches.

Every day she had walked to the wharf to monitor its progress toward completion. The masts had been raised quickly and the rigging completed with precision. When the sails were finally put in place and the craftsmen coming and going had dribbled to but a few, she knew the maiden voyage was not far off.

Over those same weeks Pierce had been much occupied with the construction, gone before the sun rose and ending his day only after the sun set. The family's merchant duties meant several long night hours in the study at home. The chances to lie in his arms had been too few, and no public announcement had yet been made of their betrothal, for they still awaited the approval of Alexandra's father.

Joshua had been told, and both he and Pierce had written to her father in England, requesting his consent and attempting to ascertain the date of his return to New England. Even though usually a jovial man, Joshua had seemed of late to float on a cloud of contentment, grinning every time Alexandra or Pierce entered a room. Joshua never had appeared at all surprised by their announcement. Some time she must find a quiet moment to learn whether he truly had plotted with her father.

A whisper of breeze brushed at her face, and more of the large black-and-white hull became visible with a slight lifting of the fog. With each passing minute, she could discern more of the neatly gathered sails attached to the yards and see the crew loading cargo and supplies.

Pierce appeared on deck and spoke with a man she knew to be the captain. A mere twenty-one years of age, the captain was the owner's son and had been seasoned during a healthy number of voyages. Still, she would have preferred an older man who had seen many more years at sea and, in all likelihood, weathered a good number of severe tempests.

Pierce towered over the captain by a good head and by stature held a much greater maturity. Hopefully, their combined talents had the ability to weather the storm she knew without a doubt waited for them.

The captain patted Pierce on the shoulder and headed below deck while Pierce leaned over the rail, looking along the wharf. He noted her scrutiny. She watched as he took the gangboard onto the wharf and strode with a serious demeanor toward her. Without a word, he offered his arm and they walked along the wharf.

"For most this day is one of excitement," he said, obviously noting the anxiety she couldn't keep from her face.

"For the sailors, maybe. I seriously doubt the women losing their sons and husbands to the call of the sea feel as such."

"You would not have that concern if it weren't for your vision. But I promise you, all has been corrected. We will come back alive. Besides, the voyage is short. We simply sail the coast with stops in New York and Newport. I will be back in Salem before the *Lucinda* continues on to China."

She stared up at the ship as its breadth was now revealed from under the fog cloak. "I can't help but remember you once told me the most dangerous part of a voyage were the waters near home."

"The captain has sailed this coast a hundred times. We have one of the best navigators, and you, if I understand your recent visits to the ship to fondle every piece of wood, have had no further visions of disaster."

She smiled at his interpretation of her visits. He was correct. She had received no visions about anything, yet she knew that personal feelings often affected her gift.

"We set sail as soon as the fog clears and the breeze fills the sails," he said as the wind wafted loose a curly lock. "I must admit, however, you are not the only one with concerns. While I am gone I implore you, stay away from Hannah. When I return, together we will search out answers to the strange quagmire you have uncovered."

"But . . ." she protested, and he immediately placed fingers to her mouth.

"I accept no protest. Hannah warned of some danger and has been proven right. And we do not know yet if she is involved in this sordid conspiracy. Until we understand what is happening, I worry over your safety."

"I can take care of myself."

"I will count on that very fact."

He stood close before her, and she wanted ever so much to be wrapped in his embrace. Social dictum, and the need for their affections still to remain private, called for no such spectacle here on the wharf. They had made their farewells, though, in private this morning.

"And can I count on you to take every caution, too?" Her voice cracked with tension.

He looked at her with those brown eyes, soft yet intense and penetrating to her very soul. "Trust in your intuition, Alexandra."

The words stung. She wanted so very much to believe all was well. Even Hannah had told her to trust in her talent. Feeling as though her heart were being torn from her very body, she leaned up and kissed his cheek. "Until you return, know that I love you."

She turned away and walked up the wharf to the street, where she found a spot to watch the *Lucinda* depart. Pierce had boarded the ship and gazed solemnly in her direction. Had she and Pierce successfully corrected the cause of the *Lucinda*'s eventual demise? Was she too brazen to believe she could truly change the future's outcome?

Joshua appeared behind Pierce and set a confident hand on

his shoulder. As the two men turned away, she felt fear and a definite lack of confidence in the visions she longed to trust.

"Please come back to me, my love," she murmured under a strained breath.

The American flag, hanging limply off the spanker gaff above Pierce, picked up a breeze and flapped gently. The time neared for sail. Joshua stood next to him, gazing off toward shore and Alexandra.

"You've made a wise choice, Son. She is the finest woman in Salem."

"In all America, I do believe," Pierce agreed. "Watch over her for me. There is something afoot in Salem which none of us understands. We have already seen just how dangerous it is. I believe part of it relates to a woman Alexandra has met named Hannah Brickford. Find her for me. Dr. Bentley has met her and may be able to help. For all I know, this woman may be in danger, too, or she may be the cause of these troubles."

"Why haven't you told me this before?"

"Because I wasn't sure she was involved. But the more I have considered the possibility—and my own lack of success in finding this woman—the more I suspect the connection."

"I'll do my best. I have hired a new man to escort Alexandra around town. Came recommended by Dr. Bentley. I also reviewed the staff in the household and stable, and anyone who I even felt had questionable loyalties, I let go. Honestly, though, I do believe your fight scared the buggers off."

"I can't be sure of anything, Father, but I know you'll do your best. I should be back in a little over a week's time." He hesitated at whether to share the next confidence with his father, then decided he had nothing to lose. "Until then, I ask one more thing of you. Start boarding the windows of the conservatory as soon as possible. There is a terrible nor'easter on the horizon. It will hit sometime later this week."

Joshua let out a surprised laugh. "By what prophetic power have you discerned such a thing? No ships have yet reported any such storm headed our way."

"I ask you to trust me on this one. I am completely serious. When the storm arrives you will experience the same amazement as I did when the bowsprit was hit by lightning."

"Make sense, Son. What is all this babble about?"

He stared confidently at his father. "I knew before the lightning struck where it would hit. Not when, but where. Someone told me as much—someone we both highly trust. This time I know that a severe storm will strike the New England coast some time this week. Please, just allow me this one appeal. If I am wrong, you are free to ridicule my foolishness for the next year."

A look of doubt fluttered across Joshua's features. "As odd as your request may be, I will do as you ask. However, you must promise me on your return to further explain what this is about."

"I shall endeavor to try and I appreciate your faith in me. I doubt many fathers would be willing to follow such unique direction."

"Unique it may be, but one thing I can't help is to trust in the son I have raised. I know you will not make a fool of me."

"Thank you, Father." The two men hugged briefly with a pat for each other on the back.

"This ship is a beauty, Son. You should be mighty proud."

"I'll be proud when I see how she sails. It's best you get to shore now or you'll be along for the ride."

"No time to play at sea," Joshua answered, headed for the gangboard. "Got to see to that parcel of land you want."

Pierce followed a few steps behind. "Do you think she will like it?"

"There's only one way to find out."

"Don't tell her. That's my surprise."

Joshua chuckled. "Oh, I wouldn't dream of such a thing. I

stay out of your personal business, remember?" He winked at his son and departed the ship.

Pierce crossed his arms, watching him go. The breeze freshened and blew across the *Lucinda* just as the fog mysteriously dissipated into a clear, cool sky. Crewmen drew in the gangboard and loosened the mooring ties.

"Hands lay aloft to set tops'ls," the mate shouted.

Pierce watched the shore as the sails filled and the ship eased into the harbor. Slowly they inched away from land as Alexandra, brave and solemn, watched and waved. He didn't relish a storm at sea, but he had confidence that his design and his foreknowledge could save the *Lucinda*. He only hoped that when the storm hit, Alexandra could weather the gale of doubts at home.

Someone pounded on the kitchen door as Joshua and Alexandra sat down for their third supper without Pierce. From the dining room they heard Mrs. Bisbey open the kitchen door and a young male voice exclaim, "The ship is in. The ship is in."

Both she and Joshua leaped to their feet and nearly ran to the kitchen. "What ship, young man?" Joshua demanded.

"Why, *Salem's Pride*, sir."

"Is that not the ship Pierce had a sizable investment in?" Alexandra asked Joshua.

"The one and only. Thank you, Son." He handed the boy a few pennies.

As Mrs. Bisbey shut the door, Joshua excitedly headed Alexandra back to the supper table. "Let's finish supper and then I must head to the wharf. Customs won't allow the ship to be unloaded till the morrow, when they can weigh and record all the goods, but I want to find out from the captain how well the trip fared."

Alexandra lightly grasped Joshua's arm. "Take me with you, I beg of you. I cannot bear to wait for the news here alone."

He vehemently shook his head. "The wharves are not a place for young women at night."

"It is yet a good hour or more before dark. I will stay in the carriage if need be."

She watched as Joshua weighed the considerations of taking her along. "As much as I should know better than to allow you to persuade me, I suppose as Pierce's intended you deserve some insight into your financial situation."

"Thank you. I promise not to be a burden." Lightly she planted a kiss on his cheek and watched as a hint of red blushed his face.

They dined in much too hasty a fashion to properly aid digestion before taking the carriage to Turner's Wharf, off which *Salem's Pride* lay at anchor. Groups of men stood and talked, some in gentlemen's attire and others obviously crewmen and their relatives. Joshua left the carriage and spoke with the gentlemen. Alexandra watched as several patted Joshua's back and shook his hand. All in all, the gentlemen's actions spoke of a positive outcome to the voyage.

Joshua returned to her with a grin seemingly stuck to his face. "By all accounts the voyage brought a greater return than expected. The captain opted not to fill his cargo completely with pepper and made another stop on the way home to take on coffee. The price of coffee actually has gone up and will bring in much more than pepper. Oh, a wise captain is a gem, quite a gem."

Joshua took the reins and set the carriage in motion.

"Where are we going?" she asked, noting that he seemed to have a destination in mind.

"Captain John's Tavern. *Salem's Pride*'s captain and Mister Chadwick, the owner, are meeting there now to go over the inventory. It may be a bit of a wait, but that tavern is acceptable for you to enter if you'd feel comfortable. However, after a ship comes into port with favorable news, it can get a bit rowdy."

"If it's all right with you, I would prefer to wait in the

carriage. The air is cool and quite delightful. The few clouds on the horizon should also make for a fantastic sunset."

They pulled up to the front of the tavern, and Joshua left the reins with Alexandra in case she cared to move the carriage. She hardly noticed the minutes passing as she watched the town slowly close down for the evening and the sun began to cast its final rays.

Sailors, dock workers, travelers, and merchants strolled by, heading home for food and relaxation. One rather grizzled worker in particular drew her attention. His jacket was draped oddly over his shoulder, as though there was something underneath. His arm, though covered in a dark shirt, appeared tucked up to his chest. A flat cap pulled low over his face made seeing any features difficult from her position, but she persisted in studying the man.

Eventually, as he stepped around someone moving in the opposite direction, his profile turned toward her. Alexandra gasped. Displayed was that cruel face she well remembered as the attacker who shoved her under the water. The man had disappeared at Ye Neck before the constable had arrived, probably whisked away by the men she saw in the boat. And now he must be hiding his injuries under that loose clothing.

She longed to follow and see where he was going, but the sheer terror of being anywhere near the man, along with common sense pointing out that he wanted her dead, made the decision to get Joshua first an easy one. Before she could even climb out of the carriage, though, the tavern door opened and Joshua stepped out.

"Hurry," she hissed as loud as she dared, not wanting her voice to carry down the street.

Joshua looked puzzled but complied as hastily as his body would allow. Alexandra set the carriage in motion before his backside even hit the leather seat.

"What's the problem?" Joshua clutched the hat on his head and took a firm hold of the carriage. "I didn't think I'd left you waiting that long."

"The man who attacked me. I just saw him. He's up ahead."

"By God, we should get the constable."

"I'm afraid we will lose him. He didn't see me, and I'd like to find out where he is going."

Joshua put a hand on her arm. "Isn't this a bit risky? What if he sees you? He might well decide to finish the job he started at Ye Neck."

Alexandra shook her head. "That's why I waited for you. Besides, his injuries are extensive. An arm appears in a sling, and he is unable to properly fit a jacket over his shoulders. Most likely he has a broken or dislocated shoulder or collarbone."

"If that hostile monster is up and moving about, I'd say he is dangerous enough." An anger she had never heard before tinged his voice. "Use caution, my dear, but I agree, let's find out where he is hiding and we can send men to get him later. This town doesn't need the likes of him."

Alexandra spurred the horse to a faster pace until Joshua pointed ahead. "Is that your assailant?"

"That's him." She slowed the carriage and kept well back. He paralleled the wharf one street over from the water, where many small homes lined the quickly darkening and narrow lanes. Eventually he turned toward the harbor down a lane where a carriage most certainly would be noticed.

"Stop the carriage," Joshua ordered softly. She did as he asked and he climbed out.

"Be careful," she whispered, "he may have friends."

Joshua looked back up at her. "I'm no hero, my dear. I don't plan on getting too close."

He left and she was alone in the carriage. The gray of dusk was now turning everything to shadows. She worried about Joshua, but under that jolly exterior of his she suspected he had a tough inner core much like his son's. She took the carriage to a place where lanes met and she could turn around.

Carefully she again approached the lane where Joshua had disappeared. A man walking with a quick gait came out of the lane and proceeded in the opposite direction. He wore what appeared to be gentleman's clothing with a hat and waistcoat, but neither his face nor features were recognizable in the dark. She wondered about Joshua and minutes passed as she worried and waited, seeing only silhouettes of a few people as they passed up the lane.

Unexpectedly, Joshua appeared from behind her and climbed into the carriage. "I do not like the implications of what I have seen."

"Tell me, what has happened?"

"We must leave. Let me take the reins, for I have to get us to the constable's house." He did not answer her question right away and seemed preoccupied for several minutes.

"Did you see a well-dressed gentleman leave the lane while I was gone?" he eventually asked.

"Yes, I did, but I was unable to recognize him."

"I'm afraid I had the same problem. The gentleman met with your friend down the lane there, and they had a hushed but heated argument. Unfortunately they departed in opposite directions. I followed the blackguard who attacked you to the Eight Bells Tavern by the wharf. It's a boozing place I'd not feel comfortable entering without a few sturdy friends."

"What do you suppose the conversation was about?"

Joshua boiled with anger. "I heard the words 'job' and 'done poorly' and suspect they were discussing what happened with you. Before the gentleman left, he seethed, 'Get it right this time.' "

"And you did not recognize the man?"

Joshua shook his head in obvious frustration. "The light was too poor and he kept his back to me. But by God, if he had anything to do with the attack, I'll find him out. To think one of the better families of Salem would champion such a dastardly act."

"Maybe if we can catch my *friend*, he will tell us who the gentleman was." Alexandra attempted to sound hopeful, but she knew the hardened man she saw on the beach was not the type to divulge his sponsor's name.

Joshua brought the carriage to a halt in front of a small cottage. "I will tell the constable what we saw, but don't expect any swift resolution. By the time he can round up help to check the tavern, our man will be long gone."

"I want this man caught."

"As do I," Joshua soundly agreed. "It would be a pleasure to have him locked in the gaol under the watchful eye of a keeper when Pierce returns. Tonight, though, there will be no more excitement for you. As soon as I pass along what we saw, I am taking you home. Night has fallen, and with these conspirators afoot, the streets are a much too dangerous place for you."

She opened her mouth to argue, then promptly shut it. The tone in Joshua's voice indicated no persuasion would change his mind, and she, too, had to agree with his assessment. "Reluctantly I must agree, but all is not lost if they don't apprehend him. We at least now realize I have a potent enemy in one of Salem's families."

A solemn frown appeared on Joshua's shadowy face. "And that in particular worries me."

"At least now we know more about them than they imagine. That may be useful to us." She set a reassuring hand on his arm. "All is not lost. This day held one satisfying event with the return of *Salem's Pride*. I assume the news the captain shared of the cargo was positive?"

Joshua seemed to stiffen in pride. "The ample return on Pierce's investment will be enough to satisfy many of his dreams."

"And if I may be so bold as to ask, what dreams are those?"

Joshua let slip a short laugh. "Oh no, my dear. I have sworn a new oath to stay out of my son's affairs. I'm sure you understand. But don't worry. He will share them with you when the time is right."

Alexandra allowed herself a smile even though, with each mention of Pierce, a longing and a bit of worry came to mind.

She offered a silent prayer that he might live long enough to enjoy some of the spoils he so greatly deserved.

Filtered sunlight brightened the wooded pathway that sloped downward past red maples, beeches, and alders as Joshua and Alexandra strolled nearer a pond.

"Do you believe our attacker will ever be found?" Alexandra asked.

Joshua was disappointed that this delightful outing had not sufficiently distracted her from the unpleasantries back in Salem. "I, too, am discouraged the man has eluded our grasp, but I don't plan on allowing him to operate freely in Salem. It may require a little determination and patience, but don't worry, my dear, we will catch him."

The path opened into a clearing, and Joshua heard Alexandra gasp at the spectacular scene. Two blue herons waded in the shallows of a dark pond. One turned its head ever so slightly to observe the newcomers.

Low bushes of variegated greens with sedges and rushes edged the water and were reflected in its glassy mirror. Joshua and Alexandra walked through the tall grasses, pausing to observe white water lilies floating delicately on the water as small pond fishes skirted underneath their broad leaves.

"This is so beautiful," Alexandra exclaimed. "Why have you waited so long to bring me here?"

"I knew you would like this place," Joshua answered, pleased with her delight. "The woods near the road are relatively unspoiled by man, and these lower back acres provide an endless array of specimens. Almost every time I come, I find something new to delight me."

He experienced great joy watching her face and taking her mind off the wait for Pierce's return. Six days had passed since Pierce set sail, and on each morning she arose and immediately walked in the gardens, checking the weather. Pierce must have shared with her the same revelation about the storm, for she offered no questions and only assistance as Joshua boarded the glass of the conservatory. Quite absently he checked the sky above and wondered if Pierce's prediction would yet come true.

"We shall come here more often if you desire. Pierce knows it well. He used to hunt this land in his youth. Now, though, he simply comes here for more serene purposes."

"I can understand why. It's absolutely captivating. Did you see the deer back in the forest?"

"Right after the garter snakes, I do believe. I must say you are one of the first women I have ever met who has handled a snake."

"I can guarantee you, I am most discerning. The poisonous ones I leave well enough alone."

Joshua laughed and, with some reluctance to leave the enchanting spot, headed them back up a poorly developed trail. The path led back through hemlocks and pines and a ground cover of partridgeberry. Near the road, the woods opened into a small clearing.

Alexandra had no knowledge that Pierce owned this piece of land and that the plans for a home to be built on this very spot were already being drawn—by his son, of course. And why not? Joshua thought, for shipwrights excelled at design. Already Pierce had ample practice, for he was the architect of Joshua's own mansion and sought out only the best craftsmen.

Joshua loaded Alexandra into the carriage and took one last look over his shoulder at the property. His heart leaped with joy at the future prospects of his family. Yes, most assuredly Alexandra's father and he had done the right thing.

A steady wind with occasional strong gusts followed their ride home. With Pierce's words of warning on his mind, he studied the horizon in all directions. No sign of an impending storm, yet something about the wind and its direction made him uncomfortable. Tonight before retiring, it might be wise to secure everything around the yard.

He spurred the horse faster, thinking himself a bit touched in the head, but then lately stranger things had happened.

Sixteen

Although the men aboard the *Lucinda* had chosen a life at sea, most couldn't swim. In this gale, Pierce thought, it mattered little. To be swept overboard by one of these wicked green waves meant certain death.

The day had started well enough, and his hope to be in Salem by midnight had been high. Since the sailing had gone nearly perfect and they approached their destination, he presumed the foretold tempest had been negated when Alexandra discovered the rudder flaw. But by the second dogwatch after the ship's light evening meal at six, the waves had started to arrive in larger and larger swells. It appeared that maybe his presumption had been in error.

The captain easily took notice of the impending storm. Pierce, however, believed it necessary to politely voice his knowledge that this storm was earmarked to become a major gale. Though young, the captain was no fool and trusted in Pierce's more mature sea sense. By the end of their talk, the winds had risen and mean clouds roiled toward them. The captain wisely ordered them into deeper water, well away from land.

"Mr. Franklin," the captain addressed the first mate, "this promises to be a bad one. Order the men to rig lifelines."

Companionway covers and the hold hatch were battened down, and the ten passengers they carried on board were directed to stay in their berths. Finally, before the winds became too dangerous for the men aloft, the captain called for all sails secured and the storm staysail set.

"Strike the topmasts and stow the stuns'l," Mr. Franklin yelled, setting the crew into action.

Barely three hours had passed since the first warning signs of the storm, and now at two bells into the first watch, the tempest beset them.

A strange purple darkness lit by lightning-torn clouds brought biting rain. A violent wind blew the neatly coiled rope ends on the deck into wild whips that dared anyone to approach. One by one the crew secured them as giant combers crested and crashed over the deck.

Stripped to a shirt and trousers and covered by an oiler, Pierce tied the end of a fifteen-foot marline around his waist. He would attach the other end of this light rope to something secure or to the lifelines stretched across the deck, giving him a safety tether and movement of more than ten feet.

Mr. Franklin appeared at Pierce's side with two long lever arms for the ship's pump. "We need every man's help," the mate yelled over the howling wind as he secured a marline to his waist.

Pierce nodded and took one of the levers. They waited as another wave slammed into the weather bow and threw the *Lucinda* off into a trough. As she rolled precariously, Pierce held onto the nearest lifeline.

The boat righted itself and he and Mr. Franklin made a dash for the mainmast, near where the pump was located. They rapidly inserted their long levers on each side, secured their marlines to a lifeline, and began to pump. Soon they were each joined by another seaman, and the water leaking below deck came spurting out before steadily flowing onto the deck and out the scuppers back to the sea.

A wave crashed over them, sweeping the seaman next to Pierce into one of the scuppers. Slowly, against the wind and avoiding fish now stranded across the deck, the seaman returned.

"Tie yourself down," Pierce yelled at him, and the man shook his head.

"Them marlines slow me down, sir. The lifelines be enough," he shouted back.

As lightning flashed, the helmsman stood eerily silhouetted, and Pierce could see him fighting with the wheel. The captain joined the helmsman and tied a marline around him. The two struggled to keep the ship on a safe heading.

Pierce's muscles screamed for relief with each push of the pump lever. Persistent waves regularly battered his aching back. As the ship again rolled steeply under an angry swell such that the coppered keel must be exposed, Pierce feared Alexandra's prediction would yet come true. He finally understood the horror she must have witnessed in her vision. He had faith, though, that the rudder was fixed, and clearly he had no intention of being swept into the violent sea.

The air suddenly sizzled, and a deafening crack split the air. Pierce knew lightning had struck the mizzenmast behind them. He glanced over to the wheel and saw neither the captain nor the helmsman.

He released the pump lever and dashed toward the wheel. Halfway there, he came up short as his safety line went taut. The unsecured seaman who had been at the pump with him rushed past. Frustrated, Pierce untied the rope at his waist. He finally made it to the wheel as the ship rolled under the next wave, forcing him to cling to the binnacle housing the compass. As the ship righted, he saw the seaman had secured the wheel. The captain was lying against a rail, and Pierce rushed to his side. The young man's eyes fluttered open; he appeared dazed but alive.

"Lightning," Pierce yelled at the captain and then searched for the helmsman.

A rope stretched taught from the wheel drum to the rail. Pierce held onto it and followed it to the rail. As he looked over, a frightened face stared up at him.

"Oh, God, help me!" the helmsman screamed. A wave

doused him and left him battered against the hull. He had only a short time to live if not pulled to safety.

Mr. Franklin appeared at Pierce's side, and they began to haul in the rope hand over hand. The helmsman, barely conscious now, could only cover his face against the waves' battery and pray. They drew the man to safety over what seemed an eternity as the storm fought against them.

Exhausted, Pierce and Mr. Franklin secured the man against the rail, then slumped to the deck, breathing heavily.

"Here, sir," Mr. Franklin said, handing his marline to Pierce. "I'll get another." Mr. Franklin clambered to his feet and staggered off across the tossing deck.

Pierce tied on the rope and headed back to the captain. He found him sitting up and holding his arm. By the look of it, Pierce assumed it was broken.

"Get me over to the wheel," the captain shouted at Pierce. They struggled to stand, and Pierce half dragged the captain. Pierce propped up and secured the captain against the binnacle, where he could give orders to the seaman now controlling the helm.

Pierce then headed back to the pump, where only one seaman now manned the device. They had to keep water out of the ship or its added weight would affect the handling.

Just as he reached the pump, a forceful gust rammed him against the mainmast. Momentarily dazed, he grasped onto some rigging near the mast. As his wits returned, he worked the free end of his marline around the mast and started to make the first loop of a knot.

"Look out," the seaman behind him yelled, and he felt the man's arms tighten about his waist as a wave taller than the ship crested above him.

It broke and slammed upon the deck with the tonnage of a stack of lumber. The water shoved them across the deck, and he watched the rail rush up. The seaman's safety rope caught and jerked them to a stop, but the water boiling on the deck grabbed at him like the fingers of death. He slid out of the seaman's grasp, and the rushing water again carried him toward the rail. As he frantically grabbed for any secure object in his path, he had a startling vision of Alexandra reaching out for him.

His hands caught the broad rail and he held on, fearing for his life. The cruel water tugged tirelessly on his body. One by one, his fingers lost their secure grip. In seconds, he would be swept to sea.

"I love you, Alexandra," he whispered as the water broke over him again.

At first Alexandra wasn't sure what had awakened her: whether it was the banging of a shutter or the strange howling of the wind. But it all too quickly became apparent that the storm of her nightmares had arrived. Her heart pounded as the vision of Pierce's ship once again played in her head.

Footsteps ran down the hallway, and muffled voices carried from the floor below. Without waiting for an invitation, Alexandra drew a blouse over her chemise and tightened a work skirt around her waist. Not pausing to put on shoes, she rushed into the hall and ran straight into Mrs. Bisbey.

Mrs. Bisbey deftly swung the single candle she carried out of Alexandra's way. "Quickly, Miss Alexandra, come help me. A terrible storm has beset us. We must secure the upstairs shutters."

Mrs. Bisbey led the way, and they started in Pierce's room. She opened the window to face a biting wind and sheeting rain. An eerie blackness enveloped them as the candle blew out, but the two determined women refused to pause. Alexandra held on to the housekeeper as she released the shutters on each side of the windows and swung them closed against the window frame. They latched the shutters in place and securely closed the window.

Mrs. Bisbey knew the house like the back of her hand and led the way to the next window. For each room on the second floor and then the third, they repeated the same drill.

Once done, they headed downstairs as a drenched Joshua literally blew in through the front door. He had completed closing all the large shutters on the first floor and had checked outside for anything left unsecured. He locked the door behind him and faced them.

"This is going to be a bad one. The gusts have already taken out a tree in the side yard." His words came out in breathless spurts as he swung off an oilskin coverall.

"The worst one in ten years," Alexandra whispered, trying not to think of the implications.

Mrs. Bisbey had headed to the kitchen and reappeared with another lit candle. "Well, we can't stand in the front hall drippin' on me floors. I'll stoke up the fire in the kitchen and we can at least get dry."

"A fine idea, Mrs. Bisbey." Joshua shook out his arms as though trying to shed water. "I could use some warm cider, too."

Mrs. Bisbey raised a brow, then added a scant smile. "A little warm brew might be good for us all."

They retreated to the kitchen, and once the fire roared warmly, they held their hands out to the flames and tried to ignore the raging storm. Mrs. Bisbey put on a pot of cider, adding cloves and cinnamon. Once the mugs were filled and handed out, they carefully sipped the steaming brew.

"Mercy me," Mrs. Bisbey gasped at one point, "listen to that moaning."

The wind whipping across the chimney produced an eerie sound. As the house creaked, Alexandra couldn't help but recall the creaking of ship's wood in her vision. Her insides knotted, and any desire to finish the cider waned. She set the mug aside and simply stared at the shifting colors of the flames. Joshua reached out and stopped her from wringing her hands. She wasn't even aware of the action.

"You look tired, my dear. Maybe it's time to retire and do our best to get some rest. There is no saying when this storm will end, but I can speak with certainty, much effort will be required to clean up its destruction."

Mrs. Bisbey pulled two chairs near the fire. "Methinks the best place is right here. If ye don't mind, I'll keep the fire company." She plopped into one and put her feet up on the second.

"Good night, then," Joshua said as he collected a candle. He took Alexandra by the elbow and headed her back upstairs. "Try to get some rest. We've survived many a storm here before, and we'll do it again."

"It's not us I'm worried about. A ship has so little protection from nature's wrath."

"Alexandra, the best place for a ship is at sea during a gale," he said gently.

"Yet a good many have been lost."

"But we both know Pierce was somehow aware of an impending storm. That knowledge will serve him well."

They stopped before her open door. "He told you about the storm?" Her stomach tightened, concerned that Pierce had revealed her unusual talent to Joshua. She tried to read the truth in Joshua's gentle but strained eyes.

He gave a half smile. "Yes, but he didn't reveal how he knew. I dishonestly told you it was predicted by the almanac, so when we boarded up the conservatory you would not think me a complete fool."

She suddenly felt a little guilty for not revealing the truth, but she believed Pierce best knew how to handle his father.

"Good night, then," she said stepping into her chamber and preparing to close the door.

"Pierce did say, though, the knowledge came from someone he and I both trust." Joshua gazed at her with an approving smile. "And considering the gale outside, I'd say his faith was rather well placed. Good night, my dear." He leaned in and gave her a peck on the cheek. "All will be well. You shall see."

As Joshua went to his room, Alexandra slowly closed her door and leaned against it. Joshua seemed to know that she had told Pierce about the storm. Fortunately, he seemed not terribly bothered by the strange implications it presented. She found that an odd reassurance on this night of doubts and fears.

The sudden quiet in the house only accentuated the fierce battle that raged outside. Rain pelted the shutters and walls, and an occasional strong gust shook the house. Rest was an impossible consideration.

The picture of Pierce's ship capsizing played over and over, no matter how she tried to rid her mind of it. Could God be so cruel as to find her a love only to snatch him away and allow her to envision the horror? The thought of her visions brought Hannah to mind, followed by the details of the research on Priscilla Gardener and the haunting, cruel life she lived. Even all of Priscilla's descendants had seemingly suffered the loss of their young husbands.

Not willing to let her mind wallow any further in self-pity, Alexandra decided to take action. Surely something could give her an insight into the outcome of Pierce's plight. Barefoot and quiet, she slipped down the hallway to his room and closed the door. Even in the darkness, she knew the placement of every piece of furniture.

She searched first for a brush or other personal item, but as her hands spread across an uncluttered washstand she realized he had taken those with him. Mrs. Bisbey had changed the linens on the day of his departure, so even they had nothing to offer to stimulate her mind.

The walnut tallboy on the wall next to the window held a good portion of his clothes. Even though he soon would be her husband, the very act of pulling out one of the smaller drawers seemed rather invasive. "Forgive me, love, but I must find something that will bring me closer to you."

With one hand, she felt inside the drawer and encountered a cold metal object recognized under her touch as a ring. Only on prominent occasions such as parties had Pierce worn jewelry of any kind. The first night they had made love, he still had it on his finger. Guiltily she removed it from the drawer and stretched out upon his bed.

As the wind howled, she swept up his quilt around her and slid the ring onto her middle finger. It hung loosely and could nearly have fit over two of her fingers. In the darkness, she felt the engravings and the smooth cut stone, trying to remember the color and design. The shiny red of a garnet was all that came to mind.

The more she concentrated on the ring, the more her thoughts whisked her back to the first party here at the mansion, when Pierce took her arm and she envisioned his kiss. How she had longed for the time when the warmth of his mouth would finally touch hers. She lay her head on a pillow and curled her knees in close, tucking the quilt tightly under her chin.

She recalled the proud look Pierce showed on the ship's tour, the adorable words he imparted under the influence of the tainted tea, and the first real heartfelt kiss he imparted. Her heart saddened as she relived his ship's sailing out of Salem Harbor. She desperately wanted some reassurance that the *Lucinda* would come home safely.

Eventually, her eyes closed as she dreamed of their nights of love. A clear picture came of them standing together, dressed in finery and in a deep embrace. Three men—Joshua, a young stranger, and her father—took Pierce by the arms and pulled him away. He struggled, but they persisted and he could but gaze sadly back into her eyes as they drew him further away.

"Stop," she screamed out and tried to follow, but someone she couldn't see held on to her waist, keeping her from following her love.

"It has to be this way," a woman whispered into her ear.

"No," Alexandra shouted, struggling fiercely. As Pierce disappeared from sight, she turned in her dream to see the mysterious Hannah holding her waist.

Alexandra's eyes abruptly popped open. She sat up breathing hard, her heart racing. Her clothing clung with perspiration to her skin.

Wind still pounded the house, and the rain came in gusty

sprays. Had the dream been a vision or just a subconscious fear? If it was a vision, did it mean she would lose Pierce? And why were those men taking him away against his will? Did they represent a wave carrying her love overboard?

"Please," she prayed, folding her hands, "protect him." The ring burned on her finger, but she refused to remove it. Twisting it around and around, she wished with all her heart for his safe return. Tears trailed from the corners of her eyes past her temples and to the pillow cradling her head.

Slowly her eyes closed again, and this time a dark and dreamless sleep brought rest to her body, if not to her mind.

The pounding on a door came loud and insistent, waking Alexandra from a deep sleep. "Alexandra, wake up. Wake up, girl," she heard Joshua speaking loudly. It took her a moment to realize the door he was speaking through was down the hall.

Light peaked through the shutter cracks into the room, and she realized it must be well into the day. Outside, the storm no longer raged. No wind screamed past the window, or rain pelted the house. Quickly she leaped off of Pierce's bed and stuck her head out his door.

"Good morning, Mister Williams. I see the storm has ceased."

Startled, he looked in her direction but offered no questions as to why she was in Pierce's chamber. "Good news, my dear. Pierce's ship has been sighted. He's headed into port as we speak."

"The ship is still in one piece?"

Joshua chuckled. " 'Tis difficult to sail any other way."

An incredible sense of joy and relief breathed fresh life into her body. "Thank you, Lord," she mumbled under her breath.

"I'm headed down to Derby Street now to wait," Joshua said, obviously anxious to get underway. "I'll take the family carriage to bring back his luggage. As soon as you are ready, come in the other. Take your time. After a storm of this magnitude, changes occur in the harbor and shallows. I guarantee the captain will be wary and will come in slow while taking continual soundings." He turned away and hustled downstairs.

Alexandra danced down the hall to her room. Even as excited as she felt, though, a mirror showed salty streaks down her face and rather red and swollen eyes. A good washing would help, plus a smile to celebrate that her love had come home.

As she raised a hand to sling her hair behind her shoulders, the ring gleamed on her finger. Footsteps sounded down the hall. She slipped the ring off and tucked it into a drawer on the washstand.

Mrs. Bisbey knocked and waltzed in moments later, humming loudly and carrying fresh water. "Good morn to ye, mum. This'll help ye to freshen up. We must look our best for Mister Pierce."

"After a night like the last, I don't believe *best* is possible. However, I will try to appear as appropriately attired as a lady should."

Mrs. Bisbey chuckled as she changed out the old water for fresh. "And a fine lady ye make. One methinks Mister Pierce is quite proud of."

Alexandra stroked a brush through her hair. The excitement of Pierce's return made it impossible for her to deny Mrs. Bisbey's comment. All she could concentrate on was getting to the wharf and holding on to Pierce for dear life. "With Pierce's ship on the horizon ready to make a triumphant return, I think we can be proud of him, too."

Mrs. Bisbey simply winked at her and hummed cheerfully as she threw open the wardrobe and thumbed through Alexandra's dresses. Finally, she pulled one out. "Methinks powder blue is perfect for today. Makes ye look real comely. I'll help ye fix up that tangle of red hair, too."

Never before had Alexandra looked on a day with such expectation and excitement. The two women brushed and primped and powdered. And finally, before dressing in blue, she dabbed rose water at various appropriate places on her body. As they hastily swept downstairs, Mrs. Bisbey told Alexandra the carriage was out front, and that under Mr. Williams's orders one of the stable hands would drive.

Before Alexandra left, Mrs. Bisbey stopped her in the front hall. There Mr. Williams had left an orchid for her hair. Carefully Mrs. Bisbey fastened it into Alexandra's curls. It now became clear why the housekeeper had discouraged Alexandra from choosing a hat.

"Can't very well kiss a man with some contraption on yer head," Mrs. Bisbey said as she finished. "Beautiful, mum. Simply beautiful."

Alexandra gave her an affectionate kiss on the cheek and flew out the door. The sight brought her feet to a stop on the top step. A branch at least two yards long lay propped up on the front iron fence. Small branches and leaves literally stripped from trees were scattered across the yard. House shingles, wood, and other unidentifiable objects added to the mess.

She quickly understood why Joshua had assigned a driver. The conditions down the road were unknown and might require some assistance.

Even though she was excited about Pierce's return, the damage about all Salem heightened her awareness of the storm's power. Picket fences lay as though blown over in one simple blast. Trees had fallen into homes and buildings, or lay on their sides with soil-covered roots exposed. Water filled every hole or low spot, and the unpaved streets were muddy at best.

If nature did this to the land, what kind of damage had she visited upon the *Lucinda*? Last night's dream of Pierce torn from her grasp rose unpleasantly to mind.

The trip to the wharves took three times longer than on a normal day. The entire town was out and about clearing, cleaning, and already repairing the damage. The clack of axes on wood and the swoosh of saws permeated the air.

As the carriage finally turned onto Derby Street, from where a good number of the wharves were visible, a black-and-white ship she had no doubt was the *Lucinda* sat docked against Turner's Wharf. With horror, she noted the upper part of the foremast was missing and a pile of sails and rigging hung tangled awkwardly from what remained. The closer they came, the harder she strained to see Pierce, but to no avail. Men busily unloaded what little cargo was brought from New York, and riggers and carpenters seemed absorbed with assessing the damage to the ship.

"Stop right here and let me out," she ordered the driver. As the carriage slowed to a stop near the wharf, Alexandra scanned the area for Joshua or any familiar face. She alighted from the carriage, never taking her eyes off the *Lucinda*.

She cursed the relative impediment of her dress and petticoats as she tried to hurry toward the ship. Two workers on the crowded wharf strolled slowly and blocked her path.

"Terrible lot that is, and he 'as no wife to mourn for 'im," she heard one exclaim.

The other nodded. "A bad omen for a new ship."

The first shook his head in disagreement. "I'd say 'tis a good omen the ship survived the storm at all."

Terrible apprehension filled Alexandra's heart as she pressed past the dockworkers. As she neared the *Lucinda*, she noticed a black cloth lying over the rail near the gangboard. Nearby, passengers who had obviously just disembarked loaded onto a stagecoach.

Apprehensively, she approached an elderly woman waiting to board the stage.

"Excuse me, Madam," Alexandra asked her. "Do you know why the cloth hangs on the ship's rail?"

"Sad thing, miss. One of the crew washed overboard. Nice young man, too. Violent storm. I hope never to live through such a nightmare again." The woman boarded the coach along with other solemn and rather bleak looking passengers.

A knife of fear pierced Alexandra's heart. A tall lanky fellow carrying a small barrel on his shoulder neared the *Lucinda*'s gangboard.

"Please, sir. Do you know if Mister Pierce Williams is aboard?"

"I'm not with the crew ma'am, sorry."

Alexandra desired greatly to dash aboard, but feared how silly she might appear running to and fro looking for someone who might not even be on the ship. Where was Joshua or his carriage? Why wasn't he here? He could easily stroll aboard and inquire about Pierce. Or had he already been here and heard the grave news that his son was lost? Panic again filled her heart.

She paced alongside the docked ship, searching the deck for Pierce, Joshua, or even the captain. Abeam of the bowsprit, she could see past the ship to Derby Wharf in the distance. A woman stood there staring in her direction. Her white dress fluttered gently in the sea breeze.

Alexandra gasped as she realized it was Hannah. Fresh in her mind was the nightmare of Pierce being pulled away from her and Hannah saying "It has to be this way." Alexandra wanted to shout "No!" across the harbor.

A cart rolled in front of her, and when it had passed, the place where Hannah had stood was empty. Why was the mysterious woman watching her?

She returned to the gangboard, determined to get on board. A workman carried off a sack of New York apples. "Is there a gentleman aboard, or the captain?" she asked.

"No, ma'am. Didn't see none. Mate's on board, if he'll do."

"Yes, could I bother you to get him for me?"

He dropped his sack onto the back of a wagon, which would haul the produce up to the scales. "No problem, if ye don't mind waitin'."

"Thank you. I'll gladly wait. By the way, do you know who the man was that died."

"No, ma'am, but Dr. Bentley was just here. He went to tell the family. Had an older gent with him." The man scratched at a scraggly beard. "Don't 'member much about him." The worker disappeared below deck.

Alexandra's mind tried to maintain some sense of calm and not panic. In all likelihood, Joshua was with Dr. Bentley and they had taken the family carriage. Were they going to look for her? Tears filled her eyes no matter how hard she fought them back. Tense and high-strung, she paced back and forth not moving more than a few yards from the gangboard, afraid she might miss the first mate.

Desperately she sought answers. Was Pierce actually swept into the sea? And if so, how could she live each day, knowing she had pictured his very demise? Never again could she enter the study to gaze upon his portrait and be taunted by the raging ocean waters in the background. Subconsciously she twisted her fingers around the place where his ring had been last night. She longed for it now, so as to hold at least some small part of him near.

Behind her, the stagecoach driver informed his passengers that the roads out of town were impassable, and the one and only stop today was at the Blue Shell Tavern. He then called his team to life. Slowly the coach pulled away, exposing with its departure a man standing on the wharf.

To her unbelieving eyes, he stood there dressed in a jacket and beaver hat, and appearing nearly as disheveled in appearance as the first day they had met.

"Pierce!" she called out with such joy it tore her breath away.

She rushed toward him, and in moments her arms wrapped snugly around his body. "I thought you had perished," she exclaimed, tears of joy running across her cheeks. She wanted so much to kiss every precious bit of him, but the general public frowned on such public displays.

He squeezed her tighter and wiped away the tears. "I promised you I'd be back and the ship wouldn't sink."

"But I heard someone washed overboard."

"I'm afraid we lost one seaman. He helped save the ship when the helmsman was injured. Refused to wear a rope, though, and a wave took him overboard."

Pierce let go of Alexandra and turned her toward the ship. A man approached them, then stopped a distance away. "I want to introduce you to the first mate. He's the reason I stand here."

Pierce waved the man closer. "Mr. Franklin, I'd like you to meet my fiancée, Miss Alexandra Gables of Boston."

Alexandra gasped, rather surprised Pierce used the title fiancée. She politely extended her hand and shook Mr. Franklin's. "Pleased to meet you. Mister Williams said he would not be standing here if it were not for you. I owe you a debt of thanks for bringing him safely home."

"It was nothin' Mister Williams hadn't already done for others."

"You are far too modest, Mr. Franklin," Pierce said. "You see, Alexandra, my life rope was not attached to the ship when a wave sent me overboard. I thought my life lost when the rope around my waist went taut. Mr. Franklin had managed to grab the other end and wrap the line about his own body."

Pierce firmly patted Mr. Franklin on the shoulder and grinned. "I'd have him show you the rope burns and bruises from such a lifesaving action, but I'm afraid his wife might disapprove. If ever I go to sea again, I'd want him at my side."

Mr. Franklin grinned in return and shook Pierce's hand. "I'd best get back to the hold, sir. Can't trust these men not to run off with the cargo. Pleased to have met you, miss." He backed away, then turned and strode proudly onto the *Lucinda*.

Pierce looked at her, and she saw a joyous contentment in his eyes. She hardly let Mr. Franklin disappear, though, before she accosted him on the subject of their betrothal. "Are you not being rather presumptuous, announcing our marriage without the consent of my father?"

To her surprise, he smiled rather smugly and entwined his arm in hers. "Oh, my dear Alexandra, you jump to such a quick judgment." They strolled down the wharf toward shore. "I have every right to announce to Salem that you have stolen my heart."

"And why do you feel so assured of that right?"

He lifted a well-worn envelope from his pocket. "While I

was in New York, a ship arrived from England. It carried letters for Salem. One in particular was from your father to me."

She snatched for the envelope and he withdrew it from her reach. "I do believe this is private mail," he teased. "But if you coax me in a proper manner, I might find it within myself to reveal its contents."

She frowned, hardly in a mood to play games after only moments ago believing him dead. Proudly she lifted her chin, trying to prove she held no further interest in the letter. "I gather by your introduction he has given his blessing to our marriage. I also assume he has given some time for his arrival home."

"Ah, I am sorely disappointed you chose not to succumb to my charms. Has my absence been so long you are no longer in need of a good man?"

She noticed he attempted to pout, but his firm chin and complete ease at her side made it impossible and instead made him deliciously attractive. "If I promise to tell a bedtime tale and kiss you good night, is that enough to coax from you the rest of my father's news?"

"That is a fair beginning. But I'd like to negotiate further for some more favorable terms."

"Granted, but I'm afraid the negotiations must be delayed for a more favorable location." With a flash of her lashes and a tilt of her chin, she eagerly flirted with him.

Pierce grinned with obvious pleasure. "I am unable to deny a request to the woman who so easily knows my every need. Your father is already on his way home and should arrive, if the winds are favorable, some time in the next week or two."

She grasped both his hands and faced him, filled with pure contentment. "I can't thank you enough for this prodigious news. I have so much to share with my father that I can barely decide what tale to tell first. Oh, I do so hope you like him." She shook her head, realizing she sounded quite giddy. "I'm sorry, the excitement has made me babble. I can scarcely believe he will arrive in August and an entire summer will have passed. Why, the time has disappeared so quickly."

"Speak for yourself," Pierce teased, prodding her toward the carriage. "I built and launched a ship, traveled to New York, almost became fodder for sharks, and had to put up with a stranger first in my house and then in my bed. I rather think the summer was quite long."

"And it is yet to be over. You must add a wedding to your rather bland list of events."

He gave the driver a few pennies to walk home, then helped Alexandra into the carriage. "Since you have mentioned the subject," he said to her, "we do need to discuss our wedding. Your father has granted permission for us to marry in Salem, if that meets with your approval. Dr. Bentley has also graciously consented to officiate in our home."

Unlike most women, Alexandra had never thought she would marry, so she had not planned or plotted her own wedding. She found no objections to the plans, except to allow her father and relatives in Boston enough time to travel to Salem.

"Nothing really matters to me as long as I have you at my side. Promise me until the wedding, though, you will plan no trips to sea."

With a short laugh, he set the carriage in motion. "I'll be too busy getting the next ship underway. Besides, for your own safety, I'd like to have the ceremony as soon as possible."

His comment brought forth the memory of Hannah watching and made her suddenly scan the streets. "I saw Hannah a few minutes ago, standing on Derby Wharf. She was staring directly at me."

"Did you see where she went?"

"No, she simply disappeared." She hesitated to bring up such a somber topic after the joy of their reunion, but she knew it was inevitable. "I also saw the attacker from Ye Neck."

"I know," Pierce said, his voice serious. "My father told me. Evidently, he has again disappeared. I plan to have someone watch for him at the Eight Bells Tavern."

He pulled the carriage to a stop on a side lane. With gentleness and affection, he held her hands. "Until Dr. Bentley announces us man and wife, and everyday thereafter, I will protect you and do my best to search out those who have hurt you. I promise to count off each passing day until, on this finger, you wear the gold band of my love." He kissed her hand in the very place the gold would soon reside. "There is nothing and no one who can stop us."

The sincerity in his soft eyes melted her heart. She imagined gazing into them as they repeated their vows in front of friends and family, holding hands just as they did now. Slowly, an eerie realization dawned over her, and for the first time she understood the meaning of her last dream. Discouraged, she bowed her head. The devastation it wreaked upon her being left her empty of emotion.

In the dream, they had stood together dressed in finery, the same finery one would wear on the occasion of a wedding. As much as she wanted and longed to believe him, for some reason he was yet to be torn from her grasp. The only consolation her dream offered was that his departure appeared against his wishes. A tear gathered in the corner of her eye. Troubling was the fact that Hannah had stood next to her, claiming it had to be that way.

Unable to understand the reason for such a terrible outcome of their love, she withheld any mention of it to Pierce. She still had time to change the future, if only she could find Hannah and discover the reason. As she looked up into his eyes again, the tear rolled down her cheek.

Delicately he touched a palm against her face, catching the tear. "A tear of joy?" he asked.

"No," she said, kissing the palm of his hand against her face. "A tear of love."

Seventeen

Never before, in Joshua's humble opinion, had Salem produced a more splendid day. He stood outside in the garden, letting the bright sun warm his face and the cool breeze keep his body at a perfectly comfortable temperature. The pungent mix of summer scents delighted him with every breath he took.

Flowers proudly bloomed in a cascade of colors. Along the side yard were tall yellow and white gladiolus, orange dog lilies and several towering sunflowers. Red geraniums, marigolds, daisies of yellow and white, and numerous flowering herbs accented the central garden.

"Fine setting," Alexandra's father, Edwin Gables, pronounced. "I wasn't sure this day would ever come."

"Ha!" Joshua exclaimed, turning to the shorter, redheaded Edwin. "I've waited a full ten years longer than you. I'd lost complete hope. Now I might even have a grandchild before I meet my Maker."

Edwin smiled and raised his chin with fatherly pride. "I have no doubt Alexandra will bring us some fine grandchildren. Bright ones, too, if the talents of our two children are combined."

Joshua shook his head, reflecting on the first night of Alexandra's visit, when she and Pierce had that little tête-à-tête at the bedroom door. How very much Alexandra was like her father: stubborn yet filled with convictions.

Joshua patted Edwin on the back. "That was a remarkable

proposal you made last year. I wasn't even certain we had it in us to make our scheme work. How ridiculous we must have sounded whining about our children's lack of romantic prospects."

"Oh, I wouldn't call it whining, ol' boy, more like complaining. I had introduced Alexandra to every worthy man in Boston and she'd have none of them. Too damn independent. When you described Pierce as the same, it simply occurred to me to pit them against each other. We had nothing to lose, wouldn't you say?"

"Assuredly," Joshua replied, noting the arrival of Dr. Bentley, who stepped from the house into the garden. "And I appreciate your confidence in me to see that things went well. They made it a bit of a challenge, though."

"Humph. Some may think you an easy man, Joshua. And that's where most fail in business against you. You're one of the most tenacious men I know."

Joshua chuckled. "Ah, I thought my success was due to the intelligent friends I chose." He scanned the faces of several relatives: some his own, and many others who had accompanied Edwin from Boston. They all seemed content, milling about and waiting for the ceremony to start not more than thirty minutes hence. The house grounds appeared secured, with one man mingling in the group watching for any trouble, as well as another man posted at the front of the house.

"Come inside and have a glass of brandy while we wait," he offered to Edwin. "I should tell you about the day Alexandra arrived."

Edwin, obviously desiring as usual to be perfectly punctual, slipped out his pocket watch. " 'Tis half past three. Do we have enough time for a nip?"

"Depends on how slowly you imbibe."

"On the contrary, I believe it depends on how liberal you are with the serving."

Joshua grinned, feeling quite pleased with himself. "On this special day, you can expect I'll be more than generous."

Edwin acquiesced with a nod, and the two contented gentlemen headed into the house, avoiding the staff who decorated and prepared food for the guests at the wedding feast.

Mrs. Bisbey stepped back to gaze at Alexandra and was pleased with the results of her handiwork. "Why, Mister Pierce's knees are goin' to buckle when he sets eyes upon ye. Dearie, I proclaim you the loveliest woman in Salem. Come, look in the mirror."

Alexandra stood in her room before a tall swing mirror, tipped appropriately to display her from head to foot. She gave a light laugh. "I can't believe whom I see is actually me."

"Why not, mum?"

"Because after all those horrid suitors in Boston, I swore no man would have my hand in marriage."

"Well, now. I guess we should know better than to make promises we can't keep."

Alexandra smiled at her comment and fluffed up the skirt. She positioned herself in various poses to see all sides of the gown. "The dress is stunning. I must proclaim my appearance is all due to you. How can I ever thank you for helping out on such short notice?"

"Me pleasure, but I can't take all the credit. I simply made changes to a dress ye already had. A fine one, too."

"As always, Mrs. Bisbey, you are too modest."

"Me, modest?" Mrs. Bisbey tweaked Alexandra's gold brocade overskirt slightly to one side to better center the opening over a silken petticoat. "I'd like Mister Joshua to hear that one."

She considered the good fortune of Mr. Pierce. For years she had wondered whom he would catch for a wife. Once Miss Alexandra had arrived, she knew almost instantly that God had meant them for each other. Happiness from within kept a smile on her face. Oh, yes, what a wonderful addition Alexandra would be to the Williams family. "Well, I must get down to help Mrs. Flamm. She's probably in a tizzy wonderin' where I got to."

"I'm sure she knows exactly where you are and understands. But before you go," Alexandra said as she moved over to the dresser, "I need one more thing from you."

Puzzled, Mrs. Bisbey waited, watching Alexandra remove from a drawer a piece of cloth of the same silk as her petticoat. A light-blue satin ribbon tied the cloth closed.

"For everything you have done to make this day special." Alexandra gave her the cloth package along with a kiss on the cheek.

Mrs. Bisbey tried to keep the tears from her eyes but didn't succeed. Carefully she untied the ribbon and unfolded the silk. Hidden inside, a delicate chain held a small silver heart.

"I've treasured that locket for years," Alexandra said warmly, "and want to pass it on to someone special."

Touched, Mrs. Bisbey couldn't hide a little sniffle. "Why, thank ye, mum. I shall always cherish it."

"Here, let me help you put it on."

Mrs. Bisbey turned and let Alexandra clasp it behind her neck. She fingered the small heart as it lay on her chest.

"I . . . I must get downstairs before Mr. Joshua riles up the staff." She hoped to appear composed, but the joy in her heart just made for a teary-eyed day. At the door she looked back. "Beautiful, mum. Just beautiful. This day is goin' to be perfect."

Surprisingly, Alexandra didn't appear happy with her comment, but instead had an almost blank and worried expression on her pretty face. Gracious, brides were an emotional lot! But Miss Alexandra needn't worry. The best housekeeper in Salem was at work, and on this special day she wouldn't let anything interfere with the happiness of her favorite young couple.

The perfect day was exactly what had Alexandra concerned. Three weeks had passed since Pierce returned from *Lucinda*'s maiden voyage, and no matter how hard or wide they searched, Hannah was not to be found.

Alexandra paced to the window and looked out over the garden. Friends and relatives were gathering, and the time for vows approached. She had the sudden urge to force Dr. Bentley to begin the proceedings now, then flee with Pierce away from Salem before what she had foreseen in her dream could come true.

Below in the garden, Dr. Bentley and Pierce appeared, creating a pleasant stir among the guests. Relief at the sight of her handsome groom made all troubles flow away. In only moments now, they would be together.

Her aunt watched silently from across the room, probably assuming she had wedding-day doubts. Doubt about marrying Pierce wasn't even a consideration. No other possible love existed on this earth except him.

A knock sounded lightly on the door, and her aunt opened it to a grinning Edwin Gables. As he caught sight of Alexandra he spread his arms wide. "Ah, my dear daughter, your beauty is truly most rare. If only your mother could see you now." His eyes grew moist, and she saw the emptiness he had felt since her death.

"Be assured she is watching," Alexandra said gently. "And I might even guess she approves of *our* choice."

Awkwardly her father adjusted his cravat in the mirror and straightened his dress coat. "Do I look worthy enough for an escort?" A hint of nervousness she had rarely seen in her father played around his eyes.

With great affection, she reached up and assisted him with the cravat. "You are the handsomest father a daughter could desire."

"Well, then, the time has arrived. Are you ready for this new adventure?"

"I'm a Gables, Father." She smiled confidently. "We are always ready for adventure." With proud chin raised, she slipped next to him in her delicate slippers and took his arm. Together they swept into the hall.

They stood at the top of the stairs: two redheads, father and daughter, teacher and student, both willful and independent.

His hand under hers shook ever so slightly, and she sensed nervousness in his excitement.

"So, what adventure have you planned next?" she asked, hoping to divert his attention to other subjects.

"Some peace and quiet back in Boston. I assume you will come visit your father once in a while?"

"I will find Boston most pleasant now that suitors won't line the street in front of our home."

"Ah, you will break many hearts this day, my dear, but I must admit you have chosen wisely."

"I have chosen? Forgive my insolence, but now that I stand ready to marry," she said with a touch of determination, "will you finally admit to your matchmaking plot with Mister Williams?"

Her father simply patted her hand and presented that endearing quirk of a smile that said he held an unshakable secret. "I will only admit to my great happiness on this day."

"I am glad to hear as much," she answered simply, "but that is truly no answer." In turn, she gently squeezed his arm with affection and looked purposefully into his eyes. It was most improper for a daughter to blackmail her father, but then these were trying times. He wanted grandchildren and she wanted a confession.

"Father, I wish to be the perfect wife and make you proud of me. You have taught me well how to study any new situation, and I think it wise to spend several years perfecting my new position as a wife. I have much to learn about cooking and household duties. Surely, though, I will master these and feel able to take on studying the art of motherhood for another appropriate time period before I bring children into the world. Don't you think such steps are wise?"

"That is all very proper, of course, but . . . but . . ." He appeared quite conflicted over exactly what to say.

"Oh, dear Father, you needn't worry about the delicate subject of marriage-bed matters. I am a woman of science. I have spent the last few weeks thoroughly researching methods to prevent conception. I apologize if that sounds rather brazen, but you have always taught me to be forthcoming."

The smile on Edwin Gables's face melted into complete astonishment, then into a doubtful frown. He had caught on to her little ploy. "By God, you are a true Gables, and such subtle manipulation will do the Williams name proud."

She offered a smug smile. "I appreciate your confidence in me. Now, unless you wish a lengthy wait for a new family generation, I believe there is the small matter of a confession."

"You promise I will not die of old age before I hold my grandchildren?"

"I'll do my best to make you happy."

Edwin once again appeared quite pleased. "Well, I cannot break an oath of secrecy to a friend, but I will admit your internship here was a roaring good adventure for me. Numerous detailed letters kept me abreast of all that passed. I was afraid you might be a little rough on the fine fellow. However, I see he survived quite well."

With a delicate poke in her father's ribs, she looked him in the eye. "And I trust in the future you will promise to stay out of my personal affairs?"

"Completely," he said too hastily, and she knew with certainty he'd continue to meddle.

Stretching to her tiptoes, she gave him a peck on the cheek. "I love you anyway."

For a moment she froze, as a picture flashed in her mind. Dear Lord, why did such a thing choose now to impinge upon her day. Instantly, she realized the vision had nothing threatening to offer. She even smiled at the implication. With a happy outlook, she smiled at her father and took her first step down the stairs. At last she was ready to become Mrs. Pierce Williams.

Pierce did his best to act nonchalant and not stare at the kitchen door, where he knew in minutes Alexandra would appear. Regardless of this attempt, his attention wandered there every few seconds. He caught Mrs. Bisbey peering out the door, a hand shielding her eyes from the sun. When her sight alighted upon him, she began to move purposefully toward him.

Pierce felt uncomfortable with the worried look etched upon her face. Dr. Bentley, standing next to him, chatted with Alexandra's uncle from Boston and hadn't noticed Mrs. Bisbey's approach. Pierce decided it best to handle whatever was on her mind well away from Bentley's ears.

"Excuse me a minute, gentlemen," he said politely, then hurried to intercept the housekeeper. He caught her near the herb garden and spoke in a lowered voice. "What is it, Mrs. Bisbey?"

"Someone came to see Miss Alexandra. I told her this wasn't a good time. But she insisted. Miss Alexandra is with her now in the study."

Instantly concerned about a stranger in the house, he took Mrs. Bisbey by the shoulders. "Was the woman named Hannah Brickford?"

"No, sir. Said her name was Mrs. Hawkes. I think ye should see her, sir. The sight was eerie, truly eerie."

"Good God, woman, what do you mean?"

Mrs. Bisbey leaned close to whisper. "Why, the woman looks just like Miss Alexandra."

"Did Mrs. Hawkes give a Christian name?"

"Why, yes. I believe she said Bridget."

"Bridget!" Pierce immediately abandoned Mrs. Bisbey in a rush for the house. He reviewed in his mind Alexandra's discussion of her visit to the lawyer's record keeper. The one triplet the woman knew of was Bridget Goodwell. Somewhere in the back of his mind, he remembered hearing that his friend Benjamin Hawkes had recently married in a hastily arranged ceremony. If the Bridget he took for his wife was the Reverend Goodwell's daughter, then he had married one of the Bennett triplets. And if Alexandra looked like Bridget . . . Good God, then Alexandra was wrong about not being adopted!

He made it into the house with a quick stride past the waiting guests. From the hall, he heard voices in the study.

A woman's voice he didn't recognize spoke urgently. "I know this is horrid timing, and please forgive me, but if you marry Pierce, he will die."

Frowning, he stepped through the doorway and took charge. "I think you had better leave." As he caught full sight of Bridget, he drew in a quick breath. A ribbon-adorned hat partially hid her red hair but did nothing to hide her face, a face that might well have belonged to Alexandra.

The number of people in the study had grown since Mrs. Bisbey had left. Pierce recognized Benjamin Hawkes, with too dour a face for this supposedly festive occasion, standing at Bridget's elbow. Pierce and Benjamin nodded at each other in acknowledgment.

Bridget appeared quite nervous, obviously uncomfortable with interrupting the wedding. Across from Alexandra stood an older woman with graying red hair. This, without a doubt, was the elusive Hannah.

Damnation, how dare these people pick his wedding day to interfere? "I can assume you are not here to celebrate our union," he said to no one in particular of the three visitors.

"They are here to stop it, I'm afraid," Alexandra said, her voice filled with disappointment, but with an odd ring of acceptance. Had she expected this all along?

"If they think a threat will stop me from matrimony, then they are sorely mistaken. There is nothing that will dissuade me from marrying you."

Benjamin stepped forward. "Please, give Hannah a few minutes to explain. We're not threatening to ruin your life; on the contrary, we're attempting to save it."

If it were not his own wedding, Pierce would have thought this scene almost comical. But he knew that nothing concerning Alexandra was ever what it seemed. He joined her and took her hand as though offering protection from the strange group now assembled. "If that be the case, then I'd rather like an explanation of why you believe I plan to meet my Maker so soon."

Hannah turned to him and nodded. "You deserve an explanation—although I am not sure how receptive you will be to much of what I have to say."

"Alexandra and I have no secrets. She has shared her research in detail with me about all matters concerning you. We have even spent these last several weeks in an extensive search to find you."

"I knew of your impending marriage and realized that you would not believe what I had to say without Bridget. She had married and left town with Benjamin, so I had to wait for their return. They only just now arrived back in town. As you can see, the similarities of the two girls have already answered many questions."

Hannah was correct about the impact that seeing Bridget had on him. Once his eyes caught her face, he had no doubt she and Alexandra were sisters. "All right, if you must. Please, explain. You have my full attention."

"As you must know by now, my true name is Mary Hannah Bennett." She looked into Alexandra's eyes. "And I am Alexandra's natural mother."

The two women seemed frozen in time, unmoving and each unsure of the other's reaction.

Finally, Alexandra slowly blinked and asked, "Why didn't you tell me this the first time we met?"

"Because you would not have believed me. Even now, facing your sister, you still have doubts in your heart. And my tale is so extraordinary, you had to be prepared for its telling."

"I am ready now."

Pierce, as well as Hannah, saw that Alexandra told the truth. Hannah faced them both with confidence. "My lineage relates back to a woman named Priscilla Gardener. Her line carries even further back to Scotland and the powerful MacInness clan, whose members were blessed with many unusual talents. You may have heard the word *sight* used to describe the ability to glimpse into the future. That is one such talent. Others of the clan were great healers or shared empathy with animals. I myself do not know all the possible talents my lineage has shared, but I and each of my children share some such talent."

He felt Alexandra shift uncomfortably next to him. The impact of learning about one's true and unexpected family history must be rather devastating. He stretched an arm around her shoulder.

"How does this relate to someone wanting to kill me?" Pierce asked. "An attack was made on Alexandra, not me."

The news of an attack concerned but did not seem to overly surprise the group. "Bridget has also been attacked," Benjamin said uncomfortably. "It shows they are worried enough to be taking drastic action."

"Who are *they?*" Alexandra demanded.

Hannah seemed drawn to the portrait of Judge Nathaniel Williams. She lightly touched the frame before turning back to Pierce and Alexandra. "A century ago during the witch trials, both Priscilla and her husband, John, were dragged toward the gallows. Judge Williams saved Priscilla from the mob because she had been legally exonerated from the charges of witchcraft. John, on the other hand, was hanged since he had confessed to the strange happenings supposedly witnessed near their home. He did it to save Priscilla and their unborn child."

With a sigh, Hannah continued, "I suppose he did not know that his wife truly was what people called a witch. She had special talents. Which ones, I do not know. The truth is that the Scottish clan had an enemy with similar powers, who also immigrated to America. It was one of their members who supposedly made the townsfolk aware of Priscilla's talents. A woman of that clan had been in love with John. But when he married, she sought revenge against Priscilla and hoped to gain John as her husband upon Priscilla's death. When her plan instead killed John, and despair and fury overcame her, she cast a curse. Each female in Priscilla's line would be destined to live a lonely life, for the men they chose to marry were now cursed to die at twenty and six years of age—the very same age at which John had hanged."

"Alexandra, we have a wedding to get on," unexpectedly boomed her father from the doorway. "I respectfully ask that these people leave—now."

All eyes turned as Edwin and Joshua entered the room. Edwin's face appeared red with anger, and Joshua's brows were drawn with doubt. From the expression on both their faces, Alexandra knew they had overheard most of the conversation. Immediately, Alexandra went to her father and gently set her hands on his crossed arms.

"Please, Father, before you say anything more, I need to ask you a question. I'd like for you to be calm and forthright with the answer. Am I . . ." She took a deep breath. "Am I an adopted child? This woman standing before us claims to be my natural mother."

Her father's jaw slackened, then flapped soundlessly for several seconds as he examined the women in the room. His eyes grew wide as they alighted on Bridget. With great affection and some sadness, he gazed into Alexandra's eyes.

"The lawyer warned us you had suffered the death of both your parents. We believed you didn't need the pain of reliving such knowledge." Sadness swirled in his eyes. "I must also admit, your mother and I feared you might feel less loved if you knew."

Alexandra's eyes filled with tears as she tenderly hugged her father. "I only wish you had trusted me enough to reveal the truth. But I understand your reasons." She stepped back slightly and took both his hands in hers. "Granted, my emotions are in turmoil, Father, but never, ever would I doubt the love you and Mother gave me. I beg your indulgence now, though. As much as this woman's story sounds incredible, would you stay here with me and listen to what she has to say?"

Edwin had no heart to deny Alexandra's request, even though obviously upset by the delay in his daughter's wedding. His lips pressed tight, and he gave a quick nod of his head.

Alexandra turned back toward Hannah. "I suspect, as grand as this tale sounds, you are telling the truth. In my own research, I noticed the coincidence of the descendants' husbands dying at the same age. But what I don't understand is why these women married if they knew the great cost."

"Because, just like me, they were not told of the curse until after marriage. I know it sounds cruel, but it was the only way to continue the family line. Because of Priscilla's own formidable powers, she was able to counter the curse by giving our family one century in order to break the curse. If it could be done in that time, then devastation would be reflected upon the woman's clan who cast the curse. The end of the one hundred years occurs this All Hallows' Eve."

A cacophony of questioning and surprised voices rose in the room. Someone uttered, "Why, that is only two months away."

"Heavens, the more this woman says, the more it sounds like gibberish," Joshua spoke out for the first time. Pierce noticed his face was puffed and red, and he tugged uncomfortably at the silk cravat wrapped around his neck. "I have never heard anything about my ancestor rescuing any witches from the gallows."

"I have," Pierce contended, realizing his father must have been listening outside the room for quite a while. "Alexandra uncovered an editorial Nathaniel wrote after the hangings, in which he criticized what had happened. And as impossible as I find any of this to believe, you yourself were amazed at Alexandra's foreknowledge of the storm."

Joshua seemed to search for something else to say, but simply shrugged.

Slowly, with arms crossed and deep in thought, Alexandra paced in her silk-and-brocade finery around Hannah. Finally, she faced her mother. "So, the basic purpose of this visit is to prevent our marriage."

With a face that said she understood Alexandra's disappointment, Hannah lowered her head. "Only until this problem is resolved. Pierce is well past twenty and six years. If he married today, his death could be imminent. We just don't know. If it is any consolation, you are not alone in this problem. Benjamin, although younger, eventually faces certain death if the curse is left unbroken. He and Bridget married before I could stop them."

Alexandra's eyes lit up as though she was suddenly endowed with some revelation. "That is why you sought a divorce," she exclaimed. "You hoped the divorce would save your husband's life."

"I tried, but the scheme failed when later a family matriarch revealed I also had to remove our love from his heart. I only knew of one way to accomplish such a feat. I had to make him believe I had perished. The decision meant I had to be separated from my daughters, but I loved him too much to simply allow him to die."

Hannah looked from Alexandra to Bridget. "I hope you will forgive me, but he was a worthy father. He had all the knowledge and love to raise you properly. On a stormy day, I took the necessary actions to make it appear I had drowned. I had hoped he would eventually find another to love, but he did not. Instead, he died at sea at twenty-six, just like all the others. I did not reside in Salem at the time of his death, for I could not chance him seeing me. By the time I heard about his death and tried to find you girls, the records were lost."

"Purposely, I'm afraid," Alexandra half whispered. "Your husband's lawyer discovered the divorce papers. He was suspicious you were still alive, and afraid you might seek us out. He is the one who destroyed the records."

An expression of many memories and much pain overtook Hannah. Pierce felt great empathy for the grief she must have endured.

"I am not surprised at his actions. I eventually discovered Bridget in town," Hannah admitted, "and revealed myself to Mr. Wynn to beg for his assistance. Instead, he threatened to disclose the divorce decree if I tried to take Bridget. The papers, of course, announced my supposed infidelity. Under such circumstances, no proper judge would return a child to my care."

Hannah's voice softened. "As much as I was devastated at the separation, I later came to realize the situation was actually best for you girls. Revealed to me by my grandmother was the fact that my children and I were the only ones left to break this wretched curse. She warned that the descendants of the evil clan thrived and lived a lavish lifestyle here in Salem, using their talents for evil purposes. If this curse is broken, they stand to loose everything. To their advantage, they have continued to hone their talents through the generations. One of us alone could not survive against them."

"But we are a force of four," Alexandra declared. "And with much more to lose. I'd say that makes us a formidable foe."

"Apparently, they held little concern about me," Bridget spoke up, "until Alexandra arrived in town. The shock of two of us in Salem must have made them feel threatened. Surely that is what precipitated the attacks on us. The fewer of us, the weaker our power against the curse. They can't afford to stop until we are all dead."

"By God, I've heard enough," Alexandra's father exclaimed, "What's this about an attack on my daughter?"

Joshua rubbed his chin and studied his shoes. "I thought it better you didn't know," he said almost under his breath.

Edwin's head wrenched toward him, and the two men began an argument of heated whispers while Pierce sought more answers from Hannah. "Do you know which family in Salem enfolds these black witches?"

Hannah appeared appropriately worried. This evidently wasn't the first time she had contemplated such a question. "I have my suspicions, but no proof. That is one thing we must gain by All Hallows' Eve."

"If your suspicions point to the Trasks," Alexandra said, her eyes narrowing and a disturbing pall covering her face, "then I believe you are right. When I first arrived in Salem, I ran into Mrs. Trask outside the Blue Shell Tavern. She was coming from the direction of the Reverend Goodwell's wagon. I later found a loose bolt that the Reverend Goodwell claimed would have killed all in the wagon—Bridget included. Mrs. Trask had ample opportunity to have done the deed, for no one was around the wagon when I arrived."

Pierce, surprised at the news, frowned at Alexandra. "You never told me about seeing Mrs. Trask there."

"At the time, I didn't connect her to anyone. She simply called me Bridget and scolded me for not helping the others."

Bridget nodded solemnly. "That's her, all right. I've known her since childhood. Cold as ice, and the haughtiest woman in Salem."

"And the deadliest," Pierce added. "She tried to poison Alexandra at a dinner party."

"What!" Joshua paled a shade. "Why didn't anyone tell me about this?"

"Because Alexandra outfoxed her and the tainted food was delivered to her daughter Phoebe." Pierce stood tall with a touch of pride.

Joshua cringed. "Oh, my, I remember how sick the dear girl was."

"And I thought I left my daughter in your safe hands," Edwin snapped.

"Please," Alexandra pleaded. "Looking back, this all seems obvious, but at the time no one knew what was happening."

Joshua plopped down into an empty chair. He appeared resigned to the fact that this wedding might not take place. Wearily he looked up at Hannah. "Just what kind of hocus-pocus must you perform to stop these people?"

Hannah spread open her palms with a shrug. "I'm not quite sure yet. Much depends on the talents and capabilities of all four of us together. I think you understand the urgency, now, of why we have to find my third daughter and protect her."

"Do you have any idea where she might be?" Pierce asked.

"At the moment, no."

Alexandra stared directly at Hannah, and Pierce read in her

face the evidence of intuition at work. "But you *do* have an idea where she will be in the near future, don't you?" Alexandra said, wandering closer to Hannah. "Your intuition, just as mine, says we are all being drawn back to Salem, where we were born. Might I also suggest this is not a coincidence?"

A weary smile crossed Hannah's face. "You have the intuition to know these things. Your power along this line is much greater than mine. But yes, I suspected years ago that we would all be drawn together once again. I simply don't know if it will be in time."

"Well, at least we have the advantage of knowing whom to search for. I can safely assume she has the same appearance as Bridget and I."

"You were identical triplets. But remember, your looks also give you away to our enemy."

Mrs. Bisbey appeared behind Edwin at the door. "Excuse me, Mister Williams," she said softly. "Can I speak with ye?"

Reluctantly Joshua rose and started for the door. "I assume the guests are wondering what has happened. I might as well be the one to break the bad news."

"Wait," Pierce said, taking Alexandra gently by the arm. "Give us a minute alone to talk this over before you cancel the ceremony."

"But there isn't anything to discuss. I can't marry you . . . yet."

Pierce faced Alexandra and did his best to exude the same confidence with which she regularly carried herself. "Marriage is a partnership, I do believe you once told me. We must make this decision together."

He held out his hand and waited for her to accept it. Tentatively she reached out, then finally grasped it and held tight. He led her from the room, leaving behind a silent crowd.

The conservatory, once again bright and glowing with the wooden window protectors removed, provided the only enclave of privacy within easy reach. To Alexandra it brought instant memories of Newton scurrying up Lydia's dress.

Frustration tore at her mind and spirit from every direction. All she wanted was to marry Pierce, lie each night by his side, and share together in their successes and dreams. But as much as she desired all these things, she could not risk the one man who shared her soul and heart. She opened her mouth to speak, but Pierce covered it with a kiss.

All her pent-up feelings exploded into the passion of the kiss. Her arms encircled him and held tight. Her hands pressed against his back, afraid that if he left her reach, he might be swept into this nightmare of a curse.

Pierce kissed every inch of her mouth, then her forehead, cheek, neck, and once again her lips. With great gentleness of his large hands, he cradled her face. "I want you as my wife, Alexandra. I'm not afraid of some hundred-year-old curse."

"This is different. I couldn't tell you before, but I foresaw this happening. This is the way it must be." The haunting words from her vision seemed awkward coming from her lips rather than Hannah's, as they had in her vision.

Newton stirred on his perch, and his head rose and beady eyes gazed in her direction. Joshua was right. She and Newton did have an affinity for each other. Was that all part of her being some kind of witch?

"I could not live my life knowing I had destroyed yours," she said softly, knowing she must be persuasive. "Can you not see the pain Hannah has lived with? At least we have a choice. Hannah said we can defeat this curse. I believe her."

"And if you don't? Am I doomed never to have the woman I love?"

Alexandra gazed up at him, serious yet seeking reassurance. "Do you truly love me?"

"Before I met you, my heart was a place I had thought forever sealed. All love and emotion wrought for any woman, I buried there. You opened that place and have put a light there I will never extinguish. There is no other woman who can take your place. As much as I had declared no need for anyone, now I cannot live without you. I love you, Alexandra. Let Dr. Bentley marry us, and together we will work to defeat this wicked family."

An intense sadness tore at the very core of her strength. "I will not risk your life even for one day. I am sorry if you think me hateful for such selfishness."

"I do not hate you. I just want you to know I'm willing to suffer the chance."

"Then you are far braver than I."

A quick yet strained laugh escaped from Pierce. "My father has oft told me love does foolish things."

She took his hands and held them to her cheek. "Don't despair. I know without any doubt, we will succeed in breaking this curse. With your love behind me, I truly believe that anything can be conquered. Please, my love, give us the few months till All Hallows' Eve. I know our fathers will protest, but we will be man and wife soon enough."

Pierce stood tall, wrapping Alexandra in his arms and pressing her head to his chest. "I cannot force you into marriage, but I pledge you my heart and protection." He released her and slipped off his finger the garnet ring that she had worn the night of the storm. "Take this as my pledge to you, and keep it close until I can put a band of our union upon your finger."

He placed the ring over her middle finger and folded his hand around it. She had never divulged the role it played that night of the storm, and had returned it to his dresser. Now, once again she could only pray the ring would bring him back to her.

"Whatever I must do to find this missing sister has my full commitment," he whispered. "I love you and will be more tenacious than Newton at protecting my interests."

She found both worry and a smile wanting to part her lips. The admission she prepared to give seemed difficult to bring forth. What would his reaction be to the news she had to offer?

"I must count on your promise of commitment. For in several months, I will surely need you at my side."

Perplexed, Pierce studied her face. "I'm afraid I don't understand."

Alexandra reached up and brought his head close to hers. "Before I came down for the ceremony, I kissed my father. I'm afraid it produced another vision."

"My God, woman, another? Does it bode well for us?"

"All I can reveal is that we must quickly find my missing sister. For I saw my father bouncing a baby on his knee."

She watched a memorable grin replace Pierce's serious demeanor. Without a doubt, her news had just made the wait and trials ahead more bearable.

"It sounds to me, Miss Alexandra Gables, that another rousing adventure is afoot."

His lips lowered slowly and softly to a kiss that lasted for what seemed a lifetime. And neither she nor Newton had any plans to stop it.

If you liked CALL DOWN THE NIGHT, be sure to look for the next book in the talented Moffett sisters' series, *The MacInness Legacy,* TO TOUCH THE SKY, available wherever books are sold September 2002.

Descended from a long line of healers, Gillian Saunders barely ekes out a living selling the herbal medicines she makes in her Gloucester cottage. Still, she remains content with her simple life, until it is turned upside down by handsome physician Spencer Reeves, whom she's called upon to heal after he's badly injured in a shipwreck. Grateful for the miraculous cure Gillian has wrought, he promises her his aid should she ever need it. Now, a violent act of revenge has destroyed her cottage, and Gillian has no choice but to go to Spencer. Offering to help him in his practice, she never expects to be swept into an irresistible passion . . . or that an ancient curse which haunts her family will soon threaten her newfound love with him. Only the power of a mysterious family legacy can offer her a way to save Spencer from a death foretold generations ago. . . .